ACCLAIM FOR

GORE VIDAL's

1876

"A glorious piece of writing. . . . Vidal's words turn each page into a tray of jewelry." —*Harper's*

"Superb. . . . Simply splendid. . . . A thoroughly grand book—must, must reading for everyone." —*Business Week*

"Crackles with life—high and low. . . . Renders the sights and sounds of New York City a century ago unforgettable."
—*New York Sunday News*

"Clearly one of Vidal's brightest works." —*The Plain Dealer*

GORE VIDAL

1876

Gore Vidal was born in 1925 at the United States Military
Academy at West Point. His first novel, *Williwaw*, written
when he was nineteen years old and serving in the Army,
appeared in the spring of 1946. Since then he has written
twenty-two novels, five plays, many screenplays, short stories, well over two hundred essays, and a memoir.

INTERNATIONAL

NARRATIVES OF EMPIRE

BY

GORE VIDAL

Burr

Lincoln

1876

Empire

Hollywood

Washington, D.C.

The Golden Age

1876

GORE VIDAL

1876

A NOVEL

VINTAGE INTERNATIONAL

VINTAGE BOOKS

A DIVISION OF RANDOM HOUSE, INC.

NEW YORK

FIRST VINTAGE INTERNATIONAL EDITION, FEBRUARY 2000

Copyright © 1976 by Gore Vidal

All rights reserved under International and Pan-American Copyright
Conventions. Published in the United States by Vintage Books, a division
of Random House, Inc., New York, and simultaneously in Canada by
Random House of Canada Limited, Toronto. Originally published in
hardcover in the United States by Random House, Inc.,
New York, in 1976.

Vintage is a registered trademark and Vintage International and colophon
are trademarks of Random House, Inc.

The Library of Congress has cataloged the Random House edition as follows:
Vidal, Gore, 1925–
1876: a novel.
1. United States—History—1865–1898—Fiction. I. Title.
PZ3.V6668Ei [PS3543.I26] 813'.5'4 75-34311
ISBN 0-394-49750-3 Trade Hardcover

Vintage ISBN: 0-375-70872-3

www.vintagebooks.com

Printed in the United States of America
10 9

For Claire Bloom

1876

One

1

"THAT IS NEW YORK." I pointed to the waterfront just ahead as if the city were mine. Ships, barges, ferry boats, four-masted schooners were shoved like a child's toys against a confused jumble of buildings quite unfamiliar to me, a mingling of red brick and brownstone, of painted wood and dull granite, of church towers that I had never seen before and odd bulbous-domed creations of—cement? More suitable for the adornment of the Golden Horn than for my native city.

"At least I *think* it is New York. Perhaps it is Brooklyn. I am told that the new Brooklyn is marvellously exotic, with a thousand churches."

Gulls swooped and howled in our wake as the stewards on a lower deck threw overboard the remains of the large breakfast fed us at dawn.

"No," said Emma. "I've just left the captain. This is really New York. And how old, how very old it looks!" Emma's excitement gave me pleasure. Of late neither of us has had much to delight in, but now she looks a girl again, her dark eyes brilliant with that all-absorbed, grave, questioning look which all her life has meant: I must know what this new thing is and how best to use it. She responds to novelty and utility rather than to beauty. I am the opposite; thus father and daughter balance each other.

Grey clouds alternated with bands of bright blue sky; sharp wind from the northwest; sun directly in our eyes, which meant that we were facing due east from the North River, and so this was indeed the island of my birth and not Brooklyn to the south nor Jersey City at our back.

I took a deep breath of sea-salt air; smelt the city's fumes of burning anthracite mingled with the smell of fish not lately caught and lying like silver ingots in a passing barge.

"So old?" I had just realized what Emma had said.

"But yes." Emma's English is almost without accent, but occasionally she translates directly from the French, betraying her foreignness. But then I am the foreign one, the American who has lived most of his life in Europe while Emma has never until now left that old world where she was born thirty-five years ago in Italy, during a cyclone that uprooted half the trees in the garden of our villa and caused the frightened midwife nearly to strangle the newborn with the umbilical cord. Whenever I see trees falling before the wind, hear thunder, observe the sea furious, I think of that December day and the paleness of the mother's face in vivid contrast to the redness of her blood, that endless haemorrhaging of blood.

(I think that a little *mémoire* in the beautiful lyric style of the above might do very well for the *Atlantic Monthly*.)

Emma shivered in the wind. "Yes, old. Dingy. Like Liverpool."

"Waterfronts are the same everywhere. But there's nothing old here. I recognize nothing. Not even City Hall, which ought to be over there where that marble tomb is. See? With all the columns . . ."

"Perhaps you've forgotten. It's been so long."

"I feel like Rip Van Winkle." Already I could see the beginning of my first piece for the New York *Herald* (unless I can interest Mr. Bonner at the New York *Ledger*; he has been known to pay a thousand dollars for a single piece). "The New Rip Van Winkle, or How Charles Schermerhorn Schuyler Sailed to Europe Almost Half a Century Ago . . ." And stayed there (asleep?). Now he's come home, to report to President Martin Van Buren who sent him abroad on a diplomatic mission, to compare foreign notes with his friend Washington Irving (who invented him after all), to dine with the poet Fitz-Greene Halleck: only to find all of them, to his astonishment, long dead.

Must stop at this point.

These pages are to be a quarry, no more. A collection of day-to-day impressions of my *new* old country.

Titles: "The United States in the Year of the Centennial." "Traveller's Return." "Old New York: A Knickerbocker's Memories." "Recollections of the Age of Jackson and Van Buren . . ." Must try these out on publishers and lecture agents.

At this moment—midnight, December 4, 1875—I am somewhat staggered at the prospect of trying in some way to encompass with words this new world until now known to me only at the farthest remove. I can of course go on and on about the past, write to order of old things by the yard; and happily there is, according to my publisher, Mr. E. P. Dutton, a considerable market for my wares whenever I am in the reminiscent mood. But the real challenge, of course, is to get the sense of the country as it is today —two, three, four times more populous than it was when I left in 1837. Yet, contemplating what I saw of New York this afternoon, I begin only now to get the range as I sit, perspiring, in the parlour of our hotel suite while dry heated air comes through metal pipes in sudden blasts like an African sirocco.

None of the Americans I have met in Europe over the past four decades saw fit to prepare me for the opulence, the grandeur, the vulgarity, the poverty, the elegance, the awful crowded abundance of this city, which, when I last saw it, was a minor seaport with such small pretensions that a mansion was a house like Madame Jumel's property on the Haarlem—no, Harlem—no, *Washington* Heights—a building that might just fill the ballroom of one of those palaces the rich are building on what is called Fifth Avenue, in my day a country road wandering through the farms north of Potter's Field, later to be known as the Parade Ground, and later still as Washington Square Park, now lined with rows of "old" houses containing the heirs of the New York gentry of my youth.

In those days, of course, the burghers lived at the south end of the island between the Battery and Broadway where now all is commercial, or worse. I can recall when St. Mark's Place was as far north as anyone would want to live. Now, I am told, a rich

woman has built herself a cream-coloured French palace on *Fifty-
seventh Street!* opposite the newly completed Central Park (how
does one "complete" a park?).

A steward hurried across the deck to Emma. *"C'est un monsieur;
il est arrivé, pour Madame la Princesse."*

Everyone told us that of all the Atlantic ships those of the
French line were the most comfortable, and so the *Pereire* proved
to be, despite winter gales that lasted from Le Havre to the
mid-Atlantic. But the captain was charming; and most impressed
by Emma's exalted rank even though her title is Napoleonic and
the second French empire is now the third French republic.
Nevertheless, the captain gave us a most regal series of staterooms
for only a hundred and fifty dollars (the usual cost of two first-
class passages is two hundred dollars).

Our fellow passengers proved to be so comfortably dull that I
was able during the eight and a half days of the crossing to
complete my article for *Harper's Monthly*, "The Empress Eugénie
in Exile," filled with facts provided by the Emperor's cousin, my
beloved Princess Mathilde who of course detests her. Conform-
ing to current American taste, the tone of the piece is ecstatic and
somewhat fraudulent.

But the Empress has always been most kind to Emma and to
me, although she once tactlessly said in my presence that literary
men give her the same sense of ennui as explorers! Well, the
writer is not unlike the explorer. We, too, are searching for lost
cities, rare tigers, the sentence never before written.

Emma's visitor was John Day Apgar. We found him in the
main salon. Rather forlornly, he stood amongst the crowd of
first-class passengers, all looking for children, maids, valets,
trunks.

Quite a number of the men were having what the Americans
so colorfully refer to as "an eye-opener" at the marble-topped bar.

"Princess!" Mr. Apgar bowed low over Emma's hand; his style
is not bad for an American. But then John, as I call him, was for
a year at our embassy in Paris. Now he is practising law in New
York.

"Mr. Apgar. You are as good as your word." Emma gave him
her direct dark gaze, not quite as intense as the one she gave New
York City, but then John, unlike the city, is a reasonably well
known and familiar object to her. "I've a carriage waiting for you
at Pier Fifty. Porters—everything. Forgive me, Mr. Schuyler."
John bowed to me; shook hands.

"How did you get on board?" I was curious. "Aren't we still in the harbour?"

"I came out on the tender. With all sorts of people who have come to greet you."

"Me?" I was genuinely surprised. I had telegraphed Jamie Bennett at the *Herald* that I was arriving on the fourth but I could hardly expect that indolent youth to pay me a dawn visit in the middle of the Hudson River. Who else knew of my arrival?

The captain enlightened us. "The American newspaper press is arrived on board to interview Monsieur Schuyler." The French pronunciation of Schuyler (Shwee-lair) is something I shall never grow used to or accept. Because of it, I feel an entirely different person in France from what I am in America. Question: Am I different? Words, after all, define us.

"How extraordinary!" Emma takes a low view of journalists despite the fact that my livelihood from now on must come from my pen, from writing for newspapers, magazines, anything and everything. The panic of 1873 wiped out my capital, such as it was. Worse, Emma's husband left her in a similar situation when he saw fit to die five years ago while ingesting a tournedos Rossini at the restaurant Lucas Carton.

Whether it was a heart attack or simply beef with foie gras lodged in the windpipe, we shall never know, since neither of us was present when the Prince d'Agrigente so abruptly departed this world during a late supper with his mistress. It was the scandal of Paris during the three days before the war with Prussia broke out. After that, Paris had other things to talk about. We did not. To this day none of us understands how it was that the Prince died *owing* the fortune that we thought he had possessed.

With the slightly shady pomp of a chamberlain at the imperial court, the captain led us across the salon to a small parlor filled with gilt chairs à la Louis Quinze where, waiting for me, was the flower of the youth of the New York press. That is to say, the new inexperienced journalists who are assigned to meet celebrities aboard ships in the harbour and, through trial and error (usually more of the second than of the first), learn the art of interviewing, of misdescribing in sprightly language odd fauna.

Twenty, thirty faces stared at me from a variety of long shabby overcoats, some open in response to the warmth of the cabin, others still tightly shut against the morning's icy wind. We have been told a hundred times today that this has been the coldest winter in memory. What winter is not?

The captain introduced me to the journalists—obviously he is well-pleased that the reduction in our fare has been so dramatically and immediately justified. I sang for all our suppers; spoke glowingly of the splendour of the French line.

Questions were hurled at me whilst a near-sighted artist scribbled a drawing of me. I caught a glimpse of one of his renderings when he flipped back the first page of his paper block: a short stout pigeon of a man with three chins lodged in an exaggerated high-winged collar (yet mine is what collars should be), and of course the snubbed nose, square jaw of a Dutchman no longer young. Dear God! Why euphemize? Of a man of sixty-two, grown very old.

Thin man from the New York *Herald*. Indolent youth from the New York *Graphic*. Sombre dwarf from *The New York Times*. The *Sun, Mail, World, Evening Post, Tribune* were also present but not immediately identified. Also half a dozen youths from the weeklies, the monthlies, the biweeklies, the bimonthlies . . . oh, New York, the United States is the Valhalla of journalism—if Valhalla is the right word. Certainly, there are more prosperous newspapers and periodicals in the United States than in all of Europe put together. As a result, today's men of letters come from the world of journalism, and never entirely leave it—unlike my generation, who turned with great reluctance to journalism in order to make a desperate, poor living of the sort that now faces me.

"What, Mr. Schuyler, are your impressions of the United States *today?*" The dwarf from *The New York Times* held his notebook before him like a missal—studying it, not me.

"I shall know better when I go ashore." Pleased chuckles from the overcoats that had begun to give off a curious musty odour of dirty wool dampened by salt spray.

Handkerchief to face, Emma stood at the door, ready for flight. But John Apgar appeared to be entirely fascinated by the Fourth Estate in all its woolly splendour.

"How long has it been, sir, since you were last in America?" A note of challenge from the *World:* it is not good form to live outside God's own country. "I left in the year 1837. That was the year that everyone went bankrupt. Now I am back and everyone has again gone bankrupt. There is a certain symmetry, don't you think?

This went down well enough. But *why* had I left?

"Because I had been appointed American vice consul at Antwerp. By President Van Buren."

I thought that this would sound impressive, but it provoked no response. I am not sure which unfamiliar phrase puzzled them more: "vice consul" or "President Van Buren." But then Americans have always lived entirely in the present, and this generation is no different from mine except that now there is more of a past for them to ignore.

Our republic (soon to be in its centennial year) was in its vivacious sixties when I left, the same age that I am now.

Although my life has spanned nearly two-thirds the life of the United States, it seems but a moment in time. Equally curious is Emma's first impression of New York: "How old it looks," she said. Yet there is hardly a building left from my youth. As I spoke to the press I did finally recognize through the window—porthole—the familiar spire of Trinity Church. At least no new fire has managed to destroy that relic of the original city.

(Noted later: my "familiar spire," according to John Day Apgar was torn down in '39. The current *un*familiar spire dates from the early forties.)

Questions came quickly. My answers were as sharp as I could make them, considering how tactful, even apologetic one must be for having stayed away so long. And if the newspaper reports of my return prove to be amiable, I will find it easy—I pray—to acquire a lecture agent, not to mention magazine commissions from—from anyone who will pay!

"Where have you been living, sir?"

"For the last few years in Paris. I came there—"

"Were you in Paris during the war, during the German occupation?"

I restrained myself; was modest; *agréable*. "Why, yes, in fact I wrote a little book about my experiences. Perhaps you know the title. *Paris Under the Commune?*"

Either my publishers have exaggerated the success of the book or journalists do not read books or even reviews of books. Yet *Harper's Weekly* referred to *Paris Under the Commune* as "a terrifying and entirely fascinating eyewitness account of the siege of Paris and the rising of the Commune, all recorded with that celebrated gift for detail which marks any utterance from Mr. Charles Schermerhorn Schuyler's pen." I recall this notice by heart, largely because the only utterance I have ever heard my pen make is a squeak.

The man from the *Sun* looked very pleased with himself as he asked, "You yourself, sir, are not a Communist?"

"No, no, dear boy." My voice filled suddenly with catarrh as I deliberately mimicked old Washington Irving at his most gracious. "I am a simple American."

"Then why have you lived so long abroad?" The *Graphic*.

"When I was an American consul in Italy, I married a Swiss lady—"

"Is that her?" The dwarf looked over his missal at Emma; in fact, pointed that object at her as if he were an imp from hell with a summons.

"My wife is dead. She died at Paris some years ago. She—"

"What is *your* name, miss?" The *World* to Emma.

"Je ne comprends pas, monsieur." Emma's face was white, her full lips a straight line of irritability. The French words snapped in the room like a whip.

"My daughter is the Princess d'Agrigente." Much confusion as we worked as one to get the spelling right. Finally, a compromise: in English she is the Princess of Agrigento. "She is a widow—" I began.

"What did the Prince *do?*" From the *Express*.

Emma started to answer, furiously, in English, but a gesture from me stopped her. Raptly John Apgar stared at us, as if at the theatre.

"The Prince had many interests. His father, as I am sure you all know, was a marshal of France and served under the first Napoleon. He was ennobled in Italy. After Waterloo, when Napoleon was defeated—" For once I was spelling out too much. Impatiently they indicated that Napoleon's defeat at Waterloo was known to them.

"Got any children, Princess?"

"Two," I answered quickly. "In Paris. With their grand-mother. The dowager Princess." Who is charging us—that sovereign bitch from hell—*five thousand francs* a year for their support, almost a thousand dollars: the entire income Emma realizes from what remains of her husband's estate. Need I say—yes, I *do* need to say, even to this journal where it is perfectly irrelevant, that I have never in my life met such a terrible woman as Emma's mother-in-law. According to legend, she was a prostitute when Lieutenant du Pont, the future marshal and Prince d'Agrigente, met her, but I doubt the story, as she must have been even then as plain—and odoriferous—as an abattoir on an August day.

"Are you planning to write about the change in New York

since you lived here?" This from the charming thin man of the
Herald, who knows me as a "valued contributor."

"Indeed. I look forward to a tour of the States. East and West.
North and South. I shall attend and write about the Centennial
Exhibition in Philadelphia when it opens—"

"For the *Herald?*" Again from the most amiable thin youth.

"Where else?" Equal amiability from me—if not total sincerity,
for I shall sell my wares to the highest bidder.

"Are you related to Mrs. William Astor?"

This was as startling a question as I have ever been asked.
"Certainly not!" I fear I was too sharp.

The mystery was promptly solved: apparently Mrs. Astor's
maiden name was the same as my mother's—Schermerhorn—
something I had not known, although even at Paris we have often
been told by amused and bemused travellers of the grandeur of
Mrs. Astor's receptions, of the gorgeous splendour of that New
York society which she dominates, having managed to unseat her
sister-in-law Mrs. John Jacob Astor III who outranks her, at least
according to primogeniture, for J.J. Astor III is the eldest son of
that family, and its head.

Once, a half-century ago, I saw the original J.J. Astor crawling
along lower Broadway; the old man wore an ermine-lined coat
and was supported by my old friend—and his secretary—the poet
Fitz-Greene Halleck. All dead.

Questions about my books. But not many. According to the
press, I am a famous author in the United States, but this set of
overcoats was not certain just *why* I am celebrated. On the other
hand, they are all familiar with my journalism, not only my
pieces for Jamie Bennett's *Herald* but also those for the *Evening
Post,* where my literary career began. I am the New York press's
perennial authority on European matters.

Politics. Sooner or later that subject always comes up with
Americans.

What did I think of the recent arrest and imprisonment of Boss
Tweed, who stole millions of dollars from the city of New York
whilst building the lavish new Court House. Piously I deplored
corruption.

What did I think of General U.S. Grant, whose second term as
president is due to end in a year's time?

I was wary. The corruption of General Grant's Administration
is a matter of some poignancy to me. My capital was administered

by the banking house of Jay Cooke, which collapsed in the fall of
1873, bringing on a panic whose effects are still with us—as my
capital is not.

Certain Wall Street criminals, among them Jay Gould and Jim
Fiske—how well I know their names!—in an attempt to corner
gold, brought on a thousand bankruptcies. Whether or not Gen-
eral Grant himself was involved in any of this is a disputed point.
Certainly he is known to take large gifts from men like Gould and
Fiske. If Grant is not himself a criminal he is a fool. Yet the
Republican party protects him, cherishes him, is loath even to let
him go now after two terms.

"Do you think General Grant will want a third term?" From
the *Times,* a newspaper particularly devoted to the Grant Administration.

"Since I have never met the General, I can hardly say. But . . ."
Deliberately I set out to make—well, not my fortune but at
least a *place* for myself where I can survive without fear of poverty the few years left me. "But," I repeated, "as you know, I am
a Democrat, of the Jackson–Van Buren persuasion . . ."

This caused some interest. There was a marked coolness from
the reporters representing the Republican interest (the majority,
I fear), but keen sympathy from the others.

"Do you favour Governor Tilden for the Democratic nomination?"

Favour him! All my hopes are based upon that fragile figure
obtaining the presidency next year. "Indeed I do. I am not, of
course, *au courant* . . ." Mistake to use French but the phrase was
out.

Odd. In France I think only in French. Now—in this hotel
room—what language do I think in? English? No. A *mélange!*

"I hardly know as much about New York's affairs as you gentlemen, but I do know that Mr. Tilden's breaking up of the
Tweed ring so pleased the honest people of the state that last year
they made him governor. After all, he has stopped the rich stealing from the poor—"

"But that sounds communist, sir." From the *Times.*

"I had no idea that honesty and communism were the same."
This evoked some applause. I find it fascinating that communism
should so distress the overcoats. Obviously the uprising in Paris
frightened the New York burghers—certainly it frightened us
Parisians when the Communards seized the city as the Germans

withdrew; even more frightening, however, was the revenge of the burghers, who butchered untold thousands for being Communards. I myself saw a child of five slaughtered in a street of Mont Rouge. The world revolution that began in 1848 is not yet finished.

At this point I raised my own banner: "When I last saw Mr. Tilden in Geneva, two summers ago—" The excitement that I had meant to create was now palpable: the overcoats positively steamed. The desultory interview with the expatriate author of successful books unknown to the newspaper press now came alive.

"*You* are a friend of the Governor?"

"Hardly. But we do correspond. We were first introduced by Mr. Gallatin, who lives in Geneva." Patiently I spelled the name; explained that Gallatin's father had been secretary of the treasury under Jefferson.

"I was struck by Mr. Tilden's, by the Governor's, extraordinary brilliance, by his intellectual grasp of every subject that he chooses to consider." This was true enough. Samuel J. Tilden is indeed a most intelligent if narrow man, and though of a cold and formal temperament, he is by no means wholly lacking in charm.

We dined nearly every day for a week on a terrace overlooking Lac Léman. Sometimes we were joined by Gallatin, whose bright European realism was often too much for the dour Americanism of S.J. Tilden.

At one point Tilden suddenly began to describe in detail precisely how he had destroyed Tweed and his ring, which included governors, judges, mayors, aldermen. As he spoke, Tilden's pale, old child's face grew flushed and the grey dull eyes suddenly reflected the lake's blue; for an instant, he was nearly handsome in his animation.

Gallatin and I (and a half dozen others) listened to the weak but compelling voice with fascination. But then Tilden struck for us Europeans (yes, I am one after so many years) a peculiarly hypocritical American note. "To think," he said to Gallatin, "what has happened to our country since your father's day! Since the time of Jefferson!"

Gallatin was astonished. "But surely everything is so much better now, Mr. Tilden. The country is so big, so very rich . . ." This was some weeks before the panic. "Railroads everywhere. Great manufactories. Floods of cheap labour from poor old

Europe. America is El Dorado now, whilst in my father's time it was just a nation of farmers—and not very good farmers at that."

"You misunderstood me, Mr. Gallatin." Tilden's sallow cheeks now each contained a smudge of brick-coloured red. "I speak of corruption. Of judges for sale. Of public men dividing amongst themselves the people's money. Of newspapers bought, *bought* by political bosses. Even the *Post.*" Tilden nodded gravely to me, knowing that I often wrote for that paper. "The *Post* took a retainer from Tweed. That's what I mean by the change in our country, this worship of the Golden Calf, of the almighty dollar, this terrible corruption."

I knew Tilden for only a week, but in that time this was the nearest to passion I had heard him come. In general he was—is —a very cold fish, as they say.

Gallatin's black eyebrows lifted, simulating amazement. "You know, Mr. Tilden, I used to talk a great deal to my father about the early days of the republic and . . . well, I do not mean to confound you, sir, but what you describe has always been the rule with us. Certainly in New York we have always given one another bribes and, whenever possible, taken the public money."

Was Tilden shocked? He has the lawyer's gift of suddenly ceasing advocacy when unexpected evidence is submitted. The spots of colour left his cheeks. He added water to the splendid Rhône wine in his glass. I noticed that he has a tremor of the hand like mine.

Then, "But surely, Mr. Gallatin, all this changed when the founder of our party, when Mr. Jefferson, was elected president?"

"Nothing ever changes, Mr. Tilden. People are people."

Is it a trick of my memory that at that moment the letters were brought to the table that assured Tilden of the Democratic nomination for the governorship of New York? I daresay I have moved things about in my memory. In any case, it was on that holiday in Switzerland—Tilden's first trip to Europe—that the summons came.

"I have no intention of being the candidate for governor." Tilden was firm as he stood in front of his hotel—trunks, companions, porters, chasseurs all about him.

"You must!" I said. "If not for the people, for the sake of our friend John Bigelow."

I got something very much like a smile on that. John Bigelow is perhaps Tilden's only friend. In the thirties the three of us were aspiring lawyers in the city. Both Tilden and Bigelow are a few years younger than I. In those days I did not know Tilden, but I often used to see John Bigelow at the Café Français, usually in the company of my friend Fitz-Greene Halleck. I seem to recall when Halleck and I played at billiards in the back room, Bigelow —a handsome, tall youth from upstate—was moderately disapproving. Once Bigelow shyly asked me to help him write for the newspaper press, and I did.

The ultra-Republican *Times* wanted to know more about my links with Tilden. "Slight. Slight," I answered truthfully. But I pray that soon our presently slight connection will be as links of steel.

"I have, at his request, written him occasionally on foreign affairs." This is true. I cannot say he precisely requested my reports, but he has shown great interest in them, particularly during the last six months when it has become apparent to everyone that he will be not only the Democratic candidate for president in '76 but the president as well, assuming that General Grant does not seek a third term.

A sudden thud like an earthquake's tremor ended my encounter with the press: the *Pereire* had docked. The overcoats fled. Emma's disgust was as plain as John Apgar's awe.

I took Emma's arm. *"C'est nécessaire, petite."*

"Comme tu veux, Papa."

I have not taken Emma into my confidence—on aesthetic grounds. She has had no real experience of the struggle that most lives are, and I would keep her innocent. My wife had a small fortune; and a family *Schloss* in Unterwalden, Switzerland. When both were lost to us at her death, Emma was safely (I thought) married to Henri d'Agrigente and for a dozen years the two lived splendidly, amassing debts in the Hôtel d'Agrigente, Boulevard de Courcelles.

Meanwhile, I did quite well with my writing; was able to support in some comfort one and a half (the half being the cost of a mistress in a good arrondissement). Then the shock of Paris falling, of Henri dying, of the banker Jay Cooke failing; and my ruin.

Now I must live by such wits as I have left. But Emma must be spared as much as possible the pain of seeing her old father like some once-beautiful *poule de luxe* of literature try once again to ply his wares on foot, as it were, in streets where once triumphantly he rode.

Well, no self-pity. The world is not easy. I only curse my luck that I am not young. At thirty I would have had no qualms. I could have conquered this city of New York in a week, like Tamburlaine when he took Persepolis!

2

JOHN DAY APGAR'S VICTORIA was at the pier as well as a curiously shaped wagon decorated with the gold legend THE FIFTH AVENUE HOTEL—"To take the trunks, sir," according to its driver, a withered son of Cork.

Amongst the thousand and one bits of information I have in the last few hours received: more than half the city's population of a million is foreign-born. Most are from Ireland (as in my day) and Germany. But representatives of the other countries are to be found in ever-increasing numbers. Whole districts of the lower island are devoted to Italians, Poles, Hebrews, Greeks, while the once charming Mott and Pell streets are now entirely occupied by *Chinese!* I cannot wait to explore this new world, more like a city from the *Arabian Nights* than that small staid English-Dutch town or village of my youth.

As the victoria left the pier and entered Orton Street, John Apgar indicated tattered beggars, holding out their hands. "We are known as the almshouse of Europe." He spoke with a mechanical bitterness, no longer even hearing the phrase on his own tongue, for everyone, I gather, uses it.

I suppose to the native New Yorker so many newcomers must be disturbing, particularly when there is not much work for them since the panic of '73, obliging them to turn to—what else? crime. But for the old New Yorkers with money this constant supply of cheap labour must be a singular joy. One can hire an excellent cook for eighteen dollars a month; a lady's maid for twelve dollars. Emma and I have been debating whether or not to indulge her in a lady's maid. Apparently we are the only occupants of a suite in the Fifth Avenue Hotel without personal servants.

The drive from the pier to the hotel was—well, Rip Van Winkle-ish. I have run out of epithets; and must remember not to use to death that hackneyed image.

I asked the driver to take us through Washington Square Park and then up the celebrated Fifth Avenue.

"You will doubtless find the avenue much changed." John's politeness is pleasing, but his gift for saying only the obvious makes him something less than the perfect companion. As a son-in-law, however, he has possibilities.

The law office of the Apgar Brothers in Chambers Street is prosperous. But I was not heartened to learn last summer in Paris that there are nine brothers and that our John is but the third son of the third brother. I think Emma regards him much as I do, but then we usually see things in exactly the same way—so much so that we seldom need to speak our thoughts, particularly on such a delicate subject as the right husband for her.

"Properly speaking, there was no Fifth Avenue in my day. A few brave souls were building houses north of the Parade Ground, as we called Washington Square. But they were thought eccentric, unduly fearful of the summer cholera, of smallpox in the lower island." I spoke without interest in what I was saying; looked this way and that; could hardly take it all in.

A white sun made vivid each detail of this new city, but gave no warmth. Beside me, Emma shivered beneath the fur rug, as enthralled as I.

Everywhere crowds of vehicles—carts, barouches, victorias, brightly painted horsecars, not to mention other and more sinister kinds of transport: when we crossed Sixth Avenue at Cornelia Street, I gasped and Emma gave a cry, as a train of cars drawn by a steam engine hurtled with deafening sound *over* our heads at thirty miles an hour!

The horses shied, whinnied; the driver swore. Like a dark rain, ashes fell from the elevated railway above our heads. Emma's cheek was smudged. Happily, we were not set afire by the bright coals that erupted from the steam engine, falling like miniature comets to the dark avenue below.

Then the cars were gone. The nervous horses were persuaded to cross the avenue and enter the quiet precinct of Washington Square Park.

"My God!" Emma put handkerchief to cheek; did not care to refine her language for Mr. John Day Apgar, who was more thrilled than not by our adventure.

"I'm sorry. I ought to have warned you. There's really nothing like it in the world, is there?"

"I'm happy to say, no, there is not." Emma's colour was now high; she looked uncommonly youthful—the sudden fright, the cold wind.

I did not repeat my now constant and, even to me, interminable refrain: How things have changed. Yet in my time (was ever any time mine?) Sixth Avenue was just a name to describe a country road that crossed isolated farms and thick marshes, where my father once took me duck shooting.

As we turned into Washington Park, I vowed I would not again make any reference to the way things were—except in print for money. More to the point, it is always difficult to discern whether or not one entertains or bores the young, since their politeness requires them to appear at all times attentive. I should know. In my youth I made my way in the world by using the old without conscience. Is there retribution awaiting me now? In the guise of some young listener smiling his betrayal as I maunder on.

I must stop this. Not dwell so much upon the past. The present is too exciting, and the small time left me must be well used to re-make Emma's fortune. At this instant I feel that nothing can stop us *if* I do not perish first of the heat.

Heat billows from the pipes, from the burning coals in the grate of the marble fireplace. I have tried and failed to open the parlour window. I positively gasp for air. But I am in my dressing gown and do not want to call a servant. Emma sleeps in her room.

Two bedrooms, parlour, and—remarkably—a private bath all for thirty dollars a day. Three meals are included, of course, whilst a fourth, supper, can be had for an additional two dollars and fifty cents. Yet even at this rate we will be penniless in three months. But the gamble is worth it. This hotel is the city's grandest; everyone of importance can be seen in the lobby, the reception rooms, the bars. So this must be our El Dorado, to be mined with care.

Curious, my pulse rate has almost doubled at the thought of money—and its absence!

I have just taken an opiate, a powerful laudanum mixed for me in Paris. So now, sleepily, I write rather as one dreams, not knowing what is real or not.

Washington Square Park is as handsome, in its way, as London's Green Park, with comfortable houses side by side, as neat and as unimaginative as a row of new American novels. In fact, the monotony of the architecture in the city's better sections takes some getting used to. But many of the newer buildings are in a different, more grandiose and—let me admit it—for *me*, more pleasing style.

We left Washington Park and began the ascent of Fifth Avenue, a pleasant boulevard not so wide or grand as the Champs-Élysées but pleasing enough, with tall ailanthus trees at regular intervals. Again, however, the avenue is lined for the most part with those sombre houses of dullest brownstone.

"Do *all* your houses look alike?" Emma was less than enchanted by fabled Fifth Avenue.

"They are dreadful, aren't they?" John's year in Paris had made him critical of what, I seem to recall in the early days of our acquaintance, he once boasted of. "You'd never recognize New York now," he would say to me. "It's every bit as fine as Paris."

"But things *are* changing uptown," he added.

"Not that your houses aren't . . . appealing." Emma smiled at him. "And obviously comfortable."

"Oh, they're that. This part"—John indicated the section between Washington Square Park and Madison Square at Twenty-third Street—"is where the old families live."

"Like the Apgars?" Emma was mischievous.

John blushed; his long face is rather like that of one of those llamas from the highlands of Peru. "Well,. we're not old in the city. We're from Philadelphia, actually. The Brothers didn't move to New York until just before I was born."

"But you live in this quarter?"

"Right along there." John pointed east, to Tenth Street. "That's my father's house. I'm staying there while looking for a place of my own—of course."

Since the conversation was now verging on the indelicate, I changed the subject, asked him about certain landmarks of my youth. No, he had never heard of the City Hotel; so that once famous center of the town has obviously been long since razed. I told him that it was the Fifth Avenue Hotel of its time.

"I thought the Astor House was."

As I heard the name I had a sudden *crise* of memory . . . a bright sultry summer afternoon when the walls of the Astor House were going up and a block of stone fell into the street, nearly killing a passer-by. Now the Astor House, once the leading hostelry of the city, "isn't what it used to be. Convenient for business people but too far downtown for the fashionables."

Today the center of the city is Madison Square and I must say its showiness provides a certain relief after the dull mile of Fifth Avenue brownstones we had driven so slowly past. I duly note that today's uptown traffic is every bit as bad as it used to be on lower Broadway.

One enters the square at the point where Broadway crosses Fifth Avenue, and immediately the eye is taken with the Fifth Avenue Hotel, a six-storey white marble palace that occupies the entire block between Twenty-third and Twenty-fourth streets. The half-colonnaded marble façade faces onto the gardens of Madison Square, and very pretty they must be in summer, though now the bare trees are like so many iron forks standing on end against a steel sky.

But . . . always the "but" in dealing with things American. Between the hotel and the park at the center of Madison Square, the avenue is wide and without much style. Half-hearted attempts have been made at paving certain sections. Asphalt, Belgian block, cobblestones succeed one another without design whilst everywhere, at irregular intervals, tall telegraph poles with their connecting wires dominate the vista just as the messages those copper wires are constantly transmitting define and govern this raw world: buy cotton, sell gold, make money. Well, I am hardly one to be condescending. Why else am I here?

John assured us that above Madison Square, as far north as Fifty-second Street, European-style mansions are going up. "While way up at Fifty-seventh Street, Mrs. Mary Mason Jones has built herself a French villa. Most extraordinary sight! Just sitting there all by itself in the wilderness with nothing around it except a few saloons and squatters' huts, and the goats."

Despite stern laws the goats are everywhere; they even invade the elegant premises of Madison Square. Emma was enthralled by the sight of a policeman attacking a half dozen dingy goats at the north end of the square, where they had taken up residence in front of a building in the process of renovation: the newest restaurant of the Delmonico family, soon to open.

We were met just outside the front door by a director of the hotel, a cousin of the late Mr. Paran Stevens, whose widow is known for her Sunday-night evenings, to which everyone goes save the most staid of the gentry like Mrs. Mary Mason Jones. I don't know why, but I do enjoy writing that name.

The opiate is beginning to take effect. I yawn. Am drowsy. Note that the heart now beats more and more slowly whilst the little drum in my head has slowed its thudding.

The Stevenses' cousin was most flattering: "A great honour, sir. To receive you and the beautiful Princess."

With much ceremony, we were led into the hotel lobby, a vast room crowded with tall palms and fat green rubber plants—a jungle contained by marble walls and red damask hangings and filled with the infernal smell of cigar smoke, of burning anthracite, of the heavy perfumes worn by the many ladies (not all, I should think, properly attended) who made their promenade either in pairs together or on the arm of a gentleman—recently met? The fact that I can no longer tell a prostitute from a fine lady is the first sign that I have been away for a very long time. As a boy, I always *knew*.

I registered us at the desk; pleasantly aware that we were the center of much attention. Obviously, I am better known than the overcoats have led me to believe. Also, the fact that I am accompanied by a bona-fide princess is stimulating. Americans care desperately for titles, for any sign of distinction. In fact, since the War Between the States, I have not met a single American of a certain age who does not insist upon being addressed as Colonel or Commodore. Invariably I promote them; address them as General, as Admiral; they preen and do not correct me.

The Stevenses' cousin . . . but I forget: he, too, is titled. The *Colonel* said that he would like personally to escort us to our suite on the sixth floor. "We shall take," he said, "the perpendicular railway."

I assumed that this was some sort of nonsense phrase and thought nothing of it as we made our regal progress across the central lobby. Many of the gentlemen bowed respectfully to the director; he is a handsome man, heavily bearded as almost everyone is nowadays except me. I continue to wear only side whiskers despite the fact that having exchanged the blond silken hair of youth for the white wiry bristle of old age, I resemble uncannily the late President Van Buren.

Halfway across the lobby, a puffy bewhiskered man of fifty, elaborately got up, with perfumed (and dyed?) whiskers, bowed low to Emma and me.

"*Princesse*, allow me to introduce myself. We met at the christening of the *prince impérial*."

The voice was Southern with a most peculiar overtone of British; the French was frightful but confident.

Emma was gracious; I, too. He told us his name; neither listened to it. Then he was gone. The Colonel, who had been talking to a huge man with a diamond stickpin, turned; his eyebrows arched at the retreating figure. "You know him?"

Emma chose to be mischievous. "Paris. The christening of the *prince impérial.*"

"Oh, yes." I could not tell if the Colonel was impressed or not. In any case, we were at that instant stopped by a nervous young man; with a sidelong glance at the disapproving Colonel, he pressed his card upon me. "I'm from Ritzman's, sir. We'd like to do you, sir. And the Princess, too, sir. If we may, sir." He took to his heels.

Emma was amused. "What will Mr. Ritzman want to do to us?"

"To photograph you." The Colonel had stopped before a mysterious grilled gate that seemed to be locked. We stopped, too.

"They have a store, across the square. Ritzman photographs everyone of importance."

"But what," asked Emma, "does he do with the pictures?"

"Sells them. Great demand for portraits of a princess like yourself . . . and a celebrated author," he added quickly as the grilled gate was flung open to reveal a small panelled chamber containing a uniformed man gravely fiddling with mysterious wheels and levers. At the Colonel's insistence we entered the closet. The door shut behind us and *we rose into the air.*

Emma is delighted, but I confess to a certain giddiness, not so much going up as when, in obedience to the law of gravity, the thing comes down and one's stomach seems not to keep up with the rest of the falling body.

Our suite is large and nicely furnished, with flowers everywhere—so many, in fact, that between the overheating and the odor of the tuberoses I have had a headache most of the evening. The private bathroom is indeed a luxury unknown in Europe's hotels, and rare in New York.

On a table in front of the marble fireplace was a stack of letters and telegrams. I could not wait to open them, but politeness required that I wait until the Colonel demonstrated for us the many conveniences of the suite, including the new calcium or lime lights that cast a rather lurid glow over everything, though they make reading particularly easy for one who is developing, as I am, cataracts.

"Mrs. Paran Stevens has invited you to her next Sunday." The Colonel indicated one of the envelopes. "She always has music. Usually someone from the opera. She hopes you will come."

"You are too kind," Emma murmured, removing furs (her mother's, I fear).

"She'll want to see you, too, Mr. Apgar." The Colonel was casually agreeable, and John blushed and said that he would be honoured.

After a demonstration of the mysterious speaking tubes that connect the suite with those bowels of the hotel where dwell valets and maids and waiters, the Colonel withdrew.

"We're really here." Emma ran to the window to look out onto the square filled with omnibuses and carriages and telegraph poles and goats (actually the goats were now trotting down East Twenty-fourth Street).

A large sign on a building just opposite implores one and all to drink Old Jacob Thompson's Sarsaparilla.

Since I still felt I was aboard ship and the floor appeared to be heaving in a most unnatural way, I sat down beside the fire and began to open telegrams whilst John showed Emma those sights of the town that are visible from the window.

"That's the Union Club over there. It's quite nice. We're all members," said John. Apparently the Apgars move in a herd up, down and all around the island.

But Emma was more concerned with the beggars.

"Why don't you do something with them?"

"Like what?"

"The Emperor would have started a war." Emma laughed. She was, however, quite serious.

"But we've just had a war."

"Well, you need another one. And very soon."

I found the invitation from Mrs. Paran Stevens for Sunday night, to hear the tenor Mario. Also, an invitation to be guest of honour at the Lotos Club any Saturday of my choosing, to give an impromptu chat. A note from Mr. Hartman, wanting to know if I would be interested in a lecture tour. A message from William Cullen Bryant (the whole name spelled out) to say that he would be happy to have me for breakfast any day, before 8:30 A.M.

I've just been counting on my fingers and my old editor at the *Evening Post*—who is still the editor of the paper—is now eighty-one years old. Everyone else from my New York youth is dead except for Bryant, whom I thought of even then as being the oldest person I knew.

There was a welcome from my publisher, Mr. Dutton, and a note delivered by hand from Richard Watson Gilder, editor of *Scribner's Monthly*, where I publish when I cannot get a decent price elsewhere; he proposes an early meeting at my convenience; he, too, wants me to address the Lotos Club. There was nothing, however, from Bonner of the *Ledger* or from Frank Leslie, whose monthly pays the best of all the magazines—I had written both men that I would be in New York on the fourth.

I was also disappointed to find no welcome from what has been for years a principal source of revenue, the New York *Herald*. But then young James Gordon Bennett is but a pale (and drunken) version of his father. Even so, he might have had the courtesy to have left at least a card.

But I found what I most wanted to find amongst the telegrams: an invitation to take tea tomorrow with John Bigelow. He is the key to my good fortune . . . if that fortune is to be good.

Words now begin to blur agreeably on the page. The opiate takes effect. In spite of the night's approach, I feel optimistic. Young. No, not young but comfortable within this carapace of old flesh as I prepare to make one last effort to place myself in such a manner that for me the setting of the sun will be the best time of my long day and Emma's noon.

3

NOON, and I am exhausted.

The opiate worked marvellously until four in the morning. Then I was wide-awake. Could not fall asleep.

I dressed. Watched the dawn. Worked for a time on my Empress Eugénie; ordered tea; made sure that the waiter was very quiet, for Emma is a light sleeper and needs all the rest she can get. New York will be a siege for her. No, a triumphant progress.

If Mr. John Day Apgar is able to support her in decent style, then I shall be reasonably pleased to have him for a son-in-law. Of course, he is a year or two younger than Emma but that hardly matters, since her beauty should have a long life whilst he has no beauty at all.

Emma is to spend the day with John's sister, visiting the shops —or stores, as they call them here. Did they always? Or have I forgotten? It is plain that I am no longer a New Yorker. But then this New York is no longer the New York that was.

Restless, the article finished and sealed in its envelope and addressed to *Harper's Monthly*, I decided to take Bryant at his word and pay him a breakfast call. He lives now at 24 West Sixteenth Street.

Without delight, I entrusted myself to the perpendicular railway. "Fine morning, sir. But near to freezing," said the operator who looked to be, at the very least, a commodore in full uniform.

The lobby was almost empty. I gave the envelope to a page who vowed he would deliver it to *Harper's;* then made my way amongst green shrubbery and bronze spittoons to the front door, where I was respectfully offered, as it were, the square by the uniformed chasseur, who also warned me of the cold and of the fineness of the day.

I had forgotten the brittle, dry exhilarating cold of the New York winter. The wet cold of Paris makes my ears ache. The clammy cold of London congests the lungs. But despite the fumes of anthracite, New York's air has a polar freshness. And everything appears new, even the sun, which this morning looked like a fresh-minted double eagle as it began its climb over the island.

Even at such an early hour the city is very much alive with horsecars rattling up and down Fifth Avenue whilst the pedestrians—mostly the poor on their way to work—walk swiftly with their heads down, exhaling clouds of steam. Many of the beggars are Civil War veterans, wearing the remains of old uniforms; armless, legless, eyeless, they sell pencils, shoelaces. "Lost my arm at Chickamauga, sir." And the dented tin cup is thrust accusingly in one's face. Italians play hurdy-gurdies; shivering monkeys dance in the terrible cold. Homeless ragged children huddle together in doorways.

I boarded a horsecar. Although the fare is five cents, I did not have any small change in my pocket—only fragments of remarkably filthy paper, some worth ten cents, twenty-five cents, or even a dollar. In my purse I carry a few half eagles: gold coins worth ten dollars apiece (to be used sparingly!). I have not yet obtained a twenty-dollar double eagle, my beautifully apt simile for this morning's sun. But then, if the New York sun does *not* resemble United States currency, this whole great country is not El Dorado but a fraud.

The horsecar swayed and rattled down Fifth Avenue. At the car's center a small potbellied stove gave off insufficient heat, and mephitic fumes. On the floor was straw as insulation. My fellow passengers were mostly men, mostly bearded, mostly potbellied like the stove. In fact, saving the desperate poor, everyone in New York is overweight: it seems to be the style. Yet when I was young (I must stop this sort of Nestorizing to myself and save it for the lecture platform and the press), the American was lean, lanky, often a bit stooped with leathery skin—and, of course, beardless. Some new race has obviously replaced the Yankees: a plump, voluptuous people, expanding gorgeously beneath their golden sun.

On the omnibus everyone was reading a newspaper. That means that the newspaper business, *my* business, is good. The headline reported the escape from prison of Boss Tweed.

I got off at the corner of Fifth Avenue and Sixteenth Street, cursing my age, for I move awkwardly. Like my countrymen, I, too, am fat, but at least have the excuse of advanced age and French cuisine.

I walked down Sixteenth Street between rows of identical brownstone houses. Irish maids swept stairs; menservants (some Negro) took in garbage pails; the knife-and-scissors-sharpener man moved jingling from house to house. Wisps of white smoke began to appear from the chimneys as this most respectable street slowly awakened.

I found William Cullen Bryant in his study, wearing a faded dressing gown and exercising with dumbbells. He did not stop, nor, I fear, did he recognize me until the maid announced my name.

"Schuyler! How good of you to come. Sit right down. I shan't be a moment."

So I sat in the dark study (the only light from two small coals burning in the grate) and watched Bryant do his exercises. He is as tall and spare as I remember, but his appearance has been entirely transformed by a vast beard that now circles his face like a mandala or a magical bush ready at a moment's notice to ignite, to emit the voice of God, but then I have always thought Bryant's voice must sound not unlike that of the Deity on one of the Creator's rare unagitated days.

"You must exercise each morning, Schuyler . . ."

"I *think* about exercise almost every day."

"The blood must flow—flow!" Then dumbbells were put away, and Bryant excused himself. Through several shut doors, I heard the sound of him splashing about in water and *knew* the water was arctic cold.

In no time at all, Bryant returned, fully clothed and the picture of, as the British say, rude health. Together we descended to the drafty downstairs dining room furnished with depressingly "sincere" Eastlake furniture.

We breakfasted alone. Bryant's wife died ten years ago and "my daughter Julia is out of the city. So I am a bachelor."

The maid served us hominy with milk, brown bread and butter. I waited for tea, for coffee—in vain.

Bryant was greatly affected by Tweed's escape from prison. "Of course he paid his gaolers. They're all alike, you know." Who "they" were he did not specify, but I assume that he meant the lower orders, the Democrats, the Irish, the enemies of the Republican *Evening Post*, which supports the Grant Administration regardless of scandal. The radical crusading spirit is now entirely dead at the *Post*. But Bryant is old.

Glumly I chewed brown bread whilst Bryant expressed himself at length on the hopeless corruption of New York City until, bored, I diverted him with an inquiry about his forthcoming history of the United States.

I was favoured with a rare smile. "Unfortunately, I have done very little of the work. My collaborator is the one who toils. But I do have a book of poetry ready for publication."

Bryant tried out a number of titles on me. We decided that *The Flood of Years* was the best. Apparently this octogenarian work is "an answer to that poem of my youth *Thanatopsis*. It's hard to believe that at seventeen I actually entertained certain doubts about the immortality of the Soul. But now, Schuyler, I have come to accept our immortality!"

At that instant, Bryant looked like Moses, despite a trace of hominy grit in his beard. I nodded respectfully; felt young again, callow, tongue-tied in the presence of America's premier poet, of the city's most distinguished newspaper editor, of the oldest man ever to exercise with dumbbells on an icy winter morning.

"But your own work has given us all much pleasure." The deep-set eyes appeared to look at me for the first time. If the blood in my congealing veins were capable of a sudden rush to *any* part of the body, I might have blushed with pleasure at praise from the only man alive who still looks upon me as young.

"I particularly admire *Paris Under the Commune.* What a time! What issues were joined!" To my surprise Bryant is not made panicky by the Communards—or communists—and he asked me intelligent questions. He also got the title of the book right; usually it is referred to as *Paris Under the Communists.*

Then we spoke of our dear mutual dead friend the editor William Leggett. I write "mutual" knowing that it is a word Bryant deplores. In fact, he has written a small book of words and phrases that are never to appear in the *Post.* Not "mutual" but "common." Not "inaugurate" but "begin." He has no liking for Latin- or Greek-derived words (yet called his most famous poem *Thanatopsis*).

It is curious that despite Bryant's great good sense about language, his own prose is so perfectly ordinary that even the liveliest topic drops dead at a single prod of his (the last in all of New York) feather quill pen.

Opening the *Herald,* Bryant found me on page three. With an amused inflection he read aloud the reporter's account of the arrival in New York of the celebrated author Charles Schermerhorn Schuyler and his daughter, the Princess Day Regent. "A Turkish title from the sound of it."

"No. Bosnian."

Bryant's humour still lurks behind that awesome face he sees fit to petrify the world with. As practising journalists, we enjoyed the confident incoherence of the interviewer; and deplored the low standards of today's journalism.

"And yet—" The maid interrupted us not with coffee or tea, as I had prayed, but with Bryant's topcoat and beaver hat.

"—the newspaper press can take a great deal of credit for having destroyed Mr. Tweed in '73."

I noticed sourly that the maid did not even attempt to help me on with *my* topcoat; and due to a rheumatic shoulder, I have more difficulty than does Bryant getting in and out of clothes.

"With some aid from Governor Tilden."

"Of course, a capital fellow. Do you know him?"

"Yes. Slightly."

We were now in the street. School-bound children carried their books in that never-out-of-date shoulder sling whilst a ragged man pulled a sort of barrow after him on which had been placed a large tin bucket of boiling water fired from beneath by a kerosene burner.

The man's hoarse cry still sounds in my head: "Here's your nice hot corn, smoking hot, smoking hot, just from the pot." I used to collect such "songs" of the street.

"What sort of corn does he find in December?" I asked as we turned into Fifth Avenue.

"From Florida. The railroads, Schuyler, the railroads! They have changed everything. For the good, for the bad." He took my arm. "Do come and see our new quarters. We moved last summer to the corner of Fulton and the Broadway—a ten-storey building —a terrible expense, frankly, but convenient. Also, the presses are hidden away at the bottom, and we even have a perpendicular railway which I refuse to set foot in. One must always walk! Walk, climb, walk, climb."

Touching his hat to those who recognized him, Bryant walked briskly south toward Washington Square Park. As best I could, I kept up with him. Each morning Bryant walks the three miles from his house to the *Evening Post.* Like a fool, I agreed to accompany him.

Now, several hours later, as I sit in the parlour of this hotel suite, waiting to take tea with John Bigelow, there is a thunderstorm in my ears whilst my fingernails have exchanged their usual healthy pink for a most disagreeable mauve tint.

I am drinking rum and tea, and hope not to die before teatime.

Assuming that I survive my gallop down Broadway with Bryant, I did do the right thing, for not only is he an editor to whom I am beholden but he knows more about the politics of the city than anyone outside prison, saving Mr. Tweed.

On every corner newspaper posters proclaim the true story of Tweed's escape from the Ludlow Street jail. Apparently, the Boss was allowed each day to go for a drive with two keepers. Yesterday, after a tour of the northern end of the island, he was allowed to pay a call on his wife in their mansion at Forty-third Street and Fifth Avenue.

Just now my hack driver pointed out to me this sinister palace

—brownstone again!—built with stolen money. In the course of yesterday's visit, Tweed went upstairs, and vanished. Obviously, he is a great rogue, but popular—at least amongst the lower orders, whom he gave, from time to time, small commissions, as it were, on the vast sums of money that he and his ring were stealing from the public at large.

During our walk Bryant showed me the new Court House. "I calculate that the money Tweed and his people stole while building that temple to Mammon could have paid off the national debt."

"But *how* did it happen?" I was genuinely curious. Most of the city's officials have always been moderately corrupt, as the younger Gallatin assured Governor Tilden; but it is not usual for the same group to remain in power year after year stealing millions in full view of the public.

But I was not to be instructed, for just then we were ambushed in City Hall Park by what at first looked to be an enormous green umbrella with no one attached to it. But then the umbrella was raised and its attachment became visible, to my astonishment and to Bryant's dismay.

The man introduced himself to us, in a piercing voice: "Citizen Train, Mr. Bryant! Your nemesis! Yours, too, sir." He gave me a courtly bow; and I noted that he was wearing a sort of French military greatcoat crossed with a broad scarlet sash.

Citizen Train indeed! The story of George Francis Train is well known to us at Paris. A New Englander, he became a millionaire in his youth from shipping. Later he helped to found the Union Pacific railroad; to finance that project, he created the infamous holding company known as *Crédit Mobilier* which set about in the most systematic way to bribe most of the Congress, including General Grant's first vice president, Schuyler Colefax.

Happily for Mr. Train, he had gone mad before all these bribes were given seven—eight?—years ago. Forced out of the Union Pacific, he went to Ireland and tried to expel the English, who put him in jail for a time. Train then moved on to France in 1870, and became a Communard; he helped organize those horrors that took so many lives—as I have described at length elsewhere.

Why am I writing *journalism?* In a moment I shall be explaining and explaining all sorts of things to you, dear reader, when none of this is meant for any eyes but mine. These notes are to be the quarry from which I hope to hack out a monument or two to decorate the republic's centennial, as well as to mark my own

American year—a year that is beginning in a most helter-skelter, breathless way: literally breathless, for I am still breathing with some difficulty despite the rum and tea.

Anyway, there in the midst of the cold windy park was mad wealthy Train with his red sash and green umbrella and all-consuming passion to be the president! Yes, after the slaughter of the Paris Communards, Train came back to the United States and ran for president in '72 as an independent—that is to say, a communist. His campaign was unusually eccentric and gave much pleasure to almost everyone. The workies were particularly amused at the spectacle of a millionaire communist whilst the press will always write at length of anyone so entirely mad as to want the vote for women, the right for labouring men to strike, and the price for a postage stamp never to exceed a penny.

"Dear Mr. Train," Bryant was uncharacteristically nervous as he backed away from that menacing green umbrella.

Train suddenly turned to me, and with an unexpected smile, said, "Forgive me, citizen, for not offering you my hand but I make it a general rule never to shake hands with anyone over the age of twelve. Intimate physical contact of that sort causes one to lose psychic energy. And vital energy, citizen, must be hoarded in these terrible times. Now, Mr. Bryant, explain yourself."

The Moseslike Bryant suddenly resembled that patriarch confronted by a bush more than usually ablaze and angry. "Explain myself?" There was a trace of stammer in his usually deliberate voice. "In what way, sir?"

"*Tweed!*" Train was becoming agitated. Nurses pushing perambulators fled our corner of the park. "I said he should be hanged! I wrote you that at the *Post*. But was my letter ever published, was it?"

"So many letters, sir . . . I mean, Citizen Train." Bryant regained a degree of composure as with a swift sidestep that would have done credit to a youthful gallant of the ballroom, he got himself round the wealthy communist, who stared at him fiercely from beneath the green umbrella (to protect him, I have been told, from malignant star rays).

"Now you can see what happens when my letters are not printed, and sensible advice is not followed . . ."

But by then Bryant had pranced—no other word—to the edge of the park with me in tow, and soon we were safely in Broadway, now filled with morning traffic.

"That man . . . !" Bryant was, comparatively, speechless. "A

perfect nuisance. Normally, he sits in the park at Madison
Square, and I can avoid him. Fate obviously instructed him to
come and wait for me here at, ah, Trivium." The classical reference did Bryant good, and gave me the occasion to congratulate
him with some insincerity on his recent translations from
Homer. Actually I could not get through them, but they are
much admired by those who have no Greek and the wrong English.

Note: Must do something with George Francis Train. The
French papers would certainly be interested. But they pay too
little. The English press? Possibly. Must inquire.

Two large new hotels dominate Broadway just below City
Hall, the St. Nicolas and the Metropolitan. Then, at Barclay
Street, I insisted that we pause a moment to look at the façade of
the Astor House. "I left when it was half-built."

"Most showy." Like me, Bryant disdains New York's attempts
at grandeur: he under the impression that they succeed and I
because they fail—at least what I have seen so far. But I do rather
like Mr. Tweed's Court House, which would not be out of place
in Paris.

Then I looked for the Park Theatre; could not find it. "What
happened?"

"Dear Schuyler, it burned to the ground! Everything here
burns up sooner or later. You know that."

I felt real anguish. "I used to review the plays there . . ."

"For me, yes. I know. What did we call you?"

"Gallery Mouse."

"Well, Gallery Mouse has a wide range of new theatres to
attend if he so chooses." A sidelong glance at me. "But surely you
don't want to write about our theatre."

"No. No."

"Because I do admire your reports from Europe. You deeply
understand that wicked old world."

I cannot think why I *deeply* resented Bryant's smug puritan
tone. After all, our wicked old Paris has never come up with a
thief on the scale of Boss Tweed.

"I had thought I might perhaps do some American pieces. You
know: what it is like to come back after so many years."

"A latter-day Rip Van Winkle?"

The phrase that I have myself been using for two days became
on his lips indescribably boring and obvious. "Well, yes. I sup-

pose that such a comparison is unavoidable."

"And our newspapers do not avoid much . . ."

"Except the truth of the matter." To my horror, this savagery escaped my lips; but Bryant took it well enough.

"Half-truths are the best we can manage, I fear. For a moment you sounded like our late friend Leggett."

"That is indeed a compliment." The passionate Leggett burned out his mind and lungs for the truth—or at least for something not unlike that elusive absolute.

Finally, we stood in front of the *Evening Post*'s new building.

"Schuyler, you have endured nobly the three miles."

Although my face was stiff from the cold, my body was leaking sweat from every pore.

"Now you must come in and meet the staff."

I entrusted myself to the compartment of the perpendicular railway whilst Bryant climbed the stairs.

The Negro operator was admiring. "There's no one like old Mr. Bryant in all New York. He'll be up there before we are."

And so he was. As I stepped onto the landing, I saw Bryant hanging from the lintel to his office door. Very slowly he chinned himself, and dropped to the floor.

"You will give *me* a heart attack." I was firm. "Just watching you is bad for *my* system."

This flattered him, and in the best of humours he took me into his new office which was simply a larger version of the old one —the same desk, chairs, open bookcases crowded with his own works; my sharp author's eye noted two books by me.

The literary editor was summoned. George Cary Eggleston is pleasant, young: "Admire *Paris and* [sic!] *the Commune* more than I can say, Mr. Schuyler."

"Would that you *had* said it, Mr. Eggleton." I seldom resist so obvious an opening. "I looked in vain for a notice of it in the *Post*."

"Is that true?" Enthroned at his desk, Bryant was Jehovah on the mountaintop.

"I must say . . . I don't know . . . perhaps . . . I shall look . . ."

That disposed of the literary editor. I was then introduced to a Mr. Henderson, the business head of the paper. The two men spoke of business. I proposed that I go.

"No, Mr. Schuyler. *I'm* the one who's going." And Mr. Henderson did go.

"Would you like to write something for us on the Centennial

Exhibition?" I had forgotten how swiftly Bryant comes to the point when he is at his desk, at work.

"Why, yes. I would."

"It opens in Philadelphia. May or June, I'm not certain. Anyway, there will be time to prepare yourself, to think through all the changes you will have noted . . ."

"Not least, amongst them, let us hope, the rates of payment at the *Post?*" How impossible it would have been for the young Charles Schermerhorn Schuyler to mention money to William Cullen Bryant. But I am old, needy, triplebound with brass, and would that it were gold. I managed to get him to agree to a flat payment of five hundred dollars for no less than ten thousand words, an excellent price for the *Post*, though hardly in the *Ledger* class.

I rose to go. "I am to take tea with our old friend John Bigelow."

Bryant was interested. "I've not seen him since the election and his . . . uh, elevation."

"What does the secretary of state of New York do?" Bigelow was elected to the post last month.

"Whatever it is, let us say that some do less of it than others. I presume *this* secretary of state will be very busy trying to elect Governor Tilden president . . ."

"That is my impression. I assume you will support Tilden."

The deep-set eyes almost vanished beneath the noble brow as he turned his head away from the window. "The *Post* is a Republican newspaper. Governor Tilden is a Democrat . . ." And so on. But Bryant's tone was pensive, tentative. This means that he is not decided; must mention this to Bigelow.

Bryant accompanied me to the office door, from which he had so recently hung. "Tilden is my lawyer, you know. A splendid man. But not perhaps strong enough for the highest place. I speak of his physical health—not mental, of course. And then, of course, he's not married. This may disturb the electorate."

"But Jackson, Van Buren, Buchanan—any number of presidents have been bachelors in the White House."

"But they once *had* wives. Saving the egregious Buchanan, they were widowers, while Samuel Tilden has never married, nor, one gathers, even contemplated matrimony. If elected, he would be our first . . . our . . . our first . . ."

"Our first *virgin* president?"

Bryant was taken aback. Then, almost shyly, he laughed through that enormous waterfall of a beard, in itself a suitable subject for ode-making.

"Dear Schuyler, you have been too long in Paris! We are simple folk in this republic."

On that amiable note we parted.

I was so exhausted from the morning's hike that I had more energy than ever: a phenomenon that Emma's father-in-law used often to remark upon as he would tell us for the thousandth time about the retreat from Moscow.

I was drawn irresistibly to the Astor House despite its decline —which is relative only to the new grandeur of the uptown hotels.

I found the lobbies crowded with people; most looked to be businessmen from nearby Wall Street and the various exchanges.

I stood at the door to the vast dining room and beheld half a thousand men at breakfast. There was hardly a woman in sight as the bearded, frock-coated, stout burghers of the district gorged themselves on plates of ham and eggs, on enormous beefsteaks and cutlets. Hungry as I was after my walk with Bryant, I could not face so many red-faced carnivores so early in the morning.

Instead I made my way to the tile-floored bar room, a dim congenial place with the longest bar that I have ever seen. Bronze Venuses and Dianas alternated as decorations with innumerable brightly polished spittoons.

Those given to heavy drink had already taken up their positions at the bar, gulping down their pick-me-ups—more put-me-downs I should think, for I dislike strong drink so early in the day.

In one corner, shaded by a spiky green plant that looked as if it might devour an entire businessman, I found a small table beside a rack containing all the morning newspapers. Not until I had sat down did I realize how truly exhausted I was: my right leg began uncontrollably to tremble from the tension of no longer having to support my considerable weight.

"What'll it be?" was the waiter's gracious question.

I said that it would be a bock beer and, perhaps, if it was possible, a cup of coffee. All things were possible, including a most astonishing array of food that I watched being laid upon a long table at a right angle to the bar.

Waiters hurried in and out, depositing platters of cold meats, lobsters, salads, cheeses, as well as large mysteriously covered dishes. This was the famous "free lunch" one has heard of for so many years, a specialty of certain New York bars. For a single five-cent glass of beer one may eat to one's heart's content the free lunch.

Possible piece for a Paris paper: how much cheaper food is here than in Europe. Just now I walked by a decent-looking restaurant that advertises a meal of hot beef "cut from the joint," bread, pickles and potatoes for seventy-five cents. In the shops, beef costs thirty-five cents the pound. John Apgar says that one can live comfortably in one's own home with three servants on six thousand a year. Unfortunately, Emma and I have less than half that amount.

Luxuriously, I read the dozen morning newspapers, so conveniently collected for me by the friendly Astor bar. Each front page was bold with Tweed's escape. Since I am not easily distressed by the familiar corruption of my native and still (to be confessed only to this page) hopelessly provincial city, I tend rather to be on the side of that large bearlike man with the small clear eyes and thick beard and I hope that Mr. Tweed manages to escape for good with all his swag. But then I tend to side with criminals. Although my sympathies in France are officially republican, at heart I delight in all Bonapartes—particularly in the first one, whose crimes were on such a large scale that they have ceased to be the stuff of moralizing and are simply history.

The inner pages of each journal announce the arrival of Charles Schermerhorn Schuyler and his beautiful daughter, the Princess Dag Regent, Degregene, Dahgreejuhnt, widow of Napoleon's famed marshal, daughter-in-law of the Emperor Napoleon III, intimate of the Empress Eugénie . . . a jumble of information, mostly false.

But I was pleased that my support of Governor Tilden was everywhere noted. Less pleased to read of the "florid, portly novelist whose fame in Europe is far greater than it is here in what was once his native land." This from the *Sun*. Although I have never written a novel, my "fame" *ought* to be more considerable here than in France where I publish seldom, unlike England where I used often to publish. Now I know how those acquaintances of my youth, Washington Irving and Fenimore Cooper, felt upon their respective returns to these States after so many years abroad: Welcome home, traitor, was the tone then—is the tone now.

Suffering a pang of hunger (hominy and milk is not my idea of
the perfect breakfast), I made my way to the buffet table—or "free
lunch counter," as the waiter called it, giving me a speculative
look that seemed to say, Is this a "dead head" (new expression to
me—it means one who travels on a railroad pass or goes to the
theatre free)? and will he, for the price of one stein of beer, eat
three meals? I daresay the state of my finances make me oversensi-
tive.

I indicated, modestly, a tureen of chipped beef. The waiter
filled my plate. "That about the size of it?"

Another new expression. I must make up a glossary. "Yes, that
is exactly the right size of it." I suspect that I gave the wrong
response.

On my way back to the blessed table beside the rack of newspapers, I was stopped by two men who had been seated at the
opposite end of the long dim bar.

"Mr. Schuyler?" asked the younger of the two, an elegantly
turned-out young gentleman with a full moustache, and what
looked to be a black orchid in his buttonhole.

"Sir?" I felt a fool, as the chipped beef slopped ever so slightly
onto my thumb.

"You don't remember me." And of course for a moment I did
fail to recognize the one man in New York I ought always to
remember, for it was none other than that exquisite athlete,
yachtsman, equestrian, millionaire publisher—*my* publisher,
James Gordon Bennett, Junior, of the New York *Herald*, in whose
pages my reports from Europe have been appearing for close to
forty years.

"Sorry, Jamie! Forgive me. I'm just off the boat. A dazzled
immigrant." I played the part of foolish elder sage, of Falstaff to
Jamie's Prince Hal—except he is now king in his own right, for
his grim Scots father who started the *Herald* as a penny horror
in '35, died three years ago, leaving Jamie as the sole proprietor
of a newspaper which has the largest (if not the best, as Bryant
would undoubtedly observe) circulation of any newspaper in the
United States.

Much of the *Herald*'s success is based on its "Personal Column"
advertisements that are nothing more than a straightforward
guide to the Sodom below Bleecker Street, to the Gomorrah of
Sixth Avenue, to every prostitute with a few dollars and a desire
to see her name in print. Good folk complain about the *Herald*'s
advertisements, but everyone reads them.

Jamie introduced me to the elderly man with him, a sort of
doleful farmer type whose name meant nothing to me.

"I've known Mr. Schuyler since I was—how old?"

"Before birth, I should think. When your mother paid us a call
in Paris, a month before you were born."

Having failed to make his way in the proud self-contained
aristocracy of New York, the older Bennett had vowed that his
son would one day prevail amongst the Knickerbocker nobles and
so sent the child off to Paris to be brought up.

My wife and I used often to see Jamie and his mother. Because
the boy was the same age as Emma, they were often together, and
I always thought that he showed some interest in her; but in those
days she was not much inclined to her father's countrymen.
Eventually Jamie returned to take with the greatest ease that
place in New York society his father had wanted for him. Everyone was enchanted by Jamie's Parisian elegance, his superb
sportsmanship and, of course, his quite unexpected gift for the
most sensational sort of newspaper publishing.

The year of old Bennett's death, Jamie arranged for one Henry
M. Stanley to search for one David Livingstone, reputedly lost in
Africa. Lavishly financed by Jamie, this entirely boring saga filled
miles of newsprint for what seemed a decade, ensuring the *Herald*
its American pre-eminence despite my own unremittingly dim
reports on such trivia as Bismarck, Garibaldi, and Napoleon III.

"I must leave you here, Mr. Bennett." The sad farmer clung a
moment to the younger man's hand; then he squeezed my elbow
and lugubriously departed.

Jamie turned to me. "Come see our offices. We're right across
the street where Barnum's used to be." But I had had my fill of
newspaper offices for one day.

"Another time. My chipped beef grows cold."

Jamie made a face at the plate. "Then I'll have a drink with
you." He joined me in my friendly green-shaded corner, and
divined why I had placed myself so close to the newspapers. "You
wanted to read all about your splendid arrival for free. A razzle-
dazzle!" He shouted this last phrase which referred not to my
arrival, as I feared, but to a perfectly terrifying cocktail that
contains, in equal parts, brandy, absinthe and ginger ale. Hard
drinkers, these New York gentlemen.

"How's Emma?"

"She would like to see you."

"Handsome as ever?"

"As always, to a father's eye."

"I shall arrange something. Perhaps the theatre. Whatever Emma likes. Mr. Schuyler, what are your politics?"

"If you'd read your own paper this morning, you'd know that I am an admirer of Governor Tilden."

"Cold as a clam. But that's good." The waiter brought Jamie his razzle-dazzle in a frozen glass, and beamed respectfully as the young lord downed the drink and asked for another. Obviously Jamie is well known at the Astor bar; but then he must be well known everywhere for New York is very much his city.

"Good that Governor Tilden is a cold clam?"

"No." Jamie wiped his moustache—handkerchief heavy with eau de Cologne. "Good that you're a Democrat. Good that you're not one of those high-minded Republicans who's willing to accept all sorts of thievery at Washington just because of the hallowed memory of Honest Ape." Yes, "Ape" for "Abe." But these New Yorkers were never partial to President Lincoln. In fact, during the late war, many distinguished New Yorkers actually favored the city's secession from the Union.

I looked at Jamie with some disapproval: not because of the reference to Lincoln but because no one ought to drink absinthe at nine in the morning. But he is not the sort of young man to take seriously anyone's criticism. He sipped the second deadly concoction. For Jamie the rule has always been, Nothing in moderation. "How would you like to interview General Grant for the *Herald?*"

"I cannot think of anything I would enjoy less."

"I know he's dull but . . ."

"Dull or not, I am your *European* correspondent."

"But it's going to be awfully interesting the next few weeks, next few days in fact."

"But he's finished, isn't he? I mean he has only one more year as president . . ."

"Unless he runs for a third time."

"Even I, in Paris, have read that he will not be a candidate again."

"Even you, in Paris, *believe* the newspapers?"

"Only yours!"

"Well, don't!" Jamie laughed. Then he looked most grave, like his father about to reduce a journalist's wage. "That old boy you met with me just now, that's Abel Corbin."

"Am I to be impressed?"

"You *have* been away! Abel's married to Grant's sister Jenny. He's the most remarkable old crook. Don't you recall . . ."

I recalled. In 1869 Abel Corbin had joined with Jay Gould and Jim Fiske in an attempt to corner the gold market. Corbin also involved his brother-in-law the President—or tried to. The subsequent panic of '73 was, in many ways, a result of that curious swindle which bankrupted a number of people, just as the disaster of '73 was to finish off the rest of us, except the very rich.

"Well, Abel Corbin's got some interesting news from Washington. Scandals are about to break . . ."

"Even if Grant turned out to be the devil himself, I can't think what I could do with him as a subject."

"You *do* your subjects very well, Mr. Schuyler." Jamie was beguiling, like a flattering son—which, of course, is the rôle he's played most of his life. "Frankly, we've had too much of the usual writing. Not that Nordhoff isn't good. He's our man at the capital. Even so, there's too much of the same old view from the same old lobby sort of thing. But if you and Emma were to descend on Washington, meet the President, his cronies—and they're such yokels they will make a great fuss over the two of you—well, your impressions of the last days of Ulysses S. Grant would be quite a coup for the *Herald.*"

"And for me?"

"Do you never tire of Bonapartes and Bismarcks?"

As Jamie talked I naturally began to think what I might be able to make of Grant. The subject certainly has its charms—or horrors. Delicately I gave Jamie to believe that I *might* be persuaded for a considerable fee to go down to Washington City in a few weeks' time and begin my investigation, and as I backed and filled most tentatively I could not help but think that here at last—and most unexpectedly—is a marvellous way for me to be of assistance to Governor Tilden.

"I am glad!" Jamie was on his feet. "I'll call on Emma tomorrow. We'll arrange something. Meanwhile prepare yourself. If that old devil Corbin is right, there will be some news this week!"

"Of what sort? On the order of the *Crédit Mobilier?*"

"Much worse." Jamie lowered his voice. "There is evidence that the President himself is about to be involved in a Tweed-ish scandal. Corbin says it looks bad, which means that for you and me it looks like purest gold!"

I am now in the thick of things rather more than I had hoped
to be, but considering my dilemma, all this activity is to the good.
I cannot say that my heart leaps with joy at the thought of "doing" General Grant, a man as famed for his silences as for his
military victories. But Washington City will provide a good setting for Emma: diplomats are to be found there as well as every
sort of politician, and so our time should be well spent. Even so,
I fear that I shall be bored to death by "court life," by all those
senators who take money from railroad tycoons at the dark of the
moon. After all, that is the custom of the country and I am no
reformer. But I daresay I shall find something of interest to write
about—if only Mrs. Grant's celebrated cross-eyes.

All in all, I've not done too badly for one morning. I have
acquired the Centennial Exhibition for the *Evening Post*; unfortunately, that won't be until May or June and we will be penniless
by then unless I can contrive an advance payment. Also, I am to
begin in February or March—Jamie is not certain—my analysis
of "Washington City in the Age of Corruption," as editors melo-
dramatically put such things.

Jamie and I have not yet agreed upon a price. He is celebrated
for his generosity (none of which has ever come my way, but then
I've not come *his* way except as an occasional correspondent since
old Bennett's death). I ought to be able to get five thousand dollars
for five pieces—no, that's just a dream. Ten for five . . . ?

I must stop this or I shall soon be writing imaginary numbers
in the margin: gleefully adding that which each day I glumly
must subtract.

On my way back to the hotel, I stopped by Brentano's book-
store at Union Park or Square. The clerks recognized me and
showed me a great number of my books on sale *in secondhand*. Yet
nowhere a copy of the *Paris Under the Commune*, which is, after all,
only two years old. I must speak to Dutton about this.

Just received a message from Mr. Dutton himself, asking if he
might call. Also a note from someone at *Harper's New Monthly*
(signature impossible to read) to tell me that the copy of my
article on the Empress Eugénie has arrived and is even now being
read with the pleasure that all my works give, etc. Enclosed, a
copy of *Harper's* December issue, containing a perfunctory discussion of Darwin, an amusing comment from the popular playwright Dion Boucicault, saying that all he wants is money and
glory *now* and posterity be hanged. A regular feature called the
Easy Chair makes a curious reference to Winant's Hotel on Staten

Island, and remarks that it was there that Colonel Aaron Burr died.

Colonel Burr has been a good deal on my mind today. Particularly when I looked into Reede Street, where his office was—and is no more. But then: "Never brood upon the past, Charlie!" he used to tell me when I was—so ineptly—pretending to be his law clerk. "Think always of the future, and how much worse it is bound to be!"

I must have dozed in my chair in front of the fire. A discreet servant has come, drawn the curtains, and gone. It is almost five. Time for tea with John Bigelow.

My fingernails are no longer mauve but the flesh is still pale. Must move with care, as if made of glass; and easily broken.

4

SLOWLY I WALKED the several blocks from the hotel to Gramercy Park, which turns out to be a homely little square on the order of London's Hanover Square but smaller, less impressive, with a tiny bleak garden at the center surrounded by a perfunctory ironwork fence and the usual narrow houses sprayed with chocolate. Apparently, no one of any pretension to respectability will live behind walls of any other shade; so unlike the vivid red-brick houses and tenements of the poor or those occasional wooden shanty houses one sees in the side streets, all smeared with bile-yellow or poison-green paint.

John Bigelow was waiting for me in his pleasant study on the second floor. In front of a cheerful fire, tea was ready for pouring. From other parts of the house I could hear the sounds of family life.

"Charlie, how are you?" Bigelow is one of the few men alive who still call me by the name of my youth.

"And you, John? or your Excellency. Just what *does* one call the secretary of the state of New York?"

"Unfortunate."

"A title you share with many."

"But curiously, peculiarly mine. Have you read the *Times* to-day?"

"Only that part about myself."

"Well, you missed a most disagreeable piece about your old friend."

Bigelow poured out the tea. I noted that there were two plates of French pastries on the trolley: tribute to my Frenchness?

"Were they as inaccurate about you as they were about me?"

We sat opposite one another before the fire. I must confess that despite their exterior hideousness, these little brownstones are most comfortable in winter. In summer, however, the rooms must be depressingly dark.

Bigelow was plainly furious but trying to contain himself. "I have 'ratted,' according to the *Times*. I have deserted the virtuous Republican party for the wicked Democrats and Tildeñ."

"Well, to be precise, you *have* done exactly that. After all, you were one of the founders of the Republican party . . ."

"But *that* Republican party did its work, and died. We abolished slavery. We preserved the Union. Now a corrupt machine continues to use our name, aided and abetted by *The New York Times* . . ."

Bitterly my old friend attacked his tormentor. I daresay the fact that Bigelow had once been, for a few months, editor of the *Times* must have hurt him doubly. "The constant *personal* attacks I find hard to take. Look at this!" He picked up from a table crowded with periodicals, a newspaper marked with dark exclamation marks. "They say that I was—look at this!—an 'embarrassment' to the United States when I was minister to France."

"Shall I write them an eyewitness account to the contrary?" I can still see the tall, grey-haired Bigelow and his wife gravely making their rounds at the Tuileries whilst the parvenue Empress smiled from behind her fan, not understanding the true dignity of these deliberately plain American republicans.

Bigelow was an excellent minister to France in the sense that he did his work conscientiously and learned to speak French perfectly. On the other hand, his political judgment was unerringly bad. Fortunately, he did his nation no harm, and that was a considerable accomplishment at a most difficult time, for he was in the consular service when the French were trying to establish a puppet empire in Mexico, and he was minister at the time of the War Between the States.

Bigelow railed against the press in general and the *Times* in particular. "But then the *Times* can never be objective. Everything is couched in personal terms. They say that I quit the Republican party in order to advance myself! Quite the contrary, I should think . . ."

"But if our friend becomes president . . ."

Bigelow did not respond to the obviousness of my approach. "I don't know why I cannot be like everyone else. Why I couldn't remain happily in the party of General Grant, and root out my *proprium*."

More in this vein. I ate several small cakes . . . which now rest somewhat heavily on my stomach. I need a purge.

When Bigelow's tirade ended, I told him that I had breakfasted with our old friend Bryant.

Immediately all was good humour. "He is astonishing, isn't he? Considering his age . . ."

"Considering his diet, which is suited only for a horse, if breakfast is typical."

"Strong as a horse, too. Well, he behaved—personally—like a gentleman when I ran for secretary of state." This election seems to obsess my old friend; but then it took place only a few weeks ago. "The *Post*, of course, supported the entire Republican ticket because that scoundrel Henderson is thick as can be with Grant, and controls the paper."

"Controls Bryant?"

"To a degree. But Bryant wrote much in praise of me, of my chairmanship last spring of the commission that broke the canal ring. You know of that?"

"Oh, yes, *yes!*" I practically brayed, knowing all that I wanted to know, which is as little as possible about those rings of corruption that Tilden and Bigelow are forever breaking up in order that the two of them may rise to the very top of the tree.

But perhaps I am unduly cynical about Bigelow. Despite his great unchannelled ambition, he has always been scrupulously high-minded. During the time he was at the *Evening Post*, he made it a financial success. Then he helped found the Republican party; was given diplomatic posts; wrote books.

If Bigelow is remembered, it will be for his resurrection of Benjamin Franklin. Until Bigelow, no one had ever thought to save that wicked old creature from the bowdlerizers. Bigelow's editing of the original texts of Franklin's works as well as the biography of Franklin he published last year have made him a fortune. Would that I could find a similar subject.

"Must you live at Albany?" I stayed his reminiscences of a thousand dragons slain in the name of good governmeni.

"The secretary of state is *supposed* to spend some time there."

"Doing what?"

"I shall tell you next month." Bigelow smiled; smoothed his heavy white side whiskers not unlike my own: he eschews the full beard of most Americans, as does Tilden.

"What," I asked, only because it has been preoccupying me since my arrival yesterday, "has happened to the American voice?"

"Voice?" Bigelow was startled by the question; his own is resonant and clear, like Bryant's.

"Yes, voice. The way Americans speak."

"You mean the immigrants? Well, it takes time . . ."

"No, I mean the Americans. Like us. When I lived here, people spoke like you, like me . . ."

"But *you* had a Dutch accent, Charlie, which you've gone and lost in Paris!"

I don't know why that should have made me want to blush, but it did. In my youth, Dutch-ness was a sort of prickly virtue to us and an occasion for dull mockery to others.

"Certainly I never . . . *we* never spoke through our noses. Or made that curious flat whining sound. One hears it everywhere. And the women! Is there anything more dreadful than an American woman's laughter?"

Bigelow was amused. After some thought, he agreed that there has been a change in the way our countrymen speak. He thinks it might be the influence of those popular fundamentalist church groups that go in for "canting"—the word for praying aloud in a whining nasal voice.

I thought that this might make an interesting article for *Harper's*, but Bigelow thought not. "No one may criticize American manners, except at a safe distance like Paris. When do you go back?"

"In a year's time." My heart's beat was now audible to me; blood pounded in my ears. I have never found it easy to ask for anything important. "I shall want to write about the election. I am also—just today—commissioned to write about the last days of General Grant, for the *Herald*."

The *Herald* was sharply analyzed for some minutes. Predictably, Bigelow did not like that paper's *Personal Topics*, its salacious gossip, its sharp attacks on anyone—that is to say, everyone—guilty of hypocrisy. But he agreed that in the end Jamie Bennett would doubtless support good government if obliged to choose. "Certainly having someone of your distinction writing about that swamp at Washington will have a powerful effect on him, not to mention on his readers."

I looked as though power was something that each day I exert like the sun its rays. Then I said, very carefully, "One of the reasons for my straying into such foreign territory is a desire to be of use to Governor Tilden."

Bigelow set down his cup; sighed; looked for a time at the fire in the grate. "Charlie, I must tell you in all confidence that I am deeply concerned about the Governor."

"Politically?"

"Never! Politically he is incorruptible. No, I fear for his health. Last February he had—" Bigelow stopped abruptly. I am fairly certain from the set of his mouth that he intended to say "a stroke." But he quickly shifted to: "He cannot stop working . . ."

"Isn't that considered admirable in this country?"

"Not the way he works. Hour after hour until he is hardly able to hold his head up or keep his eyes open. It is maniacal."

"Is there so much to do at Albany?"

"Not so much that he couldn't get others to do most of what he now does, which is to study every line of every bill as if it were—" Bigelow stopped again; plainly fearful that he had told me too much about his chief.

I was as reassuring as I could be. "But that is his nature. That is how he became a successful lawyer."

Bigelow took the plunge; told all. "The point is that he's sixty-one, and his health has never been good. Even as a young man when we first knew him . . ."

"You knew him then. I didn't."

"Well, he has a tremor of the hands—"

"Who does not—at our age?"

"Cannot digest most food. Constant dyspepsia. Spells of weakness, of costiveness. All made worse by overwork. You know that

we're supposed to be working together on his address to the
legislature in January. Well, *he* is writing it all . . ."

"But does he do it well?"

"Well enough."

"Better too much zeal than what we have been accustomed to
in high office."

"But can he live through a presidential campaign?"

"Power is, they say, a supreme tonic. He intends to run?"

After a moment's hesitation, Bigelow nodded. "But I have *said*
nothing to you, Charlie."

"Of course not." I gave him the packet that I had brought with
me. "I know that you are his principal adviser in foreign affairs,
but he did write me, some months ago, asking my views on our
relations with France, Italy, England." I did not mention Germany, since Bigelow is a devotee of all things Prussian and I am
not.

"That's good of you. Very good of you. I'll take them with me
to Albany tomorrow."

I asked when the Governor would be back in the city.

"He'll certainly be here for Christmas. You know, his house is
just there. At Number Fifteen." Bigelow's gesture seemed to take
in all Gramercy Park. "I'll let you know. He'll want to see you,
to thank you himself."

"I'd like to do whatever I can to ensure his election. I told him
as much when we met at Geneva."

I think Bigelow and I have reached an understanding, and like
most understandings between politicians it was not expressed in
words.

If I do my part, provide information, work to explore the
corruption of General Grant and whoever is chosen to succeed
him as leader of the Republican party, then I will get my heart's
desire—which Bigelow has known, since he himself achieved it
ten years ago—the legation at Paris. I can think of no better way
of spending my last years than as minister to the country where
I have lived so happily for more than a third of a century.

We spoke wistfully of Paris. I recalled the party that Bigelow
gave to celebrate the Fourth of July, some three months after the
murder of President Lincoln. Although my wife and I seldom
saw much of my fellow countrymen at Paris, we pitched in as best
we could, hiring the Pré Catalan restaurant in the Bois de Boulogne.

Every American in the city was invited—some five hundred men, women and children. It was a splendid evening with music and dancing, a wizard for the children, "The Star-Spangled Banner" for the patriotic, followed by fireworks as only the French can contrive them. Our fête ended with a sky-filling American eagle (looking suspiciously like the Napoleonic bird) and the legend "The Union Now and Forever, One and Inseparable."

"What a marvellous day!" Bigelow was misty-eyed. "Thanks to you and Emma. Mrs. Bigelow will be calling on her soon. But such a sad time, too, with President Lincoln dead and . . ." He stopped. Two weeks after the fête in the Bois de Boulogne, his young son Ernest died of fever.

It was time for me to go. At the front door Bigelow helped me into my overcoat.

"What . . . *who* are the Apgars?" I asked.

Bigelow was noncommittal. "There are a great many of them in the city. Loyal Republicans. Mostly lawyers."

"There is one called John Day Apgar."

Bigelow got the point. "He is interested in your Emma?"

"I have that impression. He was at our legation last year in Paris. We saw a good deal of him. Since then he has written her letters."

"I believe he is the one who missed the war. He bought himself a replacement."

"Do you regard that as wise or unwise?"

Bigelow laughed. "It depends on how seriously one feels about the Union."

I did not tell my old friend that I myself would certainly have stayed out of that incredibly bloody and needless war had I been of conscript age. Most New Yorkers felt the same; witness, the violent riots of those years. "Do you think I should encourage such a match?"

Bigelow's response was obvious: How does Emma feel about the young man? I do not know. John Day Apgar is known to be a competent lawyer and his family are well connected with the "cliff-dwellers"—the old nonflashy gentry who live in genteel dreariness below Madison Square. Yet, "I can't imagine the dazzling Princess d'Agrigente living out her days in West Tenth Street."

"No," I said, with perfect honesty. "I cannot see it either."

"Too far from the Tuileries, and all that imperial glitter—sham though it was. Even so, your Emma is a European, she's not one of us."

"I know. Yet she's so much a part of me that I constantly forget that she was not with us in the old days when New York was different and we were young—you, of course, so much younger than I."

"You *are* a diplomat, Charlie!"

I left him in the vestibule and made my way out into the cold darkness of Gramercy Park. The gas lamps had been lit and I found their familiar hissing a comforting note in this cold, strange city where I feel suddenly a perfect alien, entirely out of place and time.

Do the Apgars have money? More specifically, does John Day Apgar have money? Or the prospects of money?

I have found that when one starts to think of money, one cannot, finally, think on any other subject. More worries of this sort and I shall be a proper New Yorker—and so at home again, no longer alien.

TWO

1

THE BUSIEST WEEK of my life thus far (can I endure such another?) is almost over. A constant round of calls made and calls received. Of telegrams. Of flowers and candies delivered to Emma, who seems on the verge of vanishing into the vast bosom of John's family.

Although not old New York themselves, the Apgars have managed to marry into every old New York family. From Stuyvesant to Livingston, they have grafted themselves onto the old patriciate, managing, according to Jamie Bennett, always to attach themselves to the top branch but one of each noble family tree.

I was much distressed to have my memories of the Empress Eugénie returned from *Harper's* with an apologetic note; and the hope that I would do the Centennial for them. Well, that is to be *done* elsewhere, I wrote them, not pleased. The piece has now been given to Robert Bonner through a mutual (*pace*, Bryant) friend. If the *Ledger* buys it, then I shall not have to spend as many sleepless nights as I have the last few days, waiting for my plans to mature whilst each day glumly subtracting sizeable sums from our infinitesimal capital. As much as possible, I try to keep my worries from Emma. She is so forthright, so Bonapartish that she would rob a bank (or marry John Day Apgar) to save me from ruin.

"You are all that I have," Emma said suddenly yesterday. When I mentioned that she is also the mother of two sons, she was brisk, "They will be men soon. And they'll make their way at Paris. You are what matters to me now."

I was deeply moved; must not disappoint her. I must find her a splendid husband here. Failing that, I must at the least get us the American legation at Paris.

Today—Sunday—we have had a most extraordinary visitation. Emma still does not know what to make of our caller.

It began yesterday with a dozen Jacquesminot roses; and a note from a Mr. Ward McAllister, asking if he might have the pleasure of our company—should the weather be good—for a tour in his carriage of the Central Park, after church.

"Whatever time is that?" asked Emma, as pleased with the roses as she was mystified, no, taken aback, no, contemptuous of a stranger putting himself forward so boldly. "Not to mention who is this McAllister?"

John Day Apgar's arrival for tea in our suite answered both questions. The services at Grace Church (where *everyone* goes) would end at eleven-thirty, if the Reverend Dr. Potter did not go on too long. "Should you like to go to church? We have a pew?" John put the question to me but meant it for Emma.

Emma shook her head most demurely. "Remember. I am Roman Catholic."

"Oh, yes. But you, Mr. Schuyler?"

"I converted to Rome when I married Emma's mother. The conversion was more practical than serious, since I thought my wife well worth a mass!"

The reference passed the young man by. But Emma soothed him; remarked that she herself was not rigid in these matters—was indeed like so many of her class at Paris a Roman Catholic *pro forma*. In other words, if one of the marrying Apgars was to affix himself like ivy to our noble (on Emma's side) tree with its roots deep in the soil of Unterwalden, then religion need be no bar and she would marry him in the Episcopal Church without a qualm. Actually, my wife's losing battle with the Jesuits over the deed to a certain property at Feldkirch in the Vorarlberg caused her to turn violently against the Church, and as she turned, Emma was pulled part way round with her. I myself am a deist like Thomas Jefferson—that is, atheist.

"Now that we know what time Mr. McAllister will come to fetch us, who is Mr. McAllister?" Emma touched one of the silvery pink roses. They are beautiful, particularly on a cold day in winter when the New York sky is like so many tiered layers of lead.

"Oh, he is *famous!*" John's emphasis of the adjective sounded ironic but was not. The Apgar style is entirely literal (in the course of one week we have met eleven Apgars and twice as many of their connections). "I'm surprised you never met him in Europe. He used to spend a lot of time in Paris. In Florence—"

"We cannot know everyone, dear John." When I am paternal with John, I remind myself of someone that I used to know years ago and despise myself as I hear the false unction positively bubbling in my throat.

"Ward McAllister rules our society." John's eyes were wide; so the original Prince d'Agrigente used to look when he spoke of the Emperor Napoleon the First.

"But then," I said, "we must have met him at your family's house." A dash of vinegar added to my oil of unction.

"Oh, *we* don't know him. I mean we do but we move in different circles. Of course he sees Cousin Alice and Uncle Reginald . . ." Names of the grandest of the Apgar connections were then invoked; nevertheless, it became clear that the Apgar *gens* proper do not move in the McAllister high circles, for "he is the closest friend of Mrs. William Astor. And she is everything in New York, or *thinks* she is." A rebellious note; quickly modified with "Of course, Cousin Alice Chanler thinks her nice."

"But what does the best friend of this marvellous Mrs. Astor *do?*" Emma was teasing. She still cannot take seriously any New York society.

"Oh, he's rich. From the South, I think. Then he went West when he was very young and made a fortune during the Gold Rush. After that, he lived in Europe. When he came back, he decided to give us an aristocracy or an Astorocracy, as Father says. This was kind of him, since the McAllisters themselves are no one and related to no one except old Sam Ward." The Apgar concern with family connections asserts itself even negatively.

"Anyway, Mrs. Astor 'adores' him, as they say in those circles, and he helps her with her receptions, dinners, balls. The season —their season—begins the third Monday of every January with a ball at Mrs. Astor's. The guests are chosen by Mr. McAllister. Three years ago he also started something called the Patriarchs. Every Monday, during the season, twenty-five families and their guests give a dance and a supper at Delmonico's, usually after the opera."

"Do you go?" Emma's look was again teasing, but I saw something else in those dark eyes: so the eyes of justice herself must look behind their blindfold.

"Once or twice, when asked. Usually by Cousin Alice. My mother thinks the whole thing a joke in bad taste. After all, those Patriarchs aren't really the nicest people. They're simply the richest, the most ostentatious . . ." How well I know the puritan diatribe. Those whose lives are given up entirely to the making of money are the first to cast in public a stone at the Golden Calf of their not-so-secret worship.

We were joined by John's sister—a sallow maiden of thirty, appropriately named Faith, who brought with her a large box from Lord & Taylor, containing an expensive shawl for Emma, a gift from Faith herself (not from John, as that would be bad form). After many demurs, the shawl was accepted and Emma embraced Faith in the French manner, and Faith sighed with bliss.

True to his word, and not having been instructed to the contrary, Mr. Ward McAllister presented himself to us in one of the hotel's smaller reception rooms, a stuffy room off the lobby known somewhat mysteriously as the Amen Corner. I immediately recognized him as the man who had spoken to us in the lobby on the day that we arrived—a plump, corseted, lavishly turned-out dandy of fifty or so, with a bad French accent and, alas, a good deal of French to go with it.

"*Enchanté, Madame la Princesse!*" Emma's hand was kissed, and mine was weakly clasped. McAllister called me "Mr. Schermer-horn Schuyler," as though mine was a hyphenated name. More of that later.

"You are kind to let me show you the Sunday sights of our city which is so *crue* and yet so gaining each day in *ton.*" *Ton* was pronounced like "tong," and is now a favourite word with Emma and me.

McAllister's barouche was discreetly handsome. Driver and
footman wore full livery. The morning was grey but not cold;
even so, a great fuss was made over us as the fur blanket was
carefully tucked in place.

During the first half-hour McAllister did not once stop talking
to us; he also did not once look at us, for his eyes were focussed
on the occupants of all the other carriages engaged in the Sunday
passeggiata of grand New York. Certainly there were hundreds of
smart equipages; and innumerable fine horses, snorting steam
like so many railway engines: in this modern industrial age the
writer must use only mechanical references to define old-fashioned fleshly things.

Just above our hotel on Madison Square is the Hoffman House;
across from it is the Brunswick Hotel, a favourite of our cicerone.
"Personally, I think that *Madame la Princesse* might find the *ambi-
ance* there more *agréable* than the somewhat too large hotel where
you are now staying. I mean most of the people *we* know from
Europe stay at the Brunswick."

The "we" was thrown over one shoulder as he raised his hat
to a passing carriage filled with ladies. "Rutherfurds," he said, as
a quality poulterer might say "quail." "And old Mrs. Tracy." A
pheasant?

Upper Fifth Avenue is indeed an improvement on the lower
part. Although brownstone is still king, there are occasional,
encouraging variations. At Thirty-third Street we were rever-
ently shown the twin Astor houses: two tall thin slices of chocolate cake connected by a low wall. In one dwells *the* Mrs. Astor,
as McAllister refers to his heroine (also known to her intimates
as the Mystic Rose). In the other house lives the true head of the
family, John Jacob Astor III; *his* wife is charming, everyone says,
and interested in all the arts, not least in that of conversation,
whilst her junior *the* Mrs. Astor has no interest in any of the arts
save that of Italian opera, which she attends each Monday and
Friday evening during the season. Since she invariably leaves
during the second interval, it is said that she has not a clue how
any of the stories turn out. I must say I know a lot about the
Mystic Rose after this morning's ride.

But McAllister was not allowed the uninterrupted flow of gossip he is plainly used to. Suddenly Emma stopped him in mid-
discourse. "What is that?" A huge white marble palace at Thirty-
fourth Street made the neighbouring Astor twin houses look

altogether the quintessence of New York dowdy.

McAllister's small eyes looked if not steely at least penny-ish. "A Mr. Stewart, a merchant, resides there . . ."

"Not *the* Mr. Stewart of the department store?" Emma's mockery was exquisite as she invested the article before Stewart's name with the very same awe that McAllister reserves for his Mrs. Astor's unique "the."

McAllister is immune to irony, like most of those who tend to —metal again!—the brassy. "The same. But of course no one knows him. No one goes to his house."

"But *I* know him! Or I think I met him at his marvellous department store." Emma explained to me the other day that a department store—new phrase to me—is exactly that: a huge emporium in which many different kinds of things are sold, with each kind relegated to its own section or department, an innovation apparently of Mr. Stewart.

I grow disturbed—in parenthesis—by the ease with which Emma allows the family Apgar's female members to give her presents. For one thing, it is not done *before* an official engagement. For another, I do not want them to suspect that she needs such things and that we cannot pay for them.

McAllister told us the Stewart saga as we drove through the grey slow-chilling air. It is not, alas, an interesting story. Rather it is *the* American story. Poor boy comes from Scotland. Opens shop. Prospers. Becomes the richest or the second or the third richest man in the city. Builds a palace but no one will visit him, for he is *in trade!* As if all New York is not or was not within living memory in trade, or worse—the latter category to which I consign slum landlords like Mr. Astor, railroad manipulators like the Vanderbilts, not to mention anyone (including Apgars) who has chosen for a career that truly base profession the law. I know. I was nearly a lawyer.

"They say his collection of paintings is not as vulgar as the rest of the house's furnishings, but who'll ever know, now I ask you, Princess?"

"Obviously those who do visit him."

McAllister pursed his lips; hid the small grey troubling (to my eye) teeth. "A few gentlemen do dine with him. But without their ladies, don't you know?"

We were now at Forty-second Street and duly admired the huge wall of the reservoir that runs for an entire block down the west side of Fifth Avenue. It is truly a remarkable sight—something like one of those huge sloping temple walls up the Nile at Luxor. Atop the wall is a sort of rampart where sightseers get a remarkable view of the city.

As we continued uptown the carriages, like the houses, became scarce. But there are occasional architectural surprises, including an enormous unfinished church just beyond the reservoir, on the opposite side of Fifth Avenue. McAllister looked unhappy as he pointed out what proved to be a fair copy of Strasbourg Cathedral (though—for once—not nearly so brown!).

"We have a good many new Catholic immigrants," he said; then stopped himself, suspecting Emma's religion. "The spires are yet to be added. You know that my own family, on the maternal side, were French." He was confiding. "In fact, my mother is a direct descendant of the Charlotte Corday who killed that dreadful revolutionary Marat."

"But surely Mademoiselle Corday had no children? And wasn't she executed . . ."

Emma could not stem the flow. "I feel French deep inside. I said to myself when I came to Paris in the late fifties, Ward, *vous êtes chez vous enfin!* I stayed at the Hotel Meurice, and met everyone. Not the least of *tout Paris*, you, Princess, at the christening of the *prince impérial*. Remember? And of course I used to see you from time to time at the Tuileries, when you were lady-in-waiting to the *Impératrice*."

"But . . ." My hand under the fur robe nudged Emma's knee. Emma was not a lady-in-waiting until '68, by which time our devoted guide to this *paradiso* that is New York was living (he had told us earlier) elsewhere.

Nevertheless, if McAllister wants the world to believe—as obviously he does—that we were once intimate friends, then I shall be happy to oblige him. I don't care how absurd the Astors themselves are. What matters to me is the one thing that can never be absurd, their money. I am, frankly, desperate, and would sell Emma to the highest bidder. No! That is hyperbole, brought on by too much champagne this evening, and far too many new faces and old dull talk.

"There is the Central Park." McAllister pointed to a wooded area only slightly more pleasing to the eye than what surrounds it: squatters' huts, small farms, empty raw fields, and the palace of Mrs. Mary Mason Jones at Fifty-seventh Street.

"How extraordinary!" Emma was transfixed. So was I. Mrs. Jones has built herself a proper cream-coloured Paris mansion in the midst of nowhere.

McAllister smiled with sudden sweetness; and I realized that this seemingly repellent climber of the social alps is simply a small boy who has unexpectedly developed the sort of passion *vis-à-vis* aristocracy that proper small boys feel for games. "I've tricked you! Mrs. Jones wants you for lunch. But she never stirs out of the house and so she couldn't or wouldn't write you, so I was told to kidnap you both and bring you here."

"But we are to lunch at the hotel." Emma was furious enough to lie, or rather to tell the truth. We usually take lunch in the parlour of our suite, since that meal is paid for as a part of the hotel's American plan.

McAllister looked stricken—small boy again: ball lost in the bushes. "Oh, I say, Princess, I am sorry but I had thought . . ."

I made amends. Our lunch at the hotel was a casual matter, with relatives who might or might not join us. Emma's colour was high with anger, but McAllister was again happy, easily pleased. So we lunched with Mrs. Mary Mason Jones.

The house is like a Paris *hôtel particulier*, only just a bit wrong. There is an air of travesty to the painted ceilings with their nymphs, clouds, satyrs; to the gold leaf that encrusts everything save our enormously fat and very jolly hostess.

"So glad you could come." La Jones waddled forward to meet us, a necklace of huge pink pearls tried with almost no success to make itself visible through two of the pink rolls of fat that make up her neck.

There were a dozen other people for lunch. I did not learn their names (admirals, generals, of course) but I think they were all related to our hostess. We were to be included at table *en famille* and Emma was beside herself with rage. I suppose such a casual entrapment is an insult to an empress's lady-in-waiting, not to mention a princess who is in her own right a Most Eminent Highness, or so the D'Agrigentes always insisted (due to some connection with the Knights of St. John). Certainly it is true that the old man for a season or two actually reigned over his Sicilian principality, a remote place noted for bandits and Greek temples. But all this was lost to him when the first Napoleon fell.

Lately, I have begun to realize just how very foreign my daughter is even to me. For one thing, I am still afflicted with the

American casualness of my generation—now apparently su-
perseded by a new solemnity and pomp that would be vastly
amusing if the puppets involved were not so very rich and I so
very poor.

I have spent the day trying to make up to Emma and she is now
in good spirits and realizes the usefulness of our having been
acquired by the puppet master of grand New York, whose own
strings, I suspect, we shall soon be pulling.

"I saw you both any number of times when I was staying in
Paris, but no one would ever introduce me to you because you
were much too grand for the likes of me!" Thus Mrs. Mary Mason
Jones in her cheery way made us at home and made our fortune,
as it were, in the eyes of that small company, certainly in those
bright pennies of McAllister. He looked like a cat who had
managed to bring into the house and to deposit upon the best sofa
the very largest rat.

The lunch was as ample as our hostess; and we did it justice,
I must say. One grows tired of hotel food, and when we do dine
out it is usually to one or another of the Apgar houses where the
meals stick, as they say in these parts, to the ribs but no more.

The lady on my left at lunch felt obliged to tell me that I was
one of her favourite authors, and that of my works *The Bedouin
Song* was the one she most often returned to for solace, playing
it on her own piano. I thanked her politely; politely did not tell
her that I am not Bayard Taylor. With age one does grow, if not
wise, forgiving; also, forgetting—also, forgotten.

On my other side sat a very solid sort of gentleman, cousin to
our hostess. I asked him what he thought of the current scandal
at Washington City. Incidentally, Jamie was right. Shortly after
our meeting in the bar of the Astor House, President Grant's
private secretary, General Orville E. Babcock, was indicted by a
grand jury at St. Louis for his alleged part in a whisky—yes—
ring. The jury proceedings promise to be most lurid, for Babcock
is thought to have collected illegal monies from the whisky distill-
ers not only for himself but for the President.

"I know nothing of these matters." At first I wondered if perhaps my companion might be in some way involved with the
Administration and that I had been tactless. But, no, he really did
know nothing of such matters. "Because, Mr. Schermerhorn
Schuyler"—thanks to McAllister's pretensions, I am now, in
these high circles, hopelessly hyphenated—"one does not choose
to know about such squalid matters."

"I see." Apparently New York gentlemen do not discuss politics at lunch. In fact, the true gentry, according to McAllister as we drove back down the avenue in near darkness, "never for one moment refer to politics or politicians."

"Yet they are all good Republicans, are they not?"

"We never discuss how or even if we vote. It is simply not done, don't you know?" It would appear that the gentry has removed itself from the politics of the country, but do they still retain the purse-strings? or have these been surrendered to those people in trade like the ancient Commodore Vanderbilt?—"whom no one ever goes to see, because, my dear Mr. Schermerhorn Schuyler, he is *sauvage! He wears his hat indoors.*"

Emma and I duly recorded shock. Our captor was in a captivating mood. "You made a marvellous impression on Mrs. Mary Mason, she was so taken with you both."

"She makes rather a large impression herself." Emma's humour was again good. She had enjoyed the old woman's easygoing flattery, not to mention the rather stiff approval of the others who, unlike the old woman and McAllister, are little impressed by foreigners. Only Americans who have travelled a good deal abroad are capable of responding to those rare names that symbolize great deeds, old history.

Emma turned to me suddenly as we passed the Jewish synagogue (McAllister had mournfully raised his eyes when he identified it for us on the way to lunch). "Do you know why she built her house so far uptown?"

"To be in the country?"

"No," said Emma. "So Mrs. Paran Stevens could never come to call."

McAllister laughed softly into the fur collar of his topcoat. "That's just Mrs. Mary Mason's way of talking. Actually, Mrs. Paran Stevens would walk barefoot in the snow all the way up from the Battery if she thought she'd be let in, but that will never ever happen. I hope"—suddenly the small eyes looked round with fear—"that you will *not* attend any of her so-called Sunday evenings."

I spoke before Emma could say that we were, that very night, about to hear the tenor Mario sing at the Stevenses' house. "Why? Is she so disreputable?"

"Yes! Because she *pushes* herself onto people. And she is nobody, don't you know? Just the wife of a hotel manager and the daughter of a grocer from Lowell, Massachusetts, of all places."

McAllister's voice dropped a register. "You know that before they came here *they lived at Washington City!*"

"Oh, dear," was the best I could do. "Is that so very bad?"

"Of course there are nice people at the Capital, but the general "tong" . . . ! Well, I give away no secret when I say that no one goes to Washington City if he can help it."

What a lot there is to learn about these curious folk. No wonder the country is in the hands of criminals if the gentry are so fastidious—and so fatuous. I have not heard one intelligent thing said all day, neither at the Palais Jones nor the Château Stevens, where of course Emma and I went for the music, the company, the supper.

Mrs. Paran Stevens is a somewhat coarse-looking woman with a bright manner and that anxious desire to be thought amusing, which in itself never fails to amuse—me.

"We saw your picture in the window at Ritzman's!" Thus Mrs. Stevens greeted Emma, whose response was cool, for neither of us is entirely sure just what the customs of the country are. Should a lady be photographed and displayed as if she were Jenny Lind or not? I suspect not.

Nevertheless the effect of Emma's entrance into the Stevenses' drawing room was most imperial. At times Emma looks not unlike our Empress in her youth, the same dark Spanish look to the eyes, though the hair is lighter and done in the current classic style with the parting at the center. Like the Empress, Emma can appear to float—and float she did through that large gathering, through rooms not quite distinguished but complacently rich with too many of the wrong *objets*, not to mention *sujets*. Obviously the Ward McAllister manner has taken me over as I write up these notes.

It is after midnight. I sit beside the fireplace in our parlour. I can hear Emma's regular breathing from her bedroom, smell the scent that she wore, see the rose-pink camellias she thrust a moment ago into a water jug. Who sent them? I did not ask. She is like some diva in New York and I am relegated to the background, the entrepreneur who makes her bookings, manipulates the press, discourages the over-eager gentlemen, finds her a husband.

The husband that we may have found (or at least the one that we have acquired on approval) was waiting for us at Mrs. Stevens's standing beneath a portrait of our hostess disguised as the character she thinks of herself as—Madame Sans-Gêne.

Emma gave John Day Apgar a tap on the arm and a smile; then she allowed Mrs. Stevens to take her on the full circuit of the room, where nearly a hundred of New York's most elegant beaux eagerly waited to be presented. There were fewer women than men, I noted; and those women who were on hand had a somewhat too bright look to them, as if they were not really wives or at least not wives to the men they were inclined most to talk to.

"She does look splendid!" John could not take his eyes off Emma's back.

"Yes. But she feared that the effect might be less than splendid, since she is wearing the same dress that she wore in the photograph at Ritzman's."

"All New York is talking about her." I could not tell if John regards this as a good or bad thing. He speaks without much inflection. "You know how much my family likes her. Particularly Father. And my sister Faith."

The thought of Father Apgar and Sister Faith made me ever so slightly depressed. I seized a silver goblet of champagne from a passing waiter. Two long swallows and I was able to exorcize the vision of our last dinner at the Apgars, of John's grave full-fleshed parents, proud in their dullness; of Sister Faith, a horse-like bride of Christ if ever I saw one though Protestant—yet not protesting her terrible fate. Whenever Sister Faith asked about Paris, Father Apgar coughed and Mother A. changed the subject. Paris is not a subject for nice people to talk about, particularly in front of plain girls like Faith. Proper subjects in that household are the demerits of most servants, summer residences (when to open, shut), food (its cost, not its preparation), and an occasional reference to the low sort of people who are trying to take over New York society because They Have Money, like the Paran Stevenses for one, or the vulgar Commodore Vanderbilt for another, or the Astors.

At this point, I had interrupted our hostess; told her that in my youth before she was born (I think she liked *that*, presuming she is capable of liking anything other than Apgar-ishness, my new synonym for social worthiness), the original Astor in his old age was much sought after by Livingstons and Stuyvesants. Actually, I don't think that this is exactly true (the original Astor was a reclusive Medicean figure). But it does strike me as strange that after two or three generations of lawyerhood such markedly mid-

dle-class people as the Apgars should have convinced themselves
that somehow they are more special, more distinguished, more
truly *nice* than the great nobles, which, like it or not (and I like
it not), is what the Astors are; the third generation of that family
now dominates the city in what, I suspect, is perfect ignorance
of the disapproval of the nine Apgar brothers, whose sole distinction is their innumerable links with a hundred and one similar
lawyer-sailor-merchant-thief families.

But this is not the place for my eventual essay on Apgar-
ishness. That must wait until I am safely home again. I will
record only Apgar Senior's view of Governor Tilden. "The man
is so often drunk that he cannot get up in the morning." This was
announced over cigars after the ladies had gone up to the dark
cold parlour.

"But I understand General Grant is also a heavy drinker." I
tried to even the score.

"I have *never* heard that," said Apgar Senior.

Meanwhile there are pleasures here, of a sort, and Mrs. Stevens's musical Sunday evenings must count amongst them.

We sat on gold chairs and listened to a powerful Italian tenor
from the opera house. There were tears in the eyes of many of
the ladies when he ended his recital with the very loud, sobbing
solo from *Martha*. My own eyes were dry, but there was a definite
persistent ringing in my ears. This often happens when my blood
is overheated by champagne and music and the presence of, I
confess, an uncommonly handsome group of women.

Music done with, we went in to supper. Mountain ranges of a
rather inferior chicken salad were the dominant note. We were
seated at numerous small tables. I found myself between a good-
looking little woman of Emma's age and a fair little fellow in his
early forties.

I addressed myself to the lady. We introduced ourselves but
neither, at first, heard the other's name. She pointed an importantly jewelled finger at Emma across the room, and said, "Have
you got to meet the Princess yet?"

"Better than that. I *be*got her."

I was rewarded with a straightforward laugh; not at all Apgar-
ish, I was happy to note. This charming creature is called Mrs.
William Sanford. She pointed out her husband, who was seated
at Emma's right.

"I must say she is even more beautiful than her photograph.
And the way she moves!"

I accepted any number of compliments from Mrs. Sanford, learning in the process that she and her husband are building a house in Fifth Avenue, that they have a cottage at Newport, Rhode Island (plainly the most fashionable of the summer places, since the Apgars pointedly prefer Maine), and that Mr. Sanford enjoys yachting, owns race horses, and *does*—as they say here— nothing, as far as I could tell from her conversation.

All subjects were touched on. Oh, yes, she knew Mrs. Mary Mason Jones! Such a character! And dear old *silly* Ward McAllister!—with his "don't you knows." We got on famously, passing various names back and forth to establish one another's place in the scheme of things. I found her delightful; but still had no clue to the source of the Sanford fortune—was it his or hers?

After several mediocre courses, including fried oysters, which will one day be my happy death, I turned to my neighbour, who introduced himself (as if he needed an introduction to a fellow author). Although the celebrated Edmund C. Stedman is a Wall Street broker by profession, his passion, more or less requited, is for literature and for the making of taste, a sort of rustic Sainte-Beuve (whose name he did not appear to recognize—more of this cultural difference later). Last year Stedman published two volumes on (of?) Victorian poets as well as a volume of his own poetical works which I—yes, all dark things are to be confessed here—told him that I had read and admired. Actually, I did hold the book in my hand at Brentano's, and listened to the clerk's description of the author, who regularly visits the shop, presumably to encourage the clerks to sell his works.

I was rewarded for my mendacity with yet another invitation to address the Lotos Club, as well as with the assurance that I alone of all living historians of the present (*sic?*) have been able to make clear for Americans the internecine struggles of immoral old Europe. I confess that this encomium made me seem to myself like one of those seedy pitchmen at a side show, showing off for a penny the swallower of swords, the eaters of glass and of fire.

Since Stedman knows Bigelow, I tried to get the subject onto politics and the day's scandal, but once again I found myself confronted by this strange New York wall of—indifference? No, I cannot believe that they are indifferent to the ubiquitous corruption.

I can understand the gentry preferring not to acknowledge the hell that their puritan society has become even as the devils piously continue to mouth puritan nostrums. But for a man like

Stedman to shy away from *any* discussion of the Grant Administration is very odd indeed. After all, Stedman was a celebrated supporter of Lincoln. Provisionally, I take this reluctance to be a form of embarrassment at what they—I can no longer write we —have become. More to the point, the noble new party that freed the slaves and preserved the Union is the very same party that is now in cahoots with the crooked railroad tycoons and with the Wall Street cornerers of this-and-that, thus making it hard for a noble creature like Bigelow—like Stedman?—to confess to the bankruptcy of what only ten years ago was the last or latest, best or better, hope or dream of an honourable system of government.

"I much admire Bigelow's pieces from Germany. Not on a par with yours, of course . . ."

I was modest. Pressed on. "Now Bigelow goes to Albany. Is this wise?"

Like a diviner, Stedman tentatively touched a complex aspic with his fork. "It is odd, certainly. After all, we are Republicans. But then Governor Tilden is certainly—respectable. Not long ago I had the most interesting conversation with him about airships."

It took me some moments to make sense of this last phrase. When finally I did, I realized that I was in the presence of a most amiable monomaniac. "Man must fly through the air, just as he now travels across the earth at thirty or forty miles an hour and almost as swiftly over the seas. There are a number of practical methods . . ."

"Balloons . . . ?" That was my sole contribution, for Stedman did not stop in his discussion of air travel until those about us started to rise. He hoped that I would soon join him for lunch or supper at any one of those clubs that encourage Bohemian membership.

"Literary New York is eager to meet you."

"Surely they hardly know that Rip Van . . ." But I stopped myself as that dread name once again climbed out onto the end of my tongue. Fortunately Stedman was not listening.

"You will like Bayard Taylor, I'm sure. He's teaching German literature up at Cornell. But now he's in the city. Or have you already met each other in Europe?"

"No, I think not." I have been very much aware over the years of those of my literary countrymen who keep coming in what seem hordes to old Europe, where they usually stay longer than planned. Yet I have, as much as possible, avoided them. Somehow they never seem to fit our way of life at Paris: this includes Bryant, though he and I have met in Europe off and on over the years, usually in Italy. I once debated (and the negative won) taking him to Princess Mathilde's, where he might meet her circle, particularly my especial friend Taine, as well as such amusing novelists as Gautier, the Goncourt brothers and the Russian Turgenev. But somehow I could not imagine William Cullen Bryant in that circle (where even I, after forty years, am still known as the "blond wild Indian"). I fear that that brilliant circle would sooner roast a waterfowl than apostrophize it.

Lately the young journalist-writers have been descending on Europe like termites on an ancient frame house, and London has taken them very much to heart. The English can never get enough of the grotesque; they particularly delight in those Americans who seem to them truly American, preferably the ones with long hair and Western twangs, who chew tobacco and tell tall tales—ah, those tall tales of wild Indians and of drunken bears and of jumping frogs. N.P. Willis, Joaquin Miller, Mark Twain and, most interesting of all, I am told, a Californian called (I think) Pierce whose work I have not read, but whose brilliant mordant conversation has been reported to me by the Princess Mathilde who hears of him from the Empress at Chislehurst. Our Empress may be bored by literary men and explorers, but apparently a son of the American West has discovered how to make her exile amusing. Needless to say, nothing west of Seine-et-Oise interests Paris, including, alas, their former Empress.

Stedman mentioned any number of literary men I must meet and I pretended interest, although I have never found congenial the company of professional writers. Also, I do not read novels any more whilst today's poetry makes me quite angry, since, at best, it is no more than carefully ruined prose.

History and politics are my field, and New York seems not to be rich in either historians or true political writers despite the often interesting efforts of the Adams descendant who edits Boston's *North American Review*. But I am unfair to my countrymen. I have been here too short a time to judge. Also, I tend to compare the home product with Paris at a time when I think that city is, for once, what in its eternal arrogance Paris thinks itself always to be, a city of true light with Taine and Renan ablaze, and a thousand ideas stirring.

I found it amusing (the ironist's word for "discouraging") that when I spoke to Stedman of French writers, he seemed not even to know their names. He has heard of Flaubert of course; knows that *Madame Bovary* was an immoral novel that even the French tried to ban; insists that better than "all that lot, and far more daring" is an American poet much disliked by the prudish American reviewers. I promise to read this poet, who is called Whitman and lives at Camden in New Jersey; apparently, he enjoys good sales in America and good notices in England. Lucky man! The other way round would be unbearable.

Stedman moved on. I asked Mrs. Sanford if she would like to meet Emma.

"With joy! I'm French too, you know. I was born in New Orleans. My father was General Delacroix, and we're Creoles, which does *not* mean Negro, as they think up here." She laughed as we made our way across the room. "Not that I would mind one bit. But it would surely annoy my husband."

William Sanford is a tall, slender (by New York standards) man, not yet forty, with a head too small for his body, a fine aquiline nose, a glossy beard at whose center is a surprisingly small mouth, rosy-lipped as a girl's. I describe him in some detail, for he is my first important millionaire. He wore not only a diamond stickpin but a ring with a starred ruby in a heavy gold setting; in the light of the chandelier his dark evening clothes gleamed as if they, too, were made of some rich material like onyx or ebony.

I presented Mrs. Sanford to Emma. "I've enjoyed staring at you all evening," said Mrs. Sanford in a most direct way.

Emma was equal to the flattery. "And I've enjoyed staring at you, as well as listening to Mr. Sanford."

The millionaire took my hand in a firm grip, looked down into my face, as if searching in my eyes for a reflection of his own pale grey eyes. He looked to be so much at home in this particular New York world that I assumed that he, too, was old money like his wife, even Apgar-ish. But he proved to be his wife's opposite; for one thing, he speaks with a harsh New England country-folk accent in which the final "g" of any word is fiercely decapitated.

"I've decided, Mr. Schuyler, that your daughter is the best-lookin' lady in this room." The head inclined toward me; he is taller than I by rather more than that small head.

"It was my impression that Mrs. Sanford held that distinction." I was ceremonious.

Mrs. Sanford laughed without self-consciousness. "My husband is the most terrible flirt. I know. I married him. But he's
right about your daughter."

I demurred. More compliments were bestowed. Then Sanford
put his arm around my shoulder (something I detest) and led me
to a sofa for two and sat me down. He produced superb cigars.
"Rolled for me by my own firm in Cuba."

My cigar was set afire by a friction match after the ritual
circumcision with a bejewelled cutter. "Now then, you want to
know all about Orville, don't you? Well, I'm the fellow who can
tell you."

Not until Sanford had talked at some length and the blue
smoke between us had begun to have an almost narcotic effect
did I realize that Emma had told him I was to write about the
Grant Administration, and the difficulties that I had encoun-
tered in getting anyone outside the political world to so much
as respond to a name as grandly notorious as General Orville E.
Babcock.

Babcock and Sanford are friends. They were once associated in
a railroad speculation.

I fear that I have drunk too much champagne this evening,
smoked too many fine cigars, and so gorged myself on fried oysters that I cannot recall many of the details Sanford so willingly
supplied, but I do recall his offer to give me an introduction to
Babcock—to Grant, for that matter. "A good sort of man, you
know. Fact, I served on his staff." My heart sank—Major, Colonel, *General* Sanford? But whatever his title, he does not use it and
whatever it was he did or did not do in the war, he tactfully
refrained from mentioning.

"You see, the thing to be remembered is this, Mr. Schuyler.
This country isn't like anything that ever happened before. Oh,
maybe your first Romans were like us, but I doubt it. No, sir. We
are *sui generis*—of our own kind." He translated nicely for me. I
kept on nodding, eyes full of tears from the fine blue smoke
between us; his face seemed magnified, if that is possible, while
the grey eyes glared at me through the smoke. "The Millionaire
in Hell" occurred to me as a title.

"What I'm trying to tell you is, yes, we cut a few corners when
we set out to build our railroads like I did or like my father did
when he made jeans for the Westerners and those encaustic tiles
for the Easterners, regular old villain he was!" I expected a cheerful? apologetic? mitigating? laugh. But none came. Sanford saw

nothing wrong in villainy if more miles of track were laid, jeans stitched, tiles encausticized.

"Of course old Orville's in up to the handle. No doubt of it. I've warned him, 'You're too close to the wind,' I told him, oh, maybe a year ago. Not that I know a thing about this whisky ring in St. Louis. Chicken feed, I'd guess, but Orville's greedy, and if you want a *real* fortune you're never greedy."

"Are you greedy, sir? Or fortunate?" My own voice seemed disembodied to my own ears.

"Well, sir, let's say I've always known when to push myself away from the table. That's what my father used to say. From Lowell, Mass., we were. Same as Mrs. Stevens, though I don't think she admits to it now. We had the big house and her family was nearer the river, which is where our factory was. Darwin is right, you know."

The unexpected reference is, I gather, very much the Sanford style. I was not surprised to learn that he attended—but did not graduate from—Yale. His conversational style is an amazing mixture of elegance and tough low-down Yankee. I would suspect that a certain amount of art has gone into the figure he so decisively presents to the world.

"Anyhow, that's why we're the first country in the world. Fact is, we're so far ahead of the next set of monkeys on the ladder they'll never catch up. And we got the way we are because we let nothing stop us from getting what we want."

"Even that second helping of dessert?" I teased him; and the small rather pretty mouth gave me a smile.

"No, sir. You push yourself away from the table so that you can come back another day, for a whole new dinner."

I was aware that people were leaving. Out of the corner of my eye I saw Emma vanish into the room where the ladies' cloaks were kept. I got Sanford away from homilies—useful as they are to contemplate, since they appear to comprise the national philosophy—and onto the more specific, onto Governor Tilden.

"I like nothing about that sanctimonious old weasel. He did make his fortune, I'll say that for him. He's the richest lawyer in the whole country, and you don't get to be that without trailing some of your pretty dress in the mud. Anyways, if he runs for president, some of us'll have a lot to tell the world about a few of the railroad deals *he* was involved in. Oh, we'll have him forty miles down the Delaware, don't you worry."

I tried not to look worried. "Mr. Sanford, do you think that the sort of corruption we are living through now is good?"

"I do." The answer was brisk. "Who gives a goddamn if a bunch of congressmen take money for services rendered? That's the way you get things done down there. Why, I reckon we've paid off the whole pack of them one time or another."

"Including the President?"

But Sanford's brutal candour has its limits. "It's the Tildens I can't abide, and the Bigelows and the Bryants and the whole moaning tribe of old women who think we would have had all this wealth, these railroads and manufactories, just by going to church! Well, damn it to hell, we got these things by cuttin' each other's throats and stealin' whatever wasn't nailed down. Mr. Schuyler, the strong devour the weak every time, and that's the way of the world, and the law is just something you buy if you can, for it sure don't apply to any man with the dollars to buy himself a smart lawyer like Tilden—and the judge, too, if he knows how."

"You paint a dark picture, Mr. Sanford."

"It seems full of light to me, Mr. Schuyler."

Unsteadily I stood up. Emma was in the middle distance, cloaked for departure. In an instant Sanford was on his feet; he moves as gracefully as the predator he pictures himself to be. "Let us take you home."

"Mr. Apgar has us in charge."

"Ah." The single note betrayed not so much contempt as the indifference a well-feasted panther might experience at the sight of a scrawny rabbit.

Farewells were made in the marble vestibule. The Sanfords offered us the city, whatever we wanted—a box at the Academy of Music, anything. While Mrs. Stevens condemned Emma to a round of gaiety.

Mrs. Sanford took my hand in both of hers. "I don't know when I've enjoyed myself so, talking to you." She is obviously as perceptive as she is charming to look at. "And I can't tell you how . . ." She looked about to make sure that no one would hear her. We were to one side of the open door, and the freezing night. Opposite us Mr. Sanford was talking down into Emma's face while John Day Apgar attempted to draw her to the door. A footman had already announced the arrival of the Apgar carriage. Mrs. Sanford had time to impart her secret. "How very *dull* New

York parties are. No one talks about anything of the slightest interest while half the gentlemen are already in their cups *before* they come to the dinner party."

I pulled myself erect; did my best to disguise my own champagne-induced drunkenness. "I thought tonight was unusually scintillating."

"Oh, that was just me!" She laughed. "Sanford," she called to her husband. "Let the Princess go. Their carriage is waiting and that's keeping everyone else waiting, too!" She had missed nothing apparently. We vowed to see one another every day of our lives, for they are living just across the square from us at the Brunswick Hotel until their house is ready.

Snow was falling as we crossed the sidewalk to John's carriage at the head of a line of other rather grander equipages. Suddenly I found in my path the inevitable Civil War veteran; with his one arm, he held forth a tray of shoelaces. I put a coin into the tray, looked for one guilty moment into the man's face and saw almost the same face as Sanford's looking back at me—the same cold grey adamantine eyes. The veteran looked straight through me; face blue in the calcium light from Mrs. Stevens's house.

I hurried into the carriage, frozen to the bone and entirely sobered.

On the way to the hotel John told us something of the Sanfords. "She's from an old New Orleans family. She was born Denise Delacroix and she's also well-connected here. I think it was her grandmother who was a Livingston. Everyone likes her, and she's been to the house." John always speaks of those who come to his father's house in rather the same way Saint-Simon refers to the peers of France.

"*He* seems rather—rough." To my surprise, Emma was intrigued: after all, she has spent most of her adult life in Paris successfully avoiding this type of American.

"It's all a performance." John did not pretend to disguise his dislike—jealousy? "Sanford's father was a real Yankee barbarian who made money and moved down to New York, where no one ever spoke to him."

"Poor man! What punishment!" Emma, I knew, was smiling in the darkness.

"I suppose it was *hard* on him." John is a kindly boy. "But then his son married Denise Delacroix and that made the family in New York. She gave him position . . ."

"And he gave her money?" I asked.

"Oh, no. It's *her* money mostly."

This was a surprise. "Then he's not a self-made hard-drinking manipulator of railroads and briber of congressmen?"

John laughed. "Certainly not. That's why it's so funny. The way he carries on. Even Mother finds him amusing." The ultimate recognition in Apgar-land.

"He is most convincing, this actor." Emma was as surprised as I.

"Oh, he's done well himself." John made a concession. "He did make a killing on one of the Western railroads with his wife's or perhaps his father's money. But everyone says it was an accident."

"How wrong one can be about people," was my wise summing up.

I grow sleepy. I have rapidly gone through the ill-effects of overdrinking, headache and all, and have now come out the other side and note that it is only one in the morning.

Emma enjoyed herself; and I was pleased at the way she is taking hold here. If we had money . . .

But I refuse to worry. For one thing, the problem can be solved tomorrow if I want it summarily solved.

Just now, in the hotel bar where John and I went for a "night cap" after Emma had gone up to bed, he said, "I would like to marry your daughter, sir." Just like that! Although nervous, he knew exactly how the dialogue should go.

I was less certain, not having read the same novels or seen the same plays from which he had managed to achieve a proper Apgar-ishness of tone.

"My dear boy!" I knew that phrase was the right one: affection, surprise—menace? "Does she . . ." But even I could not say the expected "love you." I substituted for "love" "know?"

"Yes, sir. She knows that I would like to make her my wife. I told her how pleased my parents are."

"She must have been gratified." I could imagine Emma's response to *that*. "Let me talk to her," I said. No unseemly haste, desperate as we are for money.

"You are not opposed, sir?" The boy was actually anxious; caught in the web, the fly was trying to tempt the spider.

"Of course not. I want only . . ." Ah, I *am* getting the hang of it. George Sand once told me that writing novels was the easiest thing in the world. "Just turn on the tap," she said; and obviously the thing flows with the greatest ease, for in our stylized bourgeois world nothing ever—in conversation at least—surprises. "I want only her happiness."

Shall I tell Mr. Dutton that I would like to try my hand at novel writing? No. Because then I would have to *read* a few, and that requires more effort and a stronger stomach than I possess. The only novels of our time I can read with pleasure are those of that altogether charming Parisian-Russian Turgenev. With uncommon passion he writes only of politics, and so is able to create living men and women on the page unlike all the other novelists who are so intent on rendering in words the people they think they know or have read about that they end up with a kind of chatter not so good as the sort we hear every day of our lives.

"I want only her happiness"—"I shall do my best, sir."—"Your prospects?"—"A quarter interest in my father's share of the firm."—"Quite enough to maintain my Emma?"—"Oh, yes, sir! I've already found a house. Just opposite my parents'."—"How convenient!" So we rattled to the end of the familiar scene. I not daring to interject a single intelligent or unusual note; he not capable.

Just how much share of the firm of Nine Apgars can his father have? and of that, how much is a quarter? If Tilden does not become president, the newlyweds may have to support an aging literary relative.

2

THE *Ledger* HAS ACCEPTED my article on the Empress Eugénie, with pleasure. I am to get seven hundred and fifty dollars. Mr. Bonner himself wrote to tell me how much he liked the piece. "If you approve, we will of course want considerably to cut the text, and perhaps rearrange . . ." For all I care, they can print it backwards. I telegraphed my approval before breakfast.

In a good mood, I took Emma shopping. Both Altman's and Lord & Taylor already know the Princess, and she has unlimited credit. I must say I find bemusing these huge palaces dedicated to the selling of things by departments. They line Broadway from Stewart's white iron building at Ninth Street (replacing the old Washington Hall Hotel of my youth where Irving and Halleck used regularly to dine) all the way up to Twenty-third Street. Ladies' Mile they call it; and even on a damp winter morning, elegant ladies descend on the stores like a conquering army.

Yet along this rich mile one sees everywhere signs of the economic crisis. Innumerable beggars and prostitutes and "street rats." The "street rats" are ragged, emaciated children who paw through trash cans, collecting bones and rags. According to the *Herald*, there are more than thirty thousand homeless children adrift in the streets, living in cellarways, in barrels, packing crates. The few who manage to survive into adolescence turn to prostitution and crime.

I must say that this is a peculiarly brutal city, very different from the town of my youth where indeed there was crime and poverty—concentrated mostly in a single ward whose capital was the notorious Five Points. (Must go there soon and see what if anything has changed. At one time I knew every brothel in that neighbourhood.) Now half the city is haunted by the poor, most of them immigrants from Europe. On freezing nights they are allowed by the thousands to sleep on the floors of the police stations. The rich burghers have every reason to fear communism. This place is worse than Paris in 1871.

Emma is as horrified as I. But her solutions tend to be martial. "If they won't fight another war, then they must send the poor out West. There is room, isn't there?"

"Yes. But these people can do nothing . . ."

"Then they will die."

"It seems hard on the children."

"It is terrible." Emma was compassionate but hard. "So terrible that it is better for them to be dead."

"Or cared for."

"Your people, Papa, are not kind."

To this harsh judgment, there is no answer.

My good luck continues. When we came back to the hotel, there was a telegram from Governor Tilden. Might I join him for dinner at 15 Gramercy Park on Christmas Eve? I accepted by telegraph. There was also an invitation for Emma and me to attend the theatre with Jamie Bennett. Accepted.

Whilst Emma changed her clothes for a ladies' lunch at Mrs. Mary Mason Jones's, a pageboy arrived at the door with an elaborate floral creation of orchids.

I placed this beautiful tribute on the round marble table at the parlour's centre and then, idly, opened the attached envelope and read the enclosed card: "Pale shadows of true beauty," was the inspired message written in an odd loopy sort of hand. The signature gave me a turn: "William Sanford."

At that moment Emma came into the parlour, wearing a scarf she had bought that morning.

"*C'est beau, n'est-ce pas, Papa?*" She looked at the orchids. I gave her the card.

"I'm sorry, I opened it."

Emma did not look at the card. "Very vulgar . . . the orchids, Papa. Every bit as vulgar as Mr. Sanford."

"You knew he sent them?" In a sense I was relieved.

"Who else?" Without a glance she threw the card into the fire. "He's very bold. He knows that you're practically engaged to John. I told him."

"Am I . . . engaged?" As well as I know my daughter, there are times when I feel that she is far beyond me in her perception of things, and that she weighs with an entirely different set of balances the common morality.

I had not yet told her of last night's conversation in the bar. Now I did. She listened attentively, then burst out laughing. "Poor Papa! You of all people having to say those things!"

I laughed, too: we are as one in our sense of the absurd. I agreed that I was to be pitied. Having spent my life mastering the intricacies of the French platitude, I now must sink beneath the accumulated weight of the American.

"I can never think of this place as your country." Emma examined the orchids; she knows flowers; used to advise the Princess Mathilde on what to grow in her conservatories before the war . . . *before the war*, that phrase sums up our Eden, an entire world forever gone, and only five years ago.

"You don't like your father's city?"

"If you do, I do." That was mischievous.

"Well, it's only for a short time."

"Until I am married?" From her voice I could not guess her

mood. I suspect that this is because we now speak only English to each other and in English she is someone else, as I am. Languages do bend one morally to their grammatical requirements.

"Until I get my post as minister to France *if* I get it." I then shifted to French and that made for our old intimacy. "Do you want to marry John?"

"If you want me to."

"No. Never like that, my girl. You make your own choice."

"But you would like it?"

"He is suitable."

"Suitable!" This caused a change of colour—good! She is a Latin woman in French, and I am at home with her: her father, in fact.

"The Apgars are . . ."

"Magnificent! I know. They tell me that every day. And Sister Faith! She thinks she is the equal of a Daughter of France!"

"There is money." I was to the point.

She was, too. "But how much?"

"I should think, in time, a lot."

"Can *you* see me living here?"

Tears came to my eyes most unexpectedly. "I should not want you ever to be at any distance from me now." I did not need to say the rest. Of all living creatures, only the man of letters knows that he must die.

"John wants to announce the engagement at the New Year's." As Emma pulled on mauve gloves, she looked at herself in the pier-glass mirror whose scrollwork walnut magnificence mars the parlour of our suite rather than furnishes one of the bedrooms. I must remember to have the valet move it.

"An engagement can always be broken . . ." I began, not certain of how the sentence was to run either on my tongue or in my head. Since I am truly undecided, I did not finish. Instead I picked up the envelope from Sanford and from habit felt its surface. The type was expensively raised.

"Not easily. Not here. Not in the land of the Apgars." Emma knows the country already, better than I. She should be the one recording this world, for she really *sees* it whilst I see only the two of us, struggling to survive.

"He did mention the possibility of one day living in France." But this was weak and I knew it.

"They'll never let him go. Well"—Emma picked up her moth-

er's still-splendid sable coat—"we shall be engaged at the New
Year. I think that's best."

"And married in June?"

"At Grace Church. Where else?" Emma smiled, and the dark
hazel eyes reminded me poignantly of Aaron Burr's most beautiful luminous all-seeing eyes. "From the New Year to June is a
long time."

"Thank heaven. What do you think of him?" I was still holding
in my hand William Sanford's envelope.

"I think he is singularly brutal and wild"—she used the word
sauvage—"and overconfident."

I did not understand. "John is none of these things."

Emma watched herself look startled in the mirror. "I thought
you meant the unspeakable Mr. Sanford."

"No. No. Even for an American millionaire his manners are
not supportable. I meant John."

"Oh, John . . ." She spoke on exhalation. "Well, he'll be what
he seems. That is something. Certainly, after Henri . . ."

"John is not half bad?"

"No. Not half bad."

"But not half good?"

"Papa, I am thirty-five years old, and there is very little choice
and very little time left for me." And that was that. I have always
admired the hard French practicality even when it chills me to
the bone. Emma kissed my cheek and left me; her violet scent still
fills the room.

3

THE DAYS RUSHED BY in a constant and tiring round of encounters, mostly social. According to the popular press—of
which there is altogether too much—the glamourous Princess
d'Agrigente is the sensation of the New York season; and it is
coyly hinted that she may soon make a marriage here in "Old

Gotham" to a member of the "Knickerbockracy." The style is hideously imitable.

Not so coyly, the Apgars were told that Emma's mission on this planet would be fulfilled in June. Thanks to their kind encouragement, she told them that she is now willing to surrender the eminence of her tinselly old-world highness for the dim but oh so pregnant with distinction and true worth title of Mrs. John Day Apgar.

Sister Faith looked as if she might faint with the joy of having such a sister-in-law, whilst the Third Brother Apgar was quietly pleased and assured me, man to man, over one of his stale Park and Tilford cigars that the marriage has, as of this moment, the blessing of a two-thirds majority of the Nine Brothers. The dissenters were troubled by Emma's religion, and by *Paris.* "But they'll come round, on New Year's Day, when we make our announcement." Meanwhile, for the next week or two, the secret is known to all but not to be discussed in front of any of the principals.

Since receiving the money from Mr. Bonner of the *Ledger* I no longer wake up in the middle of the night, unable to get my breath as I wonder desperately how I am to support us. Yet even with the *Ledger*'s money, dollars do seem to melt as rapidly in this city as last night's snow.

It is now decided that we shall go to Washington City on February 15, when I begin for the *Herald* my "observations" (a good word for what I shall be doing and one that Jamie says he likes).

Mrs. Paran Stevens has given us letters to twenty intimates we must know. We are still undecided whether or not to let a house for the two or three months we shall be in the city, or simply stay at a hotel. I incline toward hotel life, as it gives one an excuse *not* to reciprocate the many kind invitations we mean to accept.

Today has been as full as all my other days. I lose Emma to the Apgars at noon. Then I lunch, usually at an oyster bar. These charming places are to be found in cellars; from the street, they are identified by a striped red and white pole with a large globe on top.

But today I had to forgo the oyster bars and have lunch with Richard Watson Gilder—at a restaurant. I firmly refused to dine with him at his house for fear of his sister. A manly girl, Jeanette is devoted to literature and has views on everything; no sooner

does she ask you a question than she answers it. Gilder's wife is
charming, but she is usually painting in her studio at the lunch
hour. I also refused to be taken yet again to either the Century
Club or the Lotos Club. One meets altogether too many writers
at those places, and not enough publishers.

I did give my promised talk at the Lotos Club last Saturday.
Everyone seemed most pleased by my comments on France since
the fall of the Empire, but there was no interest at all in the
French writers.

I met Gilder at a French restaurant reputed to be good, on
Fourteenth Street just across from the imposing Steinway Hall,
where orchestras play and lecturers bray. I believe that Charles
Dickens inaugurated the Hall on one of his visits.

Mother Linau's is a most congenial restaurant, and though
perhaps too self-consciously Bohemian (the clientele, *not* the
waiters and cooks), I quite enjoyed our lunch. I even enjoyed the
company of Gilder who is most likeable, despite a relentless
desire to get ahead in the literary world that makes me uneasy.
I see him because he is the editor of *Scribner's Monthly* and likes
to publish me. He sees me because he has developed some sort of
a passion for my—exotic-ness?

"You are so much an American writer always and yet so foreign!" The face opposite me looked pleased through the rising
mist from the excellent hot bean soup.

Happily, at Madame Linau's, there are small tables as well as
the institutional-type long tables that Americans are devoted to.
Even at the Fifth Avenue Hotel one must dine at a table set for
thirty and, worse, often occupied with as many strangers.
Democracy.

I have told the munificent Mr. Bonner that I might do him a
piece on New York's restaurants. "Make it *Paris* restaurants, and
I'll buy!" Someone at the Lotos Club told me that Bonner paid
Bryant five thousand dollars for some limp verses on the death
of Lincoln. For that amount even I would turn poet, and on any
subject.

"I don't feel in the least foreign," I lied to Gilder, enjoying the
bean soup, which I liberally seasoned with vinegar. "In fact, this
is like old times. We could be in the Shakespeare Tavern." Gilder
looked puzzled. I told him how literary and theatrical New Yorkers of the thirties used to gather in that pleasant place, long since
torn down and forgotten. He hungers for memories of Irving,

Halleck, Cooper. I do my best to amuse him.

"I suppose in those days there was more fraternity amongst our literary men than now." Gilder is younger than Emma, it suddenly occurs to me.

"We did not really think of ourselves as 'literary.' Writing was something any educated man might try his hand at for the amusement of himself, of his friends. If one was poor—like me or Mr. Bryant—why, we wrote for newspapers, often under pseudonyms because we didn't want to embarrass our friends."

"Our literature is a battlefield now, Mr. Schuyler." Gilder looked stricken. "It is a war to the very knife between the realists, as they like to call themselves, and the writers of good taste—like you, like Mr. Bryant."

I did not enjoy the joint wreath so sweetly offered, but left it unremarked. After all, my interest in these urgent literary matters is slight. As long as I don't have to read all these great new writers, I am willing to praise or condemn them as the occasion demands.

The citadel of realism is the *Atlantic Monthly*, published at Boston by a Middle-Westerner named Howells, an engaging if somewhat too literary man whom I met years ago in Venice, where he was the very young American consul—his reward for having written an exultant campaign biography of President Lincoln.

Note: remind Mr. Dutton that I am in a position to write a similar biography of Governor Tilden. Bigelow and I have corresponded on the matter and though he is the logical choice for such a work, he will be too busy with the campaign "and think you the best of all people to present the Governor to that small part of the electorate able to read."

Howells publishes realistic stories in the French manner as well as lively stories of the Far West, currently the most popular genre. In fact, if one is not a Westerner (or cannot write like one), the door of true success hereabouts is at best only half ajar. At the other end of the literary spectrum are the polite journals for which I write, including the one edited by Gilder.

"We must never forget," said Gilder loudly, perhaps suspecting that I was already beginning to forget what he was about to say even as it was being said, "that our audience is made up almost entirely of the ladies. Bless them!"

I blessed them through a chunk of decent French bread.

"That's why Howells and the *Atlantic* are losing circulation," he continued. "Because they insist on shocking or, worse, boring the ladies."

"Then our reading ladies must be as easily shocked as they are boring." Alas, I had said exactly what I meant instead of what I had only meant to say.

But like most people, Gilder heard what he expected to hear. "I don't always agree with Stedman, say, or some of our other friends at where the line should be drawn. As rough and—well, *shocking*—as Mark Twain can be, I think him a very *moral* man and a good influence."

"I think him the most contemptible music-hall performer that ever pandered to an audience of ignorant yahoos." I do detest Mark Twain, and several weeks of having to hold my peace on the subject caused me uncharacteristically to explode.

Gilder was not as astonished as I would have thought. "Of course, Twain is a sort of god in these parts," he observed mildly.

"Particularly amongst those who do not read." The fit was upon me. "He is what he is, isn't he?" For some years Twain has been lecturing around the world, telling interminable jokes and tall tales like another Davy Crockett. Unhappily, I doubt that I shall live long enough to see him duly installed at *his* Alamo.

"But surely, Mr. Schuyler, you admire the vigour of his short stories . . ."

"He is a nice comedian and I would pay to see him on a stage. But if I could burn every copy of *The Innocents Abroad* I would."

My dislike for Twain is inevitable. The professional vulgarian wandering amongst the ruins and splendours of Europe, making his jokes, displaying his contempt for civilization, in order to reassure the people back home that in their ignorance, bigotry and meanness they are like gods and if they ever should (Heaven forbid) look about them and notice the hideousness of their cities and towns and the meagreness of their lives, why, there's good old Mark to tell them that they are the best people that ever lived in the best country in the world, so let's go out and buy his book! I will say one thing for him: he is read almost entirely by people who ordinarily read no books at all. This helps us all. As everyone knows, the President's favourite (only?) book in all the world is *The Innocents Abroad*.

Gilder did his successful best to soothe me; remarked that Twain's sole attempt at writing a novel in collaboration with

Charles Dudley Warner had been a failure, though a play based
on one of the characters in *The Gilded Age* is still being performed.
"Now he seems to have failed again." Despite Gilder's liking
for Twain, he is too much the man of letters not to take joy in
the failure of another writer. "He has just this month published
what appears to be a boys' book. At Brentano's they say hardly
anyone has asked for it."

After lunch I proposed that we stroll about the Five Points.

My companion was shocked. "You're not serious, Mr. Schuyler?"

"But we must make some concession to the realists. In France
the writers haunt such places."

Gilder was grim. "I've *read* those writers and they are—un-
clean."

But finally he agreed to go with me as protection. In Broadway
we boarded a bright Yellow Bird horsecar bound for City Square
Park.

The day was not cold and it was most agreeable to take the air,
bad though the air was downtown; and see the sights, grim as
they proved to be.

At first glance, the Five Points have not changed much. As
many streets converge on a dismal acre or two of bare earth. Since
the melting of the snow, all is now mud and human excrement
in that triangle known with some bitterness to the inhabitants as
Paradise Square. A broken fence encloses the area, as if to protect
the two spindly trees that are its only decoration. Chestnut ven-
dors ply their trade in a desultory manner whilst old women of
foreign stock sit on the front stoops of tenements, grating
horseradish with filthy hands. Two young ragged tramps sit in
a doorway, swigging from a long black gin bottle. Here and there
gamblers have set up tables on the sidewalk, and despite the cold
a number of customers play three-card monte.

When I was young I used to enjoy the sense of danger, of
seduction, even of violence in this quarter. But all that is changed.
Not gone but changed, swelled by the immigrants who live
jammed in the cellars, the attics, the tiny rooms of those ram-
shackle tenements that make up the sides of the triangle. Largest
of the buildings is a one-time brewery recently turned by good
church ladies into a Mission House. On either side of this lop-
sided building are narrow lanes: one is known as Murderers'
Alley.

"Dickens was horrified when he saw this." Gilder indicated the alley in which dark figures could be seen hurrying on terrible missions.

Numerous beggars approached us. Fortunately, there are police on hand; at sundown, however, they sensibly vanish, and there is no law in the Five Points but that of the fist, the knife, the gun.

At the corner of Worth Street a black figure—literally black in clothes, face, hands (but not a Negro)—blocked our passage. "We've got the dogs for you, sirs. They're just startin' in the pit now. Down there, sirs. In the alleyway."

Gilder said we were not interested, although I must say that I'd like very much to see this new, dreadful, illegal sport. A specially trained terrier is placed in a small zinc-lined enclosure filled with rats. The terrier invariably kills each rat but also suffers horribly in the process. Meanwhile bets are placed: how many rats will the dog kill and how long will it take? Sometimes as many as a hundred rats are dispatched in a single contest.

"Most popular sport." Gilder was disapproving.

"With the poor?"

"With the rich, too. Shameful."

A number of prostitutes tried to entice us but they would not have interested anyone other than a blind-drunk sailor, for not only were they plain to look at and filthy in person but disease seemed to emanate from their every rag. I who have liked prostitutes all my life fled almost as precipitately as did the refined Gilder; it was as if even a glance from one of those poor creatures would be sufficient to make one burn and drip for a year despite the good god Mercury's best offices.

As we started down Thomas Street (discussing the sales of books—the usual subject of the New York scribbler), I noted the whorehouse where once I used to regularly spend myself in every sense of that verb. The house is unchanged. But now it is packed from cellar to dormer windows with Italian immigrants.

As we passed, children flowed like lava from the house (the image is appropriate, since all are Neapolitan), and clustered round, begging for money. I scattered pennies; spoke to them in their own language, to their astonishment. Incidentally, I speak more French, German, and Italian in New York's streets and restaurants than I do English. The entire working class save the Irish speak no English, and what the Irish speak is at best near-English.

Yet my taste for low life has now returned after two months of trying to make my way in the world of scribblers. Tonight, in fact, I was *absolutely* indulged.

Late though it is, I feel marvellous, despite exertions that at my age are more apt than not to end with the spirit's swift departure from the voluptuously overburdened flesh.

Jamie came to take us first to the theatre and then to supper at Delmonico's. I thought that he would bring his fiancée, a Baltimore belle, but he came alone, and was not entirely sober. Fortunately, after so many years, Emma is as indulgent as a sister (twenty years ago when Jamie would pull her hair she would kick his shins). So we were very much *en famille*, as he installed us in his grand victoria.

"This is going to be a rare treat." Jamie kept repeating, but though he tried to keep secret the nature of the "rare treat," we both knew what it would be since the newspapers had written of nothing else for some days.

Although the theatre was only a block or two from the hotel, we had to wait more than half an hour as each of the long line of carriages in front of us stopped and deposited its contents at the new Park Theatre (a mere shadow of the old, despite the blazing calcium lights and the enlarged proscenium arch).

"It's Oakey Hall of course!" I said the moment we joined the line in front of the theatre. "It's his opening night."

"I read of no one else in the papers but I still don't know *who* Oakey Hall is." Emma reads our newspapers with a swift but often uncomprehending eye.

"Most gorgeous creature! Isn't he, Schuyler?" Since Jamie has become sole proprietor of the *Herald* and I his special Washington observer, he has dropped the "Mister" and the "sir" with which so respectfully he addressed me all his life. Well, times change.

"He's never come my way." I turned to Emma. "He was mayor of New York. And a part of Tweed's ring. For several years they've been trying to put him in jail, too." Incidentally, Tweed is rumoured to be safe in Mexico.

"But Oakey stays out of the clink because he never stole so much as two bits." Jamie is personally fond of Hall, who is, everyone agrees, a considerable charmer as well as the best-dressed man in New York (whatever *that* must be). As mayor, he not only stole money but delighted in the title "the King of Bohemia." He has always been something of a scribbler as well as a lawyer; journalists love him as a glamourous brother.

"He has written a play. I read that much in the press."
Through the steaming glass of the carriage, the bright marquee
lights illuminated the title, *The Crucible*, elsewhere identified as a
play "leased and managed" (but actually written as well) by
Oakey Hall, who is, also, to the delight of New York, the leading
actor.

I felt the old excitement as I once again set foot in the foyer of
an American theatre. My first such occasion in New York since
1837, when quite another Park Theatre played to quite a different
audience, now for the most part gone to join the majority.

I was happy to see that even in the harsh glare of the calcium
lights Emma looked ten years younger than her age as she made
a tour of the lobby on Jamie's arm; everyone's eyes were upon
her, although half the leading actresses of the city were at the
theatre, not to mention any number of gallant ladies of fashion.

Jamie was greeted jovially by the swells; amongst them was
Commodore Vanderbilt's middle-aged heir, to whom Jamie de-
ferred. Mr. Vanderbilt looks to be a dim sort of man, and it is said
that his father (who may never die) has not much confidence in
"young" William's ability to carry on the New York Central
Railroad and the rest of the old man's huge stolen empire.

Why is it that I so much admire the Bonapartes but detest these
money-grubbers? Scale, I suppose. The Bonapartes wanted glory.
These folk just want money for its own sake. Only lately have
they begun, nervously, to spend money in what they take to be
a splendid manner by accumulating works of art, by building
mansions. I wonder if one of them will prove to be a new Augus-
tus: finding New York brownstone, he will leave it marble.

I was stopped just before the curtain rose by what I took to be
an actor. This bold-looking man's fringe of hair was long at the
back, whilst his moustaches would have looked appropriate attached to a Mexican general; he wore a leather frontiersman
jacket like Davy Crockett and carried in one hand a Mexican
cowboy hat known as a sombrero.

"Mr. Schuyler, your admirer, sir! We met in London, don't you
remember?"

The voice was resonant and resolutely Western. "Surely if we
had met, I could hardly forget it, sir." I, too, was resonant.

Of course we had never met but it made no difference. Yes, it
was Joaquin Miller, one of the horde of Western writers that the
English delight in showing off to one another. Socially Miller was
a great success in London a few seasons ago. I am told that on

occasion he would smoke three cigars simultaneously, claiming that all real Californians smoked three at a time. One memorable evening he got down on all fours and snapped at the ankles of the delighted young ladies. From time to time he publishes volumes of manly verse.

I was polite, flattered even that he would take notice of a fellow "actor" who is not only so much older but booked into (let us belabour the metaphor) an entirely different kind of theatre. Emma was also much taken with him whilst Jamie made good-natured fun of him. Apparently Miller is used to being the butt of jokes.

A number of people presented themselves to us. I was particularly taken by a tall ruddy-faced man in early middle age, elegantly dressed and with a most gracious manner. "We met for an instant at the Century, Mr. Schuyler. I'm sure you wouldn't recall. You were with Mr. Stedman. I'm right glad to meet you again, sir."

I pretended to remember him; was struck by his literary manner. As we took our seats (the curtain was an hour late), Jamie told me that my admirer was the collector of the port of New York, that extraordinarily powerful and lucrative post from which my long-dead friend and now glorious legend Sam Swartwout stole more than a million dollars. Let us hope that General—yes, another general—Arthur will be either bolder or more discreet.

General Arthur told me that in college he had read and particularly enjoyed my little book *Machiavelli and the Last Signori*. I was overwhelmed. In the old days collectors of the port knew nothing except how to add and subtract—mostly the latter.

The play was, for me, a perfect joy. The former mayor of New York is a dapper creature who wears—or wore—an odd drooping pince-nez, sports—or sported—a distinctive moustache. I change tenses because near the end of this astonishing play, the former mayor, in the interest of absolute realism, *shaved off his moustache* for a prison scene and left off wearing his pince-nez.

The result was disastrous. In the earlier acts Oakey Hall had been confident, even convincing. Now he lurched near-sightedly about the stage, running into furniture, whilst his voice became curiously indistinct as the tongue, attempting powerful consonants, sought in vain for the counterpressure of that thick overhang of moustache which had for so long made effective his usual speech.

I was weeping with laughter as he, poor man, wept with self-pity, wearing a Sing Sing prison uniform a size too large for him. Needless to say, the brave actor-author was given a standing ovation, and were I still Gallery Mouse for the *Post*, what a notice I might have written for tomorrow's paper!

Delmonico's proved to be crowded. Many of those who had been at the theatre had also made reservations for supper. In fact, we arrived at the same time as the manager, young Charles Delmonico, who respectfully greeted us outside the front door.

"Well, Charles, what did you think?" asked Jamie, perfectly willing to keep us standing on the pavement as an arctic wind roared west across Union Square. Emma gasped with cold. The polite young Delmonico hurried her inside as he answered Jamie, "I think Oakey was probably a better mayor."

Of the three Delmonico restaurants, the one at Fourteenth Street and Union Square is certainly the most fashionable. The carpeting is thick. The lamps are richly shaded. How important it is to see the food plainly, yet not to see or to be seen too closely by those one dines with! Damask curtains comfortably contained the warmth but not the heat that one so often gets in overcrowded poorly ventilated eating places.

I would dine every day at Delmonico's if I could afford it. But one cannot dine there for less than five dollars (four courses and a single bottle of claret).

The Delmonico family was originally from Ticino in Switzerland, and I have by now come to know well the autocrat of this dynasty, Lorenzo (the uncle of Charles), a man my age with a constant cough and wheeze made no better by the cigar that is never out of his mouth even when, most elegantly, he leads the ladies to their tables.

As we crossed the main dining room to Jamie's special corner, Ward McAllister rose from a table, and greeted us ceremoniously.

Jamie took Emma on to our table, as McAllister whispered into my ear, breath smelling disagreeably of port. "*She* wants you for Wednesday. For dinner! You and the Princess."

"Who?" My voice is sometimes overloud. Although my hearing is good, I am prone to the characteristic booming voice of the deaf because of the blood's most disagreeable habit of pounding against my eardrums, deafening me.

"The Mystic Rose!" He hissed the magic phrase into my ear. "Shall I say you will accept? *She* will then make the invitations.

I am her scouting party, don't you know?"

"With pleasure, of course. You are kind. So is she. I mean *she*." I babbled; withdrew.

Jamie and Emma were quoting lines from the play and laughing. But when I sat down, Jamie was curious. "I didn't know that you knew old puss."

"It's hard *not* to know him." Emma answered for me.

I turned to Emma. "Apparently the Mystic Rose would like us to come for dinner on Wednesday."

"I hope you said 'No.' " Emma was superb.

"Of course I said 'No,' Emma, but it came out 'Yes.' "

"Most awful old creature." Jamie grimaced. "I'd stay away if I were you. Boring. Boring. Bill Astor's not bad. But he won't be there. Drunk all the time."

"Stop it, Jamie!" Emma was again the Parisian schoolgirl giving sharp lessons in manners to the young barbarian from New York.

"No. I think I'll just start it, Emma!"

We supped indiscreetly but well. The lobster salad is a specialty of the house and it is as good as any dish I've ever had at Paris (paprika somehow makes the difference). Canvasback duck followed, enclosed in a savory aspic. One gets this notable bird so often at important dinner parties that for the gentry it has taken the place of the American eagle. Terrapin is another Delmonico specialty that I am learning to like. But I shall never take pleasure in what everyone regards as the chef's peculiar triumph, ice cream *with truffles*. On the other hand, Delmonico's produces an iced coffee that I cannot get too much of; half cream and half coffee and well sugared, the concoction is kept near-freezing until served in a frosted glass.

It is now two in the morning, and for some time the terrapin has been warring with the canvasback duck, whose eagle-like beak tears at my Promethean liver. Yet my pulse is normal and there is no pounding in my ears. Obviously Colonel Burr's prescription for good health and a long life was right: the discharge of the seminal vesicles as often as possible. Tonight I have added at least a month to my life's span.

Emma was taken home, and I was taken on. At first I was reluctant. "I'm much too old for this sort of thing."

"How do you know what sort of thing I have in mind? Come on. Be a sport, Charlie." The boy has now come to treat me as a contemporary. I suppose that I should be pleased. Certainly, I must allow him a degree of beard-tugging since yesterday's agreement between the *Herald* and me: a thousand dollars for each piece written during the four months preceding the Republican Convention. One long article a week would mean $16,000 by the time my tenure of office ends. Not bad!

Incidentally, the *Ledger*'s version of my Empress Eugénie will be published Saturday. I read the slips with some dismay. They have hacked everything about, trying to "improve" my poor work by adding a number of detailed descriptions of the Empress's clothes in what they take to be my style. The result is horrendous, and deeply humiliating.

When I suggested that I write a companion piece on the Princess Mathilde, I was told that no one in the United States has heard of her. But *The Last Days of Napoleon III* has been accepted. The only problem is that I know nothing about the poor man's last days except that he had a most difficult time with his prostate and bladder. I suppose I can concoct something *Ledger*-esque. After all, I saw enough of the Emperor over the years to be able to describe, with a sob in my prose, his poignant coda.

I cannot say that the coldest night in New York's memory is the best night to go aprowling with a man young enough to be my son but old enough not to get as drunk as Jamie does most nights. Unfortunately, my appetite had been morbidly whetted by the Five Points. I am drawn to prostitutes, obscure rooms, the rattle of ill-tuned pianos, the red-tasselled boots of "dancing female waiters," as they are advertised in the *Herald*. From his very own newspaper, Jamie is able to find out exactly who is where and what they are doing.

Jamie's driver knows his master well. Without a word exchanged, he headed west across Fifth Avenue; the street was a sheet of ice. A number of sleighs were to be seen even at that late hour.

We were headed, as Jamie said, sobering up somewhat, "to the Chinese Pagoda, where they've got the most beautiful creatures you've ever looked at. They know me," he added, as if I needed that reassurance.

We came to Sixth Avenue, which is now to New York what the Five Points used to be. In the daytime, from Fourteenth Street to Twenty-third Street, the avenue is in perpetual shadow from the Elevated Railway. At night the Elevated's shadow makes absolutely dark the street or "jungle," the word most used by vivid journalists. And I must say that the pillars of the Elevated do suggest sinister trees, perfect hiding places for gamblers and whores, for thieves and murderers, as well as for those who would play with them or be played by them, the victims ending, often as not, on a rag heap, to be cut up by the "street rats" who sell the remains for fat, for bone, for hair.

The street was empty, the night frosty. Our carriage clattered beneath the silent Elevated Railway. In certain windows lamps gleamed, bowls of tinted red or blue glass with the owner's name in white, *Flora, The Pearl, Amazon.* Thus the prostitutes advertise.

We stopped at a tenement. In the absolute darkness, there was no sign of life. We got out. The coachman addressed Jamie. "Do you have your pistol, sir?"

Jamie nodded and tapped his greatcoat. "And you?"

"Yes, sir. I'll wait right here. The usual place."

An alarming exchange.

Jamie rapped on the tenement's door. A grilled window was uncovered. A murmured exchange. Then we were admitted to a loud, bright, smoky hall where a band played Offenbach as a line of girls in cancan costumes danced; each girl wore red-tasselled boots. For some reason they are *de rigueur* in this sort of place. As a means of identification? or simply some manager's vice?

A large well-dressed ape of a man greeted us warmly; addressed Jamie cryptically, "Pearls but not diamonds. Rubies possible. This way, gentlemen." He led us to a plain wood stairway at the back. Feeling most uneasy, I followed them upstairs to a long corridor with a series of doors at close intervals on either side.

Our guide opened one of the doors and ushered us into a box from which we could observe everything that went on below from behind a dusty velvet curtain.

"Just give me the eye, Mr. Bennett. I'll be down there." The man pointed to a place near the stage where the girls were dancing; and left us.

"Well, Charlie, what do you think?" Jamie's drunkenness comes and goes; just as his speech becomes slurred and incoherent and the body starts to sag and be ill-coordinated, he will suddenly pull himself together, force the alcohol from his brain and appear for a time to be sober. The cold journey from the theatre had no doubt cleared the head which now he proceeded again to muddle with champagne from a cooler.

"Very elaborate," I said neutrally. "Nothing like it when I was young and living here." I must stop referring to my great age and how far back I go in time. After all, I must still convince publishers that I have the strength to drive pen efficiently across paper.

I looked down at the dancers below. Not at the girls on the stage but at the girls who were dancing with the rough sorts: fresh-looking young women despite painted faces.

At the end of the room farthest from the stage was a long, crowded bar.

"Expensive place, the Chinese Pagoda. Not that there's anything Chinese about it. They don't let just anybody in either. You've got to be a proper rake like me or a successful murderer for hire like Iron-man down there." He pointed to the bar, where there were at least twenty candidates for Iron-man.

"Now if you see anything you like, it's on me." Jamie waved graciously at the crowd beneath us.

"I fear . . ." Oh, I feared at Polonian length. Actually, despite the heavy dinner, I was slowly getting into the mood of the place. For the first time, let me confess shamefully (an adverb invariably chosen to please lady readers, but men—if any read—may substitute for "shamefully" "delightedly"), I felt that I was again in *my* New York, the world of the Five Points of forty years ago when Leggett and I would prowl like figures from the *Arabian Nights*, getting to know the good brothels of the region as now I am obliged to learn the Cabinet of General Grant, the legal victories of Governor Tilden.

A waiter-girl came to see if we wanted anything. Blond, blue-eyed and but recently from the country, she seemed terrified (did Jamie prefer the frightened "virginal type"?). "Another bottle, Polly. You are Polly?"

"Dolly, sir."

"The same! And more of the same." She took the bottle. "And my love to Polly, Dolly."

Jamie roared at his own wit and then said, suddenly, most seriously, "There was a safe out there, you know, filled with all sorts of incriminating documents. They broke into it."

"What, dear boy, are you talking about?"

"General Babcock. I'll send you my notes tomorrow. All very secret. Even the grand jury doesn't know the whole story but I do."

"Babcock himself tried to open the safe?"

"He and his friends in the whisky ring have stolen close to ten million dollars. He got his cut, of course. Oh, he's in up to the eyeballs." Jamie was drifting off: the sharpness of his first remarks was now succeeded by a slurring of words if not of thoughts.

"The safe, what about the safe?"

"Oh." This brought him to. "Babcock used Secret Service men to break it open."

"But that's illegal!" was the stupidity that came from me. The band was now playing Mexican music.

"Oh, yes! Very illegal. And that's the angle we want to play up. President's private secretary uses members of the Secret Service to burglarize a safe. If that don't touch Grant, nothing will."

Directly beneath us a dark girl was dancing on a table. Jamie whistled appreciatively. "Do you like that, Charlie?"

I could no longer maintain the Polonius role. "Yes," I said, "very much."

"It's done."

And indeed it was done. Each of the doors on the opposite side of the corridor opened into a small bedroom. I found myself not only nervous as a boy but as abashed as anyone over sixty, overweight, overtired, is bound to be when confronted with a vivid black Irish girl with gentian-blue eyes and a full, very full, figure.

"Well, you're quite the gent, I see." She gave me a smile as she started to remove her blouse. "So ring for some champagne, will you? Not for me, mind you, but Mr. Horner gets angry as can be if we don't sell the client at least one bottle of his homemade champagne. The bell's just there. Oh, these boots are killing me."

I rang for the champagne, which arrived an instant later. The old Negro waiter opened the bottle with a certain flair. I tipped him fifty cents (Jamie had instructed me in prices as well as in protocol. The girl was to get twenty dollars for which "she'll do *anything*, Charlie!").

"Anything" proved to be not much of anything except that at my age the elemental ritual must be conducted with a slowness that in my youth would have been unthinkable. Fortunately, I have not the slightest inclination to brood over my youth, since poor young Charlie Schuyler is as dead as can be, buried beneath this heavy earth-falling flesh that I with such effort still manage to animate and keep from gravity's final tug and fall, into earth.

As Cathleen—her name—helped me dress, we spoke comfortably of this and that. Like so many girls in her situation, she dreams one day of owning a shop (the young Charlie once tried to set up such a girl as a dressmaker; and terribly failed).

"But you have to be practical and money's scarce these days. And I've hardly a penny now to go see the elephant." (Whatever that means . . . the zoo?) "I had saved more than a thousand dollars, you know, and lost it all when Jay Cooke failed in '73."

I burst out laughing, and was not, amazingly, short of breath. "Why, I was caught, too! And wiped out. Just like you."

"Poor soul!" We commiserated with one another. I found her extremely knowledgeable on finance. More so than I. But then, regularly, she sees a banker who is currently enthusiastic about a certain Ohio railroad stock.

She congratulated me on my prowess. Apparently, "Half the gentlemen still haven't recovered from the Panic."

"You mean their—uh, sexual performance is affected?"

"Something tragical. They try. I try. We try. But it's no good when you've lost all that money. I do pity men, sometimes."

Jamie was already downstairs waiting for me at the bar. Feeling uncommonly pleased with myself and with the fact that I was not in the least short of breath, I started down the narrow stairway only to come face to face with a ghastly creature from the past, William de La Touche Clancey. He is as hideous as ever, face now marked with the sort of distressing eczema that sometimes afflicts those suffering from tertiary syphilis. With him was a forlorn olive-skinned youth, Turkish or Hebrew, obviously well-muscled and eager—no, desperate—for Clancey's money because only someone starving would rent himself to a creature so plainly diseased.

It was my rare good fortune that I was not recognized. Have I changed so much? Hissing and honking endearments to the young man, Clancey tottered up the stairs.

I found Jamie at the bar in the company of several swells. One or two looked familiar to me from restaurants, the theatre. One, in fact, I took for an Apgar (the fourth or fifth?) of the Nine Brothers. Would that it had been! But I was mistaken. I doubt if any member of that self-regarding fraternity would be seen in such a place where even I, a sort of Bohemian, ought not to be at my . . . no, that word no longer. I am tonight young again.

Yet for gentlemen of almost any sort, it is more usual to frequent the quiet, rich establishment of one Josie Woods where all is discretion, serenity, anonymity—and *very* expensive. Most interesting of the city's 3,300 brothels (Jamie's figure, from the *Herald's* copious file) is or was that of a Unitarian minister named Allen, whose Water Street establishment was not only as luxurious as that of Miss Woods but each of his comfortable home-like bedrooms was provided with a Bible conspicuously displayed. It has been my experience that religious Americans often prosper in this sort of business, but then most Americans from the hinterland are—or were during the thirties and forties—besotted with evangelical piety, drenched daily by itinerant preachers in the blood of the lamb.

Jamie had had the discretion not to introduce me to his friends, though I suspect I was recognized. But then it does no harm to be thought still . . . vigorous.

I confess to a slight swagger (I hope not waddle) as I took my place at the bar and ordered brandy, to revive the heart as well as take the taste of home-brewed champagne from my mouth.

"Satisfactory, Charlie?" Jamie beamed at me like a depraved nephew out on the town, with a . . . depraved uncle.

"Yes, Jamie. The dancing on the table was particularly inspiring. Even spiritual." I improvised, amusing the swells. "It seemed that the girl's boots were tapping out a message from the spirit world."

General laughter. "What was the message?" someone asked.

"Buy Southern Ohio Railroad stock, which is now selling at par."

This got more of a reception than it deserved. But then a huge man with a diamond stickpin the size of a plover's egg explained that Commodore Vanderbilt regularly communes with the dead Jim Fiske and other financiers through a pair of sisters whom he has set up in the brokerage business.

I asked Jamie about Clancey in a low voice. "Does this place also cater for catamite fanciers?"

"Well, it's an open place. But I'm sure they make Clancey pay through his nose." Jamie shuddered. "Disgusting old creature. Did you know that one of his sons is older than I am? and a member of the Union Club!"

Apparently Clancey still publishes a weekly paper financed by his wife. "Some of it's jolly funny. Clancey thought Tweed was the best thing that ever happened to New York, but then so did your friend old Bryant."

"That's not true."

"Ask the Kraut. Ask Nordhoff when you see him in Washington. He's our correspondent there. First-rate man, too. And incorruptible, as Bryant discovered. You see, the *Post* was taking a retainer from Tweed and that crook Henderson who really runs the paper thought Tweed pretty fine, and when Nordhoff wouldn't stop attacking City Hall, why, old Bryant gave him the sack. And we hired him."

I don't think that this can be true. The worst Bryant might do would be to allow *force majeure* to take its course.

In my sudden fleshly contentedness, am I sentimental and unrealistic? Otherwise why do I believe that if Bryant is not entirely honest, then there is no such creature in all the land? Obviously my critical sense has been deranged by this night's triumphant pleasures. I want Bryant to be what he ought to be, like our old friend and lover of justice William Leggett. Because of Leggett I have always felt that somewhere in this corrupt and canting American society there still exists in certain men a sense of what the good society must be.

I think I am drunk. The tears are streaming down my face as I wait for the laudanum to take its effect.

Three

1

THE FIRST DAY I have been able to sit up. A succession of doctors cannot agree amongst themselves exactly what it was that caused me simply to faint away the morning after my visit to the Chinese Pagoda.

There is talk of strain of the heart. But then what heart is not so daily strained and, with the years, so pulled and stretched that it has no choice, in time, but to stop? Happily, mine continues on about its work. And this morning, as I sit up in bed, newspapers and periodicals strewn across the counterpane and a bright sun filling the room, I feel most hearty, ready for anything.

But Emma is still concerned. "You ought not to get up just yet."

"If not now, never!" Broth for breakfast is most sustaining, and I wonder why one waits to be sick to be so well-nourished. "I've a full day. And *we* have a full evening."

"I don't think we ought to go out. Not tonight."

"If we are not at her dinner party tonight, Mrs. Astor will be laughed at in the streets and Ward McAllister will be forced to return to California, in disgrace. We must maintain the 'tong.' "

While waiting for John to take Emma to the Metropolitan
Museum and then on to lunch with yet another of the Nine
Brothers, Emma and I examined carefully the New York *Ledger's*
version of my article on the Empress Eugénie.

"It's unrecognizable!" Emma finally exclaimed.

"As my work. Or as the Empress?"

"Both. It's nothing but dress patterns, and how she does her
hair."

"Well, I've been warned that only the ladies read in this country, and presumably they like dresses and hair . . ."

"But they've got the dresses and the hair all wrong. Also, the
Empress never did much care about clothes. She'll be furious."

"I doubt if the *Ledger* will find its way to Chislehurst."

"But it will. You know her. She reads everything about herself."

"We must be brave, Emma. And hope the Empire is not restored in my lifetime, which means the next few weeks."

"Don't, Papa!" There was real concern.

Although I have suffered hardly at all from whatever it was
that felled me so suddenly, I now realize how easy it is *not* to
return from that swift sleep and so I have decided that Emma
must be married as soon as possible.

John arrived; was most solicitous. I wish he did not so deeply
bore me. "You look in fine fettle, sir!"

"That is where I hope to remain."

"Everyone's reading your article in the *Ledger.*"

"With disapproval? I know what your mother thinks of Paris."

"But there's Faith. She revels in all that sort of thing."

The talk was Apgar-ish for a time; and then the two departed
and I set to work on a study of Cavour, requested by Mr. Godkin
of *The Nation.* He pays very little but after the rather—why,
rather?—after the totally vulgar gush on the Empress I must
remind myself (and the few serious readers in the country who
admired *Paris Under the Commune*) that I still have my wits about
me.

I worked hard in bed until a light lunch was brought me—and
the usual messages, including a packet of political information
from Jamie. No one knows that I have been really ill. Emma tells
them that I am simply, "under the weather," an ominous phrase,
whose origin is no doubt nautical.

Gilder has sent me a number of books he thinks I should read. The new work by Mark Twain is all about a boy in a small town on the Mississippi. I cannot say that the doings of any boy quite seizes my attention. I suspect that this book is more in the line of William de La Touche Clancey. Thumbing through it, I did find some nice jokes, no doubt taken from the lecture hall. Yet, when it comes to raw Western vernacular, I much prefer the novels of Edward Eggleston, particularly *The Hoosier Schoolmaster.* Although a clergyman, Eggleston appears not to like Christianity, at least in its more wild evangelical frontier manifestations, and I can read him as easily as I do Balzac. I have also been fascinated by a writer named De Forest—a failure according to everyone in publishing. Gilder concedes the man's talent, "but novels are for the ladies and his are much too brutal, too close to sordid life, too full of politics." In other words too interesting and too real.

The curious thing about this ongoing "aesthetic" debate between the romantic writers on the one hand and the realists on the other is that neither school achieves anything but romantic false effects. American realists feel that to describe the workings of a factory is somehow to be vivid and truthful, and to a point they are right. But when it comes to writing about the men and women *in* the factories and what they really do to one another, particularly at work or within marriage, these realists are every bit as romantic and *un*realistic as the popular, busy women writers or even, to turn to the highest peak, that dark veiled lady of New England letters Nathaniel Hawthorne, who, faced with *any* truth about the way we are, swiftly evokes ghosts and haunted houses on those nights when silvery clouds cross a beauteous skull-like but, oh, so fictive moon.

If I were more interested I would do something on the French realists, who are not much known here. Howells at the *Atlantic* seems well-disposed; he has even written on Turgenev. Yet when one reads his own easy lady-flattering fictions, one wonders if for all his intelligence he can ever cease to be the opposite of what he affects to admire. I have several times mentioned Flaubert's *L'Éducation Sentimentale* as a novel that perfectly shows human life as it is—the undifferentiated drift down the years which most lives are—and yet the author is able to make every eddy in that slow progress glitter with some truthful light, so unlike the foolish jokes of a Mark Twain or the melodramatic romances of

Hawthorne. I think particularly of Hawthorne's last book where an age-old figure from the Roman catacombs encounters a present-day faun on the Campidoglio, a faun who must of course be destroyed, for the New England spirit requires that the natural be bent, banished, killed, even in moonlit dreams.

I think that is enough literary criticism for one morning. In any case, I have no wish to convert these proud American writers, since each is convinced that the national literature is of the highest as he waits impatiently for the next consignment of new books from London.

Now for Cavour. And some hard work.

2

FROM A LIVERY STABLE we hired a smart carriage to take us to Mrs. Astor's, and then to pick us up at midnight.

"That's the time you always have to leave, sir, from Mrs. Astor's." The concierge at the hotel who makes such arrangements did not for a moment betray his excitement at launching two of the hotel's guests to the very peak of Parnassus—if I have the right mountain. He also took quiet pleasure in showing us that he, too, was part of that great world, with a fair knowledge of who would and who would not be on the mountain's peak, as well as the exact hour that we would sit down at dinner (8:00 P.M.) and by whom the dinner would be catered, if the party happened to be too large for the chef to manage on his own.

Emma looked as if she had stepped down from a Winterhalter portrait at Schönbrunn: more Wittlesbach than Montijo empress. She wore the D'Agrigente diamonds, which are so cunningly reproduced in paste that only a jeweller with a magnifying glass could tell that they are false. I noticed with some pleasure that I am thinner than I was before the mysterious illness, and I think that we looked a most distinguished couple.

At first I was afraid that we might not know which of the two

identical Astor houses belonged to our hostess, but as Emma
pointed out, if the sisters-in-law were to give dinner parties on
the same evening, Fifth Avenue would be impassable. Incidentally, when I said that I hoped she would not be bored by the
provincialness of American society, she shook her head fiercely.

"Never bored, Papa. All that money is . . . well, like currents
of electricity in those hideous rooms, and I am absolutely thrilled!
I tingle all over. Your rich people here absolutely glow with
money, like northern lights." At times Emma can be surprisingly
literary, despite a rather vulgar taste in fiction.

As we were helped from the carriage by footmen in the Astor
livery—dark-green plush coats, gold armorial buttons, red waist-
coats, knee breeches and black silk stockings—a small crowd
watched us, despite a light snow that had begun to fall. From the
front door of 350 Fifth Avenue a red carpet had been prodigally
flung down steps, across the sidewalk and into the gutter. We
hurried inside.

What looked to be a court chamberlain directed the ladies to
their retiring or repairing room, the gentlemen to a cloakroom.
Then, properly retired and repaired, Emma and I made our way
solemnly down a long corridor to the great staircase. The house
is larger and more impressive inside than its thin wedge of choco-
late-cake look from the street would indicate.

We passed through three enfiladed drawing rooms (two in
blue, one in garnet) just as one did at the Tuileries. I was struck
by the richness of everything and, in general, the good taste of
the furnishings, though the pictures are not much good and the
sculpture insipid. Nevertheless, the light from the splendid crystal chandeliers was reflected most magically in the many silver
mirrors while everywhere there were fresh flowers—roses, orchids—and exotic plants, not to mention a proper conservatory
just past the third drawing room. It is the perfect luxury to
possess a complete tropical jungle in the midst of a freezing New
York winter.

Mrs. William Backhouse Astor née Caroline Schermerhorn
alias the Mystic Rose stood beneath a large bad portrait of herself,
receiving guests. At her side was Ward McAllister, very much in
his element, and slavishly devoted to the mysteries of his rather
full-blown rose. Mrs. Astor is not young (forty, forty-five?) and
her dead-black hair is not entirely her own, whilst the body she
has decorated with chains of diamonds and pearl moonbursts and

a stomacher of emeralds that the Great Mogul himself might envy is entirely her own (the word "body" is the subject of that last small verb: jewelled qualifying clauses now drip from my pen just as real jewels hung, fell, swayed, glittered not only from the tall stout erect figure of Mrs. Astor but from all the other ladies present).

Fifty ladies and gentlemen had been invited for this particular dinner party, Ward McAllister whispered in my ear, breath more foul with the violets that he'd been eating than the usual odour of port he wanted to disguise. "*All* New York that matters is under this roof tonight."

The Mystic Rose gave Emma a long look; then the eyes went straight to the replicas of the D'Agrigente diamonds. I feared for a moment that Mrs. Astor would suddenly produce not a lorgnette but a jeweller's magnifying glass, detect Emma's paste and order us to the door.

But Emma passed with colours that flew before the wind of our hostess's approbation like so many banners in a victory parade. "We've heard so much about you, Princess. We're so glad you could be with us tonight."

"You are most kind, Madame, to invite us." Emma's French accent was quite—deliberately?—noticeable.

"Mr. Schermerhorn Schuyler." Mrs. Astor allowed me to bow over her rather thick beringed fingers. "Mr. McAllister is confident that you and I are cousins. You see, I was born a Schermerhorn." The tone of her voice was reverent, as if she had been born a Plantagenet.

I deeply dislike McAllister's doubling of my name. In his ambition for us socially, he has managed to impose upon me a false persona, for I am connected with neither the grand Schermerhorns nor the grand Schuylers. My Schermerhorn mother was born on a poor upstate farm, one of eleven undistinguished children, all of whom had the misfortune to live while my father Schuyler kept a tavern in Greenwich Village—in those days a real village and not just a name to denote a part of this neverending city.

But I am willing to play whatever game is expected; and was complaisant. "Yes, my mother was a Schermerhorn, too. From Columbia County." All perfectly true. "Their place was near Claverack." Again perfectly honest.

"Ours is indeed a large family." Mrs. Astor gave me a gracious nod as if she were Queen Victoria and I one of a thousand German princely cousins to be suitably recognized.

Then we passed into the next drawing room, where everything was blue-green damask and rich malachite. McAllister remained beside his Rose, introducing her to people she for the most part appeared to know better than he, but then that is the task of the chamberlain in a royal household.

Emma caused some stir. Everyone knew of her. Several ladies had met her at one or another of Mrs. Mary Mason Jones's lunch parties, so she was well provided for with respectable companions of her own sex. The men eyed her most appreciatively—red-faced fat men, with eyes glazed from too many razzle-dazzles. Proudly they bear the great names of the New York that so bore me. But I am a beggar; may not choose.

"You have not been polite!" A woman's voice behind me. I turned and there was Mrs. William Sanford, as bright and cheerful as ever.

"How have I failed you?"

"You wouldn't join us for lunch at the Brunswick—"

"I was indisposed. No, really. Felled by Delmonico's splendid food—"

"—so the Princess said, but I thought you'd really dropped us."

We kept on in this vein. I was startled: Emma had not told me that she had accepted the Sanfords' invitation on the second day of my convalescence. I had been under the impression that she had retired, as usual, into Apgar-land.

"We had a charming time. I hope she did. The Belmonts were there and they took to her enormously, but then everyone does."

That explained the mysterious invitation from Mrs. August Belmont for dinner New Year's Eve. "I've not met them," I said to Emma when I saw the invitation.

"But I have," she said. "It's all right. They are charming. He's from our side of the Atlantic." Belmont—"the beautiful mountain"—was born with that name, but in German. As a Jew he occupies a somewhat equivocal place in the New York scheme of things. He is, however, a great magnate, for he represents the Rothschilds in America and since he possesses what McAllister calls true "tong," his palace and its entertainments almost rival those of the Mystic Rose.

"But Caroline won't have the Belmonts here. So narrow, I think." Mrs. Sanford was actually criticizing our hostess. I liked her more and more.

"But then I suppose she wants to draw the line somewhere,"
I said.

"Yes. And what she's done is to draw the outer perimeter so
as to contain the largest possible circle of bores that will fit comfortably into her dining room." This was a most unexpected
announcement.

"Really, Mrs. Sanford, I think you are a revolutionary."

"You'll be one, too, if you stay too long in this city, revolving
and revolving in the same orbit. Look at the gentlemen, will you!"

I said that I had already noticed them.

"Half drunk already. They leave their offices, drop in at the
Hoffman bar or at their club, have a drink or two, come home,
drink some more, quarrel with their wives. Then—well, here
they are, thinking of food and drink like buffaloes heading for the
watering hole."

"Surely Mr. Sanford does not qualify as a—buffalo."

I detected something odd in her manner, a slight turning away;
the merriment ceased. "No, no. Bill is usually most abstemious.
But he does love to go out, and I don't."

"Even now?"

"*You* are like a fresh Atlantic breeze in this hothouse, Mr.
Schuyler."

I was perfectly flattered, and responded in kind until dinner
was announced.

Ward McAllister, *in loco Astoris*, took in Emma first. I came in
last with Mrs. Astor on my arm (McAllister had earlier sent me
full verbal instructions as to protocol via the stately butler).

"Where is *Mr.* Astor?" I asked as the majestic figure beside me
set the pace for our slow walk to the long dining room.

"In Florida." She said the name of the state as though it were
something very strange and not quite nice. "He takes the boat. He
has horses there. Do you like horses, Mr. Schermerhorn Schuyler?"

I did my best with that one. In fact, I did my best through the
long luxurious dinner, for I was on Mrs. Astor's right—taking
precedence as a sort of foreigner.

The motif of the dining room was of the purest, heaviest, most
expensively wrought gold. Candelabra, epergnes, serving plates,
all was gold, even the roses (mystical?) that decorated the table
had a gold look to them.

But one works hard to sit in that high place, to eat that superb

dinner. Conversation with Mrs. Astor is not easy, for she is swift
to exclude whole subjects. As usual, I did not mention literature.
That is for others to do if they are so minded. She was not so
minded. She did not, she felt obliged to say, find much worth
reading nowadays. But, graciously, she admitted to enjoying the
illustrations to my article on the Empress Eugénie. On music she
is better. She has seen and sometimes heard the second act of all
the great operas. Painting and sculpture? No response except to
praise her own things.

I moved boldly to grave matters. I told her that I was soon to
go to Washington City. I would be dealing with the President.
My hope of impressing her was stopped dead with an absolute
exclusion. "*I* have never been to Washington myself."

"But why should you leave right here?" I babbled, implying,
idiotically, that she remain forever seated at her own dinner
table, while footmen filled golden goblets with Château Margaux.

"I go to Ferncliff." This was an announcement. It is the name
of the house that her husband has built up the Hudson at Rhine-
beck. "I also go to Newport. I have a cottage there. You and the
Princess must visit us. One goes first by the cars to Boston. Then
one changes to the cars of the Fall River line."

That, I think, gives the flavour of our conversation. At one
point she did press me hard on the Schermerhorn connection;
happily, I was able, without once lying, to convince her that we
were indeed cousins.

Since the dinner lasted three hours, I feel now that I know Mrs.
Astor as well as I shall ever want to. Alternate courses were a
relief because I had Mrs. Sanford to my right.She knew exactly
what I was going through without once making any reference to
our hostess. I must say (as a result of the contrast?) she seems to
me now a sort of angel of good sense and kindness; also, swift, oh,
very swift to get the point to things. She is remarkably like Emma
in that regard.

At about eleven Mrs. Astor rose from her place—in the middle
of a sentence to me on the difficulties of finding footmen who
would not drink up what was left in the bottles. With a marvellous silken, whispery, jingling sound, the ladies followed Mrs.
Astor to the vast art gallery that runs parallel to the dining room.
In the dining room the gentlemen huddled together, testing the
port, the madeira.

I found myself joined on the one side by the solicitous McAllister: "*She* was enchanted by you. I can tell our Rose's every mood."

And on my other side was William Sanford, looking more glamourous than ever, and already breathing cigar smoke. "So how's the old tin oven, Mr. Schuyler?" This was meant to be jovial.

I responded with all the pomp of Mrs. Astor. "If I had a tin oven, Mr. Sanford, I would hope that it worked properly."

"You must pardon an old railroad man. That's one of our expressions." He went on for a while, spinning yet another identity for himself—a sort of diamond in the rough Commodore Vanderbilt type, straight-talking and mean as a snake. I found him tiring in this vein; happily, he is not slow to see what effect he is making and so changed entirely his manner.

"We enjoyed the Princess's company at lunch. As did the Belmonts."

"So Mrs. Sanford told me." I was deliberately flat; do not really care to encourage this peculiar acquaintance.

"I hope the Princess was amused."

"She has said nothing to me about what must have been something of a gala."

"Yes." The grey eyes were very round now; and calculating—what? How to win me? But I am hardly worth the effort. "We hope that you both will visit us at Newport, Rhode Island, in June."

"June is a long time away. Besides," I added, inspired, "we're committed to Mrs. Astor."

"Beechwood's uncomfortable."

I gathered that this was the name of the Astor cottage. "Besides I may have to be at the nominating conventions. Emma is eager to see St. Louis and Cincinnati, not to mention the god Demos in action." If Sanford believed a word of this, he would, as they say here, believe anything. But I laid it on.

"Of course." Sanford was mild. "Conkling's the man, you know."

"To be nominated for president?"

Sanford nodded, slowly, deliberately, as if he himself were kingmaker. "It's all been arranged by the Stalwarts, and in spite of all your reformers like Bristow and Schurz, Tom Murphy and Chet Arthur will decide who gets nominated. Of course there'll be a row."

"Is it true that General Grant would like a third term?"

"Mrs. Grant would dearly like it and I suppose he would, too. But this Babcock thing . . ." Sanford shook his head, affecting sadness. "Not to mention the constant fussing of your reformers, going on and on about Civil Service reform, like crazy fools."

I agreed that it was foolish to want to reform the Civil Service when it is plainly not possible under the present party system which requires that the incoming political party replace everyone in the departments of the government with their own supporters who are, to a man, every bit as undeserving and as unqualified as those whose places they have usurped. This has been going on all my life. Lately, examinations have been given to would-be government workers with, predictably, farcical results. Much quoted in the town is the reply of one of Collector Arthur's pets to the examiner's question, "By what process is a statute of the United States enacted?" To which the good Republican answered, "Never saw one erected and don't know the process."

"You have not met Senator Conkling, have you?"

I said that I had met him briefly last summer.

"An impressive man, a superb orator, vain as can be, of course. The ladies think the world of him."

"Yes. Particularly our friend Mrs. Sprague."

A look of interest was bestowed on me like a prize for deportment. "Well, now, you don't say?"

"So I do say. Mrs. Sprague has been living in Paris, you know. She has an apartment near the Madeleine, in the Rue Duphot." I piled on the details.

"An uncommonly handsome woman."

"She is indeed."

"I guess Kate Chase Sprague is the closest thing to a queen we've ever had in this country." Sanford lowered his voice. "Mustn't let McAllister hear me say that or he'll push one of the Mystic Rose's thorns my way. But Mrs. Astor is just New York, while Kate was queen of Washington, of politics, right until '73. Then it was all over. Funny thing. I warned Sprague that the Panic was on its way, but there was no talking to that man. There never is. When he's not drunk—which is rare—he's just plain eccentric. Of the two, Kate has the brains."

"But apparently those brains are now at the service of Senator Conkling and not of Senator Sprague." The most talked-of Washington liaison is that between Roscoe Conkling, the beautiful senator from New York and master of his state's Republican party and Kate Chase Sprague, the beautiful daughter of the rather plain late Chief Justice and would-be president Salmon P. Chase, as well as wretched wife to the mad little senator from Rhode Island, William Sprague. Emma sees a good deal of Kate at Paris; finds her deeply embittered, resenting an exile not unlike that of our Empress but at least Kate has the good luck to be at Paris rather than at Chislehurst. Of all the Americans who have come our way in France, Emma took most to Kate, as she calls her, and I must say that despite the gloomy setting in the Rue Duphot the woman does have the curious gleam one notices in those who have been not only at a world's centre but for a time the focal point of that world's interest.

Kate has been in Paris for almost two years now; separated from her husband by an ocean—and a thousand bottles; from her lover Conkling by the force of society, not to mention that young man's ambition, for he is, as Sanford says, a contender for the presidency next year.

Sudden thought: This puts me in a curious dilemma. Should Conkling be the candidate and should I be at work for Tilden, what then ought my attitude be when the scandal of Kate and Conkling becomes a part of the ever-dingy electoral process? I shall have no attitude—and hope that the Republicans nominate Conkling's vigorous enemy the Speaker of the House of Representatives James G. Blaine.

Certainly I shall keep to myself the fact that by accident last summer, I met Senator Conkling at Mrs. Sprague's apartment. He was standing in the front doorway just *before* teatime, saying good-bye to her. She made the presentations in such a hurried, flustered way that had I not recognized from newspaper cartoons the tall, rather stout Adonis of Republican politics, I might have thought her caller some sort of overdressed professional man, like the Empress's friend and dentist Dr. Evans.

"It is a fascinating game." Sanford puffed on his cigar. "I think about it sometimes for myself."

"Politics?"

"Yes. If you have the money and the feel of the thing, why, it's as simple as can be. It would take me maybe two hundred thousand dollars to buy a seat in the Senate. Conkling paid a bit more for his seat but then New York's more prosperous than Rhode Island."

"But why would you want it? After all, don't men go to the Senate in order to acquire the sort of money that you already have?"

Sanford laughed. "Good point! I suppose it's to see if you can get the top prize. Become the president. After all, that's worth having for itself, isn't it?"

"I can't think why. As far as I can tell, our presidents have almost no function, except perhaps in wartime."

"But they are *there!* Don't you see? Now, when you worry about corruption—"

"Mr. Sanford, I promise you that I have not lost a moment's sleep at the thought of a bribe given or received."

"Sir, I know your writing. I know who your friends are. You're shocked by all this. But how else can you run a country where half the people don't even speak English and everybody's in a scramble to get his share of the pie? I'll tell you something," he told me. "Personally, I'm like you. I don't like anything about this so-called democracy. I'd like a well-run country with honest people in the government, the way they have in Prussia . . ."

"A tyranny?"

"If that's the only way to clean things up, make things run right, well, I'd accept that."

"With yourself as the tyrant, naturally."

"Oh, I'd accept *that* in a flash!" He laughed to show that he was not joking.

"Mrs. Sprague has true 'tong.'"My other ear was duly filled with the sound of McAllister's voice; he had heard a magical name and responded in character. "Whenever I hear New Yorkers say there is no society at Washington, *I* say, why, you have never been to Mrs. Sprague's for New Year's Day nor seen her enter a room, any room, with her hair done in braids like a coronet, and those marvellous jewels. Gone now, I should think. They are flat broke, don't you know? the Spragues."

This last item was added as if it were a charming detail of the poor woman's regalia.

McAllister then gave me a recipe for terrapin, "taught me by a Maryland darkey," involving a good deal of cream and butter. He also asked me if I had noticed how Americans of the same class say "sir" to one another whereas in England only servants say "sir."

"But we do say 'sir' in England. To royalty." I was benign.

Tears came to McAllister's eyes. "Some years ago, just as I was being presented to the Prince of Wales, the very instant he heard the 'Mac' part of my name, *he turned away.* "

I consoled McAllister as best I could until the evening ended at the mystical and roseate hour of midnight.

In the garnet drawing room Mrs. Astor stood, dark and commanding. As her guests filed past, they touched her hand as though it were an idol's, and certain to bring good luck.

I received the touch; so did Emma. "We hope to see a great deal of you while you are in New York." The sentence was, as it were, not said but passed.

McAllister immediately proposed, "The next Patriarchs' Ball?"

"Yes." So Queen Elizabeth might have raised from obscurity to the splendour of an earldom a common border Cecil, or Louis XIV with a nod of his wig bade a courtier to join him in the country at Marly and rich preferment.

The Sanfords said good-bye to us in the foyer. I find her entirely sympathetic but cannot warm to him. If he would only stick with a single performance, perhaps I could bear him more easily. But the constant shifts from plain-spoken man of the people, all hideously self-made, to thoughtful Darwinist and social historian is rather more than I can take.

After we got home I said to Emma, "I hadn't known you joined the Sanfords for lunch."

"I should have told you." Emma was contrite. I was already in my dressing gown before the fire, getting ready to make these notes. Emma was still in her evening gown, still Winterhalter though her face looked grey and tired, and I noted with the eye, I fear, of a realistic writer rather than with the loving gaze of an adoring father that, when tired, the lines on either side of her lower lip become deep and threaten one day to forge dewlaps like her mother's, like mine.

"At the last moment I couldn't face another excursion into Apgar-land and so I telegraphed the Sanfords 'yes' having already said 'no.' "

"Was it amusing?"

"The Belmonts are easy. Not at all American." Then Emma spoke analytically of tonight's guests. I waited for her to get round to Sanford but she did not.

"I like Mrs. Sanford." I made my move.

"So do I." Emma seemed enthusiastic. The old coals in the grate suddenly fell in upon themselves; a brief rush of flame and Emma's face was rosy, young again. "But I don't think she must have an easy time of it."

"With *him?*"

Emma nodded, staring at the flames; slowly she removed paste rings. "I have the impression he overpowers her. Forces her to do things she would rather not."

"Like go to Mrs. Astor's?"

"Worse, I should think."

"Worse? How?" I was intrigued, but Emma was not in the mood to play our usual game of penetrating the disguises people wear. "A philanderer?" was the most obvious attempt I could make to compel her attention, but Emma only smiled.

"I shouldn't think he had that sort of energy."

"What an astonishing thing to say! That is an energy few men lack. And Sanford's not yet forty."

"I don't know, Papa." Emma shifted to French. "I just said the first thing that came into my head. Perhaps he has a hundred mistresses. I wish him joy."

Emma kissed my cheek, I kissed her hand: our old ritual.

"Did he apologize for the flowers he sent you?"

"They were never mentioned. The vulgar have their own kind of tact, Papa." Then she was gone.

I cannot think why I allow Sanford to disturb me. I suppose it is because he has made it perfectly clear that he means to seduce Emma. Thank God, he has no chance if her mind is made up elsewhere, as I believe it to be in Apgar-land. Also, I suspect that Emma is not by nature amorous. She is too cool, too cautious, too possessed of a sense of the ridiculous ever to let go. I could imagine her turning from a drunken mad husband like Sprague to a man of power like Conkling, but I cannot imagine that she would ever allow herself to become involved with someone like William Sanford, a married man without glory or charm, only money. That would be out of character. Completely out of character. Yet why am I so alarmed? I do not really believe in heredity as much as I do in the ordinary circumstances that shape a life, but there is no doubt that Emma and I have in our veins most curious blood. I am the illegitimate son of Aaron Burr, and though I do not much resemble in appearance or character that elusive, marvellous, amoral man, I do sometimes see, staring at me from beneath Emma's beautiful level brows, the eyes of Aaron Burr, absolutely intense and entirely resolute—the eyes of a world conqueror. At such moments, she is as strange and magical to me as he was in life, as he is in memory.

3

THE GREAT DAY BEGAN with a snowstorm and a telegram from Governor Tilden, asking me to come see him at five o'clock, in order to talk before the dinner party.

Emma and I studied the message carefully and decided that she was not included at this meeting. "I'll come on alone for dinner." There seemed no alternative, since there is no one she could go with except the Bigelows, and they would simply walk around the corner from their own house in Gramercy Park.

At exactly five o'clock I arrived in Gramercy Park to find the air filled with a fine snow that the north wind with a most un-American fairness was trying to deposit on everything equally. The gas lamps had already been lit (because the Governor was in residence?) and their small pale halos hung in the middle air like so many purgatorial angels.

A servant showed me into an upstairs study, very much the sort of bookish retreat one would expect a wealthy lawyer with literary tastes to assemble. Seated in front of—that New York rarity —a wood fire (how sick I am of the smell of burning anthracite) was the imposing figure of a man in his fifties with short-cut dark hair and a somewhat belligerent face. As I entered the room he was entirely concentrated on reading a sheaf of papers.

When my presence was detected, the man sprang to his feet; took my hand in his and slowly crushed it. "I'm Comptroller Green, Mr. Schuyler. The Governor's resting just now. Will you take tea? Something stronger?"

Something stronger was brought me. Mr. Green took nothing. "We're still at work on the Governor's speech to the legislature next week." He struck the sheaf of papers with his fist. "This ought to set them on their ear!"

I did not ask whose ear would be set on, but assumed that he had the Republicans in mind. I drank Scotch whisky; spoke blandly, "Certainly the whole country will be listening to the Governor."

"Just what I tell that staff of his! Oh, they are . . ." But Green decided he did not know me well enough to give me his view of the Governor's staff.

"You are the comptroller of—New York City?" A foolish sort of question (though I made it sound a statement), for such men think the whole world knows them.

Green nodded gloomily. "No doubt for my sins in an earlier life. Last job in the world I wanted. But the Governor insisted. So I am heir to the Tweed debacle."

My magpie brain retains from the thousands of lines of newspaper print I feed it each day all sorts of odd useful facts. "Andrew H. Green" appeared in bold black letters behind my eyelids. The *Sun*. No, the *Herald*. I proceeded to read aloud from the newspaper in my head, "And of course we all hope that from the comptrollership you, Mr. Green, will become a reforming mayor." I let the editorial extrude smoothly, as though I had never for a day left Manhattan Island and its affairs.

Green flushed agreeably. "Well, there's been talk, but I don't think an honest comptroller of the city's finances is apt to be very popular with the bosses in the wards."

"Then let us hope you move on with the Governor to Washington."

"There is a lot of hoping but nowhere near enough organizing."

"Our friend Bigelow—"

"Does what he can." A slight edge to the voice, and I felt at home—at court again. It is all like a dim provincial version of the Tuileries, where grown men and women used to spend their days and nights plotting to arrange, as if by accident, five minutes alone with the Emperor on the stairs, in a garden, anywhere that the imperial quarry might for an instant be snared and used in order to rise in the world.

Green has been a law partner and intimate of the Governor for, he told me, thirty-three years. "A long time, isn't it?" Green shook his head at the idea of a century's third. "I was just a boy of twenty-one when I went into his law office. I thought then that he was the most brilliant man I'd ever met. I still do. He—is like an older brother to me."

I was pleasantly surprised that the somewhat chilly—even forbidding—Tilden could instill such ardour in an associate. Tilden is plainly a more complicated man than I first thought those pleasant days in Geneva when I simply saw the precise lawyer, the ruthless politician, the monomaniac—a word I have several times heard people use when referring to him. Certainly, once he has got hold of a subject, he does not easily let it go until he's shaken all the life from it, like the terrier I saw chew to bits rat after rat the other afternoon in a so-called pit just back of City Hall.

One of the doors into the study was opened by a tall young man, carrying a small valise. "The Governor's resting fine, Mr. Green."

"Thank you, Ben. You know your way out."

"Yes, sir." The young man nodded politely in my direction, acknowledging the presence of a gentleman whilst emphasizing his own position so much further down the long American social ladder.

When the lad was gone, Green identified him as "a very good giver of massages. You see, I can't get the Governor to exercise properly. He likes to ride, but nothing else, and who can ride in this weather? So naturally his blood just accumulates in the veins, which is very unhealthy. I tell him that he should be massaged every day, but I know for a fact that when he's at Albany he never stirs from his desk. Not that he isn't in the very best of health for a man of his age," Green suddenly added, realizing that the condition of a presidential candidate's body is far more important than the contents, if any, of his mind.

"Andy!" The familiar, rather feeble voice sounded from the next room. Green excused himself and joined his chief. I looked about the room. Family portraits, law books, a statuary group of a soldier fallen in the late war, head cradled in the lap of a grieving friend. I found myself wondering, idly, where the Governor kept his collection of erotic literature, which I learned about, quite by chance, from a bookseller in London; apparently the Governor has been secretly collecting lurid works for many years. Thus bachelors amuse themselves.

Green re-entered the room so silently that I started guiltily, as if I had been caught at some indiscretion by examining even in a desultory way the life-like figures created by the celebrated John Rogers. "I gave that to the Governor. If you like, you can go in. He's resting, of course . . ."

A single lamp on a table beside the bed illuminated what at first appeared to be an emaciated corpse—at least the lower part looked wasted away, for Tilden's legs as outlined beneath the single sheet that covered him are as thin as a crane's. The rest of him is more in the usual scale. Although a year younger than I, he seems to me to be very much my senior.

Cautiously I approached the bed, where the Governor lay flat on his back, arms at his sides. The hair is grey and cut almost as short as that of his friend Green. He wears no moustache, beard or side whiskers. If only for this continence, I hope that he becomes the president and sets the nation a new style. Since the war no one has actually been able to get a good look at any American face, so fantastic are the beards and whiskers, in imitation for the most part of General Grant.

In the half-light of a single kerosene lamp, Tilden looked to be all grey like a corpse. Later in the full light at dinner, his face proved to be almost as grey and corpse-like as when I found myself staring down at the sheeted figure, at the pale face with the large nose and curiously arched upper lip (dentures that do not fit?).

Then the eyes opened. I should like to report that the effect was as electrifying as, Paris friends assure me, that of the first Napoleon when suddenly he gazed upon friend or foe. But such was not the case with Governor Tilden. Rather, it was as if two large round grey clams had, of their own accord, opened and looked up at me, as from the half-shell. Were I holding a lemon, I might have squeezed it.

"Mr. Schuyler." The voice was faint. "Please draw up a chair. And forgive me for receiving you like this. You are very good to put up with me."

"Not at all." I made cheerful sounds as I placed a chair beside the bed. The Governor again shut his eyes. The lids are prominent and, even when raised, give a secret, hooded look to the dull grey eyes. I noted a slight droop to the left eyelid, the result of the mild stroke he suffered last February (and, to date, kept hidden from the public). I sat down, feeling a bit absurd, like a doctor at the wrong deathbed. For a moment there was no sound in the room but the regular soft belching of the Governor. He is a martyr to dyspepsia, and massage seems not to help the stomach's tension.

"And what, Mr. Schuyler, is *your* view of the order of the Grey Nuns?"

"Most benevolent." I improvised until I realized what he was talking about. Apparently, the Governor had signed a bill allowing the nuns to teach in the common schools. As a result, there is much Catholic-baiting going on. The *Tribune* is up in arms and the *Evening Post* wants the law repealed at the next session of the legislature.

"I must decide what position to take before next week. It is most perplexing. Much of our Democratic support is Catholic. But then there are all those Baptists and Presbyterians in the party, too. Such a noise they make . . ." Tilden sighed.

The hatred of the Catholics is still very strong in the city, particularly in such liberal circles as *Harper's Weekly*, where the celebrated cartoonist Thomas Nast, himself a German-born immigrant, wages a constant war on the papacy.

"When in doubt take no position." I was wise.

"I am neither in doubt, nor have I neglected to take a position." This was unexpectedly sharp, even presidential.

My pulse beat faster as I realized that I must not through inadvertent attempts at wit seal up the future fount of honour. "If the legislature originated the bill," I said quickly, "let them take the responsibility for it."

"Spoken like a lawyer." A slight raising of the awning-like upper lip served its owner well enough for a smile. "I must tell you, Mr. Schuyler, that I have read with care your reports on Europe and they are masterful in their detail. You have made me think new thoughts about the relationship between France and Prussia."

"You flatter me . . ."

A series, or *glissade*, of tiny belches interrupted us. Tilden is so used to them that he does not seem aware when they occur. When they ceased, he observed, "Bigelow is such a Prussian, you know."

"We have argued about that." I took my stand. "I find altogether too great a tendency here to admire the efficiency of the Germans at the expense of, let us say, the humanity and the creativity of the French."

"Yes. I have read you." Tilden was dry. Like me, he does not enjoy being told things that he already knows. "I also need your views to counterbalance Bigelow. He is convinced that in the next century there will be only three great powers—Germany, Russia and the United States."

"I lack the gift of prophecy, Governor. But in *this* century I am at your service now and—later." That was as close as I dared come to a request.

"Should there be a 'later,' I would certainly not let such a mind as yours go unused."

There it was—as good as in writing. No, better! For a lawyer as subtle as Tilden can never make a written agreement without arranging for himself, amongst the qualifying clauses, an escape hatch. The spoken word of a politician is almost always more reliable than his written bond.

We spoke a bit more of foreign affairs. I told him then of my assignment for the *Herald*.

"Not a favourite newspaper." The grey lip curled back: grey teeth shone dully. "But powerful."

"I could, I think, be of some use to the party. Not so much in what I write about General Grant, who seems already retired, but more particularly about his heirs, and your future rival."

"Blaine." The word was said softly, without emphasis.

"Conkling?"

The grey head rolled from side to side—at first, to indicate a negative, but then, finding pleasure in that rocking motion, in the easing of the muscles of the neck, the rolling continued. "I think Conkling will be no problem for us. Blaine is something else. Fortunately, he is corrupt."

"Does the public care?"

"*I* can make them care as I have made them care twice before." The feeble voice was at curious odds with the Caesarean statement. "No, Mr. Schuyler, we need fear only the good, the honest man, like Mr. Bristow at the Treasury. But such a man will never be chosen by the Republican party. Never. So—Blaine."

In the dim light I detected the makings of a most decent small-scale smile.

Green and a manservant entered. "Time to dress, Governor. The guests will be coming any minute. The Bigelows are already here."

"Thank you, Mr. Schuyler." Tilden's hand took mine for a

moment and pressed it—a relatively strong grip, I noted. "You are the sort of man we need in public life. One who is able to limit theory by practice"—there was a slight strangled sound as he held back a larger than ordinary belch—"yet enlighten practice by theory." On that high note, I joined the Bigelows in the main drawing room.

All in all, a successful evening. Emma worked hard on my behalf. She sat on Tilden's right at dinner and I think she managed to charm him, if any one can. There were a half-dozen Tilden relatives present, enjoying Christmas Eve with the family's richest and most famous member.

The Tildens are from Columbia County, close to where my mother's family lived, to where Martin Van Buren lived. In fact, the old President was a friend of Tilden's father and a benefactor to the Governor in his youth, as he was to me. But then Van Buren and I shared the same father. We were both illegitimate sons to Aaron Burr; needless to say, neither of us ever acknowledged this consanguinity to the other. Nevertheless, one of the strongest links between Tilden and me is the Van Buren connection. Tonight, when the Governor commented on my physical resemblance to the great man, I responded with an exact replica of Van Buren's secret smile which made the stony expression of the Egyptian Sphinx seem positively open and garrulous.

Bigelow was in good spirits, but tired. "We've been working night and day on the address to the legislature. I don't know how he does it." Bigelow indicated Tilden, who looked reasonably fit, the belching controlled by a constant nibbling at dry biscuits. "He lives on tea. He is an addict, I tell him."

"Better tea than whisky, as is reputed."

"You've heard those rumours?" Bigelow did not seem overly concerned.

"Only in Republican households."

"Like the Apgars?" Bigelow gave me a sidelong smile, and filled my glass with madeira. The ladies had withdrawn. Tilden drank tea, nibbled biscuits, listened as Green whispered into one of his ears and an adviser on economics named Wells in the other ear. "How does the Governor listen to two conversations simultaneously?"

"He's still got a lot of snap." Bigelow was admiring.

"You *were* worried about him, his health . . ."

"I still am. But I accept the fact that he enjoys ill health—

literally enjoys it. He also cannot stop working. So be it. After Grant, who would not work at the presidency—even had he understood the job—the Governor will be refreshing. At the moment all of us are exhausted except for the Governor. But then he has no life, you see, except the law and politics."

"If elected, will he marry?"

Bigelow tapped the half-empty glass of soda water in front of him—an abstemious group, the Tilden ring. "I think so. After all, a wife would ease his days in the White House."

"Obviously a man of passionate nature." I was moderately reckless after two glasses of madeira and a splendid hock earlier on.

"Odd, isn't it?" Bigelow took my irony in good part.

"Has he ever shown an interest in the ladies?"

Bigelow shook his head. "Never. It is curious. But also, in another way, admirable. I mean he is like a saint, absolutely removed from temptation."

"Saints, dear Bigelow, are not removed but remove themselves from temptation."

"Then he is simply chosen to be what he is, a constant worker in the public's interest. Green is the same."

"Mr. Green has never married?"

"Never. He, too, lives for his work."

"Another demi-saint?" I think the puritan Bigelow really does admire these flawed men. Not that I regard bachelorhood as a flaw; rather, the contrary. But apparently neither Tilden nor Green has had any commerce at all with women, with that half of the world who have given me, certainly, not only pleasure but a necessary measure of the common humanity. Had I not Emma, I would make another. Or, considering my advanced age, adopt, kidnap, seduce or otherwise acquire that feminine company without which I simply cannot breathe. The New York world of men's clubs and bars, of back-room politics and of sportsmen's pavilions is no world for me. I am an effete Parisian, and bloom only in the company of ladies.

Incidentally (why 'incidentally'? All-importantly!), Bigelow said, "The Governor will name you minister to almost any post you might want, saving that at St. James's."

"You don't know what this means to me." My voice grew hoarse with real emotion. Such an appointment does mean everything to me—once Emma is married, of course.

"In foreign affairs, you are one of our brightest stars, except for your unfortunate passion for the French," Bigelow added; and the mood lightened.

"Then you should be pleased with last Saturday's gush published under my name in the *Ledger*."

"It did not sound quite your style. And why did you never mention the good Dr. Evans, the Empress's ubiquitous dentist? What's become of him?"

"Still pulling teeth, I should think." Happily, we gossiped about the old good times in Paris, never to come again.

I did, delicately, try to convince Bigelow of the worthiness of Thiers and, in general, of the Third and current French Republic, but he is deeply, mysteriously anti-French. I put it down to his essential puritanism. Bigelow hates the Roman Church with a passion worthy of the true Republican he was until he became New York's secretary of state and a Democrat. For decades Bigelow has been assuring me that the wickedest and most rapacious force in the world is the papacy, which one day soon will collide in a perfect Armageddon with virtuous Protestantism, setting off a new, more bloody civil war right here in the United States, the Fort Sumter to be located in the old Sixth Ward, where the benighted Irish live.

I confess that I, too, once shared all these prejudices, particularly in regard to the Irish, whom I looked upon as a kind of disease or blight, killing my New York. Of course they and the later immigrants did indeed destroy the old Dutch-English village of my youth, but nothing valuable was lost. I daresay the fact that I have spent most of my life in Roman Catholic countries has not only made me more tolerant than Bigelow, but also convinced me that Roman Catholic societies are more agreeable to live in than Protestant ones because they are not in the slightest degree Christian.

At the end of the evening Tilden looked very tired, despite a quantity of tea and several mysterious pills.

"I hope you will come to see us at Albany, once you're finished with General Grant."

I said that I could think of no greater pleasure. Green was suddenly at Tilden's side. Handsome, rough-hewn, he physically overshadows his slight master. "Governor, did you mention to Mr. Schuyler our plans for advertisement concoctors?"

"Not yet. Not yet." Tilden's voice was low; he seemed

annoyed. But Green was not to be stopped. He turned to me.
"In the next few weeks we shall be starting a bureau, using all
sorts of writers and artists to prepare material for the newspaper
press . . ."

"Mr. Schuyler is far too distinguished a man of letters for this
sort of thing." Tilden's eyes opened very wide as he held in his
throat what must have been a powerful belch that slowly, and no
doubt painfully, he allowed to dissipate through widely flared
nostrils.

"Well, Governor, you know as well as I do that we can use all
the writers we can get and with Mr. Schuyler at the *Ledger* . . ."

"Mr. Schuyler is not *at* the *Ledger*. He is merely published *by*
them."

"But, Governor—"

I interrupted what looked to be something very like a quarrel
by saying, "Actually, I have approached my publisher about
doing a campaign biography. He is interested. Bigelow has
promised to provide me with material. So once you are nominated . . ."

Both Tilden and Green liked the sound of this; we parted in
a hail of Merry Christmases and Happy New Years. The Governor's last words to me were "I'll see you later." This curious
phrase is often on his lips.

"What did you think of Mr. Tilden?" I could not wait to quiz
Emma.

"Not the easiest man to talk to."

"A little chilly?"

"No. A passionate nature, I should think."

"That is not the impression I got, or anyone else."

"Well, there are all sorts of passions, aren't there? Like my
mother-in-law's passion for money . . ."

"Don't mention her! I can feel the blood pounding in my ears."

"Or that charming Senator Conkling's passion for Kate
Sprague."

"You liked him?"

"I saw him only that one time when we exchanged ten words."

"I remember. And you said you found him vain."

"Oh, as a peacock! With that ridiculous curl in the middle of
his forehead . . ."

"The hyacinthine curl. I suppose he's imitating Disraeli . . ."

"But when he looked at Kate, one felt *here* is a passionate man."

"Well, he had come halfway round the world to see her, incognito he thought. I don't think he fancied meeting us. Anyway, now you've met both party leaders. Which will it be? Who will be the president? Tilden or Conkling?"

"Who cares? It's only a game they play, Papa. It's not important."

I detected in her voice an echo, a variation on a theme of Sanford's. "Game or not, the result is important."

"But it is hardly like being the emperor, is it?" Emma continues to regard the United States as an overgrown Mexico.

"I admit that our presidents have very little to do. The Congress governs—and does most of the stealing. But the president has many jobs to give, particularly to deserving old writers."

"Then, *vive* Tilden!" Emma was in a good mood. "As for his passion . . ."

"Yes, how did you discover what no one has ever before noticed?"

"By listening to him talk about canals."

"Canals?"

"And railroads. And—oh, yes, justice." Emma was like a schoolgirl, recalling her lessons. "He said that he was appalled by the inequality of the American system of justice. The courts are for the rich, he said."

"He should know. He made his fortune representing the rich, particularly the railroads."

"Then, perhaps, he wants to atone for his sins. He is a good man, Papa, if absurd."

"I don't find him absurd, and doubt if he is good."

"Because you are a man. And an American. I only wish that he was less flatulent."

"A thunderer, like Prince Metternich?"

"No, a whistler like Prince Napoleon."

We laughed at the old joke. I said that I thought his real and only passion is ill health.

"No matter. I am sure that he will make a most amusing president, if such a thing is possible. Does he have a mistress?"

"You tell me."

"I think not. He is like an old capon." Thus we discussed the next president, and the restorer of our—my—fortunes.

Emma went to bed, and I worked for a time on Cavour. Not easy work. I dread the prospect of writing a campaign biography, but if I must I must. Besides, I am sure that some ambitious young man in Mr. Dutton's office will be able to take the actual task in hand, with a grace note or two from me.

Four

1

NEW YEAR'S DAY, 1876. The Year of the Centennial, as every
newspaper proclaims. I must say that if this new year
continues at the same pace as the last month of the old year, I shall
not survive until 1877.

Emma and I continue to go round and round if not up and up.
We attended a Patriarchs' Ball at Delmonico's, in the Blue Ballroom: "So difficult to decorate," complained McAllister, who
rules society whilst Mrs. Astor reigns. Earlier that evening we
had sat with the Mystic Rose in her box at the Academy of Music
and actually heard a few snatches of Verdi during those rare
moments when the gentry were silent. The ball afterwards was
of no great interest.

The Belmonts' gala proved to be much livelier than the Astor
levee, and in a way more grand, for not only were there more
Europeans but the women were far better-looking than those to
be found at Mrs. Astor's. Obviously it is Ward McAllister's ambition to be the Prince Albert of New York, creating for his Victoria a sumptuous self-satisfied and pre-eminently dull court. In

contrast, the rival court of the Belmonts is to the Astors' Windsor a sort of Tuileries: brilliant, amusing, a bit vulgar and entirely delightful. Right off, in front of Mrs. Belmont, August Belmont declared his admiration for Emma; and his wife only sighed. "Now," she said to Emma, "he will never cease to plague you. Too boring!"

But today, of course, was the day of days in Apgar-land, for there, in the cold dull living rooms of the Third Brother, the Nine Brothers with their hundreds of family connections lauded Emma on her engagement, on her translation from *French* widow to serious Apgar-ish niceness.

John was charming and awkward and rather appealing—to me. I suspect that Emma does not like him much but she has been trained like all members of her class to do what must be done gracefully and without complaint. Since there is no alternative to this marriage, Emma has accepted her rôle with every outward sign of enjoyment.

Sister Faith was scarlet with pleasure, and kept hugging Emma, speechless at their new relationship. Emma soothed Faith, charmed the rest.

Toasts were proposed in the dining room, where we dined *à la fourchette*. I was tactful. The Nine Apgars were heavy. The relatives were fascinated by this unlikely glamourous new connection.

I had forgotten, of course (why, of course? my memory is still *very* good) the old New York Dutch custom of paying calls on New Year's Day. To my surprise, it is still observed. And so not only did we enjoy the official gathering of the entire Apgar clan but we were also able to accept the congratulations of every "nice" person in the city who came to call, and if Mrs. Apgar is to be believed, only the bedridden remained at home.

"That's why we picked New Year's Day for the announcement," she told me as we stood side by side receiving an endless line of callers, most of them smelling of whisky punch. "You see, they all would be coming here anyway, so we are killing two birds with one stone."

Amongst the birds who arrived to be killed was Jamie Bennett. A majority of the Nine Brothers was noticeably cool to the proprietor of the scandalous *Herald* but Jamie carried it off well; he was only slightly drunk.

"Poor Emma!" I heard him mutter in her ear. Fortunately no

one but Emma and I heard him. She gave him her Medusa gaze, causing him to turn if not to stone to me.

"Mr. Schuyler." At least Jamie recalled some of his manners in that forbidding parlour with its dark walnut panelling, with its once-vivid rose-design rugs now faded to a suitable Apgar-ish rust.

"Mr. Bennett." I played to the hilt jovial father of the bride-to-be. "A pleasant surprise."

"But still a surprise?" Jamie leered. "Not exactly one of the houses I normally visit New Year's Day, but this time I had to, for Emma."

"The gesture is much appreciated."

"When do they get married?"

The question is still moot. There has been a good deal of talk of a Grace Church June wedding (favoured for a time by me), but we have just learned that the house that John has bought in Eleventh Street (or did the Third Brother buy it for him? Must find out) won't be habitable until October. As a result, the family is divided between the two dates. So far Emma has not expressed herself; and John will not state his own preference until she has declared hers. He did say last week that if they were married in June, they could spend the summer at his family's place in Maine . . . mosquitoes, juniper bushes, sand flies. Maine makes a very definite picture for me.

Emma will opt for October, I think. Instinctively, she postpones putting such a definite end to what once was a most beautiful life. Earlier, driving down to the Third Brother's house, she said, "We should hold a funeral for the Princess d'Agrigente."

I misunderstood her. "No such luck. That old woman will outlive us all." The old woman, incidentally, has now demanded more money than was initially agreed upon for the support of Emma's children.

"No, I meant for me. When I become Mrs. Apgar."

"Delay!" I was vehement, altogether too vehement. In fact, I have been so overwrought all day that now I pay the price and feel most unwell. I write this in bed.

"I don't think I dare."

"But you are reluctant?"

"I like John." She answered in her own fashion; and left me nothing further to say.

John took me aside after the family toasts and we stood in an alcove, sharing the cramped space with a life-size bronze deer. "I want you to know, sir, that I will do everything in my power to make Emma happy."

"Of course you will, dear boy." I was on the verge of tears, not from sentiment but from one of those premonitory signals that herald the approaching stroke. I must rest more. See fewer people. Lose weight.

"It's amazing how she fits in! Why, it's as if she'd always lived here." This was John's highest praise.

I dried my eyes. "She is not unused to society."

John did not hear; he was staring raptly at Emma. "I thought we might go to Canada on the honeymoon, *if* we are married in June, of course." Mosquitoes the size of quails filled my inner eye, not to mention gnats as big as rooks, circling carrion—if rooks eat flesh. Poor Emma. But now it is all out of my hands. I am simply an onlooker.

In fact, so passive have I become that I allowed myself to be taken in hand by Jamie, who had mysteriously sobered up at the Apgar buffet table; he insisted on taking me to pay "a very special New Year's Day call."

Since Emma was now lost to the Apgars for the rest of the day, including supper, I was able to excuse myself, pleading age and fatigue, "and perfect boredom, Papa." Emma whispered in French as she kissed my cheek and sent me off with Jamie.

Fifth Avenue was crowded with carriages. Despite the truly arctic cold, the whole town was busy paying calls.

"Where are we going?" I asked as we lurched slowly through the confusion of carriages in Madison Square.

"You'll see. I've got more news from Washington for you."

"About Babcock?"

"About a member of the President's official family who has been selling federal offices. When do you go to Washington?"

"February fifteenth."

"Well, you'll be there in time. Fireworks, I should say. How do you put up with all those Apgars?"

"The same way I endured my wife's family." But this was an exaggeration, since the Traxlers are noted for their charm as well as for their Swiss rectitude.

Approaching the spireless, raw-looking St. Patrick's Cathedral, our carriage slowed down. "Are we to go to mass, Jamie? I know that your father died in the arms of mother church but . . ."

"We go to other arms, Charlie. The most amusing in New York."

Somewhat to my horror, as well as secret delight, the carriage stopped in front of the brownstone and pink Parian marble mansion of Madame Restell, the wickedest woman in New York.

I knew the house of course. Not a single hackdriver has neglected to point out to me the mansion where for twenty years has lived in splendour the city's most celebrated abortionist. It is said that some of the very grandest ladies have visited the mansion, entering through a side door in Fifty-second Street. Most of Madame's clients, however, are catered for in her Chambers Street clinic. For thirty years the pulpits and the newspaper press have denounced this fiend, but so far she has managed, luxuriously, to survive everything and everyone by the usual expedient of buying the police and the politicians. Those she cannot buy she is usually able to intimidate, since, sooner or later, most families in New York have at least one member who requires Madame's services as "midwife," which is how she describes herself in the advertisements she places in the *Herald*, and, technically speaking, she *is* a midwife: much of her work is discreetly delivering unwanted babies and then selling them to childless families.

"I cannot imagine you ever setting foot in this house, Jamie."

"Father always said, 'Keep in good with your advertisers.' Anyway she's a rare sort."

Madame Restell indeed proved to be a rare sort. She is about my age, very richly got up in diamonds and black lace. La Restell's drawing room is as pretentious as that of Mrs. Astor except that her pictures are better and the furniture not as good. The guests are almost interchangeable. By that I mean the twenty or thirty gentlemen I met are no different in kind from Ward McAllister's chosen few; the same mixture of railroad tycoons, rich lawyers, idle clubmen. The ladies, on the other hand, are bolder and far more glittering than the ones to be seen acting as ferns and thorns to the Mystic Rose.

Madame greeted me warmly. "So good of Jamie to bring you. I've known him since he was a young lad."

"She was married to one of our compositors at the *Herald*." Jamie meant to put her in her place, but she is very much in place at all times, and that is on high.

"My husband thought the world of your dear father. In fact, when Mr. Bennett was horsewhipped in the street by that politician, what's his name?" She turned to me. "This was years ago, Mr. Schuyler. My Charlie was the first to come to old Mr. Bennett's aid."

Brava, Madame Restell, I thought to myself. Jamie glowered; then wandered off to a small parlour where a number of gentlemen were at cards. The effect of Madame Restell's rooms is not unlike that of an excellent men's club.

I spoke to her in French. She laughed. "I'm no more French than you, Mr. Schuyler. My mother was called Restell, and when I set myself up in business I took her name, not wanting to embarrass others. Actually, I'm born and bred a Gloucestershire woman." And she does still retain the accent of her country as well as of her class, which was, I should think, quite as low as now it is elevated. But she is not one for pretenses.

"Let's sit down. I've been on my feet since noon."

I sat beside her on a sofa; and took a whisky punch from a waiter in black, with a white tie like an usher at a wedding. I seem full of Hymenal images this evening, not to mention Venereal.

"Are you pleased, Mr. Schuyler, that your daughter is marrying John Apgar?" Madame Restell looked at me sharply from beneath dark-dyed gleaming curls.

"They were only engaged an hour ago. You must have been sent a telegram."

Madame was amused. "I don't need telegrams to know what's happening in New York. People tell me *everything*."

"Your—clients?"

"Friends, too. I see everyone, you know. Not your friend Mrs. Astor, of course, but I'm well acquainted with certain members of her family." Bold as a Tartar, it is quite plain why she prospers: she is in a position to blackmail half the great families of the town. "I see just about everyone. I'm most democratic. Except for clergymen." She suddenly lost her good humour. "They have hounded me all my life. As if their morals were not the worst. Hypocritical old goats!" She launched a brief tirade against one Henry Ward Beecher, a Brooklyn divine who stood trial last summer for the seduction of an associate's wife. Since the jury could not or would not make up its mind, the Reverend Beecher still continues, according to Madame Restell, "to give his Sunday sermon in the presence of twenty former mistresses."

"Such vigour!" I recently saw an illustration of the Reverend Beecher in a newspaper advertisement; he was endorsing wholeheartedly a new kind of truss. Perhaps I should buy one.

"But you must admit my house is well situated." Madame grinned more like a schoolboy than a woman dedicated to Sin and Death. "I can look right in the cathedral's windows. And they can look in mine." With relish she told me how her relentless enemy the archbishop had tried and failed to buy the land that she had built her mansion on, "simply to spite those blasted Irish good-for-nothing priests and bishops. So here we are, side by side, St. Patrick's Cathedral and me!"

All in all, I found Madame Restell beguiling. She is like a very knowing Paris concierge—a joy to talk to as long as no one ever tells you what she has said of you behind your back.

Other guests distracted her. I wandered into the parlour, where Jamie was playing at cards. He was losing money, drinking hard, and in a bad temper.

I passed on into the next room, which was a small study. A man and a woman were talking intently before the fire. Recognizing the man, I started to retreat.

But I was too late. William Sanford had seen me. If he was embarrassed—if! he was very much embarrassed—he quickly decided to play the part of debonair rake based, God knows, on what ill-observed performance in the theatre.

"Mr. Schuyler! What a surprise. I didn't know you were a friend of our hostess."

"We've only just met. If you'll excuse me . . ."

"No. No. This is Mrs. Gilray. You've seen her on the stage, I'm sure. She's appearing at Wallack's now. In that new comedy . . ."

But Mrs. Gilray (a well-known actress in these parts) was too much the dedicated professional to allow herself to be further involved in Sanford's amateur theatricals. "I must see how my friends fare with their cards. Mr. Schuyler." A regal nod; and she swept from the room, mistress of the grand exit as well as of Sanford.

"I reckon this is a relief, after all them Astors and Belmonts." Sanford was plebeian man-to-man. He offered me a cigar. Primly, I refused.

"One doesn't expect to see the same people of course." I was startled at the Apgar-ish tone of my voice. Obviously that family's dread niceness is a contagious as well as a wasting disease.

"You'd be surprised at how often the same people come here. She's a great sport, Madame Restell. And most discreet, as a lot of our lady friends could tell us but obviously won't."

"So we really have no way of knowing, do we?"

But this small play was lost on him. "My wife and I intended to come down to the engagement party. But she's been unwell since Christmas, and spending the day in bed. So I'm a bachelor."

"There's nothing seriously wrong, is there?"

"No. She's strong as an ox. Just too much going out. We're all of us pretty low between now and Easter. Will you be going South?"

"If you mean to Washington City, yes. Next month."

"I meant further down. We go to Savannah. My wife's family has a plantation just outside the town, with good shooting. It's almost like before the war. Why don't you and the Princess join us?"

"I shall be too busy. And my daughter, as you know, is engaged." I said this last very slowly, like a cue laid out carefully for a bad actor.

"I congratulate you." This was swift. Sanford tried out new approaches. "But then I suppose Apgar is really the one who should be congratulated."

"You could still send a telegram." I started to the door. I mean to make my dislike as plain as possible; to warn him off.

"I already have. And flowers to the Princess. You'll find them at the hotel."

I stopped at the door; for the first time, a flash of true anger. "*Again*, flowers?"

"From my wife and me. Yes."

"Not like the first time?"

"I was tactless, wasn't I?" Sanford's movements before the fire were boyish: he kicked at a log, then swept a hand across his small mouth as if to wipe away tell-tale stolen jam.

"My daughter is an engaged woman. And that is that, Mr. Sanford."

"That is certainly *some*thing, Mr. Schuyler." He played off me; weakly, I thought.

Now I sit in the parlour of our suite, nearly suffocated by all the flowers we have this day accumulated.

Emma came home early, and went straight to bed. When I asked her about the evening, she merely sighed. "It was like always, Papa, only a little bit more so. But I do like poor John, and with encouragement we can—maybe—get him across the Atlantic."

"Let us pray that I become American minister. Then I can give him back his old job."

"Wouldn't that be marvellous?" But the tired face did not match the enthusiastic words.

I am in a quandary. Have I done the right thing, encouraging her to marry? Obviously she must marry, and if she marries an American it must be someone like John. We could certainly have done very much worse. But what about better? That is the problem. Given time, I think we could find her someone splendid, a young Vanderbilt perhaps. Although the Vanderbilts lack "tong," the present generation is supposed to be as handsome as it is rich. But the tragedy is that we have not got the time, and so the Apgar in hand is everything for us; what may be lurking in the bush we dare not wait upon.

If I had the courage, I would persuade Emma to call off the engagement and then take our chances at Washington City, or at Newport. But I simply cannot assume that responsibility. Tilden could be defeated and Emma might find no other husband. Two lives would be ruined. There is no alternative to John but Sanford, who is married and out of the question. In any case, he makes Emma nearly as nervous as he makes me.

I have run out of laudanum. A sleepless night ahead. Not the most auspicious beginning for the new year.

2

I CANNOT BELIEVE that it has been nearly six weeks since I have written in this book.

One by one, in stately succession, the Apgar brothers have given us dinner parties. Considering their number, we shall not have completed the rounds of that family until the time of the second centennial. At present we are doing a brother a week. Last night was number five: four to go.

Emma bears up well. She makes no complaints to me or to

anyone. Outside Apgar-land, she has made only one friend, and that is Mrs. Sanford. Ordinarily, I would be alarmed at such a connection, knowing Sanford as I do or think I do. But Emma's dislike of him is now as great as mine, particularly as her friendship with Denise, as she calls her, grows more intense.

"Mr. Sanford demands a good deal of attention. So Denise and I are forced to meet like guilty lovers for lunch or tea. Once we even met at the diorama and saw the entire burning of Moscow for ten cents."

"That must have been like old times." Thanks to the rambling commentaries of Emma's late father-in-law, we both feel that we were present at that celebrated bonfire.

"She's not well." Emma frowned. "I don't know what's wrong, except that she has miscarriages and very much wants a child."

"If I were she—"

"Neither would I. Not by that man." Emma and I seldom need to finish sentences with each other—certainly not on the subject of Sanford. Fortunately, he has gone South, as promised. We saw him for the last time at Mrs. Astor's New Year's Ball, which is always held on the third Monday in January, rather like a constitutionally designated election.

For all of the Apgars' disdain of Astorocracy, the family seemed pleased enough that John Day Apgar, as Emma's fiancé, should be invited to the ball, becoming the first holder of that worthy name ever to be on the list, although, as usual, Apgar connections were everywhere, proudly bearing the great names of the city despite the fact that their right to those names is more often than not based upon some fragile cadet branch or unexpected new shoot from a famous family's old gnarled tree.

McAllister was kind to John. There is, surprisingly, a Mrs. McAllister and one or two Misses McAllister. As a mark of very special favour, John was allowed to take Mrs. McAllister in to supper.

The ball was sumptuous. I deal now only in redundancies. One formal occasion in New York is very like another. The same caterer Pinard provides the same rich complicated dishes whilst the same orchestra of Mr. Lander plays the same Offenbach and Strauss tunes for the same guests who say the same things over and over to one another as they eat and eat and drink and drink. We are not exactly slender at Paris, but few of us are as fat as these grand New Yorkers. It is especially pitiable to watch the eyes of the ladies grow round with greed as pheasants and lobsters, sorbets and desserts, are presented them. Even those who do not betray their appetite by staring, who continue to talk with animation of other subjects, give themselves away when, without warning, a polite and cultivated syllable will suddenly drown in an excess of saliva. Yet it is a reckless woman who dares take more than a small slice of some favourite dish, for should she eat as much as she likes, she will simply faint dead away, as the corsets they wear this season are of tightest whalebone.

According to Emma, many of the ladies upon arrival show off their relatively tiny waists; then they go straight to the retiring room and with the help of overwrought maids divest themselves of their cruel corsets in a wild flurry of skirts and petticoats. These bold, sensible, full-waisted ladies are invariably the most amiable table companions.

Emma and I caught a glimpse of the Sanfords in the so-called garnet drawing room, but when Mrs. Sanford saw us she turned away and Emma did the same, as if by some prearranged signal: and so that was the end of that.

A few days later Mr. Sanford was on his way to Savannah, travelling with a few men friends in his own railway car. Incidentally, half the gentlemen one meets in New York invariably want to know, solicitously, if one would like to "use the car," the way at Paris one might offer the family victoria for a day's outing.

It will be several weeks before Denise joins her husband. I hear the name Denise so much on Emma's lips that I think of her as that, though we still address each other most formally.

I ought to mention—that is to say, I certainly ought *not* to mention but cannot refrain from writing—that I saw or rather heard Sanford the day before he went South.

One of the new, to me, attractions of this city is the cigar-shop brothel. From the outside they look perfectly ordinary: the wooden Indian is in his usual tutelary place beside the door and in the window cigar boxes are displayed.

The front room also displays cigars but rather fewer than one finds in a bona-fide shop. The only false note is the much too charming saleswoman. If you are new to the establishment, she will delicately probe and should you be an actual innocent she will sell you a cigar and send you on your way. Otherwise, she will want to get a sense of your tastes, your connections. Sometimes it helps to mention the name of a girl in the house or that of a client (invariably pseudonymous). Once the mistress of the cigarine revels is satisfied that you are both serious and respectable, she will usher you into a back room where a number of girls sit about in a parlour no different from a thousand other middle-class parlours in the city. *Sotto voce,* you tell the cigar-lady which girl you want; then you go to your room upstairs and a moment later there is a rap on the door, and joy!

I have once or twice—well, three or four times—availed myself of this convenient and inexpensive service. Convenient because one can slip out of the hotel, cross Madison Square, and there in Twenty-fourth Street know rapture in the upper reaches of the Royal Havana Cigar Shop Co.

Age and health preclude the sort of performance that the young Charlie Schuyler was capable of, but to each season its pleasures; and I do believe that I feel better for my current attempts than ever I did for my youthful accomplishments.

I should say that half the respectable male population of New York use these cigar shops because of their ease, cheapness and convenience. The businessman can disport himself before lunch at his club, the family man can relieve himself before the evening meal with his loved ones whilst the lawyer en route to the Court House can reduce seminal pressures and still be present when the first session begins.

In any case, as I was seated in the parlour, drinking tea with the proprietress behind a Chinese screen (the clients are tactfully hidden from one another), I heard Sanford's voice say, "If Niobe's on hand, then so am I."

A woman's voice assured Sanford that Niobe would join him presently. I could hear his heavy tread on the carpeted stairs directly above us.

"That is my friend Mr. Sanford," I said, with absolute malice to the proprietress, a charming woman with a piquant face only slightly marred by a harelip.

"I wouldn't know his name." She lied to impress me with her discretion more than to protect him.

"He was the first to tell me about you."

"Well, whoever he is, he's a good customer. The girls do like him."

"When he comes down, do tell him that Mr. Thomas Apgar is forever in his debt."

"I will, sir." Yes, I have appropriated the name of the Third

Brother as my *nom de guerre* or rather *d'amour*. Since the proprietress is a devoted reader of the popular newspaper press, she is thrilled to have as her client such a kindly old gentleman as Mr. Thomas Apgar, whose son will soon be marrying a beauteous French princess. "That picture of her in Ritzman's really quite takes your breath away!"

"I firmly believe," I said Apgar-ishly, "that despite her being French, she will make my son a good wife."

It is now the night of February 14—no, the morning of February 15—and our trunks have already been sent on ahead to Willard's Hotel in Washington.

This afternoon, when confronted with the Fifth Avenue Hotel bill, I nearly departed this life. From January 5, when I paid our first month's bill through February 14, we owed $1,800! or slightly more than half my present fortune, since I have received only a small advance from Jamie and nothing so far from the *Ledger* for *The Last Days of Napoleon III*. *The Nation* will pay me its few pennies for Cavour only upon publication. So I was in something of a panic. Fortunately, the Stevens-related Colonel was on the premises. He showed the bill to the manager, who admitted that there were serious errors in the addition. Eventually, mercifully, the total bill was reduced by close to a third.

"Why, we should be paying you and the Princess just for the advertising your being here brings us!" The Colonel was too kind; and I said so. After all, the Fifth Avenue Hotel is the place where presidents and kings stay.

"Well, Mrs. Stevens thinks the world of you. Come on. Let's have an eye-opener." The good Colonel led me into the Amen Corner.

"Just for a moment. We're due at Mr. Peter Marié's tea party."

"You're certainly meeting the whole kit and caboodle!" exclaimed the Colonel.

The elegant Mr. Marié is the Saint-Simon of New York. No, that is not quite right. McAllister is the one who worries about precedence. The exquisite Mr. Marié is more a masculine—well, fairly masculine—Madame Récamier, who wants single-handedly to make the art of conversation flourish on Manhattan Island. Each St. Valentine's Day he writes his invitations in verse and expects one to answer in verse. A prize is given to the best acceptance poem as well as for other set pieces. He is a gallant if absurd old creature.

Those excluded from this particular social alp see only the absurdity or, as the Colonel said, "Hope you and the Princess won't be too bored."

"We are so tired that we are beyond boredom." This is perfectly true. Each of us would like to sleep for a month. I dread the plunge into Washington society, which, I gather, is even busier than New York's, as well as a good deal more raw.

At that moment Bryant entered the Amen Corner with several men, of whom one was the amiable Collector of the Port and another was Senator Roscoe Conkling, whose enormous torso always looks as if it is about to burst the tight stylish suits he affects. On this occasion Conkling towered over everyone save the Collector. The senatorial head is what lady novelists call leonine, and its thinning, wiry grey-red hair is brushed straight back from the broad forehead at whose center is a perfect curl, the celebrated hyacinthine lock. Beneath Olympian brow and ephebic twist of hair, the small light-coloured eyes are as alert as those of some jungle cat.

"Forgive me!" The Colonel leapt to his feet to greet the great men.

As I made my way past them, trying to look invisible, the ever-punctilious Bryant stopped me. "Dear Schuyler."

I was required to receive one by one the introductions Bryant made. By accident I was so close to Conkling when we shook hands that my face was almost crushed into the proud tweed curve of the Senator's upper belly or lower chest, the two having long since merged to make a Republican colossus. Happily for me, he smells most appetizingly of violet water and good cigars.

The other men proved to be leaders of the state's regular Republican party. Known as the Stalwarts, they are the enemies of every sort of reform and hence fierce supporters of General Grant and of the spoils system. I suppose old Bryant must stay in with everyone, just as everyone must stay in, or try to stay in, with him and with the *Post*.

"Mr. Schuyler is an old colleague."

The Stalwarts affected to know all about me except for Conkling, who had neither listened to my name nor looked at me. He stared over my head, lost in Olympian meditation.

Bryant was gracious. "Mr. Schuyler will be describing the Centennial Exhibition for us." He added for my benefit, "It will be opened on May tenth."

The genial Collector Arthur wanted to know: "When will you
be going back to Paris, Mr. Schuyler?"

"Not until after the election. And my daughter's marriage. . . ."
As I spoke I noted with some amusement that on the word
"Paris," Conkling's head had gone abruptly from the heights to
the foothills—that is, to me.

"Forgive me, Mr. Schuyler." The ordinarily loud and resonant
voice was now low and caressing. "I was so preoccupied that I
didn't hear your name properly."

"But then we met so briefly last summer." I was vague and
self-effacing. "And you must meet so many people."

"Not like you, Mr. Schuyler. And certainly not like your magnificent daughter . . ."

"I read that she is to be married into a good Republican
family." Bryant broke short a potentially dangerous exchange.
Whilst our finest poet spoke of politics and Apgars, I could feel
from Conkling a wave of almost electrical energy, of warning.
The man's animal force is impressive, even disturbing.

But Conkling's secret is safe enough with me; not that there is
much of a secret, since everyone in political life knows of his
affair with Kate, including her husband. Fortunately, from the
lovers' point of view, Sprague's recent bankruptcy has so ag-
gravated his drinking that he is now as invisible as Conkling's
long-suffering wife, the reclusive matron of Utica, New York.

Tea and dinner with old Mr. Marié made a fitting coda to this
phase of our New York life.

Emma and John arrived together, chaperoned by one of the
grander Apgar female connections. I came alone, not expecting
to remain much after the poetry and the tea. But when warned
that I might not stay for dinner, Mr. Marié was insistent. "You
will find many of your literary *confrères*, awaiting you with such
eagerness! Or as Racine would say . . ." And he said something
that Racine had indeed written and in an accent that Racine
might almost have understood.

Surprisingly, the master of "tong" was not present, nor was his
Mystic Rose. Since most of the non-literary guests were exactly
the same set that I have met night after night, I asked Denise
Sanford why the Sovereign had stayed away.

"Because the *other* one's here," said Denise. "The real one. And
he's here too." Then she presented me to Mr. and Mrs. John Jacob
Astor III. A bit younger than I, Mr. Astor looks not at all like his

grandfather. He is slow but agreeable, and much too red in the face.

Mrs. J.J. Astor is from South Carolina, and droll. "Every day we follow your career, Mr. Schuyler. In the newspaper press. We were particularly delighted by your daughter's engagement because it will keep her here and we need all the grace and beauty we can get. Of course, my husband and I have been longing to meet you but there was no way."

"Nothing could be simpler, Mrs. Astor—"

"Nothing could be more difficult, Mr. Schuyler. In New York, it's first come first serve. And Lina"—the family diminutive for the awesome Caroline Schermerhorn Astor!—"got you first. So we must just wait our turn." I found her delightful, and rather wish we had not been taken so quickly and so firmly in hand by McAllister, since the *other* Astor house seems in every way more appealing than that of the Mystic Rose.

I spoke to Stedman and his wife; to the Gilders (manly sister as well as girlish wife). I met Bayard Taylor, a large professional sort of writer; his verses for the evening were most charming and won the first prize. My own doggerel was read aloud by Mr. Marié, stresses in all the wrong places. Nevertheless, the company applauded.

Bryant came for tea and then departed. As America's highest-paid poet, he did not write anything for the occasion. I don't blame him.

For me the pleasantest part of the evening was sitting beside Denise on a wide Turkish leather cushion. Small, rosy, quick to comprehend everything, I like her easily the best of our new acquaintances.

"How do you find hotel life alone?" I asked.

"It is like heaven!" Obviously no grief for the departed husband. "No servants to worry about, no menus to prepare, no invitations to send out. I simply lie in bed all day and read, or look out the window and watch the snow fall in the park. And wait for Emma's visits."

"Which are daily, I gather."

"Would that they were! We are addicted to one another. She does me more good than any of the doctors. Her imitation yesterday of the Mystic Rose made me laugh so much that my doctor was furious with her, since I am not to be overstimulated."

I wanted to ask just what it is that is wrong with her but did not dare, nor has Emma been very enlightening other than to say that Denise suffers from an unnamed feminine complaint of no great seriousness.

"I don't know what I shall do without Emma. And you." She treats me like a favourite uncle and I feel old, but then I *am* old and better to be a favourite uncle than no relation at all.

"When you go South you'll come through Washington, won't you?"

Denise shook her head. "If I go South, Bill's boat will come and collect me. Sea air, the doctor says, is what I need. I must say I do hate sea air. I'm sure it's most unhealthy. Look at the natives who live all year round at Newport, Rhode Island. They're forever ill. That is, if they haven't died in childbirth."

"The men, too, or just the babies and their mothers?"

Denise's laugh is loud and unaffected. "I don't think my conversation is quite up to Mr. Marié's high standards. But children are on my poor muddled mind. You see, I can't have a child."

"Do you really want one?"

"Oh, yes! That's the whole point, isn't it?"

"I'm glad that Emma was born, but that was just luck. Most parents are as little fond of their children as their children are of them."

"That's your evil old Europe."

"I was thinking of the Vanderbilts."

"That's your evil new rich!" She was prompt. "Anyway I am not to have children, it seems. In fact, should I ever try again, I am very apt to die." This was matter-of-fact.

"Do you believe the doctors?"

"I believe my own past experiences and they have been absolutely dreadful." She shuddered; then realized the impropriety of such a subject even between old uncle and favourite niece. "Besides," she said, "I have been assured of my fatal flaw by a leading authority and friend of yours."

"Who can that be?"

"Why, Madame Restell. Bill told me he saw you there the other night, with silly young Bennett."

I was startled. Does Sanford tell his wife everything? About the cigar stores, too? "I thought husbands didn't tell their wives about their visits to Madame Restell."

"I think it's the other way round." Denise was sharp but amused. "Bill tells me whenever he goes there. Besides, Madame Restell and I are old friends."

"You have deeply shocked an old man." I moved away from her in mock horror, and almost fell off our leather cushion.

"Oh, dear!" Denise gave me a dazzling smile and a soft arm to steady myself with. "Well, it's not as bad as it sounds. You see, Madame is really a very good doctor—"

"With a degree?"

"Who knows? Who cares? What's important is that she has spent her life doing her peculiar job very well and many ladies like myself go to her."

"In order to be able to give rather than to prevent birth?"

"In my case, yes." Denise frowned. "She's a kind woman, and very direct. I am not to be *enceinte* ever again. Those are her orders."

"Is this such a burden?" I was, I suppose, shockingly intimate.

"Obviously not to my husband, who travels such a lot." She was every bit as blunt. "Anyway I am used to the idea of not having children. In a way, it is a blessing. I have fewer means of boring others." She laughed, and so did I. One of our ongoing jokes is the way that the fine New York lady only comes to life (relatively speaking) when she has got the subject round to her litter.

Curious, come to think of it, the detached manner in which Denise discusses her most intimate problems. I cannot tell if she is as detached and as cool as she seems. I suspect that she possesses naturally and to perfection that histrionic gift her husband so entirely lacks despite constant practice.

"I have, really, the best time of any one I know. I have my friends old and"—she tapped my arm—"new. I have a thousand interests, and even if I didn't, being responsible for the building and furnishing of 362 Fifth Avenue is a life's work. No." She refused champagne from a waiter. I accepted a glass. "I only worry sometimes about Bill. He does not use himself in the right way."

"You would have him in an office downtown making even more money?"

"Oh, no! There's quite enough of that going on without Bill joining the wolf pack. Besides, we have more than we need. It's just that I wish he would really *do* something. Take advantage of our—of his place."

"Boats, hunting . . ."

"Not enough for a clever man. And he is clever. I know that you think him stupid . . ."

"How do you know that?" I stupidly answered, unprepared for
the charge. "I mean, I don't think him at all stupid," I stammered;
and spilled champagne. The tremor that comes and goes is
confined only to the right hand. What does that mean?

"Oh, you do! I can tell. So does Emma. It's his manner. You see,
he's not known many intelligent people in his life. Neither have
I," she added quickly. "But I think I'm more at ease with those
cleverer than I. Certainly, I want to be in their company as much
as possible, while Bill is shy, feels that he must pretend to be
whatever he thinks the other person wants him to be—usually a
railroad magnate. I shudder for him sometimes. Particularly
when he is with you or Emma."

"But we like him. Not," I added firmly, "as much as we like
you."

"I did want you to say that!" The girl beamed at me. "I feel
that I've known the two of you all my life. Would that I had!
This"—Denise glanced at Mr. Marié's charming fussy rooms
filled with tame writers and painters as well as with quite un-
tame magnates and their wives—"is really the very best that we
can do. And it is not *chez* Princess Mathilde, is it?"

"There are *longueurs* at Paris, too."

"Not like here where there are no *courteurs*? Is there such a
word?"

"There is now. You've invented it!"

"Well, I shall want you and Emma all summer at Newport,
Rhode Island, and the days will pass like minutes as we enjoy our
courteurs."

"But Mr. Sanford . . . ?"

"I hope . . . I think he will enter politics."

"Good God!"

"I'm one of the few ladies who do not pretend to mind having
Senator Conkling as a dinner partner."

"I should've thought that that huge beautiful creature would
be in great demand."

"Not with the likes of us who want nothing from Washington.
And, of course, the poor goose is so very vain."

"And you would want your husband to be like Mr. Conkling?"

"In his own way, yes. It's not the fashion, of course, for people
like Bill to go into politics. Why should he? Why should any of
us? After all, we buy the senators who buy the elections. Even so,
I think Bill is well suited for that life. And it would give him an
interest."

"Would *you* like to live at Washington?"

"Heavens, no! I should be like Mrs. Conkling and cultivate my garden the way she does hers in—where is it? Utica!"

Emma and I both agreed that we are sorry, all in all, to be leaving New York.

"But then Washington will be an adventure." Emma is in enormously good spirits.

"For me certainly." I have not told her how much I dread the work that I must do. Daily I receive memoranda from Jamie. Lists of people I *must* meet, as well as keys to the locks of innumerable cupboards containing political skeletons.

Fortunately, I am caught up in all my other work. The truly dreadful piece on the Emperor's death is written. The long and perhaps overintricate analysis of Cavour and the House of Savoy is in Godkin's hands at *The Nation*. The campaign biography of Governor Tilden waits upon his nomination: Mr. Dutton was firm about that. Meanwhile, Bigelow and Green have set advertisement-concocters to work, assembling the raw material for a book.

I have also had several unsatisfactory meetings with a lecture agent who insists upon reminding me at regular intervals that I am not Mark Twain. I tell him that this pleases me more than not, but subtlety is lost on him. He thinks that I can do well on the lecture circuit if I stick to the dresses and hair styles of the Empress and her court. When I finally balked at this, loftily told him, "You should really book not me, not a political writer, not an historian, but my daughter the Princess d'Agrigente." The little man was all afire. "Would she do it? I can get her twelve thousand dollars for thirty nights."

Emma was much amused. "If worse comes to worse, I can keep us both. Perhaps I will. Poor Papa, you work too hard."

Just now, as I was writing in this book, Emma came in to say good night. She kissed my cheek, as always. I kissed her hand. "October," she whispered. "Not June. John's agreed."

"Good," I whispered back; we are like two conspirators. Now that she stands poised at the edge of Apgar-land, I want her with me as long as possible. To the end, I nearly wrote; have written.

Five

1

SHORTLY AFTER DAWN the hotel's carriage took us across town to the North River and then down to the Cortland Street ferry, where we embarked for Jersey City and the Pennsylvania Railroad Depot. During the ferry trip, we stayed in our carriage and watched through misty windows the shoreline of New York City become miniature.

"I used to live just there. See? That big building. Near the wharf." The building was—and still is—the Washington Market. I once lived nearby, with a girl long dead.

It is odd, in a way, that Emma should know almost nothing of my life before I met her mother. When she was young, she used to be curious about America but I told her so many made-up stories about Indians and suchlike that she took them for a kind of truth, and to this day regards my life during the twenties and thirties as, literally, fabulous. She also was brought up to regard me as something of an exotic. Early on, Princess Mathilde dubbed me the Blond Indian, and the name stuck. Most impressed, Emma would tell her school friends that her father was an authentic American Indian, from a fair-haired tribe.

The cars for Washington were luxurious; and we left on time. I was not prepared, however, for the amount of commerce that goes on. First, one is tempted by a doughnut salesman. Then a small boy appears with a large pile of magazines and cheap novels as well as bags of peanuts. Without a word, the boy shoved a ladies' magazine onto Emma's lap and a novel about the Wild West onto mine. Then he disappeared.

"Is this a present?" Emma was astonished.

"I doubt it."

When the cars pulled out of the station, we were still in possession of our unpaid-for reading matter. Meanwhile we were tempted by a fried-oyster salesman in a white coat; only a stern look from Emma kept me from devouring my favourite food, the only American dish that in France I used to dream of and could never find a cook able to approximate that marvellous mixture of Atlantic sea-taste and old lard.

The car was more comfortable than any European car, with curtains of green plush, stuffed chairs that turn this way and that, gas lamps in good cut glass, mahogany wood fittings, and, all-pervading, the smell of burning fuel mixed with that of fried oysters.

After a leisurely lunch in the restaurant car, we returned to find the young book salesman standing beside our seats. One hand pointed to the discarded novel, magazine; the other was extended to be paid. "That'll be one dollar and two bits, sir, for the two."

The subsequent battle was finally joined by the conductor, who gave the young entrepreneur a sudden kick in the shins just as I was giving him "two bits" for what he had, finally, minimally, insisted was "an out-and-out rental of my publications." With a cry of pain and triumph, he was gone.

"They always get on the cars, sir." The conductor spoke as of dust, flies. "There's nothing we can do."

As the locomotives were being changed at Baltimore we got off the car and strolled along the siding. Suddenly I heard a sound above me. I looked up and saw a dozen tramps at their ease on top of our car.

Aware of my gaze, one of them swung down onto the siding with a monkey's agility. "Ma'am." He approached Emma who was nearest him. Leering, he held out a dirty hand. "Won't you give a bit for a poor old veteran?"

Before either of us could respond, a second and a third and a fourth tramp joined their colleague. Grimacing and grasping and hideous with soot from the locomotive, they formed a menacing circle about us. I raised my stick, and Emma screamed.

In a moment two armed railroad guards appeared on the run from the nearby depot, and the tramps disappeared amongst the cars and warehouses.

This most alarming experience was made even more alarming by the conductor, who said matter-of-factly, "Nothing you can do about 'em. Soon as we're out of the depot, they'll hop right back on again. And if you're fool enough to get anywheres near them, why, they'll throw you right off the train."

Interesting and sinister note: as far as I could tell, not one of the tramps was an immigrant. All looked to be of the old American stock, wounded or debauched or both in the war, and ruined by the Panic.

Thirty years ago I would never have dreamed that there would be such a vast floating criminal class in this country, or so much grinding poverty in grisly contrast to the awful richness of the sort of people we have been seeing at New York. I pity Tilden. For all his intelligence and ambition, I doubt if he has the capacity or the will to do anything about those sooty figures which like monsters in a nightmare suddenly appear and re-appear when least expected, to remind us of the pit. Emma is still shaken, and so am I.

We arrived at Washington City in the late afternoon of what appeared, unexpectedly, to be a spring day. Though it is mid-February, the south wind was warm and languorous and the gardens and vacant lots were bright with premature spring flowers, with daffodil, narcissus, hyacinth.

In front of the Pennsylvania Station there was a long line of dilapidated hackney cabs, each in the charge of a Negro driver. Since I have always had difficulty understanding Southerners, it was Emma who finally made the arrangements for transporting us to Willard's Hotel.

"Why have you never told me about this city? It *is* a city, isn't it?"

We had just entered Pennsylvania Avenue and Emma was looking about her with absolute curiosity, and some surprise.

"I was only here once. For two days in 1836. So I don't remember much except that there was not much to remember. Now at least they've put up a city."

"Where?"

"To our left and right. A great world capital." I waved grandiloquently at the boarding houses and bars, restaurants and hotels that line Pennsylvania Avenue, only recently paved, the driver told us, with asphalt. The dingy red-brick and white frame buildings to our left and right look even smaller than they are because of the enormous width of the avenue that extends from the Capitol to the White House—or used to.

Since my last visit the direction of the avenue has been changed; it now goes in a straight line from the Capitol to the Treasury Building, and then veers off sharply to the right for a block or two when it turns to the left, dividing in half the original front lawn of the White House. The section of lawn separated from the White House by this new extension of Pennsylvania Avenue is now known as Lafayette Park, at whose center stands not a statue of Lafayette—that would be too logical—but one of Andrew Jackson, astride his horse.

I was pleased to see that the Capitol is at last finished. "It used to have a very disagreeable-looking temporary dome . . . brown, I think it was."

"A good building." Emma gave the Capitol her imprimatur. "But there is nothing really to go with it, is there?" She indicated Pennsylvania Avenue. "I mean, this won't do at all."

We were now at Sixth Street, just opposite the Metropolitan Hotel, a somewhat seedy revision of the famous old Indian Queen Hotel, where I once stayed in the high heat of a Washington summer, retching most of the night from having eaten too much of a sumptuous dinner at Andrew Jackson's White House, my one and only visit to that center of so many of our countrymen's dreams.

"And look at all the black people!"

"The Negroes have always been a majority here. Certainly, they do all the work."

"We are in Africa! And it's marvellous. But why did no one warn us?"

I suspect that Emma is more right than she knows, for Washington City *is* a curiously tropical, colonial-seeming place. Certainly, one senses a native life going on beneath the surface quite separate from that of the white visitors—a category which includes not only the transient members of the government but those native whites who are proudly known as Antiques—and bear the same relation to the political transients as those old New Yorkers who live below Madison Square bear to the flashy folk who live above.

Willard's Hotel occupies the corner where Pennsylvania Avenue turns right at the Treasury, a neoclassical building that put Emma in mind of the Church of the Madeleine at Paris. "And equally charmless."

Willard's Hotel is a six-storey building. Rather plain on the outside, the interior is elaborately decorated in that quaint American version of our Second Empire décor which many find vulgar, though, personally, I rather like the crowded, gilded, Gothic glitter of so many American houses and public places.

As we stepped beneath the marquee, amiable if not eager black servants came forward to collect our baggage. At the entrance of the main lobby stood the manager, a younger version of Ward McAllister.

"Welcome to the nation's capital, Princess. Mr. Schuyler." He bowed low. We murmured our delight at being guests of the hotel. Like a parade, we were led across the darkly frescoed main lobby, carefully avoiding in our solemn progress a thousand bronze spittoons.

"Your friends are already here, Princess. Waiting for you in the rotunda." This was said as I registered us (only ten dollars a day for a two-bedroom suite with three meals apiece). In the general flurry, neither of us quite took in what the manager had said. In fact, Emma was too busy looking at everything and everyone while I was reading a message from Charles Nordhoff, the Washington correspondent of the *Herald:* if we are not too tired, he would like to take us to dinner this evening.

The manager then led us not to our suite but to a large reception room, with a great dome supported by gilded columns. On the tessellated floor, numerous sofas and chairs contain what look to be politicians with their constituents: in their way, as alarming and dangerous-looking a group as the tramps at the Baltimore depot.

Directly beneath the dome stood a tall, formidable full-bosomed lady. "She's here!" The manager exclaimed to the lady. "I mean *they're* here. Mr. Schuyler and the Princess, your friends!"

Emma and I stopped in front of this complete stranger, who inclined her head with all the dignity of the Mystic Rose. "I," she proclaimed in a voice that echoed in the rotunda like that of the

Cumae Sybil with some curiously bad news to impart, "am Mrs. Fayette Snead."

The manager left us to the Sybil's mercies.

"I don't believe that we have had the honour . . ." I began. Emma simply stared, as though at the zoo.

"You doubtless know me as 'Fay.' " The accent was deeply Southern but altogether too easily understood, for each syllable was boomed with equal emphasis.

"As 'Fay'?" I repeated stupidly.

"That is the name I write under. For the *Washington Evening Star*. This is my daughter." A slightly larger version of "Fay" advanced upon us through the menagerie of politicians and constituents (who paid us no attention, thank Heaven, political chicanery taking precedence over mere theatre). "You doubtless know her by the pen name Miss Grundy. In real life she is Miss Augustine Snead. She also writes regularly for the *Evening Star*. Now, if you will come this way."

Obediently, blindly, we followed the two alarming women to the far end of the rotunda where I could see, through swinging doors, the blessed accoutrements of a bar room. "You may imbibe, Mr. Schuyler," said Mrs. Snead. "I am tolerant through tolerance, like all the Sneads. The darkey yonder will serve us. You, Princess, will want tea."

"Yes, yes." Emma eagerly agreed as we sat in a circle close to the bar room, from which the waiter brought me a mint julep (an excellent cocktail that McAllister often praises but never produces) and tea for the three ladies.

"Most European royalty stay at Wormley's Hotel. Why haven't you, Princess?" asked Miss Augustine Snead, a sly-looking young woman with a squint.

"I wish to be a real American like my father," said Emma. "Willard's is more democratic."

This went down well enough.

"We shall be very curious to know, in due course, your impressions of Washington, Princess," said Mrs. Fayette Snead.

"Yours, too, Mr. Schuyler," said Miss Augustine Snead. Then mother and daughter each produced a small notebook and proceeded to interview us. They were very thorough. We went through our paces with some panache, particularly Emma, who has, finally, got the range of our newspapers and will now give in the boldest, baldest way the most astonishing invented-on-the-

spot receipts for inedible dishes, not to mention arcane processes
for the maintenance of youth and beauty. "Once a week, Mrs.
Snead, I wash my hair in kerosene." Emma's eyes were aglow,
and I had to look away for fear of laughing.

"Kerosene?" Mrs. Fayette Snead's pencil paused.

"*Kerosene*, Mother!" Miss Augustine Snead knew a rare story
when it came her way. "Yes, we've heard they do that in Paris."

"It was the Empress herself who made the discovery first."
Emma's voice was hushed. "I myself find that within one hour
of the washing, my hair has the most lustrous texture. You
both must try it. Not," said Emma quickly, aware of the
rather thin lustreless heads of hair opposite her, "that you are
in any need . . ."

"Oh, yes, we are." Miss Augustine Snead was firm. "Fact,
Mother's going a bit bald on the top if the whole truth were
known."

"Let us try then to *contain* the whole truth, Gussy dear." Mrs.
Fayette fairly beamed her displeasure. Then, to Emma: "But is
there not, Princess, some danger of conflagration should one
draw too close, let us say, to a lamp?"

"No, not at all. At least not during the one hour when you must
sit absolutely still with your head held as far back as it will go so
that the loosened hairs can freely breathe."

Other subjects were handled by Emma with the smoothness of
a professional lecturer. I'm not at all sure that she ought not to
go out on the circuit. If she were not engaged to be married, I
would without conscience despatch her to thirty cities, with myself as personal manager and advertisement concocter.

The ladies knew of Emma's engagement.

"Won't you miss not being a Princess any more?" asked sly
Miss Augustine.

For the first time, Emma was irritated. But she concealed it
from the ladies. "There is no European title, Miss Snead, that is
finer than that of the simple American Missis."

"Hear, hear!" I said gravely, swallowing the last of my mint
julep. A few moments later we were in our suite, roaring with
laughter. The thought of the Sneads, mother and daughter, with
hair aflame like so many wigs of Nessus did us both a world of
good.

Bathed and rested (one must, alas, go down the hall to the
bathroom—the appointments here are not in a class with those

of the Fifth Avenue Hotel, but then neither, thank God, is the price), we met Charles Nordhoff in the lobby at seven o'clock.

I confess that at first I was somewhat intimidated by this stern Prussian-born man of forty whose profession it is to write about Washington politics for the *Herald*. I feared that he would regard me, rightly, as a presumptuous dilettante, a celebrated writer from outside sent by a frivolous publisher to take precedence over him for at least twelve weeks.

Our first encounter at the reception desk in the lobby was not encouraging. Nordhoff is a thick-set man with what I believe is known as a "nautical swagger"; at least, he walks with a peculiar lurching gait, memorial to his many years at sea. Like my old friend Leggett of the *Post*, Nordhoff's career began at sea: first with our navy, then aboard various sailing vessels. He is the author of a once-popular book that I have not read called *Nine Years a Sailor*. Nordhoff worked for Bryant at the *Post* until he was sacked because—everyone but Bryant says—of his attacks on the Tweed Ring (must ask him the truth of that story). Jamie then took him on for the *Herald*. Last year Nordhoff found time to write a most interesting book which I *have* read called *Communistic Societies of the United States*. This subject proved to be our bond.

Nordhoff clicked his heels for Emma, bowed low and kissed her hand. Warned by me of his German background, she spoke softly to him in German. Surprised and pleased, he answered. Then he took my hand, gave me a long thorough look and said, "*Paris Under the Communards* is the best and most serious work I have yet read on communism, published in any language."

I do believe I blushed. Certainly I felt giddy with this unexpected praise, so much so that I did not for once mind that he had, like everyone else, got the title wrong. I have always had bad luck with titles. I should, obviously, imitate the masters and be terse, stark, memorable. *Madame Bovary, Uncle Tom's Cabin, Bleak House*: no mistaking those titles once seen or heard.

Just before we got to the main door, Nordhoff said, "You should meet Mr. Roose. He knows everything. If you'll forgive us," he said to Emma, who smiled forgiveness.

Nordhoff then led me in to a small tobacconist's shop just to the right of the front door as you enter. Here were sold not only cigars, cigarettes and plugs of chewing tobacco, but newspapers and periodicals from all over the country. Mr. Roose is a dignified, almost senatorial figure; solemnly he welcomed me to

Washington as he gave Nordhoff an envelope (he runs a sort of post office, too). "Our special telegraph office is right there, should you be needing it, Mr. Schuyler." And sure enough, in the next room, there was indeed that modern convenience, courtesy of Western Union. Mr. Roose also promised to reserve for me each day a copy of "our" paper, the New York *Herald.*

A long line of hackney cabs is permanently stationed in front of the hotel but Nordhoff suggested that if Emma was game we walk to a restaurant called Welcher's. "It's not far from here, and there's a sidewalk most of the way."

Emma was game. "It is Africa!" she whispered to me in French as we made our way along the uneven brick sidewalk, where scores of blacks sat comfortably as though at home. Some drank, some played at dice, others made mournful music on homemade pipes whilst overall, in the distance, floating like a dream carved in whitest soap, was the Capitol, ringed by boarding houses.

Although the sun was gone, the evening was unnaturally balmy. The traffic in the broad avenue had almost ceased except for the streetcars that continued to rattle back and forth. As we turned the corner just opposite the Treasury Building, Nordhoff showed us a tall elm tree named for the painter-inventor Morse. Apparently some awesome thought like gravity occurred to him in its shade.

"How lovely," said Emma.

Nordhoff made a curious barking sound, which I now recognize is his way of laughing. "The only good thing to be said about this city is that it was worse until five years ago when we got our own Boss Tweed, a local criminal who is stealing the city blind but paving the streets in the process."

"Does no one complain?"

"About the paving? Yes, he's got the gradings all wrong, so that when it rains much of the city resembles Venice."

"I meant, complain about the stealing."

"Good God, no! That's the American way, after all. And improvements *are* being made. Also, no matter how dreary Washington is, it is still the Heavenly City to most members of the Congress. Compared to where *they* come from, this is a place of wanton luxury and dazzling architecture. There's the White House."

In the dark, through tall trees, the large white building looked like an abandoned box. "Charming," said Emma. Since my last visit a number of glass conservatories had been added to the White House; they do not improve its somewhat forlorn appearance.

"The inside is worse," said Nordhoff. Then he led us to Fifteenth Street and the restaurant, which is housed in an ordinary brick building about the size of a New York brownstone. How marvellous, by the way, to see nothing brown in this city save the Negroes. Most Washington houses are made of dark red brick, a colour that appeals to me but puts Emma in mind of dried blood.

Nordhoff led us up the stairs to the main dining room, where a black maître d'hôtel showed us to a corner table. The room was pleasant, with crimson plush curtains and an old-fashioned Turkey rug on the floor. The lighting came only from candles, a relief after New York's ubiquitous calcium glare.

Emma took her seat as if perfectly unaware of the interest the other diners showed in her. All round the dining room, mouths were forming small O's to make the word "who."

"I shall get a number of inquiries tomorrow." Nordhoff was amused. "Everyone will want to know the names of my guests."

"Guest," I said. "It is Emma they're staring at."

"Are they *all* senators?" Emma's gaze travelled swiftly about the room, as though at the theatre or viewing a diorama.

"Senators are upstairs, *Madame la Princesse*. In small dining rooms, with bottles of wine and long cigars . . ."

"And ladies?"

"Sometimes. But usually senators prefer to dine with other senators and plot ways of emptying the Treasury."

"How exciting! Then these people are . . .?" She indicated our fellow diners.

"Lobbyists. They only meet the senators in dark alleys, where money changes hands."

"It would seem," said Emma, "that the government here is simply the giving and taking of money."

"Amen!" shouted Nordhoff, startling the next table. Then he proceeded, "at Jamie's expense, of course," to order us a splendid meal (again terrapin; also, marvellous small crabs from Maryland). The wine list was admirable.

I could very easily like Washington if I did not have to write about it. Nordhoff has been kind enough to give me his notes on the Babcock affair, and I now have the makings of my first piece, which will be a general physical impression of the city after forty

years' absence, with assorted ruminations on corruption, the
Whisky Ring and O.E. Babcock.

"You'd better meet Bristow, the secretary of the treasury. He's
the one who's destroying Grant."

"His own president?" Emma is surprisingly interested in politics. I am beginning to wonder if I did not make a mistake. For
years I always took Emma with me to the Princess Mathilde at
Saint-Gratien, where all was art, when she might have been much
happier at a political salon or even at the Tuileries, trying to make
conversation with the poor Emperor, who was so entirely political, so much of a political genius, in fact, that he was, necessarily,
one of the most boring men in France, for he could never speak
candidly to anyone of anything that mattered. Happily, Emma
did have one year as lady-in-waiting to the Empress and, I suppose, heard some political talk. Unlike Napoleon III, the Empress
could talk of nothing else; she, too, was a politician but a bad one
and because of her we ("we" or "they"? *"We"!* That is or was my
country) went to war with Prussia and lost our lovely world.

Note: the incorruptible Benjamin H. Bristow of Kentucky became secretary of the treasury in June of 1874. To everyone's
surprise he turned out to be an honest man. When he discovered
that the Treasury Department was manned by thieves, he cleared
them out as best he could.

The so-called Whisky Ring began in 1870, when Grant appointed an old crony named General (naturally) John McDonald
as chief of the Revenue Office in St. Louis. Like Babcock, McDonald served with Grant at Vicksburg, and whoever served
with the great commander during that celebrated campaign may
have, if he wants, the key to the mint. In any case, the tax on
whisky in the West did not go to the government but to McDonald and his cronies, as well as to Babcock and, perhaps, to the
President himself. To date some ten million dollars have been
stolen.

"Is the President involved?" I am deeply curious.

Nordhoff shrugged. "I suspect that he is. Certainly, he's been
warned often enough about Babcock, and certainly, he is doing
everything possible to stop the investigation."

"But it is normal to try to protect your administration." Emma
was practical.

"So the Stalwarts say. Anyway, the trial goes forward in St.
Louis, and Grant has said that he is willing to testify in person
on behalf of Babcock."

"That *sounds* like an honest, stupid man," said Emma.

"Or a sly guilty one," said Nordhoff. "Anyway, the Cabinet has talked him out of going to St. Louis."

"As he no doubt intended they would." Emma is getting most eerily the range of these monsters. She has already confessed to preferring Africa to Apgar-land.

"What makes me think that Grant is guilty has been the behavior of the Attorney General. First, the U.S. attorney prosecuting the Ring was discharged. Then just before Babcock went on trial, the Attorney General ruled that the government may not obtain evidence by promising immunity or leniency to any of the witnesses. Well, that of course has stopped the prosecution cold."

"And Grant knew of this order?"

"Grant himself gave the order, to save Babcock."

"And himself?" Emma was fascinated.

"Obviously. Well, we'll soon know the verdict. The trial should end this week."

"You think that Babcock will get off?"

Nordhoff nodded. "But not the others. They will go to jail."

"Why is everyone so afraid of the President?" My question must have sounded more naïve than it really was, for Emma answered it. "Because he is the President."

"But he's not as powerful as the Congress. Or the courts. He can be impeached easily enough. Look what they did a few years ago to President Johnson, who had committed no crime of any sort."

Nordhoff put the matter for me in a different way. "Most of us here have a fair idea that Grant has been involved in a good many shady deals. But we cannot, must not, say so."

"Libel?" All things African absorb and delight Emma.

"No. Because Grant is the country's hero and the people simply cannot, will not accept that he is corrupt. I suspect a majority may secretly think that he is. They certainly know about his family and his close friends. But he is still Ulysses S. Grant who saved the Union, the greatest living general in the world—a brave and *silent* hero, ever so silent, who gives the impression that he knows nothing of politics—"

"While knowing everything." Emma nodded to me. "Like the Emperor."

"My daughter should write these reflective pieces."

Emma laughed. "I don't think—" But at that point she was interrupted by no other than the Speaker of the House of Repre-

sentatives (that is, Speaker until last November's Democratic
victory) James G. Blaine of Maine, Conkling's only serious rival
for the Republican nomination for the presidency.

Emma and I are in disagreement. I feel more force in Conkling,
as well as antipathy, than I do in Blaine. She is quite the reverse.
"Mr. Blaine is superb! A marvellous actor . . . like Coquelin
playing at an American president-to-be."

"But he is nowhere near as beautiful as Mr. Conkling. And
surely you are the first to respond to male beauty."

"But male beauty is, above all, male. Mr. Blaine positively
overwhelms with those black Indian eyes."

"You have yet to see an Indian except for your blond Indian
father."

"Well, I've seen pictures. Anyway, I am enchanted with Mr.
Blaine. Compared to him, your Mr. Conkling is a provincial
repertory *jeune premier.*"

The great man had been on his way upstairs for a supper party
with some friends when, as he put it, "I saw my very old friend
Nordhoff entertaining what looked to me to be the most beautiful
woman I'd ever seen, so here I am. Yes, I will sit with you for just
a moment. Yes, waiter, I'll have some of the wine. To drink the
health of the beautiful Princess from Far-Away, and yours, too,
Mr. Schuyler."

Apparently he, too, read in school my *Machiavelli and the Last
Signori.* If I had known thirty years ago that I was educating a
generation of American politicians, I might have taken more
pains to point a moral or two. I think they have understood my
Machiavelli too well, and missed the point to certain of the signori.

Blaine was already full of drink but not drunk. I don't suppose
he is fifty yet. The face is ruddy; the small eyes are like polished
onyxes—they look out at you so brightly that you cannot look
into them. The ears are elephantine, and often paler or rosier
than the rest of the face—do they respond to his moods first or
last? The nose is somewhat potato-shaped but, all in all, the face
(what one can see of it above the clipped General Grant beard)
is pleasing enough, as is the voice, prime requisite for a national
politician nowadays (yet everyone tells me that the late revered
President Lincoln had a weak, high, unappealing voice).

"My wife will call on you tomorrow, Princess."

"Not too early, please. We are just off the cars."

"I shall see that she applies every hour on the hour until you can receive her. Besides, it is no great distance for her. We live just down Fifteenth Street, down the road, as we say here. What an addition she is to Washington, Nordhoff!"

"Don't give me the credit. It's Mr. Schuyler and Mr. Bennett." Rather to my annoyance, Nordhoff told Blaine what I was doing in Washington, and immediately Blaine became guarded, and though no less charming, the wine that he had allowed to make him glow was suddenly banished from that sharp mind. "Well, I can't wait to see what you make of our city."

"Have you anything to tell him about General Babcock, Mr. Speaker?" Nordhoff surrounded this bland question with those little honks that are his laughter.

Comically, Blaine looked to heaven. "I am devoted to the President and to every man of our Grand Old Party . . ."

"Except Roscoe Conkling."

"There is a place in my heart even for that turkey gobbler." Blaine finished off the wine in his glass; then rose, as did Nordhoff and I (the whole room was now more or less openly watching us, and trying to eavesdrop). "Don't be too hard on us, Mr. Schuyler. We're just a bunch of poor country boys come to the big wicked city."

"I'll remember that, sir."

"Princess, you shall, I hope, honour our house soon with your presence."

In a gracious flurry the great man was gone. Nordhoff was pleased with himself and with us. "I knew he'd be here tonight, and I figured he would do exactly what he did."

"And if he hadn't?" Emma was challenging.

"Why, I'd've sent a waiter to the private dining room and asked him to come down."

"You like him?" I asked.

"It is quite impossible not to," said Nordhoff.

"And is he also corrupt?" I inquired.

"Oh, Papa! Don't you know the answer by now?"

Nordhoff first barked, very sharply; then said, "Yes, but with considerable style. I think he's the most interesting man here."

The rest of the evening—there was not much of it, for Emma and I were both exhausted—was taken up with protocol. It is usual for a lady new to this city to remain in her residence and wait for those ladies of her own rank to pay her calls—usually,

no more than the ritual leaving of a card. Nordhoff thought that
Emma, as a Most Eminent Highness, would be called upon by the
ladies of the Cabinet and the wives of the various foreign ministers. The question is what to do about Mrs. Grant. Nordhoff has
promised to investigate and let us know whether or not Emma
should call first upon her or wait and take her chances.

Our hotel suite is nowhere near as comfortable as the Fifth
Avenue Hotel but we are both too tired tonight to care. I noted,
ominously, mosquito netting about the beds but Emma noted,
with some relief, wire netting at the windows. She fell into her
bed with the faintest of good nights. I forced myself to stay awake
long enough to write these notes.

What a lot of work there is ahead.

2

I HAVE FINALLY SENT off my first piece for the *Herald*, with a good
deal of help from Nordhoff, who continues to be of a perfect
kindness. The President has also made a considerable contribution to my debut as a Washington observer, for yesterday his
personal deposition to the court at St. Louis was published.
Grant's long, rambling defence of Babcock is regarded here with
the deepest embarrassment by the Administration and with absolute joy by the opposition. At inordinate length the President—
presumably under oath—says over and over again, "I always had
great confidence in his integrity . . . I have never learned anything
that would shake that confidence; of course I know of this trial
that is progressing."

The President knows a great deal more than he deposes. For
one thing, according to Nordhoff, Grant has taken at least one
gift from the Whisky Ring. Two years ago the ringleader General
McDonald gave him a pair of full-blooded horses with a side-bar
buggy and gold-mounted harnessings. The President gave Mc-
Donald $3 as payment, whilst McDonald gave the President a
written receipt for $1,700. This is one of the ways our leaders

grow rich. But then Grant feels ill-served by the Union he saved and often remarks upon all the money and property another grateful nation bestowed on Marlborough and Wellington for their victories. Bitter at obtaining not so much as a Blenheim Palace, Grant now thinks it only fair that he take anything offered him, regardless of the source.

I sent my piece by the early morning car to New York; and have just now received a telegram from Jamie, delivered by Mr. Roose himself. "Well done" is the verdict. So now I move with more confidence through the Washington scene, this gorgeous Africa, where Emma blooms and glows.

But I am not at all certain what effect my pieces will have on our social life. At Nordhoff's urging, Emma yesterday paid her call on Mrs. Grant, who was most dignified, although she is, according to Emma, like a rich farmer's wife with hopelessly crossed eyes. "She 'allowed' we ought to enjoy Washington and that we shall be invited to her next large dinner. She emphasized the word 'large.' "

"If the President has read what I've written about him, we may not be allowed in the house."

"But you were tact itself." Emma had gone over every line. We had both agreed that my reflections would have more force if I were to describe these circles of corruption in a flat straightforward style, rather like that of a cookbook. I think, immodestly perhaps, that the result is quite interesting; certainly, it is unlike the evangelical style of most American journalists, who proclaim their partisanship in such a shrill way that even when they are telling the truth they sound false or, worse, paid for.

Emma's success has been considerable. Mrs. Hamilton Fish herself paid a call. As wife of the Secretary of State, she leads the polite society here. She is also a New York *grande dame*, and related in a complicated way to—how could she not be?—the Apgars. After Mrs. Fish left her card, the other ladies of the Cabinet did the same. In fact, the young and beautiful Mrs. William W. Belknap paid her call in person because, it seems, she had met Emma four years ago in Paris. Mr. Belknap is the secretary of war and was originally married to Mrs. Belknap's sister. When that lady died, he married the fascinating Puss, as Mrs. Belknap is known even to those who have not met her. Emma recalls her as something of a show-off at Paris. "Very *gamine*, but amusing in the Western style."

In any case, we have been taken up by the fabled Puss, and

tonight attended a dinner at her house in G Street. Incidentally, Emma often remarks upon the smallness of the houses of the great. "It is a capital city in miniature."

"But of a very large country."

"All the stranger, then, that they should live in such small, cluttered, airless rooms." Emma made a face, "Also, these celebrated rulers of your great country do not often bathe. And the men never seem to have those frock coats and trousers of theirs properly cleaned." I must say that I, too, have noticed the rather heavy odour that permeates crowded Washington gatherings. The ladies are of course drenched in French perfumes while some but not all of the men are partial to eau de Cologne. Soap, however, has no magic for the majority. I noticed that the fingernails of Blaine were black, while the portion of neck visible above Nordhoff's immaculate collar was delicately lined with grey, rather like Leonardo's silverpoint crosshatching.

Puss Belknap, however, smells like a lilac garden; and most of the ladies at dinner tonight were good to look at if somewhat countrified. The house has been packed with French furniture, and Mrs. Belknap is very pleased with the result. Emma flattered her shamelessly; never betrayed how, as she put it just now, "none of it looks right in those rooms. But what a lot of money she's spent. Anyway, she dresses well." Emma's highest compliment.

The Secretary of War is a short, barrel-chested man with a full, curly auburn beard and a most sympathetic manner. "I hear you've been writing about poor Orville. I don't dare ask what you've written."

I was not prepared for the swift confrontation. "Nothing too unpleasant. I've just tried to make some sense of what's been happening. The case is so difficult legally."

"Orville's greedy." The second time I've heard that adjective used to describe the President's secretary. "But a charming fellow. You'll like him. Fact, he lives next door to us."

"Do you think he'll be acquitted?"

"Well, you'd better ask the Attorney General about that." And there at my side was that high officer of state, Mr. G. H. Williams. But Mr. Williams (or General Williams as the Attorney General is entitled) was not about to give anything away. "I can hardly discuss a case, sir, that is at present in the courts."

"I was—ah, most interested in your ruling that the court might not extend leniency to witnesses who were willing to . . ."

"Sir, that is a weapon of the prosecution that I have never favoured. It smacks of blackmail, of bribes."

"True. True. But then when you dismissed the prosecuting attorney. . . ." I tried to lead him on, but Williams is nothing if not shrewd.

"Mr. Henderson was dismissed because of his partisanship. He was not interested in prosecuting the so-called Whisky Ring. He was interested in stopping the President from being elected to a third term by blackening the reputation of his private secretary. Sordid politics, sir. Most sordid."

"I tell you who I blame it all on." Puss Belknap swept me away from the Attorney General. "I blame it on Mr. Bristow. Ever since that man became secretary of the treasury, he has been runnin' for president. Oh, I tell you, General Grant is a saint, what he has had to put up with from that dreadful man, always talkin' about reform just like he was . . . like he was Carl Schurz!" She said the worst name that she could think of (Mr. Schurz is a German-born journalist and reformer).

"Or Governor Tilden."

"Oh, I hear he's a terrible drunk, and even worse things, too! If you know what I mean."

But I did not know, and Puss is much too much the Kentucky belle ever to speak out on unladylike subjects.

"Now I've got a real treat for you, Mr. Schuyler. I have invited, just for you, the most popular novelist in the whole country, this little lady standin' in front of you lives right here and has been livin' right here in Washington her whole life long. She is our very own and very special literary lioness, Mrs. Southworth!"

The little lady proved to be in her late forties, plain of face and lugubrious of manner. Yet Puss is right, for Mrs. Southworth may well be the most popular novelist in the country. She is certainly the richest, as Bonner publishes everything she writes in the *Ledger*. A year or two ago the public was offered—and snapped up—a complete set of her works in forty-two volumes! I know because I saw all forty-two in Mrs. Belknap's drawing room, each personally autographed.

"I've been following your work in the *Ledger*." Mrs. Southworth was both gracious and condescending, as is proper for a queen of fiction in the presence of a mere political observer.

"You are too kind."

"You have not, I believe, Mr. Schuyler, written fiction?"

"I hope not." I was sprightly. "I am mostly an historian."

"Your descriptions of the immoral court of the French Empress made me think that you have, perhaps, the gift to move with your imagination the hearts and minds of women everywhere, in every walk of life, be it the stately palace or the humble cottage."

"You do me too much credit . . ." But Mrs. Southworth had other fish to fry, as they say in these parts. "Please present me to your daughter. I am at present writing about a noblewoman of the Continent, and I should like so much to ask her a few questions."

"Emma will be thrilled." I made the presentation, to Emma's dismay, not to mention that of the Attorney General, who was making an impression on her quite as good as the bad one he had made on me.

I then met a very solemn congressman named, most happily, Clymer. He is a committee chairman and so a local colossus. "I was Mr. Belknap's roommate at Princeton," he allowed. "I do think the world of him."

But I was not interested in our charming host. I was still on the Babcock trail. Mr. Clymer, however, refused to do more than remark, "I think that General Grant has sometimes too much loyalty to his old army friends."

"I do wonder just how much the President understands what is going on about him."

"Well, he's not a fool. No matter what they may think up there in New York."

"But why would he protect Babcock, who is plainly guilty?"

"I think, sir, we must wait upon the court." I was put severely in my place.

Rather angrily, I counterattacked. "I do have some firsthand knowledge of the President's foreign appointments. I know Mr. Schenck." Actually I have only seen Mr. Schenck at a distance, shortly after he was appointed minister to the Court of St. James's. But I wanted to draw out the congressman; and did.

"I concede that this gentleman has certainly embarrassed the Administration."

"By teaching the English to play poker?" I have now learned that any sort of lightness or irony is deeply resented (when recognized) by the rulers of this country.

"I'm not aware of his diversions. I was thinking of his speculations."

"Selling stock in nonexistent mines to the English gentry?"

"I think that the President feels greatly betrayed by General Schenck."

"General—or Commodore?" One more military title, and I will entirely disgrace myself.

"General. Mr. Schenck was, I believe . . ."

"At Vicksburg."

"I thought it was at Gettysburg." Mr. Clymer did his best to outpoint me.

"So many generals," I answered, "and each has been so well rewarded by a grateful nation."

"No more than they deserve." Mr. Clymer did not, I believe, get the point.

Then we went in to dinner, where I sat on Puss's left. Protocol is an all-absorbing matter here, and who sits where is not only the visible proof of glory but the absolute manifestation of earthly power. I am told that when the charming old widow of President Tyler was in town not long ago, she had a most lonely time of it because the ladies of the Cabinet insisted that she should call on them first. Finally, Mrs. Grant showed pity and asked her to dinner.

On my other side was, alas, Mrs. Southworth, who told me the plot of her new novel, which is "set in a foreign European country where there are alps and numerous chalets. Your daughter was most helpful. But now tell me, truly, what was it that transpired between you and my old friend Mrs. Fayette Snead, known to faithful readers of the *Evening Star* as Fay?"

"Transpired? Why, she interviewed us. That's all. As did her daughter. We were charmed." In due course, each lady had written her piece (for different issues of the *Star*), and the tone was no different from what such writers always strike: a thousand adjectives, few verbs, and a great many feeble puns of the sort that Washington people are addicted to.

"Well, Mrs. Fayette Snead is in a black humour with the Princess. And I will give you a hint: it has something to do with hair."

I was filled with remorse, even alarm. "Why, has there been an accident?"

Mrs. Southworth was pleased with her cunning. "Yes, Mr. Schuyler, at the Princess's behest, Mrs. Fayette Snead washed her not exactly luxuriant hair in kerosene and—"

"Caught fire?"

"No. Worse, if possible. *Her hair fell out*, Mr. Schuyler."

"Great heavens! But—but what *sort* of kerosene did she use?"
I improvised swiftly.

"She did, she says, exactly as the Princess instructed her."

"But the Princess said *French* kerosene, which is so much
lighter than— Oh, but surely Mrs. Fayette Snead did not use
ordinary *American* kerosene?"

"I fear that she did. A misunderstanding . . . ?"

"Absolutely. Oh, we must write her. Send her flowers."

"A wig might be a more appropriate though obviously indelicate gift."

"I cannot think how she misunderstood. Emma was so specific." I think I patched things up. If not, the vengeance in the
press of Mrs. Fayette Snead known as Fay will doubtless be a
terrible one.

Emma thinks she may not sleep tonight for laughing. I note
with some interest that my pulse in this city is normal and that
I can sleep without laudanum. Obviously Africa agrees with us
both.

3

I WAS WORKING in the small parlour of our suite when Nordhoff
was announced. Emma is out for the day with Puss Belknap,
seeing the sights.

Nordhoff showed me a cable from St. Louis: Babcock has been
acquitted.

"Are you surprised?" I asked.

"I suppose not." Gloomily, he sank into a rocking chair, a
curious piece of furniture for a hotel room, but then Willard's is
a curious hotel, combining luxury and grandeur with a small-
town atmosphere. Under the hotel there is something called a
drugstore which not only sells patent medicines but also traffics
in ice cream as well as in an original concoction known as "nectar
cream soda" (cold soda water flavoured with peach or almond

extracts). If you are known to the attendants they will also place bets for you on horse races. Great city and small town exist side by side beneath the roof of Willard's Hotel.

"I hear that you've been to the Belknaps' home."

"Yes. It seems that Emma knew the delightful Puss in Paris, a charming girl. And he's rather less tiresome than the usual politician."

"Good, I guess. The fact that you've got to know them."

I did not at first notice the significance of this remark. "Emma's out driving with her now."

"I wonder if Mrs. Belknap knows."

"Knows what?"

"That the axe is about to fall on her pretty neck."

"For what?"

"Like her late sister, Puss has been in the business of selling post traderships at various military establishments around the country."

Used as I have become to the way of life here, I was not prepared to include amongst the thousand and one high-placed criminals such a charming girl. Obviously I am a sentimentalist. "What," I asked, "is a post tradership?"

"The exclusive right to maintain a store at a military post. There's a good deal of money to be made. Years ago the beautiful Puss's even more beautiful sister obtained for a Mr. Marsh the tradership at Fort Sill in the Indian Territory. Now, there was already a trader on the post and he, quite naturally, didn't want to leave, but an order from the Secretary of War is absolute. Fortunately for the incumbent, Mr. Marsh is a kindly man. He allowed the original trader to stay where he was on condition that he pay Mr. Marsh twelve thousand dollars a year. The trader thought this a fair arrangement. So did the Belknaps, who are paid each year half of Mr. Marsh's twelve thousand dollars. That is how the exquisite Puss is able to buy all that French furniture, all those gowns from Paris."

"Well," was the best that I could do.

"I sent the story to the *Herald* last night."

"What will happen?"

"A congressional committee has already got most of the evidence. They're now about to call Marsh to testify."

"Will he tell the truth?"

"I think he has no choice."

"What happens to the Secretary of War?"

"He will probably go to jail." Nordhoff was grimly pleased that at least one of the villains will be made to suffer.

"Tragic, really." I was inadequate. "That poor girl!"

"That clever girl! Except, of course, she finally got caught. You don't seem happy about it, Schuyler. Has she entranced you, too?"

"No, not really. But I do wonder what I'd have done in her place—or his place. Would I take the money?" The question that, more and more, I ask myself as I penetrate deeper and deeper into this moral Africa.

"I would not." Nordhoff was the complete Prussian.

"I might." I was honest. "Because I am weak, the way they are. And it is the custom of the country."

"You and I, Schuyler, must try to change, if not the country, its customs."

As the day was pleasant and springlike, I strolled with Nordhoff to what is known as Newspaper Row, a stretch of sidewalk just off Pennsylvania Avenue in Fourteenth Street, where the Washington journalists and their friends sit on folding chairs beneath tall shady trees whilst copy boys hurry back and forth with slips or proofsheets. Here members of the Congress, eager for publicity, pay court to the press, and Negro waiters from a nearby barroom pass to and fro serving mint juleps and shooing away the cows that sometimes get loose and wander along the sidewalks, sensibly avoiding that mortal enemy of cowdom the streetcar.

Nordhoff was greeted warmly by the other journalists. He is much respected, as he should be. They treat me amicably but not seriously. They are not book-reading men; and the sort of journalism that I do impresses them not at all. Besides, in a few weeks, I shall be gone. They can afford to be tolerant.

"Mark Twain used to sit here all day long when he was writing *The Gilded Age,*" said Nordhoff, ordering cold soda water for both of us. "All the while telling us how it just wasn't possible to write about this place."

"As he proved." I found *The Gilded Age* entirely unsatisfying: a half-dozen good jokes embedded in a Mrs. Southworth plot. I prefer De Forest's novel *Honest John Vane,* which deals with much the same material and in a sharper way. But no one I have met has even heard of the book, except Nordhoff; he admires De Forest, too.

Needless to say, most of the talk along the Row was of Babcock's acquittal. The conversation of any journalist is always more interesting than anything that he writes. Although each is obviously inhibited by the prejudices of the proprietor of the newspaper he works for, I have the impression that given perfect freedom to write what he knows, he would still manage somehow not to be interesting or truthful if only because he is too much involved with the politicians he writes about. I think I met half the Congress this afternoon; and a good number of these men of state were not so secretly spreading about the money they themselves get from the lobby in order to hire as concocters of personal advertisements the residents of the Row. Everyone appears to have his price.

I heard a dozen good Babcock stories. The man's greed is legendary. When the Whisky Ring sent him a diamond stickpin worth several thousand dollars, he found a tiny flaw in it and demanded as replacement an even larger, purer stone; and got it. He is expected back at the White House tomorrow, and Grant is expected to keep him on as private secretary. There was also a good deal of talk about the Belknaps—most of it confused. Nordhoff (who has got the march on all the other journalists) pretended to know nothing.

"Mr. Schuyler!" I heard a voice that I should have recognized but did not, for it was in the wrong place. I turned. Striding toward me was John Day Apgar.

I left Nordhoff and met John at the beginning of the Row.

"I came down to do some legal work for the Days—my uncle, you remember him, don't you? At the New Year's party?"

I did not but said that I did. The Days are a merchant family who have lived in Washington since the days of President Monroe. "Real Antiques, as they say here." John was dutifully proud. "I've also seen Mrs. Fish, who is a cousin of Hiram Apgar's wife. She says they're planning to give a dinner for you and Emma very soon."

"That's most kind of them." We have received nothing from Mrs. Fish save a calling card, which Emma answered with one of her own.

John and I walked back to Willard's. "This will be a nice surprise for Emma. You didn't warn her, did you?"

"No. I wanted it to be a surprise."

A surprise it was. Emma gave a fine impression of joy at the news when she came back for tea, to find me hard at work in our parlour.

"John wants to take us to Chamberlain's for dinner." This is the most distinguished of the city's restaurants, more like a club than a restaurant, for Mr. Chamberlain only allows those who please him to gamble as well as dine in the mansion that was until recently the British legation, far out on a country road grandly known as Connecticut Avenue.

Emma said that she would be delighted. Then she poured us both tea and announced rather than asked, "You know about Puss, don't you?"

"Nordhoff told me something, yes."

"Poor girl. She's been weeping her eyes out."

"She confided in you?"

"She had to talk to someone, and I'm an outsider, which helps. And another woman, which helps, too. Besides, it will be no secret tomorrow. She told me the press has got the story."

"Is she innocent?"

Emma was thoughtful. Then: "Let us say, she is contradictory. She blames everything on a Mrs. Marsh, the wife of the man who is supposed to have divided the money with her. She and Mrs. Marsh used to be close friends. They even went to Europe together. But then I suspect that Puss became a little too grand for her old friend, and was resented. Anyway, the Marshes are in town. He is going to testify tomorrow, I think, before a congressional committee. Mrs. Marsh insists that he tell the truth, while Puss has begged him to deny everything."

"So she admits to her guilt."

"She does and she doesn't. She says it was all a misunderstanding. That she had no idea what arrangements her dead sister had made with the Marshes, and so on."

"But she has been taking the money?"

Emma nodded. "Yes, I should say that she has. And Marsh is going to testify that he has been paying off the Belknaps for some years, at the rate of six thousand dollars a year. Not very much, is it, Papa?"

"For us—now—a fortune."

"But for the Secretary of War?"

"No. It's striking, really, the smallness of the sums these people will take."

"I suspect they find it simpler and less dangerous to take a great many small bribes rather than an occasional large one."

Emma, as usual, managed to hit upon the obvious, which had, as usual, not occurred to me. If the Belknaps are now known to have sold one post tradership, then they have probably sold a dozen others that no one will ever know about.

"We are moving, Emma, in the best circles. No doubt of that."

But Emma did not laugh. "I don't think I really understand your people, Papa. Why is it so wrong to take money in this way? Who is hurt?"

"The original trader at Fort Sill is hurt—"

"Nonsense! He is making a fortune. And he probably paid a bribe to get the position in the first place. And then all this fuss over the gifts that General Grant receives—"

"It's not the gifts. It's what he does in exchange for them. Like trying, just now—successfully—to obstruct the course of justice in St. Louis. Babcock has been acquitted because Grant removed the prosecutor in the middle of the trial and then refused to grant leniency to the prosecution's witnesses and then, to top it off, lied under oath to the court. The country's First Magistrate is a criminal."

"But in Europe everyone steals?"

"But we are not Europeans. We are Protestants and believe in sin and in retribution and in the absolute necessity of being good."

"I shall never be an American." Emma was firm.

"Then let us hope you manage to make John a Frenchman."

"I'll have no choice, will I?" For an instant we were on the verge of a dangerous candour. But neither could face that prospect; and so we prepared ourselves for dinner. I quite like John and I think Emma does, too. But it is really all wrong, this bringing together of two entirely different cultures. Well, Emma will triumph at whatever she decides to do. I have perfect faith in the power of her will, and in the subtlety of her mind. There is nothing that she will not do in order to prevail. She is, in her way, a Bonaparte.

Mr. John Chamberlain greeted us warmly. He did not appear to recollect John specifically but the name Apgar did have reverberations for him, whilst Emma and I, thanks to the Sneads, mother and daughter, are local celebrities.

We were assigned to the most elegant of the dining rooms: a rather dark room, made sombre with that black walnut panelling which so appeals to my countrymen and so puts me in mind of funerals.

John was full of news from Apgar-land. Emma glowed with what looked to be interest. "Your first piece for the *Herald* was well received, Mr. Schuyler. Even Father thought it was sound, though of course he'll hear no ill of the Republican party."

"Then I suggest that like Odysseus he seal his ears, for presently we will be in Sirenland, and the Republican barque is headed for the rocks."

"Oh," was the only response to this fine aria. "Have you been to the White House yet?" John was curious to see how Emma would respond to American grandeur. But she was demure. "Only to pay a call on Mrs. Grant. We are, she said, to be invited to her next 'large' dinner. She emphasized the 'large.' Unless, of course, Papa offends the President with his pieces."

"Then you've not seen the President, Mr. Schuyler?"

"Oh, I've seen him, yes, but I've not met him." I should have noted earlier in these pages that two days ago, at about ten o'clock in the evening the President appeared in the rotunda of Willard's Hotel. I had been warned that he often likes to stroll over from the White House to sit in the lobby and smoke a cigar, to speak to no one, and then go home. The hotel people respect his incognito, if that's the word. But sometimes he is recognized by the guests, as he was by Nordhoff and me.

Nordhoff saw him first. We were seated at the far end of the rotunda, going over my second piece. "Here he comes. Don't stare."

I glanced casually toward the main door and there stood General Grant. None of the other guests recognized him, but then he is not, to say the least, a vivid-looking man. For one thing he is a good deal smaller than I had expected, and though, ostensibly, robust of build, he seems curiously fragile because of the way he moves: the upper part of the body inclines forward as he walks, while the head is held slightly to one side. I would suspect that he is pigeon-toed, with one leg shorter than the other like my mother, whose gait resembled his. The hair is short, turning grey, and parted on the left side (it is said that he has a violent prejudice against men who part their hair in the middle). The famous beard is neatly tended and covers, or rather masks, the entire lower part of the face. Clenched between his teeth was a long black cigar that remained unlit for the whole time he sat in the lobby: he chewed rather than smoked. Just back of his chair stood the sole detective who guards the President on his strolls.

Ears, nose, eyes are unexceptional, but the face in repose is very curious. There is something hurt, damaged, puzzled in the expression.

"Does he always look so wretched?" I asked.

"Pretty much. He laughs little, smiles less. And for an army man he is most prudish. He'll walk out of the room if someone tells a dirty story—"

"But he drinks, doesn't he?"

"He used to. Certainly before and even during the war he was often drunk. But now I think he's rather abstinent. Most of his time is spent with horses. In fact, he will only talk to you about horses or the war. He gets upset at any mention of politics."

"Quite understandable."

"He has no interest in the arts. He actively dislikes music. Yet he is partial, curiously enough, to flowers."

"Men are not easy to fathom, are they?"

"Heroes least of all." So we stared for half an hour at General Grant as he took his ease, chewed his cigar, looked at the people coming and going like any other war veteran come home to grow old, to sit on the courthouse steps of an evening and watch others live.

Finally, the President was recognized. Two political types (of the lobby, not the Congress: I've got so I can tell them apart with a glance) emerged from the barroom and, rather drunkenly, presented themselves for Grant's attention. The hero's face did not once lose its puzzled expression while the blue eyes did not, to say the least, invite any intimacy with the strangers.

As Grant got to his feet one of the men seized his hand. The President allowed the hand to be held for an instant. Then he pulled it—and himself—away. The two men suddenly were faced not with the President but with the tall detective who had placed his large presence between them and the retreating small figure. In an instant the scene was done.

"Is he stupid?" I asked, genuinely curious.

"No. But limited. Without much curiosity. Yet he has come to know a good deal more about government than most people suspect. But he has—obviously—no gift for presiding over this country."

I laughed, at the odd way Nordhoff expressed himself, like a translation from the German. "Who *could* govern such a place?"

"Tilden, I think."

"Not Blaine?"

"Too corrupt."

"Conkling?"

"Too proud, too unyielding."

"Is there anyone else?"

"A hundred candidates, but none of any distinction. I have a personal fondness for Congressman Garfield. He is a scholar. A cultivated man. But weak in character. Like almost all of the Congress, he took money from the *Crédit Mobilier*, that company which owned the Union Pacific Railroad."

General (of course) James Garfield is a member of the House of Representatives from Ohio. He is relatively ungreedy, since "He took only three hundred and twenty-nine dollars from the Union Pacific. I believe he called it a dividend against some stock that may never have existed. By the way, I saw him this morning and he said that he would like to meet you."

"For three hundred and twenty-nine dollars, tell him that I shall be his creature, and concoct advertisements for him."

But Nordhoff has not much lightness when the subject is *his* subject, the politics of the United States. Garfield is a classicist. Simultaneously, he can write Greek with one hand and Latin with the other—the result must be dreadful; he belongs to Washington's most intellectual literary club; he particularly admires the works of Washington Irving and wants to meet me, largely, I suspect, because he knows that I go back to that era.

I don't know why, but any hour spent with any Apgar seems to contain not the sixty precious passing minutes that old men are supposed to cherish but more like ninety minutes of marking rather than living time. It has been a tiring day.

Tomorrow Emma will devote herself to the Day family; and perhaps take tea with Mrs. Fish. I shall attend the hearing of the House Committee on Expenditures in the War Department, and listen to what Mr. Marsh has to say.

Six

1

NORDHOFF INTRODUCED ME to Congressman General Garfield in the huge gloomy rotunda of the Capitol where squalid booths have been set up by enterprising businessmen to sell visitors everything from food to patriotic knickknacks.

I must say that I was pleasantly impressed by the golden-bearded, blue-eyed Garfield. He is about six feet tall and not, astonishingly, *too* fat, considering his age (forty-five?) and position in the world.

"Now that we have met, Mr. Schuyler, I hope that you will do us the honour of coming to the house . . ." The usual formula was offered and responded to. Meanwhile Garfield was shepherding Nordhoff and me down a frescoed corridor, through jostling crowds of congressmen, lobbyists, mere citizens. Finally, we stopped at the door to that committee room which, for several hours today, was the focal point of the nation's political life.

Outside the door sergeants-at-arms were pushing members of the newspaper press back. "We're full up, gentlemen. Full up!" But after a whispered word from Congressman Garfield, Nord-

hoff and I were able to slip into the crowded committee room and
squeeze places for ourselves just back of a row of fashionable
ladies, all jammed together on narrow benches.

At a long table sat the members of the committee, chaired, to
my astonishment, by Representative Clymer. I whispered to
Nordhoff how I had met Clymer at the Belknaps' house. Nordhoff was fascinated. "He actually told you he was Belknap's roommate at Princeton?"

"Yes. And his oldest friend."

Nordhoff whistled. "They must've been trying to fix something at that dinner party because Clymer has known about
Marsh for weeks."

All in all, the human drama that unfolded seemed even more
unreal to me than, say, Oakey Hall's play. The members of Congress (or at least these particular members) deported themselves
like the very worst sort of actors trying to look like Roman senators whilst sounding like country Jonathans.

The hero—or heroine—of the day proved to be Mrs. Marsh, a
good-looking woman, who wept noisily, stared boldly at members of the committee, allowed them glimpses of her ankles as,
deliberately, she crossed and re-crossed them during her husband's testimony.

I think Mr. Marsh made a good impression on the committee,
for he sounded like a man telling the whole truth, and thereby
delivering a death sentence upon the Belknaps. He even described a recent evening with that desperate couple; told how
Mrs. Belknap had asked him to perjure himself, but he would not,
could not, had not.

All through this recital I watched Mr. Clymer. "Pained" best
describes his expression. Not once did he address a question of
any importance to the witness. On the other hand, Mr. Clymer
made no effort to save his friend. He simply sat there and listened
as the Belknaps were destroyed.

When the hearing was over, Nordhoff and the other day-to-day
journalists hurried to the Capitol telegraph office to send the
story out on the wires.

Left to my own devices, I spent a bemused hour observing the
Senate and the House of Representatives. The two chambers
have recently been renovated, and the old red hangings and
tobacco-stained rugs have been replaced by a delicate grey décor
with hints here and there of imperial gilt. Although there is less

spitting of tobacco nowadays, there are quite as many spittoons in the two chambers as in the old days.

At one point I found myself actually on the floor of the Senate without having had to undergo the tedium of the electoral process. I had seen a crowd of lobbyists hurrying through frosted-glass swinging doors into a long narrow chamber. Out of curiosity I followed them.

At first I had no idea what this dim, peculiarly shaped room was. Against one sombre wall black leather sofas alternated with black walnut writing desks. In the opposite wall several swinging doors opened onto what, I soon realized, was the Senate chamber.

As the doors swung to and fro, a declaiming voice could be heard but not, happily, understood. Senators wandered back and forth from chamber to cloakroom, as the room where I was is known. But the cloakroom is not exclusively for senators. I found it crowded with the men of the lobby as well as with journalists and, here and there, a citizen or two.

All in all, I was somewhat amazed at the lack of formality, considering the awesome self-esteem of the American senator. But then, torn between maintaining a proud reserve suitable to one who has been elected to the highest legislature of the greatest nation the world has ever known and doing business with lobbyists, the practical tribune of the people prefers making himself easily accessible to those who want to give him money.

Today, of course, was a day like no other. The usual trafficking in favours had been replaced by speculations on the Belknap scandal and its possible ramifications.

A journalist held enthralled a group of senators with a description of Mr. Marsh's testimony. Since I had seen and heard for myself what he was plainly unable to record accurately (journalism, not justice, ought to be portrayed blind, holding a loaded set of scales), I walked over to one of the swinging doors, hoping to get a glimpse of the Senate floor.

Suddenly a senator pushed past me; and sent me stumbling toward the high dais from which, constitutionally, the vice president presides. Since that personage died some months ago, his place is filled by various ranking senators. Today a large solemn man was in the chair, reading what looked to be a novel. So absorbed was he in his book that he did not once glance my way despite the noise of my entrance into politics.

Fortunately, I was well sponsored, cradled as I promptly was

in the arms of Senator Roscoe Conkling. Whoever had pushed me
through the swinging doors had done so just as Conkling was
about to leave the floor; and into his powerful arms I fell.

I looked up at him; he down at me. The magnificent face,
finally, broke into a smile. " 'Senator' Schuyler, you seem in a
great hurry!"

"I was pushed, sir. And stumbled. I must thank you for catching me."

"I had no choice." By then we were not only standing apart but
as I am prone to do with tall men, I was beginning to make that
necessary distance between us which minimizes differences in
height. Conkling was resplendent in a brocaded vest and white
flannel trousers (in February!).

"A rambunctious lot, our lobbyists."

"And much at home here, it would seem."

"Too much at home." Conkling shook his head gravely, deplor-
ing with that gesture the common corruption. "But now that you
are a senator too, come look at your new home."

Conkling took my arm. I hesitated. "Isn't it forbidden?"

"Of course. Everything is forbidden. Otherwise there would be
no pleasure." With that he led me onto the Senate floor: a semicir-
cle of desks faced the dais of the presiding officer. Daylight from
a skylight above reflected coolly off grey walls and hangings. In
the press gallery I saw a few familiar faces. The public galleries,
however, were nearly empty. Those few who had come to observe the democratic process seemed mostly to be simple country
people who behaved—quite rightly—as if they were at the circus;
they chewed tobacco, shelled peanuts, ate popped corn, a newly
contrived delicacy with the consistency and, I should think, the
flavor of new paper currency.

Perhaps a dozen senators were at their desks, reading newspapers, chewing tobacco, chatting with one another as a noble-
browed Southerner made an impassioned speech whose subject
was the continuing minatory presence of Federal troops in certain of the Southern states a decade after the end of what he did
not call the Civil War.

Conkling motioned for me to sit at an empty desk. He then sat
at the desk just in front, graciously turning toward me the magnificent head and torso. "You are now seated at the desk where
the late Senator Charles Sumner of Massachusetts was nearly
beaten to death with a cane."

"Which am I to anticipate? His ghost or that of the cane?"

Conkling's smile revealed dingy teeth. "Both are long since exorcized. A superior man, Sumner, but unbelievably arrogant." Curious how we always detect (and despise) in others our own faults. "When someone told General Grant that Senator Sumner did not believe in the Bible, General Grant said, 'Only because he did not write it.'"

I laughed spontaneously, and with some surprise. "I had not thought General Grant a wit."

"Oh, he is a shrewd, quiet, odd little man, and today"—Conkling exhaled a long breath—"he has been murdered."

"By Mr. Marsh?"

Conkling nodded. "Any hope for a third term was just now butchered in that committee room." He waved in the offending direction, like Edwin Forrest as Othello confronting Iago.

"Were you at the hearing?"

Conkling shook his head. "We've known for some days what would be said, and done."

"Will Mr. Belknap be impeached?"

"I think *that* at least can be avoided."

"But is he—are they not plainly guilty? I believe that over the years Mr. Marsh paid the Belknaps something like forty thousand dollars."

"Yes." But the word was not an affirmation. Simply a form of punctuation. "So much is for sale, Mr. Schuyler."

"Apparently. I am told that to obtain a cadetship at West Point you must give your member of Congress five thousand dollars."

"I believe the price is higher if he is from New York." Conkling looked both amused and bleak. "Senate seats are also expensive. My admirers are said to have spent a quarter of a million dollars to get me this plain chair and table." He slapped the desk in front of him.

I was taken aback, as he no doubt intended me to be. "But surely you, of all people, did not need money to be elected."

"Senators are chosen by state legislatures and the legislators of New York are spoiled men—as well as spoilsmen." He laughed at his own play on words. I laughed, too, a bit weakly, not at all sure what he was trying to tell me.

"Is the price too high then?" I was tentative.

"It is all money nowadays, Mr. Schuyler, and it is all too high. I do believe in my party, though." The look of sincerity in those pale eyes was so perfectly convincing that I knew myself to be in the presence of a truly deceitful man. "I still believe in Grant, though God knows he makes it hard for us over here, with those war cronies of his . . ."

"Does he know they steal?"

Conkling again gave me his sudden charming if dingy-toothed smile. "Oh, Mr. Schuyler! I know that you'll put whatever I say into Jamie's *Herald* just to help your friend—and mine too—good old Sam Tilden, who'll use anything to beat us at the polls. Not that he'll succeed, mind you. Not in the end."

"If that is the case, Senator, and if you are his opponent, the country will be in good hands no matter what the result of the canvass." I was every bit as dishonest as Conkling, who then proceeded to startle me.

"Spoken like a true minister to France, Mr. Schuyler. And may I say that if I should ever become the president, I'd have more than half a mind to appoint you myself."

At that instant I could not think how in Heaven's name my ambition was known to Roscoe Conkling, since only three people on this earth are aware of it and I cannot imagine Emma, Bigelow or Tilden mentioning the matter to anyone. My response was, I hope, cool; certainly not brilliant. "What little I do for the Governor is simply *pro bono publico.*"

"That goes without saying, as the French say. Why, when General Grant wanted to appoint me Chief Justice two years ago, I told him, privately, more or less the same thing. How it was in the public interest that I stay on here, doing what I can to help his Administration."

"And then, in due course, take *his* place, which is certainly more splendid than that of the late Chief Justice Chase."

I put in the knife without remorse. Conkling had taken me for a fool. Having somehow learned my ambition, he thought that by appearing to equal Tilden's offer I would then keep silent about his affair with the daughter of the late Chief Justice Chase. Yet I cannot imagine how I or anyone could make political use of this affair. Only the injured party, the mad little Senator Sprague, could make trouble. If he were to join forces with Blaine or Tilden in defeating his wife's lover . . . I must take all this up with Bigelow.

I shall never know how Conkling intended to respond, for just then a sergeant-at-arms came over to say that some Senate busi-

ness was about to be transacted and that strangers must vanish.
We shook hands with every appearance of warmth. "I shall
hope to see you soon, and the Princess, too, of course."

A few minutes ago I asked Emma if she had ever mentioned to
anyone my desire to be minister to France.

"Never, Papa! Not in this country of wolves—or I suppose,
since we're in Africa, it's jackals."

But when I told her what Conkling had said, she looked suddenly knowing, and somewhat abashed. "I have discussed it,
Papa. I'm sorry. I told Kate Sprague."

"My God!"

"It's not that bad." Emma was soothing; kissed my cheek (I
have a slight fever this evening, and catarrh). "I mean, of course
I should not have mentioned it to anyone, but Kate was in tears
and had told me so much about her affairs that I thought a fair
exchange no robbery." Emma had shifted to French. "She told
me that Mr. Conkling would marry her if she could ever have her
husband legally put away. I don't know what the process is,
but . . ."

"But there is still the very sane Mrs. Conkling, the gardener of
Utica."

"Well, that was what *I* said, too, and Kate got quite confused
—for her. She is always so clear and hard. She spoke of divorce
and—"

"And an end to the career of Mr. Conkling."

"So I thought, and I know nothing of such matters. Anyway,
Kate must have told Mr. Conkling that she had been indiscreet.
I'm sorry."

I cannot say that I like Conkling any better for his attempt to
make me an ally or to disarm me but his fierce boldness is certainly most presidential—no, most imperial—and so *not* a proper
style for this time, place.

Our evening with John's relatives the Day family proved to be
Apgar-ish, Confederate style. In fact, though their house is of
brick, it looked suspiciously *brown* by the time the evening was
over.

Rather like the grand New Yorkers, the Days and their fellow
Antiques seldom speak of politics, ignoring as much as possible
those transients, the politicians. But tonight even these authen-
ticated—positively signed—Antiques are forced to admit that
they were intrigued by the Belknap scandal. They had known the

first Mrs. Belknap; thought the second Mrs. Belknap a trifle
flashy; deplored corruption, naturally.

"There is really no one in this Administration you would want
to know except poor Cousin Julia, and she just seems to ignore
everything unpleasant." Poor Cousin Julia is Mrs. Hamilton
Fish, whose formal dinner in our honour has yet to materialize.

"A wretched business, politics," declared Mr. Day, a stout man
with a patch over one eye that gave him the look of a pirate. "A
business for the bent." To which a six-year-old nephew from
somewhere in the South piped up, "Well, I want to be a senator!"
Much laughter (this was before dinner); the boy was duly
removed from the parlour, which was a perfect re-creation of any
one of the New York parlours of the Worthy Nine despite the
African provenance.

Mrs. Day's appearance might be improved by a patch over one
eye or perhaps both eyes, since she suffers, poor woman, from
some sort of lurid eye infection; she asked me the familiar question, "Why aren't you at Wormley's? It's the only *nice* place,
really. I always say that to stay at Willard's is about as bad as
staying in the Capitol itself for all the low types you see in the
public rooms."

I begged expediency. Emma smiled and smiled. She looked
radiant and smiled yet again when John proposed a toast in her
honour (I could not see the label on the wine but think it homemade: the source of tonight's fever?).

"To my future wife!" John looked rather red and embarrassed
as he made the toast, and I rather like him. He does indeed love
Emma, and there is a lot to be said for such a strong emotion, even
in marriage.

Then the ladies left the table, and John and I were entertained
by ten gentlemen of Washington, Antiques to a man and entirely
Southern in manner and accent, not to mention politics. "I would
vote for a yellow dog if he was runnin' as a Democrat," said one,
explaining not too flatteringly his support of Governor Tilden.
Although politics does not much interest them, they are furious
at Blaine, who recently made a speech on the necessity of denying
civil rights to Jefferson Davis, the former president of the former
Confederacy. As for the Republican party, they will abhor it "so
long as a single Federal soldier stands with bayonet in hand
before the capitol of any Southern state!" boomed one Antique.

It is curious that after ten years the late conflict is still so much

on their minds. But then the signs of war are everywhere. The
city is ringed by derelict forts, and all the flimsy, ugly buildings
thrown up to house troops, the wounded, and government offices
still temporarily stand. Then, too, the Days and their friends are
Southerners, and Washington is the paradigm of a Southern city,
African to the core, and a most peculiar place from which to
conduct a war against the rest of the South. It is a wonder that
Mr. Lincoln escaped assassination as long as he did. Yet I find it
startling that, even now, Federal troops are still on duty in states
like Louisiana, Florida and South Carolina.

"I have been invited to Newport, Rhode Island, this summer,"
said John as the others discussed real estate, the one subject that
enthralls the true Antique, since a good many of them live by
selling or renting houses to the despised political transients.

"The Sanfords?"

"Yes. They—*she* said that you and Emma would be there in
July. Is this true?"

"I think so." Actually, I have not made up my mind. Although
Emma and I would like to stay with Denise, neither of us is happy
at the thought of playing audience day after day to William Sanford's incorrigible performances. I would prefer to stay with
Mrs. Astor, and visit Denise as much as possible. Unfortunately,
despite hints, there has been no invitation from Mystic Rose or
from loyal chamberlain. I told John that nothing was definite.

"My parents are very nervous." And John laughed very nervously. "They think Newport, Rhode Island, almost as terrible
a place as Long Branch, where the President goes."

"What standards!" I exclaimed. (I am certain it was the wine:
I am now feeling sick to my stomach and in need of a purge).

When we joined the ladies, Mr. Day gave a number of samples
of Antique wit, particularly calculated to thrill and titillate mixed
company.

"Why," Mr. Day asked Emma, "did the Devil never learn to
skate?"

"Learn to *what?*" Emma has not all our verbs at her command.

"Ice-skate. You know, skate on ice."

"Ah, did the Devil wish to ice-skate?"

"No, no. Well, yes, I guess he must've. But why did he never
learn? why couldn't he learn to ice-skate?"

"I am baffled," said Emma.

"Because how in hell could he!" Mr. Day and the Antique

gentlemen laughed at what, I gather, is an old, even antique story, whilst the ladies clucked disapprovingly at the sly way profanity had been legitimately used in their presence.

Emma simply smiled. Saint-Gratien seems a world away, and entirely lost.

2

THE LAST FEW DAYS would have brought down any parliamentary government. As it is, the Grant Administration is in a shambles, and there is even talk that the President might resign.

Events are moving so rapidly that I have become a sort of writing machine into which Nordhoff pours whatever information I need. He is most generous. But then he is writing every day, while I write, thank God, only once a week.

On March 1, Babcock resigned as the President's private secretary. Ill-advised as ever, the President has just appointed his own son to take Babcock's place. Apparently Grant wanted to retain Babcock, but Mr. Fish said that if he did he would then have to find himself a new Secretary of State. But Babcock will not want. The President has rewarded him with the superintendency of Washington's public buildings where he can steal himself a second fortune. Happily, Babcock is about to be indicted for the burglarization of that famous safe in St. Louis and there is still a chance of putting him in prison.

Nordhoff is very grim these days; also, very pleased. The Augean stables of American politics may yet be cleansed once the public sees what condition they are in. Poor Tilden. He will have to play Hercules.

On March 2, Belknap resigned as secretary of war. I was with the Belknaps earlier today, so I now have their version of what happened. It varies significantly from what Nordhoff thinks happened.

Terrified at the thought of impeachment in the House and trial by the Senate, Belknap went to the White House on the morning of March 2. With him was Secretary of the Interior Zachariah Chandler, a Michigan politician close to the President. This sequence of events was supplied me by Nordhoff and seems plausible.

According to General Grant's defenders, the President had been so preoccupied with the Babcock affair that he had not been aware of the charges against Belknap . . . Just writing these words makes me think that if Grant did *not* know of this business, then he is indeed the village idiot. I realize that there are those who would consign him to that category, but I am not one of them. No fool could ever command for any length of time a great army, much less defeat a resourceful and splendid enemy. But I must set down the story as Nordhoff tells it.

Shortly before the arrival of Belknap and Chandler, Secretary of the Treasury Bristow (rapidly becoming the President's nemesis) interrupted General Grant at breakfast with the request that he receive at noon a certain New York congressman who would give the President full details of the Belknap scandal. General Grant agreed to meet the congressman.

Query: Wouldn't Bristow have mentioned *why* the congressman wanted to talk to the President? And if he had, then the President must have known that Belknap was on the verge of impeachment. The question is crucial.

Bristow departs. The President orders his carriage to take him to the studio of a painter who is doing his portrait. Just as General Grant is coming downstairs from the family living quarters, a messenger tells him that the Secretaries of War and Interior wish, urgently, to see him. They are in the Red Dining Room. The President goes to them.

Belknap says that he wants to resign immediately as secretary of war; he babbles incoherently. Chandler is direct, if not honest. He gives Grant the impression that Belknap must resign in order to protect his wife, who has been involved in something of an illegal nature. Without returning to his office, Grant sends for his son Ulysses, and orders him to write out a letter accepting Belknap's resignation; then he tears up his son's letter (it is too cool in tone), and himself writes the letter of acceptance, and signs it. Exeunt Belknap and Chandler.

As the President is about to get into his carriage, enter two Republican senators who explain to him for the first(!) time the

Belknap affair. The senators are shocked. The President is shocked, and, I should think, alarmed, for by allowing Belknap to resign, Grant inadvertently (the adverb used by his supporters) made it impossible for Belknap to be impeached, because in the eyes of many constitutional authorities an official may not be impeached, much less convicted of a crime committed in office, when he no longer holds that office.

After this disheartening news, General Grant went and sat for his portrait, and the artist later reported that the President was as serene as ever. I find it curious that the ordinarily suspicious Nordhoff tends to believe that Grant knew nothing of the Belknap scandal *before* the arrival of the two senators. It seems to me inconceivable that he would accept so quickly the resignation of an old friend on the grounds that, out of office, Belknap might be able to protect his wife—a perfect *non sequitur*, since a high official is always in a better position to thwart justice than the plain citizen. I think that General Grant understood perfectly what he was doing. But I think that even the most partisan of Democrats will prefer to believe that Grant did not understand the matter, for if he did, he is guilty of obstructing the course of justice and is as much a criminal as Belknap.

Now for General and Puss Belknap besieged at 2022 G Street in their lovely home, as Mrs. Fayette Snead would say, crammed with French furniture; no, not besieged—kept under guard in order to prevent them from escaping to Europe. We arrived at teatime, in response to an urgent message from Puss not to "abandon" her.

"May we go in?" I asked the policeman. I was tentative, not certain of the protocol in these matters.

"Suit yourself," was that genial officer's response.

The scene in the downstairs parlour resembled a lying-in. Heavy curtains were drawn against the daylight. Large funereal candles stationed at strategic points created a dim but attractive setting for the room's centerpiece, a blue velvet chaise longue, on which reclined Puss, swathed attractively in lace, features pale and interesting. On a papier-mâché table at her side a glass of port stood next to smelling salts.

The Negro servant showed us into the presence. "Bring them tea," a tiny voice whispered from amidst the lace, "and tell the General our friends are here. Our only friends!" The servant vanished just as the tears fell. I suspect that this dialogue and those tears have been often repeated these last few days.

Dramatically, Puss held wide her arms to receive Emma, who dutifully filled those arms, allowing the rain of Puss's tears to fall onto her shoulder. I stood awkwardly to one side, as men must do at such times, wishing I were elsewhere.

But then tea came. Puss poured. Respectfully we sat around the bier and heard her version of what had happened. "It is beyond me how anybody on this earth could believe a word that Mr. Marsh said, much less the word of that—that *woman* he is married to, that viper I once like a perfect fool befriended! Sugar? Milk?"

We instructed her. Puss was now in full command of herself. Our tea was handed us without a tremor. "The truth is that my late sister, an angel if ever there was one loose on this terrible earth, *did* know the Marshes, and did have some kind of business dealin's with them which I knew nothin' about, bein' unable to add two and two, much less able to do—what that awful woman got that stupid husband of hers to say I did."

"Then Mr. Marsh never paid you anything?"

"Of course he paid me what he *owed* us!" The answer was swift. She has learned her part. "And I did, in my ignorance, use him to look after certain business affairs of my late sister's and took his word for everything, since I have no head for such things, and should probably be hung for my stupidity, seein' as how my poor husband has been forced to resign . . ."

"But Mr. Marsh said that he paid both you *and* your husband."

"It's that awful Mr. Bristow! Oh, I tell you this, Mr. Schuyler, before that man is through he is goin' to drive General Grant himself from office. He'll have the President of the United States, the greatest hero of all time, in jail —"

"For what?"

Although Puss's rambling commentaries never exactly responded to any question asked, they were conducted for a definite purpose. "I shudder every time I pick up a copy of the New York *Herald, shudder* when I read what your friend Mr. Nordhoff is writin' about us as if we were criminals! Did you know that they came here and arrested my husband because Mr. Nordhoff had said we were plannin' to flee to Belgium, which has no extradition treaty with the U.S. . . . ?"

"I don't think Mr. Nordhoff intended to . . ."

"Well, it's all craziness! We're not goin' anywhere. As if we could! Because after my poor husband was arrested and they let

him come home, they put that policeman outside the house, and
when I begged the man to at least come inside and sit in the
vestibule, where he would be less visible, he just laughed in my
face. I hope Mr. Nordhoff is satisfied. And I hope you at least will
give the world *our* side, somethin' nobody else will even dare to
do."

That explained the invitation to tea. I must say my position is
delicate. I cannot contradict anything that Nordhoff has written,
and harsh splendid stuff it is; also, in general, I think that he is
right. Certainly, I am absolutely convinced of Puss's guilt. But
the mysterious figure in all this is Grant. I must meet him; see
him at close range. Yet I shall not be able to meet him if my next
piece for the *Herald* describes my suspicion . . . no, my conviction
that the President is involved right "up to the handle," as Sanford
in the rôle of rough-hewn railroad man would say. Meanwhile,
I've solved the matter of this week's piece. I shall simply describe
in flat detail the committee hearings, the behaviour of Mr. Marsh
as well as Mrs. Marsh (this will please Puss), and allow the reader
to make up his own mind as to the Belknaps' criminality.

We were joined by Belknap and a square-jawed, clean-shaven
man of about my age, who proved to be the Secretary of the
Interior, Zachariah (or Zach., as everyone calls him) Chandler.
Belknap looked properly distraught. Chandler, however, was
very cool, and very much in control.

With a trembling voice, Belknap said, "Princess, Mr. Schuyler,
you don't know what this means to Puss and to me, your rallying
around at this terrible moment in our country's history."

I was much amazed that what was, after all, old-fashioned
grand larceny should have so suddenly become a crisis in the
affairs of a great nation. But then, I suppose, in a way, Belknap
is right. As Conkling said, any hope of a third term for Grant has
been butchered by the Belknap affair, and the prospects of Conkling or whomever the Republicans choose to run against Tilden
will hardly be enhanced by these revelations.

Then Belknap turned to Chandler. "You tell her," he whispered, turning to face the empty fireplace, head down as if praying; from the rear, he looked like a solid keg covered in black
cloth.

"Clymer has started the impeachment process. He spoke to the
House just an hour ago."

"God save us!" Puss was not performing now. She looked more

drawn than ever, and very intelligent: fox in a trap, ready if necessary to gnaw off its own leg.

Chandler was as soothing as he could be under the circumstances. "I must say it was a terrible strain on him, being such a good friend to you both. At one point, I thought he was going to break down."

"A pity that he didn't. What happens now?" Puss looked to her husband, but the dark keg of a man was impassive.

"There will be a trial," said Chandler. "We can't avoid it now. But they haven't got the votes to convict us." The "us" was very nice. "They'll need two-thirds of the Senate which they haven't got. Besides, there are quite a few senators who've already said that you can't impeach and convict a man no longer in office."

"What effect, Mr. Secretary, will this have, do you think, on the coming election?" I spoke in my rôle of solemn but friendly journalist.

"It is quite possible that the Republican party will lose." Zach. Chandler was matter-of-fact.

The keg spun around. "And all on account of the damnable Marsh—forgive me, Princess—and that she-devil of a wife!"

"Evil is a constant in human affairs," intoned Zach. Chandler. They were marvellous. The guilt had been transferred to the Marshes in order that that obscure couple would be held responsible through all eternity not only for the end to Grant's hope of a third term but for a possible end to sixteen golden years of Republican rule.

I looked at Emma, afraid that she might burst out laughing, but she was as grave as any mourner. I felt a traitor in that room, for with every word Zach. Chandler spoke I saw with growing certainty—and joy—the fact of a Tilden Administration.

But Zach. Chandler thinks otherwise. "The man who will benefit from all this is Bristow."

"Will your party nominate him?" I ought not to have said "your," but Chandler seemed not to notice; treated me as one of them.

"If they do, I'll kill him! I swear it!" That from the blue velvet sofa.

"He will have a difficult time." Chandler was mild. "I don't think the Stalwarts will take to a man who has covered General Grant in mud."

Belknap sat down in a chair opposite us. I felt truly sorry for him. He has taken money for favours given, but I cannot regard him as a bad man. Rather, he is a victim of this place, and I mean not Emma's delicious Africa, the national capital, but the country itself; this vigorous, ugly, turbulent realm devoted to moneymaking by any means. Certainly, if true justice were meted out to one and all, impartially, most of the congressmen would be in prison while Mrs. Astor's parties would be decimated at the very least.

As for Grant himself—well, that is for me a deep mystery to which Belknap added when he said, "I told General Grant when I last saw him, after all this started, I said, 'What a long strange way we've come, you and I, since Shiloh and Vicksburg,' and he said, 'The end's not yet in sight,' whatever that may mean."

3

MIDNIGHT. Emma has gone to bed exhausted, and I must try to make some sense of our evening at the White House.

The long-awaited invitation for the "large" dinner arrived, to honor the dean of the diplomatic corps, Baron Jacobi, the minister from Bulgaria. Of a hundred guests perhaps half were diplomats or visiting foreigners, a category to which the social aides at the White House have decided that Emma and I belong.

"It should be interesting." Nordhoff had joined me for a peach-nectar cream soda in the drugstore beneath the hotel. "Keep a close eye on Mrs. Grant."

"Why? Is she apt to take one's wallet?" Thus do we speak of our masters.

"No. But she's apt to be a bit shaken today. This afternoon she marched uninvited into a Cabinet meeting and, to the embarrassment of everyone, paid tearful tribute to the goodness of her friend Puss and the probity of General Belknap."

"I was not aware she was so politically minded."

"She's not, as her appeal plainly demonstrates. Anyway, something was ventured but nothing was gained. The trial continues."

At exactly seven o'clock the rented carriage containing Emma and me joined the long line of carriages in front of the White House portico, or "piazza," as Mrs. Grant calls it. Emma was again in her Winterhalter Empress Elizabeth gown and the long gauzy train quite filled the back seat. We had both of us to struggle with it to avoid smothering.

"What do I call the President?" Emma asked.

"Mr. President, I should think, or perhaps General Grant."

"Not Highness, or Excellency?"

"No, no! None of that. Here we are all equal."

"It is a pretty house," said Emma as we alighted. A Negro usher showed us into the entrance hall, where most of the guests were already gathered, a somewhat un-Washington assortment, thanks to the preponderance of foreigners.

Baron Jacobi is a fine bright little man more fluent in French than English; and he presented himself to Emma. "With delight! I have been following you day by day in the press as you make your way through the gilded salons of the Capital, and I have been hoping, praying that one day we would meet."

Emma was charmed. The Baron is a bachelor, and as protocol does not obtain before the President's arrival, the Baron took Emma in to the East Room.

I followed, looking about for familiar faces (Blaine was there, but not Conkling; I bowed to Zach. Chandler and to General Garfield). I also looked to see what changes had been made since my only other visit to the White House forty years ago. A single glance convinced me that nothing is as it was. The hand of Mrs. Grant can be seen in every room, and it is not a light hand. Where, before, everything was bright and airy (if a bit dusty and run-down), now all is dark, rich, and thickly gilded.

The East Room is unrecognizable in its new Galena, Illinois, Gothic style. Rows of squat wooden columns now break into three small areas what once had been a splendid large room. The wallpaper is dark with dim gold figures. The furniture is of ebony and gold. The effect is deeply sombre, even disturbing. I trust that Tilden will take an axe to the Grant additions.

Of all the guests assembled in the East Room, the diplomats seemed most at home, but then that is their minimal function. I was pleased that since Emma was on Baron Jacobi's arm, everyone was eager to meet her. She looked most fetching, despite the sombre setting.

"A splendid-looking woman, that child of yours." Blaine was at my side—face red with wine, black eyes aglitter with reflected candlelight. Side by side, we stood in the doorway, surveying the room.

"Well, French ladies do make the most of themselves." I cannot think why I was so stupid as to emphasize Emma's foreignness, which of course can only throw in doubt my own Americanness. But I was distracted by the room, the people, the occasion, trying to absorb the experience in order to turn it into words, the writer's glum task that forever keeps him at one remove from life.

"Did my daughter call upon Mrs. Blaine?" I had forgotten whether or not the ladies had done their duty.

"Indeed she did. And they had tea, at an hour chosen deliberately so that I would be safely at the Capitol. I hope, on some other occasion, you'll do us the honour . . ." Another invitation.

"You must be most harried, Mr. Blaine. This seems an unusually busy session of the Congress." I did my duty as a journalist.

"Busy? Not me!" Blaine laughed. "I've never been lazier. When we Republicans lost our majority last fall, I said, 'Now I'm out of jail. I don't have to be the Speaker.'" At some length he told me how much he enjoyed not being Speaker. "You can't imagine how dull it is up there, listening to all that bad oratory. But what have I said? You won't quote me, will you? I am at your mercy."

"Your secret is safe with me, sir."

Blaine gave me a curiously sly sort of smile. "Well, now. You *might* be able to quote me as saying that I find the oratory on the *other* side of the Capitol not quite so fascinating. Five minutes of Senator Conkling's glorious voice and I am as one chained to Morpheus's slow carriage and, like a prisoner, am borne irresistibly to the land of dreams."

"That will go into my next piece for the *Herald*."

During all this, Blaine was constantly beaming, shaking hands, greeting one and all, as he talked to me. "I'm glad you're not as hard on us as Charlie Nordhoff. Now, he's what I call something fierce."

"That's because I'm just the curious man from the outside, while Nordhoff is the furious man on the inside." Nice, I thought to myself (and duly record here for possible use later).

"Ever since the Democrats won the House away from us, they've been smelling blood. They're on our trail. And November they'll try their very best to get their hands on this fine old house, too." Expansively Blaine gestured, striking General Grant a light blow on the shoulder.

Feeling his arm in contact with someone else, Blaine turned to apologize; then his eyes went wide when he realized that it was the President he had struck. The Grants were now at the center of the doorway, preparing to make their entrance.

"My God! I mean, my General. I didn't see you."

"Quite all right, Mr. Blaine. This season it is the custom to strike the President on sight." Grant's face did not lose its usual hurt puzzled expression, but the drollery was swift and engaging. As I anticipated, he is no fool. I was not prepared, however, for the quality of his voice, which is low and musical and not at all what one would expect in a military man. The late Prince d'Agrigente, marshal of France, had a voice like that of a whooping crane, and easily audible, I should have thought, from Moscow to St. Petersburg (shrieking, "Retreat!").

Side by side the Grants marched (or, in his case, tottered) toward one end of the East Room. We were then lined up to be presented. Behind the President stood some sort of master of protocol who murmured our names as we were presented. I was gratified that Emma was the first lady to be presented, since little Baron Jacobi had no intention of letting her go and, as guest of honour, he took precedence. Lacking any rank, I was amongst the last to touch hands, for that is about all that either General or Mrs. Grant does.

Close to, one finds that the General's eyes are still alert, though the sharp clear blue of the early portraits has gone somewhat cloudy with age. The hair must have been a rust colour originally; now it is mostly grey. A prominent wart to one side of the beard is the last part of the face that one can see, for mouth and chin are entirely hidden by the famous neatly cropped beard.

The President, I should mention, wore evening dress. I don't know why, but I had expected him to be in full uniform, wearing a hundred bright medals. When my name was mentioned, I saw that he knew exactly who I was. He frowned. Perhaps he also smiled as well; it is hard to tell, since the mouth is hidden. He muttered something that I could not hear. I suspect it was "Good evening."

I moved on to Mrs. Grant. A small stout counterpart of her husband, Julia Dent Grant is uncommonly plain, with eyes that look toward each other, giving her face a slightly crazed expression, as if one eye could not fathom why the other eye was staring into it. The senior James Gordon Bennett's eyes were equally crossed, but stared only toward Heaven.

"I've had the pleasure earlier of meeting your daughter, the Princess, Mr. Schuyler." The voice was nasal and somewhat Southern (she comes originally from Missouri); the manner was easy.

"You are too kind to invite us here . . ." I was polite, even apologetic, feeling something of a traitor in that room.

"I also know that you have both been *more* than kind to my *friends* General and Mrs. Belknap." This was said firmly and more loudly than was needful. I looked at the President. He had heard, and was not pleased. With the gesture of a rider transferring the reins of a horse to a groom, he handed the guest he had just greeted over to Mrs. Grant, forcing me to move on.

"You remember Colonel Claypoole," said the President loudly, and I was swiftly succeeded by the Colonel, whom Mrs. Grant did remember.

So much for my first encounter with the world's most famous general. I must say, right off, that I found Grant less impressive than Andrew Jackson, whose hand I had also shaken in that same room. Yet I do detect some strange quality in Grant that is very deep. (Yes, I recall that Hawthorne said of his old friend President Pierce that he was "deep, deep, deep" when of course Pierce was shallow, shallow, shallow). But where Jackson was entirely the splendid border aristocrat, visibly pleased with himself and his place in history, Grant is—well, not deep but puzzling. For one thing, the hurt face is perfectly contradicted by the confident voice, by the swift intelligent gaze that simultaneously takes in and dismisses—reflective of a military genius that for some reason has not translated into politics as it ought to have done, for, contrary to legend, generals are almost by definition adept politicians.

Presently we were led in to dinner. The state dining room reflects the taste of Mrs. Grant: nightmarishly rich, complicated, and dark.

We sat at a huge horseshoe table. I was something like a mile below the salt. On my right I had the wife of a French diplomat (an omen?); and on the other side Mrs. James Garfield. She bears the resonant name of Lucretia, and appears to be a woman of strong character; she is pleasant-looking with auburn hair piled high on her head, contrary to the prevailing fashion. "I've met the Princess already," she confided, as the slow procession of huge platters of hammered gold, of worked silver, made the rounds; all told, we were served twenty-five courses and six *good* wines. "She was at poor Puss Belknap's house."

"Oh, yes. Emma told me," I lied. It is curious how secretive Emma is. Although we talk, I think, with perfect frankness about everything and everyone, I am forever startled to discover that, unknown to me, she has dined with the Belmonts, say, or chatted with Lucretia Garfield at the Belknaps' house. Emma finds it easy to keep a secret. I don't. But then she is a secret, and I am not.

"Naturally, I asked her if she knew poor Kate Sprague." It would seem that all ladies are "poor" to proud Lucretia.

"Yes, Emma sees her often at Paris. I'm afraid I hardly know her."

"What a comedown in the world it must be for her." Mrs. Garfield could not hide her pleasure, which was increased, as was mine, by the arrival of those Maryland crabs I have developed such a taste for. She, too, is addicted to Maryland crab. "Even though it took me years to get up the nerve to eat one. I mean, they don't grow them back in Ohio." She ate a crab—shell, claws and all; and kept on talking. "I used to be so jealous of Kate I couldn't bear to be in the same room with her."

This confidence was most unusual. Jealousy is one emotion never admitted to by those who live on the political and social heights. "You see, General Garfield was a protégé of her father, Chief Justice Chase. We're all from Ohio, you know, and of course it's no secret that before my husband married me, he was out of his head for Kate, so pretty she was in those days, though General Garfield did tell me that he thought her nose a trifle pug. But I think he just said that to keep me quiet. Anyway, she was the absolute queen of Washington from Mr. Lincoln's time right up to the Panic, when she lost everything and had to move to Europe." The pleasure in learning that others have lost money is apparently a universal one. Aaron Burr used to brighten visibly when he heard that yet another of the republic's founders had gone bankrupt.

"Not *everything*," I was to the point. "She has acquired Senator Conkling."

This took some wind from Lucretia's voluminous sails. But they soon filled again. "True. But I cannot see what earthly good it will do either of them. Rather the contrary, since each is married."

"Divorce?"

"She has grounds, I'll say that, poor girl. And no one would mind. I mean Bill Sprague is mad as a hatter, and a drunk, and dangerous. But Mrs. Conkling is a perfect lady."

"Then come next January Mrs. Conkling will be in this room, doing the honours." I gestured toward Mrs. Grant, whose eyes managed most diplomatically to fix the attention of each dinner partner simultaneously.

"Oh, I'm not so sure of that." Lucretia Garfield refused claret, which I drank (too much of, I fear; my tremor has returned, but the low recurring fever of the last few days is gone). "I should say that Mrs. Blaine will be at the head of this table, poor woman. She has such a good mind. But *six* children! I mean she has no peace."

"But Mr. Blaine is not, as far as I know, a general, and I thought the people only elect generals nowadays."

"Senator Conkling isn't a general either, and he's the President's personal choice." This is the first indication, if true, that Grant has a preference.

"Not that General Grant will try to interfere," Mrs. Garfield continued. "That's not his way. But he'd like to see Senator Conkling get the nomination. If Mr. Conkling doesn't get it—and of course he can't, for ever so many reasons, among them poor Kate—the President would like to see poor Mr. Fish as president, and he can't be nominated either. So it will have to be Mr. Blaine, or so my husband thinks," she added, for the first time ceasing to be an expert in her own right and acknowledging her satellite-ship to Garfield's sun.

The wife of the French diplomat was more amused than amusing. Although entirely tactful, she managed to make fun of our great republic's leaders; and I confess that looking about the dining room, at the grim small President thoughtfully chewing a piece of charred beef (the best thing I have heard about Grant is that he cannot bear the sight of blood; nor will he "eat anything that walks," as he puts it, "on two legs," removing poultry and the human race from his diet); at the plump solemn officers of state got up in mouldy black (Emma is quite right: the odour of Washington's imperfectly washed and laundered statesmen is oppressive); at the overdressed preening ladies, looking like so many farmers' wives in fancy dress, I could not help but agree that our social scene is seriously lacking in "tong." But while I regard it as perfectly natural for *me* to make sharp comments, I find it peculiarly unbearable to hear my own criticisms voiced by a decidedly second-rate Frenchwoman.

"It is the strength of this republic," I spoke sententiously, in the rolling French periods of a Chateaubriand, "to take from *every* class its leaders, particularly in time of war. Naturally, you will say"—the poor woman was not about to say anything—"that by constantly changing those leaders we fail to create a continuing sense of splendour and of hierarchy but—and bear this forever in mind—by so doing we avoid the tyrant's sway." I can do this sort of thing in French by the hour. In fact, I once competed at Saint-Gratien with the novelist Flaubert, who also has a pet characterization known as *l'idiot*. After one hour of listening to the two of us, I with my gracious Dr. Pangloss looking forever foolishly on the bright side and Flaubert with his idiot, prone not only to rapturous arias in which not one original thing is said ("I adore the Gothic! It aspires to be!") but to the most alarming facial tics and inadvertent lunges of the body, Princess Mathilde agreed that we were equally horrendous. When dinner was done, the French lady fled me gratefully.

The gentlemen stood about after the ladies retired. Baron Jacobi sought me out. "I am desolate to think that your daughter —and you, too, sir—will not be permanent in this city."

"I am sad, too. We've been most marvellously entertained here." The Baron conducted the conversation in German, a language I speak not too easily.

"I read, of course, your piece on the last days of the Emperor Napoleon—" I detected a malicious glitter in his eyes, and stopped him in his tracks.

"Perfect rubbish," I said. "But one cannot live by *The Nation* alone."

"I admired your *Cavour*. I knew him." The little man reads everything; spoke knowledgeably of Cavour; also, mentioned some old pieces of mine for the *North American Review*, and asked if I knew its current editor. I said that I did not.

"A splendid man, a fine scholar—"

We were interrupted by the genial Mr. Blaine. "What is this strange language that I hear?"

Baron Jacobi shifted to English; told Blaine of our common admiration for the editor of the *North American Review*. "In fact,

I believe that the editor's father, Mr. Charles Francis Adams, is being spoken of to lead your party. That is, if *you*, Mr. Blaine, should not choose to succeed General Grant." This was a most mischievous remark for a diplomat to make, I thought, but then mischief is, apparently, Baron Jacobi's style.

"My dear Baron, I have no idea, nor does anyone save the Almighty, if that cup will pass to me or, if it does, whether I will drink thereof." Blaine has a fine comic style when he chooses, cheerfully willing to parody the ponderous locutions of the American statesman, so like the ubiquitous carnival salesman of snakeroot oil. "But I can tell you one thing. If any Adams should ever again be elected president, he will kill his own party just as dead as the other two President Adamses killed theirs. Show me a President Adams, sir, and I will show you a particide."

The Baron was called away, and for a moment I had Blaine to myself. "How do you think the election will be fought? On what issues . . . General?"

Blaine gave me a most comical look. "Mr. Schuyler, I served my country in the late conflict as best I could by editing the *Kennebec Journal*, and supporting with fiery editorials the Union cause, not to mention each and every one of our brave boys in blue."

Kennebec reminded me suddenly of Benedict Arnold's invasion of Canada during the Revolution. I mentioned this. Blaine was intrigued. "We've got all sorts of legends about Arnold up in those parts. Aaron Burr, too, who was with him. You were a protégé of Colonel Burr, weren't you?" A polite euphemism, often employed by the press. I acknowledged a relationship and passed quickly on to the election.

"Well, your friend Mr. Tilden will make a great noise about corruption in Washington, and I must say after Babcock, Schenck, and Belknap, all three so fast in a row, he'll be able to make some good points. But I don't think that corruption ever really excites the people one way or the other."

"What does?"

Blaine indicated the silent stubby figure of the President, held captive by a number of his eager guests as well as by his high office. "The fear of the North at the South. The resentment of the South at the North."

"The war's been over for ten years. There are other issues. Civil service reform—"

I was interrupted graciously but firmly. "Our people vote only against what they fear, what they dislike. Since more people resent the South than fear the North, we shall win, as usual, providing things cool down a bit."

"No more scandals?"

"Not *too* many more." Blaine smiled, the shiny black eyes alert. "Besides, if your friend Governor Tilden is nominated, I suspect he is going to have to spend most of his time explaining—well, about this and that. I mean he *was* a railroad lawyer, and precious few of them ever taught Sunday School."

But my interview with what now looks to be the next president was causing jealousy; and Blaine was taken from me. I found myself with a member of Congress from somewhere in the West who said, "I have a subject for your literary talents, Mr. Schuyler. I suggest we collaborate, as I have not the time to write the narrative myself. We would split the profits, naturally. What about sixty per cent for me, forty for you?"

I felt positively giddy—*jeune fille* or, rather, *jeune poule*, being bid for. "I don't, I fear, collaborate . . ."

"You will, on this story." The man—I still don't know his name—looked about furtively to make sure that no one was listening. Needless to say, no one was. Each of the powerful men had managed to collect a crowd about him. Blaine's was the largest, as he is expected to be the next president. Grant's was next in size (although he *is* the president, he will be gone in less than a year and so does not need cultivating). Garfield, Chandler and others I did not recognize stood at the centers of lesser groups beneath the smoking chandeliers.

"I know who murdered Abraham Lincoln."

"So do I." I did my best. "The actor Booth."

The man shook his head pityingly. "You believe that, too, I see."

"Well, Booth was observed behaving in a most suspicious way after the murder, jumping onto the stage of Ford's Theatre, denouncing the President . . ."

"But, Mr. Schuyler, *cui bono?* Who profits?"

"Mr. Booth's histrionic mania."

"But who, *above all*, profited?"

"The Vice President, I suppose, who succeeded him, Mr. Johnson."

"Exactly."

"But he, too, is dead now. So—"

"*Others* are alive, sir. And certain of those who were responsible for Lincoln's murder are present in this very room tonight."

I fled the madman by attaching myself to General Garfield, who was now working his own way toward the President. As I bade Garfield good evening, the handsome face beamed down at me and he took my hand. Because of a twisted arm, he has an odd habit when shaking hands of slowly and powerfully first pulling, then turning you toward him. "Lucretia certainly enjoyed her talk with you, and insists you and the Princess come see us."

Incidentally and *à propos* nothing, I did *not* celebrate my sixty-third birthday today. Both Emma and I had forgotten it entirely. As of 1:00 A.M., March 27, I have nothing to say about old age and death, except to note how unsettling it is to find oneself so much older than the leaders of this country. Garfield and Blaine and Conkling are in their mid-forties; each young enough to be my son. The world hero General Grant is almost a decade younger than I; yet in his sombre presence, I feel myself reduced to boyish irrelevance.

The time I was allowed to spend in that high presence was not long. Garfield graciously started to present me, but the President cut him short, not rudely but firmly. "We have had the honour." Again I was struck by the beautiful voice emerging from that grizzled and—well, stupid-looking—face.

"Perhaps you've read Mr. Schuyler in the *Ledger* on the Emperor Napoleon . . ." Garfield did his best, but it was not enough.

"I think Chancellor Bismarck the greatest man in Europe. I would like to meet him." Tangential but significant statement: Bismarck destroyed the Emperor and the Empire.

"The Chancellor certainly understands the uses and the ends of power." I rallied: my *North American Review* style can, usually, dominate any discussion.

"Then he must be lonely." There was a sort of twitch at the beard's center that might have been a smile.

"Lonely because no one else knows what he knows?"

"Yes, sir." For a moment there was silence. General Grant had simply stopped. I am told that this is a familiar tactic of his, calculated to put the other person on the defensive as well as to save himself from boredom, not to mention indiscretion. But then, uncharacteristically, as Garfield said later, the President suddenly began to speak, most fluently. "For me the use of power was simply a trust, given me to maintain the Union at any cost."

"And using that power, you achieved the end you wanted."

"Well, when a war stops there is a halt, but I don't know that it's an end. The fight goes on in other ways, doesn't it, General?" He turned to Garfield, who proceeded to speak so eloquently and so animatedly that I cannot remember one word he said, so busy was I staring at General Grant, as if there might be some external clue, some magical wart that would explain him to me.

". . . as in the case of Santo Domingo." I did hear Garfield say *that* because it was—is—the wrong subject to mention in Grant's presence.

The President scowled. "Sir, we had every right to intervene in Santo Domingo. And if I had not been stopped by the Congress that island would be ours today, and prosperous. After all, it was their own president who asked us in."

Note (added later): According to Nordhoff, at the beginning of Grant's Administration, the ubiquitous Babcock had worked out a plan with the corrupt president of Santo Domingo for the United States to annex that country for a price which was then to be divided by the Santo Domingan president, Babcock and (enemies say) Grant himself. Congress refused to pay for the annexation, to Grant's fury.

Garfield was soothing. "There were so many misunderstandings at that time."

Emboldened by wine (and by my sixty-third birthday: what have I to fear of any man? particularly a soon-to-be *former* President), I said, "I have often wondered, sir, at the change in your own policy. You condemned the Mexican War of '47 which ended in our seizing from Mexico all the land north of the Rio Grande. Yet twenty years later you wanted to annex Santo Domingo without consulting that nation's people."

I shall not be asked to the White House again during the Grant Administration. But I think that my impolite and highly apposite challenge was worthwhile. At least I did not have to listen to the usual tedious discourse on horses that most people are treated to by this canny and deliberately dull little man who is, I would say, like the first Bonaparte, entirely immoral or amoral, but unlike the Emperor, burdened with the Puritan's sense of sin and retribution. This combination can make for confusion.

I got a long stare from the President: the eyes suddenly very clear, very bright with anger. Garfield was plainly distraught at my *lèse-majesté*.

When General Grant's response finally came, it was character-istic. "The president of Mexico did not invite us to invade his country and attach a part of it to the United States. The president of Santo Domingo *offered* me his country for a fair price. By wanting to buy this island I did no more than Mr. Jefferson when he agreed to buy Louisiana, or than Mr. Johnson when he agreed to buy Alaska."

The audience was at an end. The President led the way into the Red Room, where Mrs. Grant reigned.

"Well," said Garfield, somewhat shaken, "I never thought I'd hear anybody tax General Grant on that subject, and in the White House."

"Bad manners, I know." I was reckless because of the sixty-third birthday; also, the Grant Administration must of necessity be the chief target of Governor Tilden and I must do what I can to help prepare the case for the prosecution. "But I was curious. And he did bring up the subject first, in a way, by mentioning Bismarck."

We followed the crowd of men into the Red Room.

"I've almost never heard anyone get him on the defensive like that."

"It is the privilege, General, of the historian, and of the old."

Happily, while I was shutting for myself the White House doors, Emma was opening them wide for herself. Mrs. Grant has taken a fancy to her, and Emma is to return soon to the mansion for a ladies' afternoon.

"She also told me how she found out the President wasn't going to stand for a third term."

We were preparing for bed, the long evening at an end.

"From the newspapers?"

"Almost. She said that she'd gone into the President's office on a Sunday afternoon. He wasn't there, but the Cabinet was all present, which she thought very strange because the Cabinet never meets on a Sunday. When she asked the ministers *why* they were all there, they said it was simply coincidence. Then the President came in and she said, 'Ulys'—she calls him that—'what's happening?' and he said, 'Just wait till I light this cigar.' And then he told her that he had met with the Cabinet and had read to them his statement that he would not be a candidate for president. Then while she had been talking to the ministers, he had sent off the letter. She was furious with Ulys. 'Why didn't you read *me* the letter, too?' And he said, 'Because if I had, I'd never have been allowed to post it and I don't want to stay here another four years.' She was quite fierce because she would like to spend the rest of her days in those hideous rooms."

It is late. I am tired. I am no wiser on the subject of General Grant than before. I suspect that he is as corrupt as those about him; otherwise, he would not have such men as intimates. Certainly, I shall never believe the usual Stalwart explanation: that Grant is a simpleton and does not understand politics or people. He understands both very well indeed and, I suspect, likes neither.

It is late. I am tired. I am—but it is not possible!—sixty-three.

Seven

1

NORDHOFF CAME to the suite this morning with a long telegram from Jamie, requesting more "snap" in my pieces "because you are much too cool, just like the recording angel."

"Well," I turned to Nordhoff, "that is what I try to be while *you* are the snappy one."

"Ignore him," was Nordhoff's good advice. I had not seen Nordhoff since my White House evening over a week ago. He had been amused by my confrontation with the President.

"I suspect that's the first political statement any guest has ever got out of him. Usually, he goes on and on about the war and who was where and when and why, or about his horses. You know, some years ago, Grant is supposed to have told General Sherman that he had decided, deliberately, to interest himself in horses because, he said, 'If you don't pick your own hobby, the press will pick one for you, and then you're really in for it.' "

"Like drink?"

"Or like the ladies." Nordhoff is disapproving of loose morals, as are so many ex-sailors.

"There are those who deny Grant was ever drunk."
Nordhoff shook his head. "I know for a fact that there were
times in the war when he was never sober. But now he seems all
right, though a few years ago at a dinner in New York with Jim
Fiske and some low-life cronies, Grant got so drunk that he put
his cigar wrong way round in his mouth, and singed his beard."
Nordhoff gave me the day's scandal as I waited for Emma to
return from a visit to Mrs. Fish (the ladies have now met but I
have yet to set eyes on the Secretary of State and his wife). "The
President's younger brother Orvil is mixed up in the Babcock
affair. He's scheduled to go before Clymer's committee . . ."
"And lie?"
"What else?" Nordhoff's glee at the wickedness each day revealed alternates with gloom as he then contemplates the meaning of the wickedness revealed. That is why his style is so much
more vivid, more journalistic than mine. I try for balance, to
consider the true nature of this Africa, while he plunges wildly
through the jungle, amazed, horrified, outraged by exotic flora,
dangerous fauna.

The Garfields had proposed a picnic if this day, Sunday, proved
to be pleasant. The day was lovely and so apicknicking we went
beside the Rock Creek, a charming small river that winds between laurel-covered hills in a forest at the edge of the city.

The Garfields had also invited Baron Jacobi and Madame José
García. This extraordinary lady is the wife of a Peruvian diplomat, the daughter or niece of some South American autocrat, and
the authoress of a number of novels, including *Love in the Pampas*,
a gorgeous trashy work that Emma dearly loved when it was
published some years ago. Madame García is very rich, very
lavish in her entertainments and very, very fat even by the leni-
ent standards of this plump society.

We were deposited by our carriages on a mossy bank just above
the creek where, beneath slender trees in newest leaf, Lucretia
Garfield and Emma unpacked the picnic hamper. Seated on a
fallen log, Madame García allowed her many diamonds (small
picnic ones) to take the air, to sparkle in April light, while their
large owner praised nature: "The air! So fresh. And the amusing
flowers! Look, Baron Jacobi, a primrose, no?"
"No, my dear. A poppy."
"And, hark, the sound of water purling over rocks."
"Purling, yes." Baron Jacobi gave me his quick amused lizard's

glance. "I have never before heard anyone actually say that word."

"In that case, we must celebrate." Garfield was most charming. He opened a bottle of wine and we all drank to "purling."

"A common English word surely." Madame García flashed her black eyes at the company. "I encounter it every day—in poetry, of course. I read nothing else. I find that poetry makes me more alive, more quick to seize the passing moment! To extract from it true pleasure, made by art divine."

Between the sly wit of Baron Jacobi and the sheer splendour of Madame García's person and pronouncements, Emma and I were much amused, as the Garfields had intended. Later, Baron Jacobi napped in the warm sun while Madame García nodded over a volume of verse (not slim but every bit as fat as she). Emma and Mrs. Garfield spoke in low voices of important matters. I looked at General Garfield expectantly. Nothing here is ever done at random, even a picnic.

"Shall we take a stroll?" Garfield is a restless, active man. I am neither. I said that nothing would please me more. Heart sinking (and pounding), I accompanied my host through the woods. I do not much care for nature, and believe that flowers belong in vases rather than loose and untidy on the ground.

But I do feel better for that stroll; when I shut my eyes, I can still see the shimmering vivid green effect of sunlight filtered through new leaves, emphasizing the darker green of low-growing laurel. I am beginning to write the way Madame García speaks. "I revel in *all* of glorious nature!" she had confided to me, methodically killing ants with a small rock.

At the top of a low hill, we paused. There was not much view, just more hills similarly wooded. Behind a hedge of lilac bushes I could make out a small dilapidated cabin. "An ex-slave lives there. A nice old man who is supposed to make a most superior whisky."

"What an incredible institution, slavery." I don't know why but the sight of the slave cabin made me actually think of the *fact* of slavery, something difficult to do, since the word itself (like the institution) has for so long been made meaningless by too much furious prose, both for and against, not to mention by all the killing done in its name. When one hears too much of a subject, one ceases to comprehend it at all.

"We are well rid of it. Now we must worry about the Chinese

who are being imported by the thousands, and taking jobs away
from our own people."

A few more remarks on the Chinese; then we sat on two tree
stumps, only a few feet apart. As we smoked cigars my host
gradually came to the point. "I read your last piece . . ."

"Filled with errors, I know."

"I saw only one which might not be an error, after all, if . . ."
There was a pause. A new beginning. "You seemed fairly certain
that our party will nominate Mr. Blaine for president."

"I thought that was your opinion too."

"It's my *wish*, certainly. But . . . well, I must tell you in all
confidence, there is about to be yet another scandal."

"Involving Blaine?"

Garfield nodded. "We have not had much luck these last few
months, have we?"

"Perhaps your party has been too long in power."

"Perhaps. Though I don't think your friend Tilden will order
things any better."

"But between a Babcock, say, and a Bigelow you must admit
there is a world of difference."

But Garfield is not much interested in what the reform element
calls "good government." He is a conventional party man whose
only singularity is his reputation for honesty. Except for that one
small slip with *Crédit Mobilier*, no scandal has ever been attached
to him (for the record, I must add that all-important word "yet").

Garfield came to the point. "About seven years ago when
Blaine was Speaker of the House, he became involved with a Mr.
Warren Fisher, a Boston contractor who was to build a railroad
called the Little Rock and Fort Smith." Garfield's mind is such
an orderly one that he was able to make what must be a very
complicated business so plain that even I am now able to understand it . . . up to a point (up to the point intended?). "Mr. Blaine
thought very highly of Mr. Fisher and of his railroad. So he sold
a number of the railroad's first mortgage bonds to some friends."

"Was Mr. Blaine a bond salesman before he went to Congress
or only after?" This small pleasantry did not charm my companion, who puffed very hard at his cigar and looked above my head,
as though expecting to see a storm cloud in the bright sky.

"Mr. Blaine is much too good-natured a man." Garfield's answer was not to the point. "Also, he is casual in his business
affairs. Certainly, he ought never to have involved himself with

Mr. Fisher. In any case, shortly after the bonds were sold, the railroad nearly failed."

"And the bonds he had sold his friends were worthless."

"Until the Little Rock and Fort Smith was bought by three other railroads, of which one was the Union Pacific." It was with real distaste that Garfield said the name of his only known corrupter. "As a result, the bonds of Mr. Fisher's railroad regained their value. But there were—there are—those who think it was Mr. Blaine who persuaded the three railroads to help out Mr. Fisher in order to save his friends."

"I see no harm in that," I said, beginning to make out the vague shape of a familiar crime.

"Nor do I. The reverse, in fact. Mr. Blaine was embarrassed. He felt he had let down his friends. So he set out to save Mr. Fisher's railroad and succeeded."

"On the other hand," I was now able to make out certain features of that no longer so vague shape, "there will be those who think that Mr. Blaine may have done some favour for the three rescuing companies. Otherwise they would not have wanted to buy a worthless railroad."

"Far from worthless, Mr. Schuyler. I am told the Little Rock is as sound as any road in the country." Garfield exhaled blue smoke slowly, and through the haze I saw resting on the branch of a tree a red bird, known in these parts as a cardinal. I decided to regard this bird as a good omen.

"So you believe that this transaction is going to be used to damage Mr. Blaine."

Garfield let his cigar fall to the ground; then with the heel of his boot, he buried the stub deep in soft moist earth. "Yes. And it's going to be used against him in a most diabolical way. Just before the Republican Convention, in June, the . . . the enemy will make those charges, figuring that by the time Blaine has been able to prove himself innocent, the convention will have chosen someone else."

"Senator Conkling?"

"Probably. Certainly, we will *never* nominate Mr. Bristow." The usually mellifluous warm voice was suddenly flat, nasal, hard.

"And you think that Mr. Bristow is behind these charges?"

"Who else? He wants desperately to be president. And in his mad way, he thinks that by destroying, one by one, the leaders of our party, he will be nominated on a wave of reform. Well, he will be greatly surprised. Meanwhile . . ." Garfield stopped.

It was now my turn. I took it. Did what was expected of me. "You think that if I were to write this story for the *Herald* and publish it next week, say, that Mr. Blaine would then have nearly three months in which to defuse, if I may use a military metaphor, the scandal."

"I see no reason *why* you should be helpful, Mr. Schuyler." The bright April blue eyes were moist, sincere, quite irresistible. I felt, for a moment, as if I were in the presence of the handsome son that I never had (or, for that matter, wanted). "I know that you are a Democrat and a friend of Governor Tilden. I also believe that you are a fair historian and that you would not like to see a . . . well, a great man, as I think Blaine is, not only falsely accused but unable to defend himself until it is too late for him, and for the country." Garfield was absolutely winning, and so I was won, though not absolutely.

We made our way back to Rock Creek. Madame García was reading from her book of verse; the powerful voice echoed against the rocks, the hills. In the trees frightened birds chattered warnings to one another. Then suddenly the sun went behind a hill and the blue shadows turned cold.

"Time to go!" Lucretia Garfield was on her feet at the sight of us. "I think I'm getting a chill."

Baron Jacobi helped Emma to her feet while Garfield and I used our combined strength to set Madame García upright.

"What a successful picnic!" exclaimed Baron Jacobi. He looked closely at Garfield and me. "I suspect a plot, gentlemen."

"Tonight," said Garfield to me, "the Atlantic cable will bear a message to the Bulgarian government of the most sinister portent, in cipher."

"Except that my secretary mislaid the cipher and I've sent no messages for a month. Your plots are safe with me, gentlemen. Besides, what the Balkans do not know will not harm them."

We then divided ourselves so that Baron Jacobi and I were with Garfield while the three ladies travelled in the second carriage. Had Madame García been less large we could all have travelled in a single victoria. Lucretia insisted that the men travel together because, "They will want to smoke like chimneys."

But we did not smoke. We spoke instead of history. Garfield is a devoted reader of the classics. Baron Jacobi has read the classics but is not devoted to them as history—"only as literature. Who, after all, believes a word that Julius Caesar wrote? His little 'history' was simply a sort of leg up for his political career."

"But if we can't believe those classical writers whose works have come down to us, then how can we ever know *any* history?" Garfield is passionate on the subject.

"I think, General, the answer to that is very simple. We *cannot* know any history, truly. I suppose somewhere, in Heaven perhaps, there is a Platonic history of the world, a precise true record. But what we think to be history is nothing but fiction. Isn't that so, Mr. Schuyler? I appeal to you, perversely, since you are a historian."

"And therefore a novelist?"

"*Malgré vous.*"

"I agree, Baron. There is no *absolute* record. When I was trying to write about the Communards in Paris—and I was there at the time—I could seldom find out just who was killed by whom."

"But surely, gentlemen, there is a winnowing process. History is distilled from many conflicting witnesses. We do *know* that President Lincoln was murdered, that General Grant commanded the Union army."

"But no one knows the name Achilles took when he hid himself among the ladies or the lyrics of those songs the sirens sang. If Mr. Schuyler will forgive me, I prefer fiction to history, particularly if the narrative involves people that once lived, like Alexander the Great."

"I must disagree," I said, thinking of those dreadful novels by Dumas. "I always want to know what is true, if anyone knows it."

"But no one does except the subject, and he—like Caesar—is more apt than not to lie."

"But," said Garfield, "we now have letters, diaries, newspaper cuttings—"

"Dear General, is there a newspaper in the United States— other than *The New York Times*—whose reports *you* believe?"

Garfield saw the humour. He laughed. "Well, if future historians will read only the *Times*—"

"They will think that the Grant Administration was absolutely superb—as does the minister from Bulgaria," added the Baron quickly, "and entirely free of corruption. As for letters, journals, who ever writes the truth about himself?"

"You are too cynical for me, Baron," said Garfield, himself every bit as cynical but in the agreeably open American way.

"I would make a bonfire of all historians, except Mr. Schuyler, and the early fabulists like Livy . . ."

"But how then would you learn about the past?"

"From Dante, Shakespeare, Scott—all fiction writers."

"But Shakespeare's history is always wrong."

"But his characters are always *right*. Anyway if you want to know what Julius Caesar or James G. Blaine or our own delicious James Garfield is really like, then look into a mirror and study with perfect attention what is reflected there."

After supper, I sat with Nordhoff in the rotunda at Willard's and repeated to him what Garfield had told me about Blaine.

"Very clever," was Nordhoff's verdict, delivered through a half-dozen amused barks.

"Then Blaine did do—favours for the three railroads?"

"Favours! He is in their pocket. He is also in Fisher's pocket. When Blaine sold his friends all those Little Rock and Fort Smith bonds, Fisher made him a present of a hundred and twenty-five thousand dollars' worth of land-grant bonds and thirty-two thousand five hundred dollars of first mortgage bonds."

Also, I learned that Blaine had used his influence as Speaker of the House to see that Fisher's railroad was awarded a crucial land grant by the Congress. "Then he's in very deep," was the most I could think to say.

"Over his head, I'd say. But you can never tell in Washington."

"Garfield seems to think Bristow is behind this."

"The Stalwarts think Bristow is behind everything. But if Blaine is destroyed, it won't be the work of Bristow. It will be because for the first time in years there is a Democratic majority in the House and they are out for blood."

Blood Red. I thought of the red bird on the green bough, my good omen. "Garfield is clever, then, to want me to tell the story now, in his version."

"Yes. Because then the scandal will have come and—he hopes —have gone before the convention in June."

"I think I must write it, don't you?"

Nordhoff was thoughtful. "Certainly it is very useful for us— for you—to have General Garfield as a friend."

"Then I should write the story in such a way as to please both him and Blaine."

"Yes. Then *I* shall follow up, day after day, with all the terrible details."

"And that will be the end of Blaine?"

"That *ought* to be the end, but he is very shrewd, as well as the most intelligent, most likable man down here."

"So then let us allow him to be the president."

Nordhoff found this amusing. "I don't think it's really up to us, worse luck. The Democrats will take care of him in due course, preferably just before the convention. But, in a way, you *are* helping him by publishing part of the story now. As for letting him be the president—now, really, Schuyler."

"Yes, yes. I know. He is too corrupt."

"Isn't that enough?"

"Not, it would appear, for the American people."

"You are hard on us. I want this election to be a reveille. I want everyone to wake up. And we can do it, too, you and I and a few others."

"Make history? But there is no history," I said, trying out in my own voice Baron Jacobi's theory, "only fictions of varying degrees of plausibility."

"What?"

"I meant to tell you that I had an amusing conversation with Garfield about history. He assured me that one can learn the truth about the past through old newspapers, letters, diaries. Then he proposed to help me write, as it were, the history of Mr. Blaine, by setting down in the *Herald* all the lies he would like to see in print."

"But now you know the truth. And the truth always comes out."

"Dear Nordhoff, in this case I know only what *you* tell me is the truth. And you could be mistaken. As for the truth always coming out, why, I think it never does. But even if it did, who would know?"

2

JAMIE BENNETT TELEGRAPHED: "Your report on Blaine will in-sure nomination of Conkling and election of Tilden talk of nothing else in New York congratulations" while a long letter from John Bigelow was most flattering, not to mention promising: "Just an hour ago I was in the Governor's office and he was reading aloud to several friends your astonishing—well, your definitive—revelations about Mr. Blaine. The Governor was delighted, and praised you highly. Secretly we are both a little sad because we saw Mr. Blaine as the candidate, and an easy one to defeat. Conkling will be more difficult, and Bristow most difficult of all. Fortunately, Bristow is hated by the Stalwarts; in fact, Chet Arthur has told a number of people that Bristow will never hold office again, as a Republican. The Governor said, 'I did not imagine your friend Mr. Schuyler was going to be such a kingmaker!' Of course the world has yet to hear from Mr. Blaine."

Indeed the world had not when Bigelow wrote me. But today —April 24—the beleaguered colossus of the Republican party rose to his feet in the House of Representatives and, on a point of personal privilege, proceeded to make one of the most eloquent speeches in the history of that body, or so everyone says. I would not know, for I was at the dentist having a back tooth pulled. I am still groggy from the nitrous oxide I was given, and my right jaw, which for some years has not been exactly what Mrs. Southworth would call "lean," is still grotesquely swollen.

But Emma was at the Capitol with Nordhoff; and when the speech was done, both came to see me on or, rather, in my sick rocking chair. Nordhoff promptly seated himself at the desk and began to write his piece for tomorrow's *Herald* while Emma described the apotheosis of James G. Blaine, with a bark or two from Nordhoff.

"He was *adorable*, Papa!" Emma is truly stimulated by this city's peculiar theatre.

"What a word!" Nordhoff said, continuing to write rapidly.

"But he was! You've never seen so many enthusiastic people. And everyone was there."

"Except me," I mumbled through swollen jaw. "The cause of it all."

"Poor Papa! I never asked about the tooth. Was it painful?" We despatched the tooth as a subject, and returned to Blaine's performance.

"His voice shook. He sobbed at one point . . ."

"Like an actor," said Nordhoff, and proceeded, I am sure, to write the phrase at the same time he was saying it, "a *bad* actor."

"He convinced me." But then Emma was thoughtful. "Well, perhaps he did not convince but he overwhelmed us all. There were even cheers from the people in the press gallery while in the ladies' gallery where I was, well, you've never seen so many handkerchiefs waved, heard so many hurrays!" With gusto, Emma imitated the nasal brazen sound that my countrywomen make when they publicly express their pleasure.

"I am sure he was marvellous." I spoke wetly, for blood and saliva have been filling my mouth all day and I must keep mopping my lips with cotton wool. I turned to Nordhoff. "But what did Blaine actually *say?*"

Nordhoff put down his pen. "Very little. He claimed he was being persecuted in the press . . ."

"Did he mention the *Herald?*" I was keen to know if Blaine had made reference to me, but though my article was the very first to expose him, he had named no names. I was, I fear, piqued at this omission. The speech was about political partisans and their unrelenting hostility to good government and to the party that had saved the Union, freed the slaves, and honoured James G. Blaine.

"But what about the charges that I—that we have made?" I would like to take *all* the credit for the bold exposure, but with some effort I acknowledge Nordhoff's assistance. "Why did those railroads buy the worthless stock of the Little Rock and Fort Smith?"

"He read a letter." Nordhoff was grimly amused.

"He read that letter superbly well," added Emma.

"From whom?"

"From the treasurer of the Union Pacific Railroad." Nordhoff looked down at his notebook. "Dated March thirty-first, saying that the railroad had never paid any money to Blaine."

"As if the treasurer would have written anything else to Blaine." I must say the man is bold, the public gullible.

A series of barks from Nordhoff, and a demur from Emma: "There were other letters. But the point is that he was so forthright. So honest. So—well, charming in the African style," she added, dropping her voice so that Nordhoff would not hear, but he was intent on composition.

I am afraid that neither Emma nor Nordhoff has been able to give me any idea of *what* Blaine actually said, but the way that he said whatever it was that so delighted his listeners has saved at least this one day for him.

Nordhoff finished his story and rang for a page to take it down to Mr. Roose to send on by telegraph to the *Herald*. Then Nordhoff delivered his verdict. "Blaine's got away with it."

"And I did the wrong thing? From our point of view?" I must say that I am revelling in a most uncharacteristic and charmless way in my sudden fame. For two weeks I have been known from one end of the country to the other as the brave and fearless journalist who dared to expose the clandestine activities of the former Speaker of the House of Representatives. Wherever I go in Washington, the most celebrated people gather about me, and listen respectfully to my every word. During these last few days it has got so that I want no one to talk of anything else but me, ever again! But after this day's vivid and historic performance, Blaine's is now the central rôle and I am eclipsed, at best a pale ghost of a moon hardly visible as his sun blazes.

"This is just the beginning." Nordhoff assumed his special secret face that I have come to recognize as prelude to some devastating revelation.

"Then there is more?" Emma was intensely curious.

"Oh, yes." I, too, did my best to achieve a secret face despite a swollen jaw. "There is more to come."

"Oh, dear!" Emma is now a complete Blaine partisan. She looked at Nordhoff and then at me and back again, but we refused to satisfy her curiosity. Then a second page appeared and presented me with a copy of Washington's *Evening Star*.

"This was sent you, sir."

"By whom?" I gave him a coin.

"Don't know, sir. Just came. That's all."

The vengeance of Mrs. Fayette Snead known as Fay was like

that terrible swift sword so savagely celebrated in the blood-
thirsty "hymn" of one Julia Ward Howe, a denizen of "the evening dews and damps" of Beacon Hill.

With numerous asterisks and blanks for names and horrendous
puns, the P*** d'A*** was linked romantically with the B***
J*** while, in far-off New York, a youthful American suitor did
not dream that he had been jilted by this frivolous *French* woman.

Nordhoff was surprised at how lightly Emma and I took Fay's
vengeance. We explained to him about the kerosene. Emma was
not at all contrite. "How was I to know that her hair would fall
out? It must not have been attached very firmly to the scalp. I
shall send her a hat." Emma went in to dress for dinner. I walked
Nordhoff to the door.

"What next?" I asked.

"We accumulate more evidence." Again the secret look.

"Where do you get it from?"

"Ah!" Nordhoff was maddening.

"From Bristow?"

"Bristow is an honest man. That is a fact."

"But hardly loyal to his president, to his party . . ."

"He is loyal to principle."

"*That!*" I am heartily sick of principles, affected or real.

"Anyway, I'll let you know in due course. It should be amusing
tonight for you to visit the enemy's camp."

"I find it hard to think of the Garfields as enemies. After all,
he is a devoted reader of mine."

"Not to mention collaborator."

I was unexpectedly embarrassed. I do like Garfield, and dislike
deceiving him. But then of course he lied to me; got me to provide
Blaine with time enough to answer the charges against him. Yet
I am uneasy whenever I dine at Garfield's house and he takes me
into his confidence . . . but then I am *not* taken into his confidence.
I must stop this sentimentalizing. I am with ravenous wolves.
This is Africa.

Emma and I arrived late for dinner, delayed by a tremendous
tropical storm that suddenly broke over the city at sundown.
Much thunder and lightning and gusts of wind full of rain turned
the unpaved streets to thick mud while horses stumbled, carriages
slid, umbrellas turned inside out.

Finally our carriage stopped at the corner of Thirteenth Street
and I, and we braved the storm that flung us like flimsy dolls hard

against the Garfields' pleasant red-brick house, so like all the other pleasant red-brick houses of the town. We were then propelled by the wind through the front door held half open by a delighted servant.

The interior of the house is pretty much like all the other houses that we have visited. On the left of the entrance hall is the parlour with its inevitable upright piano and slate-mantelled fireplace. On the right of the hall, the family sitting room is at the front of the house and the dining room is at the back.

The dinner guests were in the parlour: a room whose only distinction proved to be a pair of tall Chinese vases that were, according to Emma, "most lovely," and Lucretia Garfield was visibly pleased to have her own taste confirmed by Emma, who is thought to be an authority on every sort of "tong."

A dozen guests had already assembled, amongst them the dread Madame García who has taken to flirting with me in a most alarming way, thundering her heavily accented French into my ear whilst allowing me vistas of what appear to be four very large breasts encased by all too fragile whalebone beneath a purple muslin marquee or tent.

As I record her bold advances I am suddenly aware that I have not had a single amatory encounter during all this time in Washington City. Nordhoff is too much the puritan to be of any use. In fact, when I made a delicate inquiry or two, he pretended that I was joking. I daresay he thinks me too old for this sort of thing. One of the waiters in the bar at Willard's did propose sponsoring me at an establishment on Ninth Street, but I was not feeling sufficiently hearty at the time. Since then, my would-be cicerone has been dismissed.

The specialty of the town is the mulatto, or "high yellow," girl and I confess that, once or twice, I have seen truly marvellous-looking half-breed girls in the street of the sort to inspire languorous daydreams even at congressional hearings. If only Jamie Bennett were here to guide his old uncle!

Garfield introduced me about the room. For the dozenth time I met the courtly Horatio King, who organizes literary evenings at which Garfield shines. I have so far avoided these Parnassian revels but "Soon, Mr. Schuyler, soon we shall have the pleasure I am sure."

Madame García threw me a flashing black-eyed glance. "*I* shall bring him, Mr. King! He too shares our passion for Art and for

Life writ large!" On the gale of her explosive sounding of the
word "passion," I was propelled toward Baron Jacobi, who took
both my hands in his and exclaimed, "To think, Mr. Schuyler,
that I shall soon be able to address you as Father!"

Lucretia Garfield thought this in the poorest taste, and said so.
But Emma and I were both amused. Everyone, needless to say,
had read Fay.

Emma was serene, "I never dreamed Mrs. Fayette Snead's revenge would be so charming, and so flattering." With that, I lost
Emma to the Baron while I met the British minister Sir Edward
Thornton and his wife, a couple that are produced in considerable quantity by the British Foreign Office. Zach. Chandler was
also present; just as we were shaking hands Garfield was called
away to greet new arrivals, fugitives from the storm that still
thundered and whistled about the house. "Well, sir, how did you
like Mr. Blaine's answer today?" asked Chandler.

"I didn't hear him. I was having a tooth extracted." I touched
my lips with the handkerchief that I have been clutching all day.
"Answer?" The anesthetizing gas had made me slow; in fact, this
whole stormy day and evening linger in my memory like a dream.
"You felt that he was answering *me?*"

"Oh, don't be modest, sir. You've caused a considerable com-
motion." Chandler smiled down at me—a formidable grey face,
much lined, with a shark's mouth and dead eyes. I cannot say that
the Secretary of the Interior charms me.

"At least," I rallied, "our friends the Belknaps are off the front
page for a time."

Chandler nodded. "A blessing, small but appreciated."

"Does the impeachment continue?"

"Since the Democrats control the House, there will be an impeachment. Of course the whole thing is illegal. How can you
impeach and try and perhaps remove from office a member of the
Cabinet who is no longer *in* the Cabinet?"

I did not make any contribution to this subtle constitutional
question because, like the Devil himself, with a clap of thunder
and a gust of wind, James G. Blaine had entered the room from
the vestibule and stood in the doorway. Garfield promptly seized
him in that peculiar way of his which is almost an embrace; as
he pulled the hero close to his side, he quite blocked from view
the charming Mrs. Blaine.

Applause from everyone in the parlour, save the foreigners—

and myself. Then the great man made a slow progress through the parlour, receiving compliments with a gracious smile until he came to me and the smile became gaily conspiratorial.

"Mr. Schuyler, I guess you know by now that I spoke only to you this morning. Yes, sir, to you directly. From the very first moment that I saw you up there in the gallery, I said to myself, If I don't convince Mr. Schuyler who's sitting there, looking down at me with that skeptical look of his, then I had better quit politics forthwith and go back to Kennebec. So . . ." He paused dramatically. "What did you think? Tell me the unvarnished truth?"

"The unvarnished truth, sir, is that I was *not* in the gallery but at the dentist's."

"That was *not* you?" Caught in his splendid lie, Blaine responded splendidly. "Then I addressed myself with all my heart to your double, to a counterfeit Charles Schermerhorn Schuyler!"

"But from what everyone tells me, your speech itself was purest gold, and in no way counterfeit."

For the first time Blaine gave me a truly amused and interested look; it is obvious that he enjoys his own performances and is more amused than not to find his art appreciated, even at the expense of his plausibility. It may well be that Blaine is what the country needs (and deserves?). In any case, as of today, it looks as if Blaine is what the country is going to get, at least as Republican nominee for president.

Garfield was euphoric. He got me to one side, looked at me with those beautiful blue eyes, and said in a low voice, "You have saved us."

"You exaggerate, General." I was uneasy, not wanting anyone else to hear this undeserved and dangerous (to me) compliment.

"No. Your article was perfectly balanced. You repeated the charges that were being whispered, and so, by bringing everything to a head, Mr. Blaine was able to answer his enemies, to clear his name."

"But has he?" I was perverse and irritable. Those who use do not like being used.

"To the satisfaction of everyone. Obviously die-hard partisans will not be convinced, but I've just learned that *The Nation* is going to support Mr. Blaine, and all as a result of his speech today." I suppose Garfield thought that I would be impressed by

The Nation, a most intelligent and virtuous journal, and as capable
of making errors as any other paper.

"You think the matter is ended?" I was genuinely curious,
recalling Nordhoff's secret face. "There'll be no more revelations
about Mr. Blaine and the railroads?"

"It's a dead issue." Garfield was emphatic. "Oh, there's some
talk among the Democrats in the House about an investigation,
but they won't get far. That's a promise. Fact, after today, I have
a hunch they'll all dry up pretty fast."

At dinner I sat next to Mrs. Blaine. Not unnaturally, she was
somewhat prickly, but I did my best to convince her of my impartiality. I don't think that she is in on the plot. If she is, then she
is as good a performer as her husband. In any case, we did not
mention *l'affaire* Blaine. Other topics concerned us. Although she
spoke at length of her admiration for General and Mrs. Grant,
there was a mocking edge to some of her stories. But then Grant
is supporting in a not-so-secret way Blaine's rival and bitter
enemy Conkling.

"I know that people complain of General Grant's silences but
let me tell you they are to be preferred sometimes to his actual
conversation. Just the other day I sat next to him at dinner and
I tell you, Mr. Schuyler, that man talked about himself for three
hours without a stop. All about how ungrateful the country is and
how he is always being held responsible for everything that goes
wrong, and how the newspapers have always been against him
even during the war when they were guilty of treason for what
they wrote in support of the South, and how the British gave so
much money and property to Marlborough and to Wellington for
saving their country while he got nothing at all from us Americans but a job he never wanted. It was something of an earful."

Mrs. Blaine also told me of a recent day spent with Emma. I
pretended I knew all about it, but, again, Emma has surprised me.
Apparently she has met Mrs. Grant *twice* since our dinner at the
White House. I knew of the first visit with: "All the ladies of the
town, drinking tea. And very dull they are."

But day before yesterday Emma met Mrs. Grant at the house
of Mrs. Fish. Mrs. Blaine was also there, and spoke glowingly of
Emma. "She is certainly the best-looking woman Washington has
seen in many a moon. And so patient! Mrs. Grant kept asking her
all these questions about Paris and what places she and her 'Ulys'
ought to visit when they go around the world after they leave the
White House."

I have just asked Emma about the tea party *chez* Fish. Emma looked genuinely surprised. "But I told you all about it, didn't I?" "Not a word. And you know how I still covet an invitation to the house of the cousin of Hiram Apgar's wife!"

Emma assured me that I had missed nothing. Emma found Julia Fish polite, dim, Apgar-ish. Mr. Fish was not present. As for Mrs. Grant, "Well, she took me aside, and looked me very close in the face, left eye into my left eye, right eye into my right eye, and said, 'My mother once spent a night in a cabin with a part of Colonel Aaron Burr's army in the West, and she told me that they were *perfect* gentlemen.' I can't think why she felt I ought to know this. Of course you used to work for Colonel Burr, but even so . . ."

Obviously Emma and I do not entirely confide in each other. I cannot think why I feel hurt when she does not tell me every detail of her life, no matter how insignificant; yet I have never told her the most singular fact about myself, that I am—as was the late President Martin Van Buren—presumed to be an illegitimate son of Colonel Burr. Although I did publish *Conversations with Aaron Burr*, I have never alluded publicly to any connection between the Colonel and me other than a professional one.

Conversation after dinner: the American gentlemen praised Blaine extravagantly to his face while the British minister looked uncomfortable and Baron Jacobi looked alert. I suspect that even as I write this late at night, the Atlantic cable is buzzing with ciphered Balkan wit.

Recalling the Antiques' fury at Blaine, I asked him why he was so unrelentingly hostile to Jefferson Davis when the civil rights of all the other officers of the Confederacy have been restored.

"Andersonville, Mr. Schuyler." The black eyes narrowed. "Thousands of our men died in that camp and all because of Davis. He knew what was happening to those prisoners of war. Yet he did nothing."

"But surely others were even more responsible."

"Davis, as president of the Confederacy, had the power of life and death. And he chose death for our brave men." From the slight roar of catarrh at the back of Blaine's throat, from the deep rumble in his chest, I knew that I was listening to what will be a major theme in his campaign for the presidency: playing on the hostility of the North toward the South, waving on high the so-called bloody shirt in order to keep alive the passions of the war.

Blaine also told me that the Democrats in Congress would be blamed for denying appropriations for the War Department; particularly hurt has been the Army of the Frontier which protects Western settlers from the ever-irritable Indian tribes.

When we joined the ladies, Blaine went straight to Emma, "Well, at least I saw *you* very plainly in the gallery!"

"And no doubt *heard* me, too, cheering in the commonest way." Emma was aglow in the presence of her favourite African chief.

"I do like him, Papa," she said just now.

"But he's an absolute scoundrel."

"So was Napoleon—the First *and* the Third. Anyway the world is made for scoundrels, isn't it? Certainly, they always manage to do with it as they please."

"I'm afraid we have been here too long. You are becoming African before my eyes."

"I was *born* African, Papa. And presently I shall put a bone through my nose and eat human flesh." On that high note, Emma retired to bed.

The swelling in my jaw has gone down, but I am still oozing blood in the most disgusting way. Old bodies take so long to heal.

Eight

1

THE NIGHT of May 10 to May 11, at Philadelphia. I am so weary that I think it most unlikely I shall be able to write more than a few words. Emma is also exhausted and has gone to her room on the opposite side of the hotel. There was no suite of rooms to be had. In fact, only a series of telegrams from Bryant demanding rooms for us in the name of the *Evening Post* kept us from spending a night in the streets, for the Centennial Exhibition opened this morning and every room in the city is taken. I realize now that I am much too old for this kind of journalism, but as a beggar I am in no position to choose where I go or what I do. I feel most unwell.

Although this is my first visit to Philadelphia, I shall *not* record here my first impressions of the old capital of the republic—other than to say that whatever virtues the city may possess are entirely obscured by the several hundred thousand visitors who have made the town a nightmare of stalled carriages and horsecars, of crowded sidewalks and restaurants.

After a sleepless night (the walls of our hotel might just as well have been made of paper like those of the Japanese pavilion at the Fair), we got up at dawn to the merry sounds of hawking and spitting, of yawning and groaning, not to mention a number of loud domestic quarrels.

Emma and I met in the hotel restaurant for breakfast, only to find that the groaners, hawkers, spitters, yawners and domestic battlers were already in possession. So with empty stomachs and nerves stretched taut, we proceeded through a fine hot drizzle to the depot of one of the three new steam railways that connect the city with Fairmount Park, where an entire new city has been erected on some two hundred acres. Thirty-eight foreign nations have each put up a characteristic building, as have the various states of the Union. A specially built railroad circles the Fair. It is . . . No! I shall save all that for the *Evening Post*.

At about 8:00 A.M. the clouds lifted; the sun shone; and we were able to find seats on the special railway car reserved for "honoured guests." I was well equipped with all sorts of documents, ensuring Emma and me the very best accommodations everywhere, as befitting the representative of the nation's most distinguished newspaper.

"It is like the Paris Exhibition." Emma was delighted by the splendid new exotic buildings. Many are *literally* exotic: built by Japanese, Turks, Tunisians; others because they represent the very latest in architectural styles.

The honoured guests were allowed to sweep past thousands of early arrivals who were waiting in line at the turnstiles. We chosen few (there proved to be four thousand of us) were then admitted to the south door of the Main Building. Here each of us was given a map of the seating arrangements in front of the Memorial Hall at the opposite end of the Grand Plaza. Emma and I had been placed just behind the presidential party, thanks to Bryant.

The Main Building covers twenty-three acres (I cannot keep out the statistics that have all day been poured into my head); it is made of glass with a central nave nearly 2,000 feet long. One would have the sense of being in the world's largest railway station were it not for the huge imperial eagles on plinths—and, of course, the exhibits.

With our fellow four thousand, we left the Main Building by the north door. Immediately overhead was a temporary platform built to support an enormous orchestra and chorus. Beyond the shadow of the platform was the Grand Plaza, a sea of gummy red earth ending in the grandiose Memorial Hall. Here wooden stands covered with miles of red, white and blue bunting had been built to contain the notables.

In the center of the plaza two colossal statues make hideous the prospect (for the *Post*, I shall be more tactful). One colossus is of Pegasus; the other is of an Amazon standing beside a horse slightly smaller than she. Emma thinks that it is not a horse but a big dog.

Once we had found our seats, the orchestra began to warm up, and the public was admitted. Some two hundred thousand people, I am told, filled the Grand Plaza. Certainly, it was a considerable mob. I was happy to note that the two dreadful statues were soon hidden from view by dozens of boys who seated themselves on Pegasus's back and wings, and on the Amazon's broad shoulders and thick head.

Our fellow honoured guests proved to be so distinguished that Emma and I spent the better part of an hour gawking, like country folk come to the fair. The entire diplomatic corps from Washington City was on hand, all aglitter with gold braid and orders. Baron Jacobi's costume was vaguely Hungarian; he waved his fur-lined cap at Emma. We decided that he had invented his own costume in the name of Bulgaria.

The Justices of the Supreme Court, the leaders of the Congress, the principal generals and admirals were all to be seen in the grandstands. Or nearly all. The very greatest of the personages delayed their entrances until the rest of us were safely seated and the crowd was more or less quiet and expectant.

"It is just like the theatre!" Emma was having a marvellous time. Particularly when, to the strains of some military march (*not* "Marching Through Georgia"), the erect figure of General William Tecumseh Sherman appeared. To much whistling and shouting, the General made his way to the empty presidential box. Like so many of our warriors and statesmen (at least in the early days of the republic), Sherman is red-haired. General Philip Sheridan was then applauded. So, too, was a genial-looking man in a frock coat. I asked the man sitting next to me (a member of the Pennsylvania Supreme Court) who this civilian hero was. "That's the Secretary of the Treasury, Mr. Bristow." My informant was obviously a Stalwart Republican; he did not applaud. The applause for Bristow was slow to get started (in appear-

ance he is an unprepossessing man, but he holds himself well, as
if certain of some unique destiny). Plainly aware that unlike the
famous warriors his appearance is less known to the crowd, Bristow paused in front of our grandstand and waited for the word
to spread throughout the huge muddy plaza, now entirely filled
with men in holiday black, with women in bright hats.

Gradually one heard, louder and louder, the sibilant in Bristow's name until the fervent applause of those nearest him was
taken up by concentric ring after concentric ring of humanity
until, at its crescendo, he turned to the people—his people-to-be?
—removed his hat, bowed, and took his place with the rest of the
Cabinet. Emma was amused. "The other Cabinet ministers don't
seem at all pleased. Look at Mr. Fish. He seems to be asleep."

"In an election year, all politicians dream of glory."

Then James G. Blaine was in the Grand Plaza, riding the mob's
thunder as if it were a wild horse to be broken. He waved his hat
as he turned to left, to right; bowed and grinned. No doubt about
it, between him and the people there is a powerful bond.

"He could sell the White House to a speculator," I heard myself
observe to Emma, "pocket the cash, and the people would still
love him." I do admire the man's audacity.

"It's because he is one of them. Because they'd do the same
thing if they dared but they don't dare because they know they'd
be caught and they know he'll *never* be caught!" Emma was
breathless from cheering Blaine. I saw Baron Jacobi watching her
with amusement—and watching with equal amusement me
watching the whole extraordinary spectacle.

As Blaine moved toward the grandstand the people almost
engulfed him; but then soldiers in blue swiftly formed a cordon
and pushed back the crowd.

Next appeared Dom Pedro, the emperor of Brazil, with his
empress. This eccentric gentleman has been for some time at
Washington incognito; although he is furious if any official pays
the slightest attention to him, he is even more furious when he
is not treated in a manner properly befitting the ruler of the
world's largest jungle.

Dom Pedro was very much cognito today and plainly over-
joyed by the sensation he caused. Bowing, smiling, waving, with
his white moustaches and goatee, he looks like an elderly version
of Napoleon III. As Dom Pedro is the only foreign chief of state
at the Exhibition, he is duly cherished by the mob for his conde-

scension. He is also in his element, for he loves science, and spent much of the day listening to a new invention called the telephone which makes it possible for two people at a distance of miles to conduct a conversation. "It talks!" Dom Pedro kept shouting.

We were then treated by the orchestra of Mr. Theodore Thomas to the national anthems of *thirteen* countries. The orchestra was very loud, and I am edified to have heard not only Argentina's "Marcha de la República" but Austria's "Gott erhalte Franz der Kaiser" all in one morning. Exhausted by so much patriotic ardour, we were not prepared for the next extraordinary effort on the part of Maestro Thomas, an "Inaugural March," especially written for the occasion by Richard Wagner.

"Astonishing!" murmured Emma. "Are there no American composers?"

"None so good apparently." As one who likes the new music, I think it amazingly intelligent, not to mention courageous, of the Centennial Committee to have given the commission to Wagner and not to some local sweet-singer. Emma prefers Offenbach.

Simultaneous with the beginning of Wagner's march, the presidential party came into view. To the sound of French horns, the President appeared with Mrs. Grant on his arm. As the music continued, the two little figures and their entourage took their places in the central box just below us. I was somewhat startled that the President's entrance had been covered by music, that he had not been allowed the sort of ovation the other great men had received. I soon discovered that whoever had planned the pageantry knew exactly what he was doing.

By the time the orchestra was silent, the presidential party was seated and a bishop was on his feet, speaking at awful length, as bishops will. This holy man favoured peace, commerce and God, in that order. When he sat down, the chorus treated us to a very loud hymn, whose words had been written especially for the occasion by the American poet J.G. Whittier, who piously hoped that America's future would be bright.

Next the head of the Centennial Committee made a speech, which, I think, turned everything over to the government; this was duly accepted, at some length, by a general. We were then obliged to listen to a very long poem by a Mr. Sidney Lanier, entitled *Cantata*. So badly was this long poem delivered that hardly anyone but me heard the actual words. Due to some acoustical vagary, I heard every line. Not surprisingly, the poet praised the United States. He, too, hoped for a better future. "At least we have American poets," I said to Emma, who sighed.

It was now close to noon. We were all beginning to wilt from the warm sun, from the odour of too many distinguished people too closely pressed together about us, from the relentless music, poetry, oratory.

Then the accepting general (must get his name; I've mislaid the schedule of events) spoke at length; he ended by presenting to the people their President.

General Grant got to his feet. From our seats just above the presidential box, we had an excellent view of his back. He moved slowly toward the lectern. This is the moment, I thought, in which all the earlier displays of delight will be surpassed.

Grant was now in full view of the crowd, the text of his speech clutched in one hand. He paused. He looked straight ahead. He waited. But there was nothing, nothing at all from the crowd: only silence, an absolute dead silence for the hero of Vicksburg and Shiloh, for the saviour of the Union, for the twice-elected President of the United States.

I saw Mrs. Grant turn suddenly to the person next to her; even in profile, and at a distance, one saw the alarm in her face.

For a long dull moment the President simply stood there, speech in hand. Finally, someone cheered him. Then a second cheer went up, which made it even worse, for after that there were no more cheers.

At last, in a resonant and dignified voice, General Grant read his speech, which was graceful and mercifully short. He even struck a modest note, a sound seldom heard in this self-regarding land. "While proud of what we have done, we regret that we have not done more." I think that this reasonable sentiment must have distressed his audience (it is usual for their masters to sing their praises), for when the President finished, the original silence that had greeted him was now replaced with quite a number of jeers, whistles, and booing.

Emma looked at me in amazement. "They have turned against him?"

"It would seem so."

"But I thought he was their hero."

"No one is a hero in this place for very long. Let's hope it will be Governor Tilden's turn to be hero next."

As we spoke, I caught a glimpse of Grant's face as he turned away from the mob to take his seat. Most of the distinguished guests were applauding him. In fact, the Emperor of Brazil was waving his hat over his head like a cowboy. The bleakness of Grant's face, however, was not altered by the applause of friends. He had just been given harsh proof that he had lost the people who once had worshipped him, and any hope that he might have entertained of continuing in office was now entirely at an end.

Meanwhile, a hundred-cannon salute was being fired and a huge American flag went up a pole at the center of the plaza, while orchestra and singers deafened us with the "Hallelujah" chorus. Then it was over.

Led by the presidential party, we moved on to Machinery Hall, which proved to be nearly as large as the Main Building. At the center of the hall is something very large called the Corliss engine. I have not yet found out what this machine is supposed to do (mercifully, the directors of the fair are providing us journalists with elaborate descriptions of the various exhibits), but I must say that the size of this double engine is most impressive; it is about six times the height of a man, made of some dark gleaming metal.

On a platform at the base of the machine General Grant moved into the place of honour, the Brazilian Empress on his arm; he was followed by Mrs. Grant on the arm of the Brazilian Emperor. Mrs. Grant looked very grim. General Grant's expression was, as usual, puzzled and withdrawn.

Rather dementedly, and certainly tactlessly, the Brazilian Emperor kept waving his hat in the air rather more times than was entirely necessary, emphasizing the uncomfortable fact that the crowd was deliberately cheering him and not the President.

At a signal from an official of the fair, the President and the Empress moved toward a . . . what? a small mechanical something. The President turned politely to the Empress, said something to her, and she, very firmly, pushed a valve. The huge engine began to pump away most impressively, if to no immediate or practical purpose that I could see. This was the occasion for more cheers, more waves of the Emperor's hat, more scowls from Mrs. Grant.

Then, like the sea receding from some mechanical or "automated" (new word) shore, we distinguished guests left the building and our distinctions behind in order to join the humble thousands, as well as Mr. and Mrs. William Sanford, who were gazing rather blankly at the nearby State of Pennsylvania Building.

Denise and Emma embraced like sisters united after years of separation. Sanford and I shook hands, our common distaste in abeyance for the sake of the ladies. Apparently, the Sanfords had also been in our grandstand.

"We saw you and I waved and waved but you never looked the right way!" Denise took one of my arms and one of Emma's. Sanford led us to Les Trois Frères, a re-creation of the Paris restaurant.

"I hear it's first-rate Provençal cooking." Sanford always knows whatever is best wherever he is.

"That means garlic, which I love," said Denise, in a most un-ladylike way.

"And truffles, which I love," I said, rather greedily, for we had had no breakfast.

"But truffles are from the Dordogne," said Sanford, wishing successfully to enrage.

The restaurant was already crowded, but a few whispered words from Sanford brought the maître d'hôtel over to Emma. In the rapid French of the *Midi,* he said how delighted he was to receive her, a countrywoman whom he had long admired. Emma was gracious. The rest of us were hungry, and the food was good though ridiculously expensive.

I asked the Sanfords where they were staying. "In the car," he said, as if I ought to have known. It took me a moment to realize what he meant. Like a number of other magnates who had not been able to find proper shelter in the crowded city, the Sanfords chose to sleep in their private railway car. "Just go to the Broad Street depot, and there we are," said Denise. "Next to the U.S. mail."

And to the depot we went, rather self-consciously, in full evening dress ("Giving a little dinner for Senator Conkling," said Sanford. "You both must come.") On a siding, we found the glossy, highly ornamented car of the Sanfords.

"Very odd, dining in a railway station." Emma was much amused; also much pleased to see Denise again. So, too, was I. We both found her unexpectedly glowing and happy.

Feeling a bit strange, we made our way into the long, narrow (what other shape?) salon of the railway car. A dozen guests were already assembled. Senator Conkling was not one of them.

"Deserted us." Sanford was cool. "There's some reception for the President tonight, and he thought he should go."

"We'll survive." Denise took Emma round to meet the guests. Sanford did the same for me. The gentlemen looked rather like the ones at Madame Restell's. The ladies were like those at Mrs. Paran Stevens's, which is to say they are handsomer than those at Mrs. Astor's but less brilliant than those at Mrs. Belmont's.

We were waited on most efficiently by two black butlers, and the small kitchen, or galley, of the car produced a surprisingly elaborate dinner. Had it not been for the occasional coming or going of a train, one might have been seated in any luxurious if peculiarly shaped New York dining room.

The lady next to me at dinner was large, elderly, coarse-looking, but with good eyes and a marvellous speaking voice that sounded hauntingly familiar. She spoke with delight of the Exhibition. "Two years ago I bought and learned to use the Sholes printing machine. That was the first of those many lovely new typewriters we saw today. Do you use a typewriter, Mr. Schuyler?"

"No. I am frightened of machinery."

"I am devoted to machines. They are so much more reliable than people."

I worried about her all through the evening. Was she an author? Another Mrs. Southworth? Why else would she own and operate a typewriter? She also spoke knowledgeably of politics. "I must say that I am surprised General Grant had the bad taste to appear at the Exhibition today. He was superb in the war, of course."

She was violently against slavery. She told me that she had lived at the South before the war; yet she speaks with an English accent. I could not begin to figure her out. Not until we were leaving did I discover from Denise that I had been talking to Fanny Kemble.

"The idol of my youth!" I was stunned. "Why, I saw her when she first performed in New York forty years ago."

Colonel Burr and I had gone to see her, and found her a marvel. She was the most extraordinary actress of at least two generations. When very young, she interrupted her career to marry a slave-owning Southerner. She was so appalled by the peculiar institution that she turned fiery author. She now lives in Philadelphia. Through ignorance, I missed an opportunity to talk of old days.

I did have a chance to talk of new days, with Denise after dinner (there was no lingering of gentlemen at table in that tiny dining room). Denise and I sat in a loveseat. Most of the others preferred to stand. One half expected a conductor to come through and ask for our tickets.

"Emma says she will come to Newport, Rhode Island, in June, *if* you agree. That means I must force you to say yes. I shall use any and every weapon."

I had not expected such a sudden assault. "But I shall be in Washington City then, and after that I may go to Cincinnati for the convention—"

"You are not going to drag Emma off to Cincinnati, are you? You would not be that cruel. And Washington in June is like Cairo in August."

"No, no." Actually I have been counting on Mrs. Astor to invite Emma to stay with her next month when I begin my deep plunge into the electoral process. But to date only silence from the roseate mystery.

Denise is delicate in these matters; guessed at my dilemma. "You're both coming to New York next week. So why not let Emma stay with me at the Brunswick. Then when you go back to Washington, she'll stay on with me until you know your plans."

"If she would like that, why, of course—"

"She does, and it's done!" Denise was luminous with pleasure at having got her way. I looked about for Emma, wanting confirmation. But she was not in the salon.

Denise saw my puzzlement; she put her hand on my arm. "Emma's with Bill. In the office." Denise indicated a door covered with red velvet. "Don't worry. We know what we're doing."

"I wish *I* knew what you two are doing."

"Well, it's for a good purpose. Oh, I can't wait for all of us to be in Newport together! It will be heaven on earth for me."

"For him, too?"

Denise smiled. "I must say, we . . . Bill and I . . . have never got on better. I can't think why. But then no woman is supposed to understand her husband."

"I think you've got *that* the wrong way round."

Denise suggested that I go into the office. "Quite by accident, of course. And see how the plot is progressing."

Somewhat baffled, I walked the length of the salon; tried not to step on toes in that small space.

Behind the red velvet curtain the office proved to be a tiny cubicle almost entirely filled by a mahogany desk, at which sat Emma like some corporation president; she was frowning most seriously at Sanford, who was sitting opposite her, his back to me. "You are certain it will work?" Sanford sounded anxious. "Absolutely." Emma's voice was firm. Then she looked up and saw me and smiled and said, "Papa, we are making presidents." Sanford leapt to his feet. He seemed agitated. "And presidents-to-be," she added.

"Your daughter wants me to jump into the arena."

"Only because I can't do it myself!" Emma rose. "It's so unfair, this exclusion of women." And she meant what she said, for, to my astonishment, she has succumbed to African fever just like Blaine and all the others.

On our way back to this sinister hotel, Emma told me of the plot with Denise. "Mr. Sanford knows I don't like him, and he knows how you despise him . . ."

" 'Despise' is too strong a word." Our conversation was a long one, since we were caught for almost one hour in traffic. The night was like daytime and very gala with thousands of revellers in the streets, mostly drunk.

"Anyway, Denise wanted me to charm him."

"I think you've already done that."

"The flowers? No. Or at least that phase of the charm ended when Denise and I got to be friends and he became jealous of the way we've excluded him, or so he thinks."

"And tonight?"

"Denise wanted me to prepare him for the summer. To make him like me."

"It is not often, Emma, that I sound like a father but all this —plotting is very dangerous."

"Dangerous?" I could not see her face in the half-light from a pair of gas lamps used to illuminate an advertisement for "I.L. Baker's Celebrated Sugar Pop-Corn Machine, at the Exhibition." Emma shifted to French. "I don't think so. Certainly Denise and I, we can handle him. I was, I thought, rather ingenious."

"Proposing that he go into politics one day?"

"Better than that. I thought he should go to work for Monsieur Blaine. I told him that, if necessary, I could help him—remove Senator Conkling from the race."

"The business with Kate?"

"Yes. She told me a great deal in the Rue Duphot."

I was shocked; and said so.

"Papa." Emma was firm. "You don't like Senator Conkling. Kate is no friend of mine. And I do have this already notorious passion for Monsieur Blaine. So why not involve Sanford? Will it work? he wonders. I said, 'Absolutely, yes.' Actually I don't care one way or the other. The point is to get him away from Newport during June while I'm there."

"You are—elaborate, Emma."

In the now three-quarter light from a theatre's marquee, she smiled, and squeezed my hand. "Don't worry, Papa. Your Governor Tilden is bound to defeat my Monsieur Blaine."

"So I pray. Certainly, I don't think your plot will come to anything politically. I can't imagine Sanford as a successful *intrigueur*. But if you can keep him away from Newport while we're there, you have my blessing."

Emma wanted to know if I approved of her staying at the Brunswick with Denise.

"I never give, never withhold approval where you're concerned. You're a grown woman. Do what you like."

"It will certainly save money."

"But will *he* be there?"

"Not if he gets involved with M. Blaine. And I think he will. I think he took the bait."

"It *is* a pity that you cannot be in politics."

Emma laughed. "I should probably be as big a fool as our Empress."

"What about John?"

The response was quick. "He can visit me as easily at the Brunswick as at the Fifth Avenue Hotel."

"And at Newport?"

"Denise will invite him to stay. 'I'll be your duenna,' she said. She is a marvellous woman, Papa. We are lucky to know her."

2

My piece on the Centennial Exhibition is finally finished and set in type. It was not easy to do, for Bryant is still very much the stern editor of my youth. Exhausting arguments over words, grammar, wit; the last is a quality he does not enjoy even on those occasions when he recognizes it.

"But surely, Schuyler, Cleopatra is *not* the most beautiful of all the exhibits. Everyone else says that the work is in bad taste."

I had written an apostrophe to the astonishing life-size waxen Cleopatra in the Annex. This popular exhibit shows the famous lady reclining on her barge, one waxy wrist supporting a stuffed parrot whose wings at regular intervals open and shut. The Serpent of the Nile is accompanied by pink wax Cupids whose heads turn from left to right while their mistress's eyes blink in a manner suggestive not so much of lust as of the early stages of glaucoma.

Bryant forced me to jettison a number of telling adverbs, and all irony. On the other hand, he found most interesting my account of the receptions for Grant, Bristow, Blaine. He listened attentively, sitting very straight at his desk: the Moses-head seemed all afire from a convenient sunset just back of him.

"We shall be meeting at your hotel tomorrow," he said, tickling one ear with the tip of his feather pen. "A number of—virtuous liberal Republicans. We are trying to find a way of salvaging our poor country's reputation."

"This might be done by voting for the other party."

Bryant sighed. Then: "I was at Albany right after Governor Tilden was inaugurated. He was kind enough to present me to the legislators, a truly generous act. You know, he is one of my oldest and dearest friends."

"But you cannot vote for him."

The magnificent head shook angrily. "That is not the point! I mistrust his party. And would like to revive the Republican party."

"With Bristow?"

"I know that many of our group prefer him to the other candidates. But Bristow will only accept the Republican nomination. He'll never run on a separate ticket, the way Greeley did. Bristow is from Kentucky, he keeps telling us, and so a party regular."

"Except that he is honest."

"What a terrible thing it is, Schuyler! Imagine demanding nothing more of a president than that he not steal money."

"How have things managed to go so very wrong with us?" I was genuinely curious to hear what Bryant would say.

"The war." The answer was quick, and already thought out. "So much money had to be raised and spent in order to put down the rebellion. And whenever there is a lot of money being spent, there will be a lot of corruption. The railroads have also made their contribution. The scramble for government grants, for rights of way, for the votes of individual congressmen. Well, it would take a strong man to say no forever to temptation."

"As you said no to Tweed." I cannot think why I was so tactless, even cruel. Could it be resentment at what he had done to my Cleopatra?

"I had no dealings with Mr. Tweed." The answer was smooth and oblique. But Bryant has been a famous public man for more than half a century and he cannot be taken by surprise. "At one time I believe the *Post* took some money from City Hall. But when your friend Nordhoff attacked the Tweed Ring in our columns, I was in no way disturbed. But then you saw his statement of April 21."

"Yes. He showed it to me before it was published."

"Then you know that he has said, categorically, that I did not let him go because of his attacks on the Tweed Ring."

"But *why* was he let go?"

"Other reasons entirely. But he is a splendid journalist and I compliment the two of you for what you have done in the way of illuminating Mr. Blaine. In fact . . ." And so on.

My other publisher is more to my taste. I met Jamie at five o'clock at the Hoffman House, in what is reputedly the largest bar room in New York. This congenial place is much frequented by the most elegant of the politicians as well as the sportiest of the magnates.

Back of the long bar hangs a huge painting by the French Bouguereau: ponderous nudes peek through bushes, all rendered in New York sepia. The bar itself is much gilded and medallioned, and not a square inch of ceiling or of wall is unmirrored or undecorated. I like it very much.

Before Jamie arrived, I visited the long table on which was arranged the city's most elaborate free lunch. After helping myself to a lobster salad very nearly as good as Delmonico's, I sat happily at a small table and drank a mint julep, and watched as the bar room began to fill with stout burghers.

I was in a mood of some euphoria (though—again—short of breath) due to a satisfactory visit to the Royal Havana Cigar Shop Co. just after my conference with Bryant. I don't know whether or not it is simply the fine spring weather but I feel very much the young journalist again, and quite disregard the ominous difficulty that I have in breathing on the sensible ground it will one day be resolved by my simply dispensing altogether with this monotonous and ultimately futile labour.

Jamie was relatively sober; and highly pleased with himself and me. He was still shaking my hand when a razzle-dazzle was placed in front of him by an obsequious waiter. Obviously Jamie's appearance in any bar in the city causes razzle-dazzles to form themselves of their own accord for the privilege of being poured down that youthful throat.

"I never thought you'd be such a winner, Charlie!"

"How flattering!" I was not pleased.

"No. No. I only meant you're usually so serious. So much a—historian." He said the word with true dislike. "And historians don't have snap. But you do. You smoked out old Blaine like a possum. Now he's in the open."

"Partly in the open."

Jamie frowned at the glass that had so recently been filled to the brim and was now, mysteriously, treacherously, empty. "You're right there. Listen, you're going back soon, aren't you?"

"Well, we had agreed on six pieces . . ."

"Charlie, I'm doubling your price, which was too high to begin with."

"You will turn my head, dear boy." And I turned my own head, having caught a glimpse of the elegant Collector of the Port and a few of his cronies.

"But you must go back before the end of the month. Then I'll want you to cover the convention at Cincinnati."

"I am too old to go to Cincinnati. Send Nordhoff."

"Can't. I'm sending him South. He's going to write about the cotton states and . . ."

"I don't know that I should speak to the two of you," spoke Collector Arthur, tall, smiling, brutally charming, with brown eyes aglimmer in the blazing gaslight (the Hoffman Bar is extravagantly lit all day and most of the night). We shook hands. The Stalwart cronies at the bar eyed us with disapproval.

"Chet, you're a Conkling man, ain't you?" Jamie enjoys politicians. But then, like Emma, he is spiritually African. "So be happy that Charlie here has gone and put Mr. Blaine in a pinewood box and sent him home to Maine."

"I wouldn't count on that, Jamie." Arthur beamed at both of us as if he truly liked us; his manner is not unlike Blaine's, though he lacks the master's irony and mischievous self-deprecatory style. "We're going to have quite a fine little dust-up at Cincinnati. Will you be there, Mr. Schuyler?"

"Indeed he will!" Jamie answered for me. "It's Charlie's dream to get to know the *real* America! The West. The rolling plains. The wide—uh, Missouri, isn't it?"

"I wouldn't know." The Collector gave a mock shudder. "For me it's all Indians west of Jersey City."

"Anyway tell Roscoe the *Herald*'s going to get him the nomination."

"He'll be delighted."

"And then tell him how Tilden will beat him in November."

"He'll be amused—to hear that. I hope to see you in Cincinnati, Mr. Schuyler."

The Collector joined his friends at the bar. "A good man, for a Stalwart. Don't think he steals too much at the custom house. But he sure knows how to collect money for campaigns. Charlie, I'm serious. I want you to write about the Indians."

I heard Indians as Africans and nodded; then realized that Jamie does not know of my joke with Emma; *then* realized that he had said "Indians." "What on earth is one to write about Indians?"

"They're out there, Charlie." Jamie pointed in the general direction of Madison Square. "They're wild, brutish. They hate the white man. Civilization. After Cincinnati, you take the cars to Chicago, then . . ."

"Dear Jamie, *you* take the cars. I have no desire to see the Indians or the West."

"But you'll go to Cincinnati. That's settled." Somehow he got me to agree that I shall return to Washington at the end of the month and then on to Cincinnati for the Republican Convention in the second week of June. "But after that I go to Newport. I am through with journalism."

"Surely, you'll want to see your friend Governor Tilden nominated at the end of June. And of course you'll be writing about the election in November. Are you absolutely certain that you don't want to look at the Indians in between?"

"As certain as I shall be of anything."

But Jamie was not listening; he was staring past me at the bar. I turned and saw that the stately Collector was talking intently with a dim-looking bearded gnome of a man. The Collector was leaning down from his great height as though eager, by diminishing himself, to elevate the little man.

"That," said Jamie, "is Jay Gould."

By cornering gold in '69, Jay Gould helped bring on the Panic of '73 that ruined so many of us. I was satisfied to observe that this true villain is as wretched a physical specimen as I have ever seen.

"I can tell you what they're talking about, too." Jamie waved for yet another of his terrible cocktails. "Chet is getting money from Gould for Conkling."

"Will Gould give it?"

"Of course. Did you know that the House is investigating Blaine?" Jamie's shifts in subject are swift. And one must be alert.

"There was talk of it. The Democrats . . ."

"They're meeting secretly now. It's going to be just like the Belknap investigation."

"Do they have anything *provable* against him?"

Jamie nodded. "If Mark Twain wasn't so rich, I'd send *him* West. He'd be good on Indians. Show their savagery. Brutishness." Jamie was now a bit drunk. "But he lives in Hartford. Can you imagine that? Mark Twain a Connecticut gentleman. It's too much. On the other hand, that last book of his didn't go over so well. Damn it, I'll try him. Why not?"

In the best of humours, I walked (next door practically) to the Fifth Avenue Hotel. The early evening was unusually fine, with bright stars appearing one by one over Madison Park. At this hour the handsomest and most expensive of the prostitutes cruise up and down Fifth Avenue, dressed in the highest fashion (they are, in fact, known locally as "cruisers" or, in low quarters, as "hookers" from the way the girls will suddenly hook arms with a likely-looking suspect). But I was tranquil, beyond lust, as a result of this afternoon's cigarine dalliance.

I went up to my single room, and found it rather lonely. Emma is now sharing the Sanford suite with Denise. Emma believes that Sanford has taken the bait and is even now at Washington making an alliance with Blaine. I hope so. I am not as confident of her ability to manipulate Sanford as she is. But whatever he is doing or not doing, at least he is away from New York, and Emma and Denise are like two school girls in the luxurious suite at the Brunswick where the Sanfords maintain *three* personal servants, housed under the hotel's eaves.

Tonight Emma made a journey into Apgar-land, and I dined with John Bigelow in Gramercy Park. Dinner was set for the two of us in his study. The family is at his place up the Hudson.

"When I'm here, there's no room for them. There's hardly room for me. All the comings and goings." He looked tired and strained. "This is the first time I've been alone all day."

"Not quite alone."

Bigelow was amiable; even produced claret for me as an Irish maid served us dinner. A vase filled with splendid purple iris made me sneeze uncontrollably but he took no notice. It's curious that in some years the pollen of certain spring flowers will bring on these attacks of sneezing, while in other years I am not distressed.

I accepted with my by-now habitual greed Bigelow's praise for the Blaine articles. I told him, using Nordhoff's secret face, "There is more to come. I go back to Washington in a fortnight."

"I cannot wait! Now if you'd do the same for Bristow . . ."

"You fear the honest man?"

"Actually, we fear no one at all. The Governor is going to be nominated, and he is going to be elected by a good plurality. But . . ." Bigelow frowned at the beef on his plate.

I sneezed into my napkin and softly blew my nose. I don't think he noticed.

"We're going to have difficulty carrying New York State." I found this hard to believe, but as Bigelow explained it, I see that there is indeed some danger for the Governor, whose assaults on Tammany Hall have not made him popular with the braves, particularly with the leader of Tammany Hall, one John Kelly who delights in the misnomer "Honest John." Kelly has vowed to make mischief at the convention. "And if he doesn't stop the Governor at St. Louis—and he won't—he'll see to it that Tammany will let the city go to the Republicans."

"What can you do?"

I was told at such elaborate length that I soon realized that there is nothing for the Tilden forces to do but hope to get so many votes elsewhere that the defection of Tammany will not matter.

"Outside New York we're strong. Also, to be attacked by Tammany will prejudice many in our favour. And we have the South. We have California. We also have an excellent Newspaper Popularity Bureau."

"I'm still ready to do the campaign biography."

"What you're doing now is far better. Anyway, we've hired someone named Cook, who's busy potboiling away." Bigelow wanted to know Bryant's mood because "He is an odd creature and never exactly where you think he ought to be."

Bigelow is also curious about the two hundred Liberal Republicans who are currently meeting at the Fifth Avenue Hotel. Many of them are literary men, and all of them are reformers with names like Adams, Lodge, Godwin. They are preparing a denunciation of Grantism. But "they're not ready to come over to us." Bigelow was sad.

"Even when—if—when the Governor is nominated?"

Bigelow nodded. "They really believe in the Republican party."

"So did you."

"But when it outgrew its original purpose, I left it. They should, too."

"Perhaps they'll nominate their own candidate, as they did the last time."

But Bigelow thought not, pointing out that when the Liberal Republicans bolted the party in '72 in order to nominate Horace Greeley (who was also nominated by the Democrats), Grant's victory over the forces of virtue was absolute. The American electorate deeply dislikes the idea of reform, of good government, of militant honesty. So let us hope this year they will see in Tilden something sinister, corrupt, American!

By the time our dinner was over, Green and a dozen other

planners and advertisement-concocters had arrived. After a decent interval, during which I saw to it that each person would have his chance to praise my articles on Blaine ("Powerful work!" Mr. Green nearly broke my hand, so fervent was his clasp), I took my leave.

3

AMARVELLOUS AND ENTIRELY RELAXING DAY that began with a noon rendezvous in the new Grand Central depot at Forty-second Street. This was the first time that I had been inside Commodore Vanderbilt's monument to a lifetime of triumphant rascality; yet it must be said in the old villain's favour that before he managed through theft, violence, and fraud to put together his railroad empire, a passenger from New York City to Chicago was obliged to change trains seventeen times during the course of the journey. Now, thanks to Vanderbilt's ruthless elimination of his rivals, the public is better served.

The huge building, with its mansard-roofed towers, looks rather like the Tuileries, whilst the vast interior is reminiscent of the buildings at the Centennial Exhibition. But large as the depot is, it was filled with hurrying people. Americans seem always to be on the move these days. In my youth, we stayed at home.

With some difficulty I found the Sanford car, where Emma and Denise were waiting for me (my luggage had been sent on earlier by the hotel).

The two girls— I can't think why I keep regarding these two women in their thirties as girls, but they seem so to me, and to themselves, too, from the most uncharacteristic (for Emma at least) way they giggle and whisper to each other as if just let out of school, no, convent, for a holiday in the country, which is exactly where we are now and what we are now doing.

There is a good deal to be said for being rich, particularly in this country. I begin to see now the reality behind my old friend

Washington Irving's memorable phrase "The Almighty Dollar." Not only is there a fascination in amassing huge quantities of money, preferably by illegal means and at the expense of everyone else in the country, but there is also the marvellous comfort and privacy that these riches confer. In Europe we are used to splendid houses, servants, "tong" by the ton, but a private railway car is something enjoyed only by an emperor. Here this luxury is quite common—at least in the high circles we frequent!

With a sudden jerk our car was attached to a train just after noon. As we were borne north of the city, the hauntingly beautiful Hudson River was ever in our view while we contentedly dined.

"It is really the loveliest river in the world," was Emma's sincere verdict, and I must say I, too, was overwhelmed by the sight of my natal river, viewed like a diorama from our moving dinner table.

By the time lunch was comfortably digested, our car was detached at the Rhinecliff depot. Waiting for us on the siding were Ward McAllister and a pair of grooms from the Astor household. In frock coat and silk hat, McAllister looked remarkably out of place in that green rustic setting.

Like an ambassador from one sovereign to another, he came aboard, full of compliments. "What a handsomely appointed car! Such good taste, Mrs. Sanford. Truly good taste."

McAllister touched the Brussels-lace antimacassars approvingly. I half expected him to examine the silver coffeepot for its markings. Then he told us that Mrs. Astor was "pleased" that we had made the arduous journey to stay with her at Ferncliff. "You will find a number of most charming people in the house. All friends, I am sure."

On that note, we climbed a great many steps (the town of Rhinecliff is indeed built on a cliff) to where the Astor carriage was waiting for us.

In solemn state we drove along a charming country lane lined with stone houses from our Dutch period as well as with the frame houses of our English successors. But "successor" is not the right word, since we Dutch are still a majority in this county. Our English *conquerors* is more like what they were—and still continue to be, though their predominance is now being threatened by the Irish and by the Italians.

At the end of a driveway lined with splendid elm trees was

Ferncliff, a large new mansion of *wood!* Emma was as surprised as I. No doubt the Astors thought to save money, since wood is in such ample supply. Even so, the effect is very odd.

As we approached the main entrance a sudden warm wind overpowered us with the scent of lilies-of-the-valley. For the first time Emma is beginning to feel—if not at home—at ease in this country, which until now she has regarded as, at best, exotic; at worst, provincial.

We were shown to comfortable rooms, each with a splendid vista through trees of the bright river far below, not to mention the railroad. The sound of the trains carries eerily well, and all the magnates who have built houses along this high cliff are forced to listen to the trains just the way the humble folk who live beneath the Sixth Avenue Elevated Railway are deafened at regular intervals all through the day. Unfortunately, Commodore Vanderbilt's trains continue through the night as well as the day and, perversely (at his orders?), they blow their whistles just as they pass beneath Ferncliff. But saving the trains, this is an idyllic house and setting. The guests are somewhat less idyllic and our hostess least of all. (I should have a padlock made for this book, but somehow I cannot see Mrs. Astor turning the pages, looking for references to herself). Yet she does her best—such as it is— to be agreeable, if not entertaining.

There are a dozen other guests in the house. I think we have met all of them before and I certainly know all of their names, but fitting names to faces is no easy task. Stuyvesant, who *ought* to be the plump, pink snub-nosed man, turns out to be the slender Italianate old man, and so on. Ward McAllister does all that he can to make things go easily and as a result, they do not, really, go at all. But the food is good and the neighbours who join us from time to time (all named Chanler or Livingston) are considerably more amusing than the house guests, not to mention the Mystic Rose herself, on whose left I sat on the first night.

"I cannot think how it all began." *She* began *in medias res.* "I like and have always liked James Van Alen." She fixed me with a stern look over the plate of pale hothouse asparagus that the footman was holding between us. I helped myself and quite agreed that James Van Alen is likeable, though I had not a clue as to what she was talking about.

"People make such trouble."

"That has been my experience."

"They *will* gossip."

"True."

"They will tell untruths, Mr. Schemerhorn Schuyler."

"I have heard them tell untruths, Mrs. Astor, and quite gratuitously, too."

She frowned, not liking, I suspect, the long word which no doubt made her think of overtipping.

"There was and has never been trouble between my husband and the Van Alen family."

"I should think not."

"We favoured the marriage."

"Naturally."

"Not 'naturally'!" She looked unusually roseate about the gills —to which were attached enormous pendant rubies. "Our Emily should have remained free a little while longer."

"Ah, Emily, yes." A newspaper account of the recent wedding of an Astor daughter surfaced through the miles of newsprint that my poor head contains.

"But she fell in love. Girls fall in love, Mr. Schemerhorn Schuyler."

"Boys, too." I wished to keep my side of the conversation as witty and vivacious as possible.

"I don't think they really do. Men are different. But we were pleased when James Van Alen became our son-in-law. And the rest is a tissue of lies."

"Envy, Mrs. Astor." I murmured sadly, easily resisting an impulse to pat her large heavily jewelled hand.

"My husband *never* said he did not want our daughter to marry into the Van Alen family."

"How could he? They are most distinguished."

This was the wrong response. The rose showed me a thorn. "There are those who might disagree. But"—the large hand resting on the highly polished mahogany table made itself into a very dangerous-looking fist—"not only did Mr. Astor *not* make the remark in question but old General Van Alen did *not* . . ."

At this high point in the drama a train passed beneath the house causing the crystals in the chandeliers to chatter. Those guests from elsewhere stopped speaking, while those native to the region continued to talk right through the long, mournful, deafening whistle, as did Mrs. Astor, thus leaving me in perfect suspense about what General Van Alen did or did not do, for by the time the train was gone she had turned to address her other partner at table.

After dinner, Ward McAllister (who had acted as host, once again *in loco Astoris*) explained to me what a scandal there had been in March, when General Van Alen was told that Mr. Astor had allegedly said, "No daughter of mine is going to marry into *that* family!"

When McAllister was out of range, a wild-eyed Chanler lady told me, "Of course Bill Astor said it. He was drunk. He's always drunk. And General Van Alen challenged him to a duel. But then, at the last moment, the duel was called off. Too exasperating!"

The wedding took place in Grace Church without incident. During the reception afterward Mr. Astor fled the city. So we amuse ourselves at Ferncliff.

4

A WEEK OF HEAVY EATING and, I fear, heavier company made bearable by the fine weather and the girls. Now it is time to go.

"So soon?" asked the Mystic Rose. She seemed genuinely displeased when I showed her the telegram from Jamie: "*Blaine to go before Committee They have got the goods You must go to Washington.*"

"Who is this Mr. Blaine?" asked Mrs. Astor.

I told her. I could not determine if she is really ignorant or if she simply prefers not to acknowledge that politicians exist. I should note that not one member of the house party admits to having read my articles for the *Herald*. But then, of course, the *Herald* is not really a respectable newspaper and perhaps they mean to do me a kindness by not mentioning my shameful connection with it. The talk is of food, clothes, horses, servants, children, arrivals and departures. Like money, the arts are never mentioned. Unlike money, the arts are never thought of.

Mrs. Astor has taken to Emma and they have long grave conversations under the elm trees. But when I ask Emma what they talk about, she just laughs and says, "I have no idea. She declares things and I agree to her declarations."

Although Mrs. Astor does not go visiting in the neighbourhood except on state occasions, we are encouraged to drive about, visiting Chanlers and Livingstons and the rest of the gentry whose estates adjoin one another on a forested bluff high above the river and the railroad. Some of these county seats date back to the eighteenth century and are very fine—like Clermont, the principal Livingston house. Most, however, are new, and in the heavy, gloomy Gothic style made popular hereabouts by the novels of Sir Walter Scott. Thank God, Scott is unknown in France and we have no Gothic revival, only the Gothic itself (I'm beginning to sound like Flaubert's idiot: it is the company I keep).

After lunch, McAllister, the girls and I drove north along the river road to a charming estate owned by some people whose name I never learned but whose house is a fine example of the Greek style that was so popular in my youth. Six tall columns form a portico that overlooks a sweep of lawn ending in willow trees and the Hudson River. The house is beautifully proportioned, with a north wing consisting of a single octagonal room two storeys high and lit by a glass cupola that must make it unpleasantly hot in the summer and impossible to heat in the winter.

But none of this matters to the owners. "We are simply camping out, that's all," said our hostess, a vigorous middle-aged woman who had greeted us in front of the house. "We're never here any more. We've given up. What's the use—" She was interrupted by a noise rather like an explosion close by, then a deafening shrill whistle.

We looked and saw just back of the house one of Commodore Vanderbilt's monsters: some thirty freight cars jerked and rattled past as smoke and burning cinders erupted from the locomotive, making a huge cloud that obscured half the sky.

During this visitation even the natives did not speak. We stood mute, motionless, as ashes fell about us like a dark rain.

"It is Vesuvian," said Emma, for once tactless in her surprise.

"Would that it were!" said our hostess. "Then the place would be covered with lava and we'd never have to come back. It's all the fault of my husband's father. He said, 'Oh, how marvellous!' when they wanted to put the railroad through. 'It'll stop and pick us up whenever we want!' Well!"

Poor woman, another fine place blighted by this railway age.
But between trains the prospect was delicious, and we strolled
contentedly about the lawn in the company of a most sensitive,
wide-eyed, rather plump young man from, I think, Boston. "I
read you faithfully, Mr. Schuyler." We were standing beneath a
willow tree at the river's edge. The smell of rank river mud
mingled most agreeably with the scent of lilies. Across the silvery
water the delicately irregular line of the pale-blue Catskills was
like the flourish beneath Washington Irving's signature.

"You are the first reader I've met, my dear sir, in this valley."
I did not mean to sound petulant, but I fear that was the impression I gave. Quickly I modified my tone. "But then one cannot
expect the gentry to read the *Herald*."

"I fear the *Herald* is perfectly beyond me, too, if I may say so."
The young man's manners were exquisite. "No, I have read you
on Turgenev, on Flaubert; read you with passion, let me here-
with confess."

"Well, I am pleased . . ." But I got no further. A torrent of
praise for me and for the French writers quite engulfed me and
I was ravished by so much understanding. The young man is a
writer—of course! Who else would find Turgenev interesting in
this awful age—and country—of Mark Twain and Mrs. Southworth? My young admirer writes for the *Atlantic Monthly*; he will
send me his newly published first novel before he goes "to live
in Paris, the sort of life *you* have led, Mr. Schuyler."

"I am hardly a worthwhile model." He made so bold as to
contradict me, and in an ecstasy of communality we crossed the
lawn to the hostess (she is in some way his relative) and a group
of valley neighbours.

Everything was most casual, and there was to be, I soon saw,
no shape to our visit. I did notice a servant setting up the ap-
paratus for tea on a table beneath a small sort of hut.

When my young admirer was detached from me by the hostess,
Emma and I strolled through a grove of locust trees, of all trees
my favourite, particularly now when they are in bloom and their
white petals are everywhere, causing me—this spring at least—
to sneeze constantly. I am only able to get through the meals at
Ferncliff with the aid of smelling salts. I must say that between
the sneezing and the smelling salts, I have yet to taste anything
that I've eaten.

"Denise wants me to go on from here to Newport."

"We are getting to be true New Yorkers of 'tong.' We discuss only travel plans."

But Emma was thoughtful. "I don't think John likes the idea."

"He will come, too, won't he?"

"Not until the end of June. I think he'd rather I stayed in New York."

"I give no advice." I have often said, and always believed, that my success as a parent is based entirely on this indolent rule.

"Then there are the children. Should they come over before or after the wedding." This is a subject that we have both been avoiding. When I last saw my eldest grandchild he was not only taller than I but had the beginnings of a precocious moustache. At fourteen he looks a man; fortunately, his eight-year-old brother will look more suitable in the role of putative ring bearer or cherub-in-attendance at Grace Church. Yet I have been somewhat disturbed at the prospective tableau of Apgars in serried ranks, staring at Emma, the magnificent young bride, as she is attended by a young Frenchman who looks to be more than half the groom's age. It is a delicate matter.

"Would the Sanfords take the children?"

"Oh, yes. Denise insists, in fact. But then . . ."

"But then . . ." We think alike, as always.

We now found ourselves on a retaining wall at the river's edge. In the shadow of a willow tree stood a gazebo so divided into four sections that a couple seated in one section would not be observed by those in the other three. Slowly we walked around the gazebo. In the section that faced the river two figures were entwined most lovingly.

Emma gasped. The figures quickly separated. A shocked second as the four of us stared at one another; then we all burst out laughing and Denise and Sanford got to their feet, looking as confused as guilty lovers.

"I suppose," said Denise, "our behaviour would be considered very wicked in Paris."

"Quite the contrary," I said. "You would be put on permanent exhibition at the zoo. The loving *married* couple. People would come from all over the world to look at you."

It appears that Sanford arrived today in his car. Not wanting to interrupt lunch at Ferncliff, he had come here to see old friends, intending to present himself to Mrs. Astor this evening. Denise had discovered him, "Quite by accident. I was in the

garden over there when he leapt out at me from behind a lilac
bush, clapped his hand over my mouth and said, 'I'm a veteran,
ma'am, a Union soldier, and I'm going to . . .' The rest you can
imagine."

"How exciting!" Emma beamed her pleasure, but as soon as the
loving couple moved on ahead of us, she frowned, was pensive.

"Did you know he was coming?"

"No. I don't . . ." She did not finish the sentence. We stopped
a few yards from the tea hut, where a dozen guests were gathered
about Sanford, apparently spellbound by one of his performances.

"You don't what?"

"I don't trust him." Between Emma and me fell a single white
locust petal.

"Does it matter that *you* trust him?"

"For Denise's sake, yes, it does matter." She was herself again.
"But it's none of my business. We must be neutral, as you always
say."

"But seldom am."

I found Sanford unusually boring, even by his previous high
standards. But he did bring news from Washington. "I was with
Mr. Blaine on several occasions." He sounded quietly important.
We were in the carriage on our way back to Ferncliff, the light
of the setting sun making a green fire of those leaves that come
together like a roof over the river road.

"What does he say about the secret investigation?"

"That it's a secret, ain't it?" Sanford cackled, like a Union
veteran tramp-rapist. But seeing the look of dismay—disgust?—
on my face, he assumed his grave statesman's voice, rather worse,
all in all, than the tramp's. "Blaine says they've got nothing on
him except some letters that aren't incriminating but might be
twisted about. He's going to be nominated. We've seen to that."

Emma and I exchanged a quick glance. Denise was half-asleep,
head resting on her husband's shoulder. Sanford, as far as I can
tell, knows nothing useful.

Before dinner tonight, Emma and I met in the large drawing
room; the others had not yet appeared. Masses of flowers everywhere made lovely the great room whilst causing my mucous
membranes to swell. Although the smelling salts stop the sneezing, I am beginning to feel most odd, and wonder if, in time,
they'll stop the heart, too.

"I think you should go on to Newport with them," I said, giving that advice which I am celebrated for never giving.

"I would like to go with you back to . . . to . . ."

"To the jungle?"

"To the zoo! I am pining for Mr. Blaine. But I agree, I think it's best I go with Denise." Without thinking, Emma started to re-arrange a vase of perfectly arranged Madonna lilies. "She needs looking after."

"What are you afraid of?"

"If I knew, I would warn her." This was swift. "I've just written John—with her permission—asking him to come to Newport as soon as possible."

"For protection?"

Emma nodded. "In a way, yes. Also, it will look better. One needs, at times, a counter . . ."

"A pawn?"

Emma gave me a sidelong mischievous look, "Oh, no, a knight, and a knight's gambit often takes the queen."

Ward McAllister sailed across the room, gorgeous in evening dress. "I have won a great victory, my dears! We are having *old* champagne with the shad! For years the Rose and I have argued. *I* say that ten-year-old champagne is superb with fish, particularly if it is flat as can be—the wine, not the fish—so, secretly, I smuggled several cases into the house and this afternoon she agreed, at the eleventh hour, to let it be served! Isn't it terrible what the trains have done to that lovely house?" With McAllister there are no pauses in conversation, unlike his Rose.

I was again at Mrs. Astor's side, and she declared that she would be sad to see me go. "Your beautiful daughter, too. The Princess is a charming addition to society. And quite my favourite *distant* cousin."

I got the subject as quickly as possible from our dubious cousinage. "But then, we shall see you at Newport next month. We are staying with the Sanfords."

"You *were* to stay with me." Accusation in her voice; emeralds upon her poitrine.

"Perhaps another time."

"Why is she marrying . . . I have forgot the name?"

"Apgar." Although Mrs. Astor is perfectly aware that the Apgars are related to almost everyone she knows, she has decided that they themselves are not yet knowable. The Astorocracy is stern: Vanderbilts and Belmonts are too glossy, Apgars too numerous and dim. "They are in love. And as you said yourself, girls do fall in love."

For the first time in our acquaintance, I saw in Mrs. Astor's face a look not only of intelligence but even of humour. "Oh, yes. That's right. I did say that." She took a sip from her glass and made a face. "I *hate* old champagne. How am I to tell Mr. McAllister?"

I am packed and ready to take the morning train from Rhinecliff (gone are my regal days of private cars). I have just said good night to Emma, who will not be up when I leave.

We talked of the Sanfords, and of how they have managed in some mysterious way to get themselves at the very centre of our lives. Emma's attitude toward Sanford is openly hostile, and I can only put it down to straightforward jealousy. She wants Denise for herself. I find all this perfectly acceptable if surprising, since Emma has never before had a close woman friend.

I have just thrown the vial of smelling salts out the window. I am sure it was responsible for the alarming stops and starts of the heart that I have been experiencing during the last few days.

Nine

1

NORDHOFF'S FACE is no longer secret. "We've known for months about Mr. Mulligan."

I write this on my lap, seated in a crowded committee room of the Capitol. Mr. Mulligan is testifying, or was testifying a few moments ago. I am so hemmed in that I can barely write in this book. Against the wall, opposite me, sit the members of the special committee charged with investigating Blaine's financial arrangements. A majority of the committee is Democratic, and scent blood. The chairman is a hard-faced man called Proctor Knott.

Just beyond me, Blaine is seated in the front row; Garfield beside him. Nordhoff is behind me, bony knees gouging my back; his sharp barks punctuate the speeches of Blaine's defenders, a beleaguered minority.

James Mulligan is from Boston. I still don't know who discovered him. But he is a plausible, deliberate sort of man, an accountant, who once kept the books for Warren Fisher, creator of the now infamous Little Rock & Fort Smith railway. Some minutes ago he told the committee that a director of the Union Pacific named Elisha Atkins told him that Blaine turned over $75,000 in Little Rock & Fort Smith bonds to the president of the Texas & Pacific, Tom Scott, who insisted that the railroad give Blaine $64,000 for the worthless bonds.

I think I have got this straight. There have been so many interruptions. The Republicans on the committee make it as difficult as they can for Mulligan to testify. Blaine also interferes; from time to time, he whispers to one of the committee members.

Procedural matters at the moment. Speeches. Nordhoff just whispered in my ear, "More to come."

I whispered back, "So far it's Mulligan's word against Blaine's."

"Wait."

Not long to wait. A Democratic member of the committee has just asked Mulligan if he has any correspondence that might be relevant to the Blaine-Fisher connection.

Blaine sits up very straight; the ears are now paler than his face. Beside him Garfield slumps.

The members of the committee seem not to know what to expect. One is trying, pitiably, with weakened teeth to bite off a large chaw of tobacco.

Mulligan clears his throat. Looks about vaguely. "Well," he says at last, staring at the still-intact plug of tobacco. "Yes, sir. I do happen to have some . . . I mean, a number of letters from Mr. Blaine to Mr. Fisher . . ."

But Mulligan's voice is drowned in the sudden uproar. "Liar!" a man shouts. There is some hooting, some cheering. Blaine is now on his feet, talking to a member of the committee who then whispers something in the ear of Chairman Knott, who meanwhile is banging his gavel for silence. The appearance of sergeants-at-arms quiets the room.

The chairman says, "It has been moved by the ranking minority member that this committee be adjourned until tomorrow . . ." More shouts from the audience: fearful that we would be robbed of our drama, and we were.

The motion was seconded, and on a narrow vote was carried. The committee stood adjourned. Blaine slipped out a side door. I am now back at Willard's, writing this late at night. No doubt about it, even for a non-African, this was a most exciting day.

I had dinner with the Garfields even though I feared that

amongst the guests would be Madame García, whose passion for me is like some prairie fire quite out of control in the subequatorial pampas, assuming that a pampas is not the same thing as a prairie.

My fears were justified. Once again the huge black eyes flashed their terrible invitation whilst the four breasts heaved in near unison whenever she looked my way, which was often.

"I prayed to our Lady of Santiago that you would return, and our Lady has answered my prayers!" So Madame greeted me.

"My own cup runneth over," I said, rallying as best I could. Fortunately, Garfield drew me to one side. "How are things with your friend Tilden?"

"I suspect he will win."

Garfield frowned. "That would be a terrible thing, you know. Not that Governor Tilden is not an honourable man," quickly added. "But if he does succeed it will be due to a damnable combination of former Confederates, Catholics and the whisky interest."

I was amused by Garfield's sincere bigotry; and liked him no less for so perfectly reflecting the prejudices of his class and party.

We were eight at dinner, and to my surprise one of the eight was Puss Belknap. "I think she has suffered quite enough," said Lucretia Garfield, in an aside to me. "Poor Puss," she added on principle.

"I have so missed you and your lovely Emma!" Puss was in excellent form. "I will never, truly *never* forget the way you two rallied round me in my hour of agony, which still goes on, of course."

"Will there be a trial in the Senate?" I have not been keeping up with the Belknaps as I should.

"Oh, yes!" Puss was bitter. "This is an election year, remember? And the Democrats will do *anything* to blacken us, which is why my angel will go on trial next month even though, as Senator Conkling himself said only the other day, the Senate has *no* jurisdiction at all because my angel is no longer a member of the Cabinet. Oh, they wish us to know the very depths of disgrace, the absolute bitterness of martyrdom!" But for all Puss's Southern rhetoric, she seems to be enjoying herself; in any case, there is little likelihood of the Senate obtaining the two-thirds vote needed to convict.

"Now, of course, that demon from the lower depths, that Mr. Bristow, is after Mr. Blaine, who is as honest a man as ever served his country in the halls of Congress."

"I am certain of that." Puss did not notice my small joke. She blames all of the Administration's troubles on the ambitions of Bristow combined with the savagery of the Democrats.

"Why, it is a positive duty of a congressman to help those railroads which have made this country of ours what it is today. Of course Mr. Blaine may have been a little bit careless, now and then, along the way, 'cause he's got no head for business, you know. And he certainly made a big mistake when he took that mortgage for his Fifteenth Street house—a very good investment, by the way—from Mr. Jay Cooke."

This was startling, I have just mentioned the matter to Nordhoff, who will look into it; he was suitably grim; he believes there is no end to Blaine's corruption. At times I wish that I could take all of this as seriously as Nordhoff does. But I cannot. I regard the politics of the country as an ongoing comedy, which, this evening, has suddenly sheered off into wildest farce.

After dinner, while the gentlemen were still at table and working their way through a quantity of madeira, a messenger arrived for Garfield, who excused himself. From the parlour I could hear Madame García not only thumping out on the upright piano a ballad of unrequited Argentinian love but singing as well in a voice as piercing and as brazen as Fate, *my* fate.

Garfield returned; handsome face very thoughtful. We were expectant.

"What news?" From a Western senator; long white beard stained with tobacco juice.

"I suppose everyone will know by tomorrow." Garfield sat down; manner most grave. "A note from Mr. Blaine. This afternoon he visited Mr. Mulligan at his hotel and they had a—well, a sort of reconciliation. Anyway, Mr. Blaine is now studying the letters and . . ."

"Mr. Blaine has got the letters in *his* possession?" I was not certain that I had heard right.

Garfield nodded. "Yes. Mr. Mulligan was—obviously—most agreeable. Certainly he realized the importance of those letters to Mr. Blaine, not to mention to the leadership of our party and, of course, to the whole country."

The Western senator applauded. "That Blaine has got more nerve than any man I know."

"Well," said Garfield, as though quoting Cicero, "a pound of pluck is worth a ton of luck." I think he meant what he said, assuming that he was listening to himself.

I could not wait to tell Nordhoff, who was waiting for me in the bar at Willard's. As usual, Nordhoff knew even more than I. "I've just been with Mulligan. God never made a greater fool." Nordhoff was not entirely sober—something very rare with him. He was also in a state of fury.

Apparently, "Mulligan was having his hair cut in the barber shop at the Riggs House when Blaine appeared. Needless to say, their conversation was overheard." Nordhoff is a great one for getting people to tell him what he wants to know, but then he has often likened himself to a detective on the trail of a kidnapped heiress; in the present case, the heiress is the republic itself and the abductors are the duly elected representative of the people.

"Blaine said, 'Well, you're an enemy of mine, I see.' Then Blaine recalled that Mulligan had worked as a bookkeeper for Blaine's brother-in-law and once, in a dispute between the brother-in-law and Mulligan, Blaine had ruled against Mulligan. Clever of Blaine to bring that up. Setting the stage in advance. Establishing malice." The black waiter brought us yet another round of whisky—I now have a terrible headache. Incidentally, I find it curious that the sneezing has stopped altogether. But then the season is later here than in the Hudson Valley and the pollen —or whatever it is—has gone away.

"Blaine then conferred privately with Mulligan. There were no witnesses. Shortly afterward I spoke to Mulligan—we have a friend in common."

"Imaginary?"

A brief yelp. "Almost. Anyway I was able to get him to talk. Not that he made much sense. He just stood there in the lobby of the Riggs House, looking as if he'd been struck on the head with a rock—something I'd like to do to him.

"How did Blaine get the letters from him?"

"Tears. Appeals to patriotism. To the flag. Not to mention an offer to *buy* the letters."

"How much?"

"Blaine does these things with style, and with the Treasury's money. He offered Mulligan a consulship."

"Good God!" I thought for an instant nostalgically of my old rank, conferred on me by President Van Buren simply because

we were half-brothers. "So he accepted the consulship, and
Blaine got the letters."

Nordhoff shook his head. "He got nothing at all. Or so he
swears. Oh, he did get Blaine's promise to return the letters after
he and his lawyers have studied them. I ask you, Schuyler, has
there ever been such a beguiling monster as Blaine since the
Serpent in the Garden?"

"Surely Mr. Mulligan does not expect ever to see those letters
again."

"How—how—how does he do it?" Nordhoff slammed his glass
hard on the bar, alarming the Negro waiter. Fortunately we were
the only customers in the room.

"Obviously he is a clever man. And, obviously, he means to be
president."

"No! Never! He's trapped this time."

2

I AM SITTING in the press gallery of the House of Representatives. Despite the crowding, I am fairly comfortable and able
to write without too much difficulty. All the galleries are filled.
Most of the Senate has converged on the floor of the House;
senators are sitting, standing, leaning. The whole country is waiting for Blaine's speech.

It is now June 5. In nine days the Republican Convention will
meet at Cincinnati. If Blaine is to be nominated, then today's
speech must be the most eloquent, not to mention plausible, of
his remarkable career. There is a sense of history being made in
this chamber—certainly, of theatre.

I have already sent off one piece to the *Herald* describing how
Blaine got Mulligan to give up the letters "for temporary
perusal." Needless to say, Blaine has not only refused to give the
letters back to Mulligan but he has also refused to present them
to the committee. He is now in danger of being held in contempt

of Congress, and there is even a movement amongst certain of the
more rabid Democrats to have him expelled from the House of
Representatives. To every question of "why" and "what" and
"how," he has said, "Wait until Monday."

Well, it is Monday . . . And Blaine just appeared on the floor.
Republican members of both Houses surround him. There is
much shaking of hands, pinching of arms, whispers into those
large now-rather-red ears. Blaine is poised and serene.

Blaine has just looked up at the press gallery. When he sees me,
he touches his jaw and winks, reminding me of the extracted
tooth and the other speech not heard by me. He waves to various
friends in the gallery. He sits at his desk. All eyes upon him as
he slowly removes from inside his frock coat a thick packet. A
long exhalation of breath throughout the chamber: *The Letters.*

Casually Blaine places the packet on top of his desk. A sudden
expectant hush in the House (I am now writing this back at
Willard's). It was, suddenly, the moment.

Blaine stood up, and the Speaker, Mr. Kerr (a sickly man recently accused of having sold a cadetship to West Point), recognized the honourable gentleman from Maine on a point of personal privilege.

Blaine began pianissimo. He spoke, sadly, of partisanship in
the House. He felt obliged to remind us that two members of the
committee which had been hounding him had seen service in the
rebel army during the late Civil War. This brought forth a few
jeers from Southern members, and some louder ones directed
against the Southerners by Republican partisans. Mr. Kerr
pounded for order.

Blaine struck his usual note: false charges are to be expected
when the fevers of a terrible conflict still course through the body
politic. Because of his notorious love for the Union, he has enemies. He knows it. He forgives them.

Letters. Blaine spoke warmly of the sacred and inviolable nature of private communication between gentlemen. What was
meant for one man's eyes was no business of any other man on
this earth. He made this somewhat dubious assertion sound as if
it were the very foundation of the American Constitution and of
all civilized law.

But then Blaine's voice began to rise, and his face turned as
scarlet as his ears. The black eyes burned. The voice rumbled like
an organ as stop after stop was pulled out. "I have defied the

power of the House to compel me to produce these letters. But I am not afraid to show the letters." I write this from memory, and must paraphrase. "Thank God Almighty, I am not ashamed to show them." He picked up the packet. "There they are!" Blaine held the packet above his head for all to see. "There is the very original package. And with some sense of humiliation, with a mortification I do not pretend to conceal, with a sense of" —and the voice now sounded like a trumpet when he let loose the word—"*outrage*, any man in my position would feel, I invite the confidence of forty-four million of my countrymen while I read these letters from this desk."

It was a delectable, impudent performance. Blaine read here and there, skipped about, commented on this and that—all with such apparent candour, such a confiding *honest* manner, that as we listened, even those of us who are convinced that James G. Blaine is one of the most gorgeous villains in American life, we were, one by one, swept along with the man.

Although a child of nine would have known that Blaine was reading us only what he chose, it made no difference. One could have listened to that righteous yet charming voice by the hour. And by the hour we did, until I was aware that my left leg had lost all sensation, that I had been too long cramped in the same position. At that exact instant, Blaine, as if in perfect harmony with my leg and consequent diminution of attention, slammed down the letters on his desk, as if thoroughly weary of the whole matter.

"Enough! The letters are now part of the record of this Congress for the world to read. But will my persecutors continue in their sordid task? Will they?"

Blaine turned dramatically to the aisle that separates Democrats from Republicans. He pointed to Proctor Knott. "You, sir, are the honourable chairman of the committee that has shown so much interest in my affairs, even to my most private, most sacred correspondence. I trust you are satisfied." A good stroke *not* to pose a question but, rather, to make a statement.

Blaine then said that his innocence hinged on the word of one Josiah Caldwell in London. Blaine asked Chairman Knott if he had heard from Mr. Caldwell.

Knott rose, obviously irritated. He said that he had not been able to obtain Mr. Caldwell's address.

Blaine: But did you receive a despatch from him?

Knott: I'll answer that in a moment.

Blaine: I want a categorical answer.

Much tension in the chamber: all eyes on the two men.

Knott: I have received a despatch *purporting* to be from Mr. Caldwell.

Now Blaine moved swiftly for the kill. When did the cable arrive? Why was it not admitted as evidence? Knott stammered. Blaine roared, "You got a despatch last Thursday evening at eight o'clock from Josiah Caldwell, completely and absolutely exonerating me from this charge, and you have suppressed it!"

Blaine sat down to the most extraordinary demonstration. Republicans were on their feet roaring his name. Rebel yells from many Southern Democrats. Gavel pounding from the Speaker. Cries from the ladies' gallery . . .

Nordhoff and I walked slowly back to Willard's. The day was hot and overcast. Heat lightning flashed at the far end of Pennsylvania Avenue. Nordhoff was in despair. I was elated, the way one is after a good—no, great—performance in the theatre. "It is all bunkum," was Nordhoff's verdict. "Caldwell means nothing. The cable was probably a fixed-up job. The letters make no sense, as he read them."

"Sense has nothing to do with such—music! What *sense* is there in Wagner?"

"The letters will eventually be printed. And they'll show that he is guilty as sin."

"But he'll be nominated nine days from now. There won't be time to stop him, at least not with Mr. Mulligan's letters."

"Perhaps. Have you seen this?" Nordhoff showed me a letter in the form of a circular, signed by Tilden as chairman of the New York State Democratic party, and dated October 27, 1868. The text was a request from Tilden to the various Democratic county leaders to telegraph as soon as possible what looked to be the vote in their area to William M. Tweed at Tammany Hall. "The object being to let Tweed know how many false votes he would have to provide to counteract the Democratic losses upstate."

"I understand, dear Nordhoff, the object of the letter. I also suggest that it is a forgery."

"So your friend Tilden says. Anyway, we're in for a lively campaign."

3

I AM IN *Cincinnati*. I cannot think how Jamie got me to make the
trip. After all, the Associated Press does this sort of reporting
far better than I. But here I am, after a sleepless night in the cars.

A room at the Gibson Hotel had been prepared for me but
when I discovered that I would be obliged to share it with three
members of the Indiana delegation (and only two beds), I made
my way, pathetically, valise in hand, along the steep streets (the
city is built on a series of bluffs overlooking the Ohio River) until
I came to a solid blue limestone building with what Mrs. Grant
would call a "piazza," and threw myself on the mercy of the
family, whose head, a man of my age, proved to be a native of
Wiesbaden in Germany.

"Half the town is German," he told me, pleased to be able to
speak his native tongue. From my bedroom (three dollars a day),
I have a fine view of the Miami and Erie Canal, known to the
natives as the Rhine; the area where the German population lives
is referred to as "over the Rhine."

Today was the first day of the convention. Armed with various
identifying documents, I presented myself at the huge Exhibition
Hall at Elm and Fourteenth Street, and mingled with the press
and the delegates while avoiding, as much as possible, the oratory.
The party is now assembling that platform on which the eventual
nominee must stand or run or fall or whatever. The issue that
most grips me is monogamy for Utah. Many otherwise quite sane
politicians become livid at the mention of the Mormons, a curious
sect recently invented by a "prophet" and confined for the most
part to the Utah desert, where Mormon women live in harems
and breed incontinently. They sound very nice to me, if overly
energetic.

I have just learned that a group of New York Stalwarts headed
by "Chet" Arthur has been in town for almost a week, preparing

the way for Conkling, who is supported not only by the New York delegation but by some fifteen hundred eager workers, wearing blue badges.

In front of the Gibson House a FOR PRESIDENT, ROSCOE CONKLING sign has been hung just below that of the New York Reform Club, an elegant high-minded group of some sixty gentlemen who have been in the town for several days, elegantly and high-mindedly working for Mr. Bristow.

"But the man to watch," according to Nordhoff, whom I found earlier this evening in the bar of the Gibson House, "is Oliver P. Morton." This gentleman is a senator from Indiana, an enemy of Conkling and popular at the South. If Conkling and Blaine stop Bristow and then each other, Morton is expected to win. There are a number of other minor candidates, known rather glumly as "favourite sons"; these include the governors of Ohio and Pennsylvania.

4

I AM MUCH EXCITED, despite my better judgment. We are in Exhibition Hall. On the platform sit various party leaders. None of the candidates is visible. Apparently, they never are during a convention. They stay at home, awaiting the people's summons.

Conkling's name and face are everywhere displayed. The New York delegation has taken over the Grand Hotel, which they have decorated with a huge, not very subtle banner that warns: "Conkling's Nomination Assures the Thirty-five Electoral Votes of New York." This sign has inspired everyone to quote a recent remark of Blaine: "Conkling can't even carry his own state against Tilden. His candidacy is an absurdity." There is also a good deal of gossip about the Senator and Kate Sprague. In fact, a pamphlet on the subject has been distributed to each of the delegates. Sanford at work?

Blaine is the man of the hour—as of this minute. I am not
listening to a very long nomination speech in favour of a former
postmaster general called Jewell. The oratory, so far, has been
tedious. The interior of the hall is stifling; but now the sun has
begun to go down, and we are a bit more comfortable.

Rumours abound. The latest: Blaine is a dying man. Last Sunday Blaine arrived at a church in Washington and fainted dead
away. Sunstroke, his followers say. Something worse, say the
others, naming all sorts of enticing diseases, each in its terminal
phase. Most likely of the diseases is committee-itis. By appearing
to be ill, Blaine has obliged the committee to postpone its investigation until after the convention. Then, worried, that he might
be thought moribund, Blaine appeared in public with Secretary
Fish the day before the convention. During this outing one of
Blaine's sons was heard to remark, "This ought to have a right
good effect in Cincinnati." So it has had.

According to the program for today, we are to be favoured with
sixteen speeches, putting in nomination the various leaders. I
drink bottle after bottle of sarsaparilla and eat handfuls of popped
corn, a novelty I have unexpectedly developed a liking for.

Late afternoon. None of the speeches has caught fire, nor has
any of the candidates. Nordhoff tells me to pay particular attention to a young Illinois lawyer and politician named Ingersoll. He
will nominate Blaine, if the current speaker ever sits down. According to Nordhoff, Ingersoll is a proud agnostic, something not
easy to be, I should think, in God's very special Illinois wilderness.

Ingersoll is reputed to have said, "Calvin was as near like the
God of the Old Testament as his health would allow." I warm to
him.

Warm to him? Ingersoll has set me afire. It is now a half-hour
since Ingersoll stopped speaking, yet the demonstration for
Blaine continues. Although I am immune—allergic to political
oratory—I have never heard such a performance, nor has anyone
else. I cannot recall a line of what he said—only the tone, the
fierce exultation. How primitive we are at best.

The Blaine forces are calling for a vote, but the chairman of the
convention has just announced, "I am informed that the gaslights
of this hall are in such condition that they cannot safely be
lighted." We adjourned on account of darkness. Blaine's forces

are in a rage. They blame the chairman. The followers of Bristow. The city of Cincinnati.

June 15. The first ballot has just been taken. I am somewhat ill, after an all-night drinking session with the New York Reform delegation: elegant high-minded drinking, may I say, in the Gibson Hotel bar. Although eager for Bristow to win, the Reformers agree that had the balloting begun last night Blaine would have swept the convention, or as the editor of *Harper's Weekly* said, "There has never been a better speech than Ingersoll's in a worse cause."

The phrase of Ingersoll that everyone quotes (save me: was I listening or just hearing?) is his reference to Blaine as "the plumed Knight." I suppose my ear rejected this image because of its silliness. Blaine is many marvellous things but hardly a knight; if anything fabulous, he is more dragon than plumed knight.

To be nominated, the candidate must acquire at least 378 votes. The result of the first ballot was inconclusive . . . except for Conkling, who got only 99 votes and is now no longer a serious candidate. Blaine led the field with 285 votes; then Bristow, 213; Morton, 124; Hayes, the governor of Ohio, 61; Hartranft, the governor of Pennsylvania, 58; Jewell, Grant's former Postmaster General, 11; and somebody named Wheeler of New York, 3.

Word is now spreading that Conkling is about to withdraw. Who will get his 99 votes?

"Morton," says Nordhoff. "Certainly not Blaine. Ever!"

5

THE REPUBLICAN NOMINEE for president of the United States is one Rutherford Birchard Hayes, three times governor of Ohio, a general of no distinction in the late war, and a man entirely unknown to most of the convention that has just nominated him. When I came back to the house and told my host the news, he said, "The Governor is honest but a bigot. He is always campaigning against the Catholics." My host is a Roman Catholic. "Even worse," said the good man from Wiesbaden, pouring us each a mug of beer, "he is a Son of Temperance, and would outlaw alcohol."

I have spent most of the night preparing my piece for the *Herald*. It is not easy to say exactly what happened after Conkling's collapse on the first ballot, but as far as I can tell, *in*exactly, Blaine not only held his own but continued to gain support until, by the sixth ballot, he had 308 votes. During this time, Morton mysteriously declined while Bristow's candidacy never took fire.

At some point between the sixth and seventh ballots, the anti-Blaine and pro-reform groups decided to drop Bristow and Morton and to take their chances with the dim governor of Ohio. On the seventh ballot New York abandoned Conkling to support, for the most part, Blaine. Yet the final vote was Hayes, 384; Blaine, 351; Bristow, 21. The anti-Conkling New Yorker Wheeler was then selected as vice-presidential candidate. Roscoe Conkling is now as dead politically as his friend Ulysses S. Grant.

Nordhoff assures me that one of the chief reasons behind the last-minute coalition to support Hayes is that he is willing, unlike Grant, to withdraw Federal troops from the South, and allow that febrile region home rule.

6

I am literally breathless from too much crisscrossing of the country. Governor Tilden's doctor has come and gone, and although he did nothing of a constructive or curative nature, I feel somewhat better, no doubt due to an enforced rest here in a most pleasant suite at the Delavan House in Albany.

It is now June 27, and I lie in bed, scribbling these notes. The Democratic National Convention is meeting in St. Louis, without me.

Jamie was upset when I told him that, first, I had no intention of going to Fremont, Ohio, to interview Rutherford B. Hayes, who is, this morning's paper informs us, fifty-three years old, five feet eight inches tall, and weighs one hundred and seventy pounds—which is plainly wishful thinking on the part of the Governor, who must weigh, according to his photograph, about two hundred pounds; he has a long grizzled beard, an aquiline nose, and a fierce gaze. I have no desire to meet him, nor, as I told Jamie firmly in the bar of the Hoffman House, "have I the slightest desire to go to St. Louis."

"But, Charlie, you made Cincinnati sound so exciting."

"It was. But St. Louis will be boring. Tilden will be nominated on the first ballot." I have become extraordinarily glib in my political pronouncements—the result, I suppose, of the excellent response to the last few pieces from Washington and Cincinnati, but then my style, as I continue to impress on Jamie, is only as good as the price he pays me. Lately, my words have been winged.

"I shall compromise, dear boy. I'll go to Albany, and write you a piece on Tilden's reaction to his nomination."

"Reaction? How does a dead fish react to anything?" Jamie drank his third razzle-dazzle in one long swallow. "You should have done those Indians, Charlie. By God, I had a hunch and I was right."

"And I was right to come straight back to New York. I have no intention of losing my scalp, not even for the *Herald*." This was the day that every newspaper in the country was filled with the lurid details of a brutal massacre by Sioux Indians of some two hundred Federal troops at a place in the Far West called Little Big Horn. Amongst those killed was a Civil War hero (Northern side) named General George A. Custer, whose book *My Life on the Plains* was a fair success a year or so ago.

As usual, General Grant—I almost wrote "poor" General Grant—is being held responsible because of Belknap's famed retrenchment at the War Department. In any case, the country talks of nothing but the victor at the Little Big Horn, a chief of the Sioux nation called Sitting Bull and of his colleague Chief Rain-in-the-Face who cut out the heart of a young Federal officer and ate it.

"It's a pity you didn't engage Mr. Mark Twain to report on the Indian tribes."

"You know, I never tried. Damn it! And I should've. And he'd have gone. I'm positive. Great God, what a story I would've had, with him to write it!"

"Or, better yet, to be the *subject* of a story. 'Mark Twain Scalped'—I see the headline now—'An Exclusive to the *Herald* by Sitting Bull.' What joy you have denied us, Jamie!"

That day I took the cars to Albany; had dinner with two of Tilden's aides (Bigelow is at St. Louis); lost all my breath during the fish course; turned quite blue and was put to bed—and here I am. Everyone has been most considerate. Tomorrow, just as the balloting starts in St. Louis, I shall be with the Governor, waiting for the news.

7

THE LONG CRUCIAL DAY has come and gone. I *seem* in good health. At least, I have no trouble breathing. My legs, however, are curiously weak, and every now and then I see, for just an instant, objects mysteriously and disagreeably doubled. Tilden takes a tremendous interest in my symptoms, which is flattering when one considers what this day has meant to him.

At noon I drove up to the Governor's house in Eagle Street. The house is a comfortable if rather gloomy affair, the sort of place that someone retired from the wool trade might have built. Not surprisingly, Albany is much changed since I was last here forty years ago. On all sides new "Gothic" buildings are going up while the charming old brick Dutch houses are coming down.

I was shown into the drawing room, though I suppose the word "parlour" suits better the taste of the retired wool merchant. I was greeted by the Governor's sister, Mrs. William T. Pelton, born Mary Tilden. She and her husband are living with the Governor. In fact, "my husband found this lovely home for my brother just after he was elected governor. Would you believe it that they have no governor's house up here? Which means that the poor governors must rent whatever they can find. It's not at all expensive," she added, as though I had asked. Mrs. Pelton is an amiable woman, with a face very like Tilden's except that her colouring is a pleasant pink as opposed to his distinctive grey.

"Do sit down. The Governor's with Mr. Carter, a lawyer from the city. They're working ever so hard but they'll be down for lunch. You know Mr. Green, don't you?"

Green approached, with his usual forceful stride. This time I allowed my hand (to his visible disgust) to go absolutely limp, and so avoided the rolling and crushing of my old delicate bones. "Mr. Schuyler, we've been deeply impressed by your articles in the *Herald*."

"You're very kind." But, alas, this praise was cut short by the arrival of a messenger boy from the state capitol, the first of what must have been a hundred such interruptions in the course of the day. Green glanced at the message, thanked the boy, and sent him on his way.

"Is it from St. Louis?" During the day, Mrs. Pelton's attempts at emulating her brother's sang-froid grew less and less convincing. She was enormously excited, and showed it.

Green nodded. "Nothing very interesting yet." He turned to me. "We've got a special telegraph line at the capitol, direct from St. Louis to the Governor's office. But, as you see, he's spending the day here."

"I do wish he'd let *me* sit by the wire." Mrs. Pelton started nervously as a servant dropped a dish in the dining room.

"I'm surprised the Governor should be practising law today of all days."

Green looked at me gravely, spoke slowly, to make absolutely certain that I got the story entirely straight. "It's not by choice, Mr. Schuyler. There is a very complicated legal suit in which Mr. Tilden figures. A highly technical civil suit that goes back to the days when he was actively practising law. Mr. Carter is now handling the case but needs the Governor's help, his advice, his recollection of the intricacies of the suit." Green continued to explain, and I used this restful interlude to take, surreptitiously, my own pulse; I found it only a little fast.

Then Tilden and Carter joined us. The Governor looked no more tired than when I saw him last. He was entirely at ease and showed none of the excitement that the rest of us kept betraying in small ways. Green bit his knuckles during lunch when there was nothing else to bite; while Mrs. Pelton fussed with the servants, and Carter kept remarking, at large, "The Governor's concentration is truly amazing! Amazing! He recalls *every* detail of the case, after all these years."

The principal actor in this high drama was very much as always. He nibbled his biscuits, drank his tea, took his pills, controlled as best he could his belches while asking most solicitously about my health. But for once that ever-attractive subject did not hold my attention. Like everyone else, I wanted to know what was happening at St. Louis.

"Yesterday was most lively, I'm told." Tilden was mild. " 'Honest' John Kelly arrived with one hundred and fifty loyal Tammany men, dedicated to my defeat."

"He's mad. And a villain!" Green was properly partisan.

"I doubt if he'll do us much harm." Tilden did wince as a plate was dropped just back of his chair. The maid fled in confusion. Mrs. Pelton sighed.

"But surely," I said, "you and Mr. Kelly were once allies."

Cold eyes like those of a fish behind the glass of an aquarium turned my way. "It is true that Mr. Kelly supported me for governor but . . ."

"Kelly's demands!" Green answered for his leader. "The patronage he wanted! The criminals he proposed for jobs."

"Hardly criminals. At least"—the curiously shaped upper lip arched to make the smallest of Tilden's small smiles—"they must be presumed innocent until found guilty. Looking back, I see now that it was inevitable that we would one day come to a parting of the ways. But I am surprised at his bitterness."

"Did you know that he arrived in St. Louis with a banner saying 'Tilden Can't Carry New York'!" Green bit first a knuckle, then a roll.

"I shall carry New York." Tilden's voice was soft, his face quite hard. "If I am nominated, of course," he added with another miniature smile.

"You know, Mr. Schuyler, our common friend President Van Buren used to say that he never knew anyone with as little ambition as me."

"He was not known as the 'little magician' for nothing."

"Meaning his magic wand touched me, and here I am?" Tilden looked amused. "But now tell us about General Hayes, Mr. Schuyler. After all, you come to us straight from the hurly-burly of Republicanism."

"I know nothing more of him, Governor, than what I have read in my own articles, and that is very little."

"One would have preferred an out-and-out true-blue Republican villain, like Blaine." Tilden looked for a moment sad. "General Hayes *appears* to be an honest man."

"But no reformer!" This from the loyal Green.

"No. There will be only one reform candidate this year." Tilden swallowed a pill. "I find it most curious that Hayes *appears* to be repudiating General Grant. That was very pointed of him, wasn't it? When he said he would definitely *not* seek a second term—if elected of course."

"I don't think the occasion will arise!" Mrs. Pelton was not to be left out of the discussion. "What's happening now? This very minute. At St. Louis?"

Green looked at his watch. "Nothing. The convention has recessed until two o'clock. Then when the balloting begins . . ."

"Mr. Carter and I will be trying to find our way through a most complicated legal labyrinth." With that, Tilden and Carter withdrew, and I accompanied Green to the hideous state capitol, where we spent most of the day in the Governor's office, reading on ticker tape the constant stream of messages from St. Louis.

Finally, late in the day, the balloting began. To win, Tilden needed 492 votes. On the first ballot Tilden got 404 1/2 votes; Governor Hendricks of Illinois got 140 1/2 votes; the remaining hundred odd votes were divided amongst five candidates.

I sat next to Green. He had a small notebook in which he kept careful count of each state's vote.

"Will he win?" After all, Blaine had been in the lead until the favourite sons' votes had gone against him. The same thing could happen to Tilden.

But Green was confident. "He's going to win right now. On the second ballot." So we sat in the ornate executive office until nine-thirty in the evening, staring at the ribbon of paper as it extruded numbers.

It was all over on the second ballot. The first numbers came through: Tilden, 508, Hendricks, 75 . . . but by then there was pandemonium in the office, and Green and I hurried back to the house in Eagle Street to congratulate the Democratic nominee for president.

Green had hoped to be the first with the news, but someone else had already told the Governor. Tilden was in the parlour, holding a cup of tea in his left hand while well-wishers shook the right hand.

I stood with the lawyer Carter during this tableau, and he told me that when their work was done in the early evening, "The Governor said, 'Let's go driving,' and I said, 'Aren't you afraid the news will come while you're away from the house?' And he said, 'We will know at exactly nine-thirty.' Uncanny, isn't it? Anyway, he drove me himself all about the town and I must say that I feared for my life. The horse was lively, but the Governor paid no attention to it. Instead he spoke quite beautifully of what the next president must do, with me all the while ready to jump out of that carriage if the horse should bolt. When we got back and the word came that he'd been nominated at nine-thirty, just as he'd predicted, all he said was, 'Is that so?' "

As the room filled with more and more people word came that the state capitol had been illuminated, that a brass band was playing, that the people had assembled to see "the president-to-be." So Tilden and his party got into several carriages, and we drove to the capitol.

I sat opposite Tilden and found him, for the first time, impressive. Toward the end of lunch, I had asked him why he had not joined the Republican party, since, politically, he is little different from the Bryants and the Adamses. Someone had interrupted us, and he had not been able to answer—had not wanted to answer, I thought. But now, without prompting, Tilden returned to the subject, his voice less and less audible as the noise of the band at the capitol grew.

"I was never a Republican, Mr. Schuyler, because those gentlemen you mentioned, distinguished as they are, have only one real interest, and that is the making of special laws in order to protect their fortunes. I know. In my day I was employed by them as a working lawyer. I also know that they have no compassion for the masses of the people in this country who are without money and who are, many of them, thanks to General Grant and his friends, without food or houses. I have always thought that only as a Democrat, reflecting Jefferson and Jackson—and our common friend Van Buren—could justice ever be done the people because, at this moment in history, ours is the only party which is even faintly responsive to the force of ideas. That is why I mean to do my very best to fire a majority of the people with a desire for true reform. I also have every intention of succeeding. To fail now would be cruel and unthinkable!"

I was deeply impressed not only by this statement but by Tilden's power of concentration, and recollection. With a band playing, a crowd cheering, fireworks exploding, the nomination for the presidency in his hand, he took the time to answer me eloquently, even passionately, considering his habitual coolness.

Is it possible, I wonder, that in this gaudy centennial year these states have produced a great man? I am half convinced that such is the case, and unless the people of the country are even more stupid than one suspects, there is not a chance of Samuel Tilden, in the name of reform, failing to be elected nineteenth president of the United States.

Ten

1

I HAVE, MOST HAPPILY, mislaid July, lost every single day of it in a sea-brightness that fair dazzles me. The world of little men pursuing power seems far away. I dream quite other dreams in this lotus sleep, induced by the high summer scent of peonies and of roses, of sea-salt spray.

Idle days succeed one another like blue Atlantic waves on Newport's seaweed-strewn lion's-skin-coloured beach. Oh, let me stay here forever upon (or even under) these marvellous moist green lawns, in the shade of serious old trees whilst the dulcet voice of Ward McAllister sounds in my ear throughout all eternity, giving me his darkey's receipts for terrapin, for black stew Baltimore or Trenton (add cream, butter), cooked in a chafing dish.

Jamie sends me urgent telegrams. Colonel Pelton wants me to join the Tilden "Speakers Bureau" and exhort the public in the small towns of the republic. But I plead ill health, having never been in better form—form in the mental, *not* in the corporeal sense, for my legs are weakening, I am too fat, and my lungs give every indication that the effort demanded of them will soon be

too much, not to mention the monotony of in-out, in-out. But
accepting the fact that I am in my penultimate phase, I have been
entirely content—until perhaps this afternoon, when something
very like a cloud crossed our gilded Newport sun.

We were invited by McAllister for a picnic. This is an occasion
much looked forward to by the Newporters, because McAllister
does take pains, and to echo the style of Mrs. Fayette Snead
known as Fay, there are many pains here to be taken.

A special train left at noon from the town to McAllister's place,
Bayside Farm; another train at 4:45 P.M. returned us from farm
to town. The journey to Bayside takes exactly six minutes and is
an occasion for much good cheer as Watteau ladies pretend to be
Breughel women, each carrying a single dish as her chef's contribution to the picnic.

Emma, Denise, John Apgar and I joined the other revellers.
The Mystic Rose was indisposed, but there were enough minor
Astors to give "tong" to the day. McAllister's cottage is not much
more than a farmhouse which makes it unique, for at Newport
"cottage" means mansion, like the Sanford palace (built by
Denise's father), a white and grey marble replica of the Grand
Trianon, half again as large. Here twenty servants look after us,
and Saint-Gratien seems cottagey by comparison. I have, incidentally, just received a charming but sad note from Princess Mathilde. She complains that too many of our friends have had the bad
taste to die. She is quite right to be indignant.

Sanford is mostly on his yacht. When he does visit us, he speaks
warmly of his old friend General Hayes, and I suppose that they
must, by now, have met. Lately he has been threatening to take
us on a cruise but Denise has said, firmly, no.

John Apgar has been with us for ten days, and goes back to
New York Monday: "To work. All the family is now in Maine,
except me." If John is resentful of the way Emma has elected to
spend her summer, he has said nothing to her, or if he has she has
not repeated it to me. Although, on occasion, I see him looking
down or, rather, up the Apgar nose at some element of grandeur
that would not be in good taste south of Madison Square, he takes
well to Sanford luxury.

Today the girls were very much *en fleur*, at least, at the beginning of the picnic. McAllister greeted us effusively. "Fish off the
rocks, do! Catch us a lobster." And some of the guests actually did
take fishing rods and sat on the rocks, impersonating fishermen.

Others strolled about McAllister's farm—a real farm with real tenant farmers got up for the day to look like honest yeomen, but, thank Heaven, their sly, disgruntled Yankee faces quite nullified McAllister's feudal intention.

Denise and I sat beneath a tall shady tree, and drank a well-chilled '74 champagne brut. Emma and John walked arm in arm to where a small orchestra played waltzes and couples danced on a raised platform. The women of the farmers' families arranged the various dishes on a long trestle table beneath a grape arbour.

"I like John." It was the first time Denise had mentioned to me her—rival? No, that confuses rather than defines an odd and delicate relationship between two women, neither of whom has ever before had a woman friend. Although Denise did tell me of a first cousin back in New Orleans "who was like my sister, the way Emma is now. Only she died when she was seventeen. Of the bloody flux, as they call dysentery in the South. Too terrible! I thought I'd never get over it, her dying. But I did."

"John is devoted," I said. That's really the best thing that one can say of him. "And I like him, too . . ."

"I think they'll be happy. I hope so, anyway."

"What does Emma say to you?" I was deeply curious. On the subject of John, Emma tends to obliqueness.

"Very little." Denise opened her eighteenth-century fan and stirred warm air redolent of new-cut grass and cow. "It's a pity we can't go on like this forever."

"More pity for me, my girl." I took her hand. I treat her like a daughter but could easily be her lover—well, not easily. Nothing on that order is easy for me now, but in my day . . .

No! I must confine myself to the events and non-events of *this* day, which is so evidently not to be mine. "I'm the one who wants to make time stop. I don't want any part of the future. Just let me have this present frozen forever in"—since my eye was on the buffet table I fear that instead of saying "amber" I said—"aspic."

Denise laughed until her face was quite scarlet. Then we drank to our future *en gelée*. "Bill has found an interest, thanks to you."

"Not me."

Denise shook her head. "No. You've done it. I don't know how. He wants to prove to you that he's . . ."

"What?"

"Worthwhile. Powerful. All the things he pretends to be. Not that he couldn't be any of them, mind you. And I think that he will be. Now."

"And *I* have been his inspiration?"

Denise nodded. "He respects you. He's a little afraid of you. And he wants very much to impress you. As do I."

"You are good—to *say* that." Looking at her in that—oh, for a superior word! lambent?—light framed in that fragment of time already lost as I write this late at night, I had the terrible sad sense that I would never be so happy again with anyone whom I so much—not loved, for that word is too suggestive of pain, not to mention banality—delighted in. She is twin to my Emma, but not, like Emma, a part of me and therein lies a world of difference, tempering beautifully response.

But, as always, interruption. Denise was led away by McAllister. Emma danced with a minor Astor connection while I walked slowly amongst the rocks at the sea's edge, my arm through John Apgar's arm—a gesture that looked to be more affectionate than it was, because with my curiously weakened legs I do fear falling.

"Are you enjoying Newport, sir?" The question suggested that a negative softly sounded might strike an Apgar note. But I chose to sound enthusiastic; praised the sea, weather, cottages—and Sanfords.

"Oh, *she* is very nice. In fact, her father . . ."

"Is a connection of your family. Yes!" I was perhaps too swift in cutting short Apgar genealogy. "It is nice for Emma to have a friend like Denise." I stopped to catch my breath, to watch the gulls and sailboats. For an instant I could not tell which was which. A trick of perspective combined with bright summer's vivid sea and sky had so eliminated the horizon that distant sails and gulls' wings seemed all the same: free-moving bits of white in a blue creation.

"Mrs. Sanford has been more than kind." John cleared his throat. I sat down carefully on a rock; breathed deeply, deliberately, filling lungs with sea air, the best of tonics. John unfolded the largest white handkerchief that I have ever seen and spread it on the mosses and the lichens beside my rock; then he sat cross-legged and looked up at me, his Adam's apple mysteriously bobbing up and down, as regularly as Mr. Corliss's steam engine and to as little evident purpose.

"But you would rather Emma had gone to Maine."

"The family had expected it, of course. But I can see how this must—amuse her more." Wanting, I think, gently to condemn, John merely sounded wistful. Although an Apgar, he responds as any young man might to the rich pleasures of this place as opposed to what must be the rather austere arrangements at Maine.

"Emma is a foreigner in a strange land, and though she has her father, and her husband-to-be"—I managed a sweet smile for my son-in-law-to-be—"she is still without friends, without any sense of belonging. Denise—Mrs. Sanford"—I must stop making this slip—"has given her that sense, has given her true friendship, and women, dear boy, need each other in a way that we can never understand." I let fall this nonsense with impressive gravity, like a newly engraved brick found at the base of Sinai.

"I hope," said John, astonishing me, "that I don't lose her."

"What makes you think there's any danger of that?"

"This is not the life . . ." He gestured at the handsome picknickers strolling amongst the rocks, dancing beneath the trees. "I mean we are very different in our family."

"Has Emma said that she does not—enjoy your family?"

"No. No. She is an angel, as you know. She is most tactful. And most self-contained."

I cannot think why I have got into the habit of thinking John stupid when he is not. I suppose his social limitations and want of imagination have misled me. He is an acute observer in matters that concern him (as who is not?). "I don't, I hope, betray a secret, John, when I say that both Emma and I rather hope that you will, perhaps, consider seriously the possibility of one day living at Paris." There. It was said.

John's response was swift and, to a point, heartening. "I would like nothing better. And I've told Emma that repeatedly." I find it curious that Emma has never said a word of this to me. She has remarked, from time to time, that it might be possible one day to persuade John to come to Europe, but she has never told me that he is actually *eager* to make the move.

"But your family . . ." No need to finish that sentence.

"My family would survive." This was very dry; and rather disloyal to the Gens Apgar. "But it would take some arranging. I would have to separate my share of the estate from that of the Brothers. I would also have to find employment."

"But surely the estate is sufficient?" I shall soon be like one of those Americans who goes about asking everyone how much money he has.

John ever so slightly winced at my crudeness. "I mean, sir, I cannot be idle. I must practise law or do something useful."

"Of course. Of course." I was encouraging, spoke of various American and English law firms with offices at Paris.

John interrupted me. "I know, sir. I have even made inquiries. But when I talk about all this in any detail, Emma seems not to be interested."

"But I assure you, she is!"

"That's not my impression. She is—I don't know. Drifting out to sea, as they say." And confirming the metaphor physically, he hurled a piece of juniper wood toward the rocks. It vanished in the foam of a breaking wave.

Somewhat alarmed, I did and said all that I could to reassure him. I think I succeeded. At least he was more cheerful as we made our way back to the picnic, to the music, to the champagne, to Ward McAllister's excited anecdotes of the various great personages he has peeped at. Apparently, he once was allowed to watch, from a pantry at Windsor, Queen Victoria's private dinner table being set.

I had it out with Emma after dinner. Denise did not join us; sent word that she had had too much sun and picnic. So we dined *à trois* in the cavernous dining room.

After dinner we went into the drawing room and Emma played Offenbach while John and I smoked cigars (we had been given dispensation by Denise). Then John went to bed early. Tomorrow he goes to Providence to do business, even though it is a Sunday. Emma and Denise will, as usual, go to early mass while I will, as usual, lie in bed until noon.

When John had gone, I told Emma of our conversation at the rocks. She listened intently, still seated at the piano. Finally, she sighed and said, "Well, is he right? Am I drifting away?"

"You must tell me."

Emma did scales. Not my favourite sound. "No." She spoke very precisely. "I feel the same way about this marriage as I did when it was first proposed."

"Perhaps *that* is what John fears."

Emma glanced at me, with half a smile and half a frown. "I keep my bargain, Papa." She shifted to her native language, where she is entirely at ease with every nuance and where I am at ease but doomed to a slow decorous correctness, unlike my conversation—and behaviour—in English.

"What have you done, to make him uneasy?"

Emma struck chords. "It is probably what I've *not* done. In affairs like this, there is supposed to be some sort of progress. Well, he has moved and I have not. I've stayed the same, from the beginning."

"All things considered, that is not abnormal. But he is more intelligent than we think."

"Oh, Papa! Of course he is. And I'm not intelligent at all, as you must've noticed in our thirty-five years together."

"Thirty-two, *chérie!*" That is the age we have agreed is most plausible, given the accursedly premature moustache of my oldest grandson. "And you are as intelligent as a doting father who was himself—" I was going to say "son to a doting father," meaning Colonel Burr, but stopped, for she still thinks me the son of James Schuyler, the cuckolded tavern keeper of Greenwich Village.

Emma had just begun a new set of scales when Denise's maid entered—a thick-boned, good-hearted woman from the Auvergne. She was very red in the face and out of breath. "It's Madame. She wants you. She's not well."

Emma hurried after the maid, and I sat alone in that dim summery drawing room and wondered how and by what route I have come to be who I am, old, derelict, unreal to myself, a victim of the sheer incomprehensible randomness of living, and of the atrocious running out of time. Why am I I, and not another? Young, not old? Or unborn, rather than (result of a most random conjoining) made flesh and deposited in a hard world, to flourish, mate, and now presently to die.

This sombre train of thought was made even worse by Emma's visit to me here in my room half an hour ago. She told me that Denise's doctor had come and gone.

"What is it?" I asked. "What's wrong with her?"

Emma looked weary. She has been with Denise since dinner and it is now midnight. "She's pregnant, Papa."

I felt my own stomach contract, as if in sympathy. "But I thought she could not have a child, ever."

"So did she. So did everyone. But Madame Restell . . . You know who I mean?"

"Yes, my dear. I have even met the infamous lady."

"Well, Madame Restell says that with proper rest, and a new concoction—to be taken every day, to relax the muscles, or whatever—Denise can have a normal childbirth."

"Then what was the trouble just now?"

Emma shrugged. "It's the third month. Her responses are normal. She felt ill. Some nausea . . . You don't really want to know all the secrets of our maternal art, do you?"

"No. Spare me the details. But if everything is so normal, why the doctor tonight?"

"Because she's easily frightened. And more than anything, *that* could make the birth difficult. Anyway, I trust Madame Restell, and so does Denise."

"How curious that Denise would want a child. She told me in New York how pleased she was not to be like the other ladies."

"When she said that, she was making the best of it. She has always wanted a child. After all, she's a *good* Catholic, not like us. Be fruitful, multiply. She is being obedient and very happy."

2

"**P**OLO," SAID JAMIE, mopping his sweaty face with a towel, "is perhaps the oldest game in the world. And thanks to me, as you can see, it's on its way to being the most popular American sport."

"Popular?" I indicated the thirty or forty bewildered spectators, most if not all of them related to the players on the green meadow at the edge of the Central Park.

"Don't worry. The *Herald* will make it popular." Jamie was his usual airy self. We were seated beneath a shady tree. Today the weather has been formidably hot, and both horses and riders looked exhausted. For the last two years polo has been the rage in England. Not to be outdone by our—by *his*—British cousins, Jamie has now formed his own club, and a number of young men have taken to the game. Mounted on horses, the players try to hit a small wooden ball with a long mallet. Like so many games, polo is more amusing to play than to watch.

Between matches, we were able to do a little business.

"You are missed at the *Herald.*" Jamie looked at me accusingly.

I looked at him most innocently, rather struck by the trimness of his figure considering the amount of absinthe he daily pours into it. "Nothing from Schuyler in July. Nothing in August. Next week it's September. A new season."

"But what is there *new* to write about? I mean politically. No one seems very interested in either candidate." This is true, and I find it astonishing, considering the issues involved. Yet all summer long the country has been entirely preoccupied with the Centennial Exhibition, with sewing machines, Japanese vases, popped corn, typewriters and telephones, not to mention incessant praise for those paladins who created this perfect nation, this envied Eden, exactly one century ago.

"Things will heat up, Charlie, and you're the man to do the heating."

"No, Jamie. Nordhoff heats the pot, which I simply stir from time to time."

"That's all right, too." He gave me a passing grade for this conceit. "Zach. Chandler has ordered the Interior Department to investigate Tilden's taxes. Back in '62, during the worst of the war, Tilden said that his income for the year was only seven thousand dollars. Actually, it was more than a hundred thousand."

"I should think that by *not* paying the infamous tax on income, Tilden would be something of a hero."

"Boys in blue," said Jamie, combing his moustache with his fingers. "Union in peril. Slaves to be freed. Every dollar needed. Patriotic duty. Down with Copperhead Democrats. Oh, *The New York Times* is getting ready to pour it on. There is no crime their editors would not commit to help the Republican party."

"I don't think that I can be lyric on the subject of taxes not paid."

"There's good stuff assembled. And something very sweet about Hayes." Jamie looked suddenly happy. "Some years ago he shot his mother with a pistol, in a sudden fit of insanity."

"This need not make him unpopular." I thought Jamie was joking. But apparently he was repeating the latest rumour to make the rounds.

All in all, I do not think that democracy, as practised in these states, is a success. While Tilden grimly, laboriously presents to the people his plans to reform what is, probably, the most corrupt society in the Western world, the press is busy with idiotic ir-

relevancies about Tilden's alleged drunkenness, syphilis, close-
ness to Tweed—all set to music in a pretty song called "Sly Sam,
the Railroad Thief."

Hayes's taxes are also under review, since he, too, is a rich
lawyer who did not pay, it is rumoured, any tax at all in '68 and
'69. Lately he has been accused of stealing the money entrusted
him by one of his soldiers killed in the war.

"Charlie, go South. Please. I beg you. Get that pony out of the
sun, you stupid Irish bastard!" shouted Jamie to his groom.

"Even the heat at Newport is too much for me. I would perish
at the South. Besides, Nordhoff's already done you proud." Nordhoff's pieces for the *Herald* on the so-called cotton states have been
most sympathetic and vivid; he appears to want some sort of
re-alignment to the present political balance.

"Always a breeze at New Orleans, and Florida is a paradise this
time of year. That's where the trouble's going to be."

"How do you know?" Although I have no high opinion of
Jamie's general intelligence (certainly he has managed to keep
well outside Western civilization and all its works), I am constantly impressed by his sense of this country. He is a sort of
human barometer, able to anticipate before anyone else a political
scandal, an Indian massacre.

"South Carolina, Florida, and Louisiana are all under Federal
control. Grant's got the troops down there."

"Less than three thousand in the whole South." I am, after all,
An Authority.

Jamie ignored my Authoritativeness. "So what's going to happen if they vote Democratic?"

"But they *will* vote Democratic, and Tilden will be the president."

"That's only a part of it." Jamie looked about him vaguely. "I'll
give you half again as much as I've been overpaying you if you
just go to New Orleans, talk to the leaders there . . ."

I was firm. I refused to go South. But I did agree to resume my
weekly pieces in September, since the last eight weeks of a presidential election are the crucial ones. At least from the point of
view of learning who stole what from whom.

"Did Hayes really shoot his mother?" I was curious about that
detail.

Jamie was donning his helmet, pony at hand. "Certainly."

"Shot her dead?"

"No. Just winged the old cow. But then he never could shoot straight. Missed his own fat mother from six foot away. That's no president, now, is it?"

As Jamie mounted his pony and I prepared to go back to the hotel, I asked him if Madame Restell was in the city. "Oh, Charlie! You've no need of her for a friend, have you? Some lady you have wronged?"

"No, dear boy. I want to chat with her about a common friend."

"Well, she's away. Nobody's in town in August, except the *first* American polo team!" He returned to his game; I returned to the Fifth Avenue Hotel.

Denise has been in excellent spirits, faithfully taking her powders twice a day, and there have been no more recurrences of panic. Emma is constantly with her, while Sanford is constantly at sea in his yacht. I would be critical of his behaviour if it did not so absolutely suit the three of us to have him at a distance.

I had hoped my first evening in town to pay a call on Madame Restell and report on her patient's progress, but instead of an evening at Madame Restell's amusing atelier, I had an unexpectedly fascinating time with John Apgar, who had got us tickets for a new play called *Two Men of Sandy Bar* by Bret Harte, one of the numerous imitators of Mark Twain.

"They say the play isn't very good." John was apologetic. "But there is supposed to be a most comical Chinese character in it."

I started to tell John about the Chinese club at Paris where a number of us go from time to time to smoke opium but then thought better of it: lately there have been a good number of attacks in the press on the Chinese, whose supposed addiction to opium is always mentioned as proof of their undesirability as citizens. I have always found it strange that a nation whose prosperity is based entirely upon cheap immigrant labour should be so unrelentingly xenophobic.

Since the notices for Mr. Harte's play had been unenthusiastic, the audience was small; also, late August is not the best time to open a play. The Union Square Theatre was so hot that it would have been difficult to enjoy any play, much less this one, on such a night. John tells me that Mr. Harte is best known for a poem about the "Heathen Chinee," and regards himself as a friend to that beleaguered race; he writes, however, like an enemy.

John apologized for the play, as if he'd written it. But I pre-

tended to be amused, and in due course was very much amused
when during the entr'acte, John pointed out to me Samuel L.
Clemens, better known as Mark Twain, in whose wiry small
frame is concentrated everything that I most dislike in American
life—or thought I disliked.

"Would you like to meet him, sir?" asked John.

"No." And I meant "no." I have never particularly liked the
company of professional writers, and certainly this music-hall
comedian and newspaper-writing Yahoo is quintessentially the
professional. But my "no" coincided with the approach of Twain
and the phrase "no go" on his lips seemed to echo me. He was
talking to the play's author, who looked every bit as distracted as
playwrights are supposed to look on such occasions.

"Good evening, Mr. Clemens," said John as Twain suddenly
veered in our direction, as if eager for a distraction.

"Why, good evening. Uh . . ."

"Apgar, and this is Mr. Charles Schuyler—"

"Charles *Schermerhorn* Schuyler?" I was surprised to note that
Twain's normal voice is not much different from that of any
other resident of Hartford, Connecticut. But when he is "in character," as it were, the voice becomes very Western and yokel-ish;
he also has the careful, artful delivery of a professional actor.

"Well, I confess now that this is very like to being an honour,
sir, meeting you." Twain slipped into character as, warmly, he
shook my hand. For the record, Twain's hair is wiry and still
fox-red. He is not tall, not stout. The face's expression is very
much sly-Yankee, in the pre-Civil War sense.

"Your confession delights me, Mr. Clemens." Does one address
him as Clemens or Twain? I wondered. Following the usually
impeccable Apgar lead, I called him Clemens.

"Always hoped we might get a glimpse of you and your beautiful daughter in Paris but we never did, though we heard tell of
you, naturally." I could see that Twain was idling, hoping to
strike the right note.

I was benign as befits a sixty-three-year-old writer of only
modest fame in the presence of a world-famous celebrity of
thirty-nine.

The playwright muttered something in Twain's ear and moved
away. "Let's have us a drink at Delmonico's," said Twain, plainly
relieved at Harte's departure, "as soon as this—well, accident is
over. Old Bret won't be joining us right away. Says they're going

to rehearse the company right after the show. Sort of like giving a haircut to a corpse. Does no good, but the family feels better for the effort."

When the play eventually ended, we walked the short distance to Delmonico's. John and I were not allowed to forget just how privileged we were, for everyone knows Mark Twain; even the hack men would shout, "Hey, Mark!" as they rattled down Fourteenth Street. Meanwhile, the great man talked what is known as a "blue streak."

We were greeted by Charles Delmonico, who told us that we were to be amongst the very last to dine at this branch of Delmonico's "because we're shutting down for good. Next month we open the place on Madison Square."

"You hear that?" Twain shook his head theatrically. "Now I ask you, how can you have any kind of tradition in a country where as soon as you get used to a place like this where the food is passable in spite of the Frenchified trimmings, they go and tear it down?"

But Charles Delmonico sang the praises of the family's new restaurant and invited us all to the grand opening. He then assigned us a table close to the main entrance where, according to Twain, "we can keep an eye on the comings and goings because, let me tell you, it's a lot more entertaining in here than it is at any of the theatres in this town. Oh, that play!"

Then Twain proceeded to drink the first of several Scotch Old Fashioneds whilst John and I shared a bottle of claret. I listened to him very carefully, in order to be able to record here everything America's—no, the world's—idol said.

"And to think that my old friend wrote that thing, or, I reckon, just let it happen to him, like measles. Well, it's plain no go, that play. And I'm sorry. Old Bret's had a terrible time, poor man. First he comes East. Which is a fatal mistake—for some people. Then he gets himself this nice contract to write for the *Atlantic Monthly*. Then promptly forgets how to write like he used to, which is just plain peculiar. Then he goes out lecturing.

"Now, there's not a word to be said against lecturing, at least not by me, because there's a whole heap of money to be made at it *if* you've got the knack. But old Bret, why, he can't get up and talk worth a hill of beans. Which is again most peculiar, come to think of it, since he's a natural-born liar. Anyway, now he's trying the theatre, which is the gold mine in our trade.

"Not yours, of course, Mr. Schuyler. Oh, I've got the greatest respect for your—uh, history-writing. But for us journalists, it's the lecture hall or trying to please the ladies in the magazines, which is a Christ-awful labour, if you'll forgive my language. But I have to say that the most or certainly the *easiest* money that I ever did make—and am still making—is from that play they made out of *The Gilded Age*—"

"I saw it, Mr. Clemens." John is an eager theatregoer. "I thought it most enjoyable, sir. Colonel Sellers is a wonderful character."

"Glad you did, because if you and a lot of others didn't enjoy it, why, I wouldn't be getting those weekly royalties that so delight my soul. Particularly after the bad time I had with the press when the book first came out and the *Chicago Tribune*, may it burn to the ground all over again, said I had written a *hoax*, which, as it developed, as attacks go, was nothing compared to what that bastard Whitelaw Reid did to me in the *Tribune*. I guess you saw that. But I made him back down just the way I made the *Evening Post* haul water. I reckon you know what the *Post* did to me. Well, maybe you missed that, living in Europe. *They said I had paid out of my own pocket for a testimonial dinner to myself!* Well, I sued and I won. Oh, I tell you that old Bryant is as sanctimonious an old weasel as ever got loose in a hen house."

This went on for some time. Mark Twain takes very seriously what the press says about him. Obviously this is the price one must pay for his kind of popularity; yet there is not a popular newspaper in the United States which an intelligent man need take seriously on any subject.

But Twain was only beginning to warm up. He reverted again to play-writing and all the money that could be made in the theatre. "Fact, I've told Harte I'll collaborate with him on his next play. We're going to use that character of his, the Heathen Chinee. Which is what the public is going for in a big way right now, you know, comical Chinese characters. Then there's some talk they may be doing that new book of mine for the stage."

"*Tom Sawyer?*" To my astonishment, the proper John Apgar was bedazzled by the splendid figure at our table, and knows his career in great detail.

"Yes. I can't say that the sales have been anything like what I had hoped for. We've sold just under twenty-five thousand copies since December—a fraction of what *Innocents Abroad* did in its first year. But if we can get a play out of the book . . ."

Twain began a second Old Fashioned and I ordered my usual lobster salad. "Anyway, I told the managers that I see the two boys, Tom and Huck, being played by two really good-looking girls. That's always popular, you know." Tom and Huck are, I gather, two characters in the new book.

"But would young women be convincing in the parts?" Yes, John has actually read the book, which I only glanced at. "Surely they are—well, *real* boys in your story."

"But that's just a story. The stage is something else again. A gold mine for those who have the gift—not that I personally seem to have it on my own, so far, but you never can tell."

Until now, Twain the professional writer was living up to my grimmest expectation. But then he shifted to unexpected ground. "I must say I'd like to give up this whole damned thing here and light out with the Madam for Europe. The way you did, Mr. Schuyler. Not Paris, mind you. There's nothing on this earth anywhere near as absurd as a Frenchman. But England—now, that's a place where you can really *use* the past they got there . . . awful as it is. But if you stay on here, you find you're obliged to wear yourself out just trying to keep up to the minute."

"But your last book, sir, was very fine. And that was about the old days, wasn't it? Your own boyhood." John was reverent.

"Yes, but it's not the same thing as all that history they've got in Europe. And then, like I said, the sales have been very, very disappointing. No, I'm now interested in the *truly* historical sort of tale."

I made the mistake of asking him if he'd read Flaubert's *Salammbô*. "An immoral sort of writer, I believe." Twain looked stern.

"But a most distinguished style—"

"Mr. Schuyler, if I am forced to read a distinguished writer and suffer in consequences the torments of the damned, I will apply myself to the interminable distinction of our very own Mr. Charles Francis Adams."

"But I should think that with your great satiric gift"—I laid it on—"you would want to stay here where there is so much absurdity."

The answer to that was prompt. "Mr. Schuyler, no man can write good satire unless he's in a good mood. Well, sir, I am in a terrible mood. Which means I can't satirize anything at the moment." The blue-grey eyes were as cold and as bright as the ice in the third Old Fashioned, which he held tight in his hand, as though fearful it might escape his clutch. "I want to take a stick, an axe, a club, and smash it all to bits."

"Smash *what?*" I had never suspected that at the heart of this beloved popular entertainer there would be so much rage.

"Anything, everything! Look at those congressmen you've been writing about! Every last one a thief. You know their motto, don't you? Addition and division and silence. They are all crooks —and why? Because of universal suffrage. Wicked, ungodly universal suffrage!

"Now, you watch me real close because I am about to foam at the mouth! I always do at this point. How, I ask you, can you have any kind of a country when every idiot male of twenty-one or more can vote? And how, I ask you, can anyone with half a mind want to make equal what God has made unequal? I tell you to do that is a wrong and a shame."

"Then who ought to vote?"

"The rich man ought to have that many more votes than the poor man, based on what he's been able through his own intelligence and hard work to acquire."

"But I read somewhere, Mr. Twain—Clemens—that you, like me, had been nearly wiped out when Jay Cooke failed. Do you think that when we lost our money, we should've lost the right to vote?"

Twain laughed suddenly, the fierceness quite gone. "Well, since we proved we were two precious fools for getting ourselves caught with our pants down, then I don't think our votes ought to have been counted—at least not for that year."

The arrival of Bret Harte and several theatrical-looking personages ended this most sympathetic encounter.

"Hope you enjoy the animals, Mr. Schuyler" were the last words to me of the menagerie's favourite writer-performer.

A nice paradox: although Mark Twain is himself one of those animals (otherwise, they would not worship him, for nothing truly alien can ever be popular), he hates them for all the right reasons and so must hate himself. Had he the character to be *un*popular, he might have been greater than Swift, another Voltaire, a new Rabelais . . . I seem to be rather overdoing this but Twain fascinates me. In any case, whatever he might have been, he is, for now at least, hurt Caliban, a monster who has had the ill-luck to see his own face mirrored in the composite looking-glass of a million adoring countrymen. By cunningly playing the fool, Twain has become rich and beloved; he has also come to hate himself, but lacks the courage either to crack the mirror or to change, if he could, that deliberately common face which it so faithfully reflects.

There! That is enough Mark Twain. It does me a world of good to pity *him*.

3

I HAVE BECOME a typewriter. Jamie has linked me inextricably with this loud and uncongenial machine, which I do not play myself but shout above its clatter my rolling periods to a young man who takes them down directly upon the machine.

At first, it is marvellous to see all those words so swiftly become print. But when one looks carefully at the neat pages, one suffers the recurrent nightmare of every author I've ever known well enough to exchange nightmares. The new book has arrived from the printers. Eagerly one opens it. Immediately the binding crumbles. The folios separate. Worst of all, words are misspelled, sentences run backward, chaos.

As a result, I drive my typewriter-machinist from draft to draft until each weekly piece is as right as I can make it.

I am fairly open about my allegiance to Governor Tilden as I do my best to counteract the libels of *The New York Times* whilst scrutinizing the long, dim career of Rutherford B. Hayes.

Every other day Denise writes me faithfully from Newport; and Emma adds postscripts (it ought to be the other way round). The pregnancy goes well. Both girls agree that September is an idyllic month at Newport, because, one by one, the magnates are departing; even Ward McAllister has returned to the city, Mystic Rose in his buttonhole. Odd that I have seen neither him nor the Rose. But then my days are busy with journalism, with politicians, with Bigelow.

By happy coincidence, Republican headquarters are here in the Fifth Avenue Hotel, and I often see the national chairman of the party, the inscrutable Zach. Chandler in the lobby or in the Amen Corner. We bow to each other, but seldom speak.

Tilden himself spends most of his time in the city (he has not resigned as governor and is much criticized by partisans for holding on to office). He makes occasional trips about the country, as does Hayes. Yesterday (September 21), Tilden received a splendid ovation in Philadelphia, where it was the Centennial Exhibition's New York Day.

Both candidates are having a difficult time attracting the interest of the people or, perhaps I should say, of the press. Thanks to the unremitting scandals of the Grant regime, all politicians are suspect.

Some weeks ago when Belknap finally came to trial before the Senate, he was duly acquitted on a party vote; yet there was little public indignation. The press prefers (sensibly?) to go on and on about such novelties as the telephone, about such grisly horrors as the last hours of General Custer and his gallant men, eaten raw by Indians.

This morning, after I had finished the last draft of my weekly piece, I went to the Everett House, where I found the suite of rooms occupied by the Democratic National Committee packed with political hangers-on. Ticker tape pours in political intelligence from all about the country. There is a good deal of bustle but to no useful end, according to the critical Bigelow.

The new party chairman, Abram S. Hewitt, is an amiable but inexperienced political manager, unable to make that necessary distance between himself and those would-be officeholders who fill the rooms at the Everett House, an all-important distance superbly kept by Tilden himself.

Bigelow told me that the other night Tilden was sitting up late with a pair of powerful New York politicians, hungry for spoils. Relaxing over the Governor's best hock, one of them said, "Now tell us, Governor, what's in it for us when you come into the Kingdom?"

"Why, boys," whispered the great man, smiling his small smile, left eyelid drooping with fatigue, "you know that you don't want office for yourselves, because that would do your character more harm than good. What you really want is influence with the administration. That's what counts."

Tilden is as splendidly ambiguous when it comes to the dark

side of politics as he is fiercely forthright when it comes to the
issues of the day; thus, he is the reverse of every important politician in the country.

Physically, the Governor is holding up well, according to Bigelow. I have not seen him since the banquet in July at Delmonico's
where those wealthy magnificoes who support reform (I cannot
think why) pledged their fealty over canvasback duck.

As I was rather forlornly inquiring for Bigelow in the Everett
House confusion, Hewitt himself appeared at my side and said,
"He's down at Liberty Street. Where the *real* work is done."

Before I could commiserate, the national chairman was borne
away by clubhouse types. Like his leader, Hewitt is a martyr to
dyspepsia. He is, also, I have just discovered, a son-in-law of the
eccentric millionaire Peter Cooper, who is the Greenback candidate for president. "Soft" versus "hard" currency is one of the
battles being fought between—and within—all the parties.

With difficulty, I got through the crowd of future postmasters,
consuls and custom house men. Victory is in the air. Faithful and
faithless gather round.

At 59 Liberty Street the Literary Bureau has been installed,
with its own printing press; also, the Speakers Bureau. Tilden's
brother-in-law Colonel Pelton officially runs both, but Bigelow
assures me that the actual administration of the entire campaign
is the work of Tilden himself. Hewitt complains that he has too
little access to the Governor.

In a windowless office the size of my hotel closet I found Bigelow at a table piled high with newspapers. In the next room some
twenty men and several women sat at long tables, answering piles
of correspondence by hand. There are, apparently, too few type-
writer-machinists to take over this burdensome task.

"Even so, the Governor wants every letter answered."

Bigelow shut the door to the closet. I was disagreeably aware
that the wick of the kerosene lamp on his table wanted trimming.

Bigelow was in high good spirits. "You read about the ovation
he got in Philadelphia?" "He," said in a certain voice, is always
Tilden.

"I've mentioned it in my next piece."

Bigelow gave me a quick smile. "Your pieces in the *Herald* are
being reproduced in every small-town newspaper in the country."

"Without permission?" I affected horror.

"They do us a world of good. Oh, we're on our way." Bigelow

clapped his hands; then ran a hand through hair that tends to arrange itself in grey tufts, rather like those sharp mountain peaks in the Dolomites.

"Our only trouble now is money."

"Of all things!" I was surprised. "The Governor . . ."

". . . is a rich man. *Ergo*, other rich men say, 'Why should we give him the money that he already has?' "

"So *why* doesn't he pay for the campaign himself?"

"His *proprium*, I suppose. He doesn't want people to say he bought the election."

"Which they do." *Harper's* have outdone themselves with caricatures of Tilden pouring forth money from a barrel.

"As it is, he's forced to pay for most of this." Bigelow indicated 59 Liberty Street with a sweep of an ink-stained hand. "But he has hoped all along to win on the issues."

"But the people dislike issues. They prefer scandal."

"Some people. By the way, we've just solved the income-tax problem."

I think Bigelow is unduly sanguine. For weeks now the Republican newspapers have been going on and on about Tilden's taxes. Last month *The New York Times* made thirteen charges against Tilden, accusing him of various tax frauds. After much labour, Tilden answered the charges so skillfully that *The Nation*, which had previously regarded the whole business as "an ugly flaw" in the candidate's history, now praises him.

Best of all, Bryant is angry at the unfairness of the attacks and he has promised to defend—if not support—his old colleague. Meanwhile, the egregious editors of *The New York Times* promise to reveal "new rascalities of Tilden": theirs is a most inventive newspaper. I am certain that Tilden underpaid his taxes, but all the rich do, including Hayes.

Day after day, political orators range up and down the country. "We've the best organization, by far," said Bigelow. "But the Republicans have the best speakers. What with Blaine" (two months ago translated from House to Senate by his native state, causing the House to drop its investigation of his crimes), "Ingersoll, Garfield, Mark Twain, General Sherman . . ."

"What about Conkling?"

"Silence. Illness, they say. He lies in a darkened room at Utica." Bigelow was enjoying the warrior's defeat altogether too much.

•

"Emma has had a letter from Kate Sprague. She's coming home this fall."

"When they meet, I should like to be—what is it our French friends say?—a fly on that wall."

Colonel Pelton joined us. I offered him my chair, the only chair aside from Bigelow's, but he preferred, nervously, to pace the tiny room. "We've got to get more money into both Ohio and Indiana. And we haven't got it. Belmont's come through but the others . . ." He shook his head.

They treat me as one of the family, and speak of the most arcane matters in my presence. Indiana and Ohio are crucial; although Election Day is November 7, these two states will hold local elections on October 10, and whoever wins the two states—both ordinarily Republican—will be sure to win the country.

The Democratic organization in Ohio has been indolent. Yet "Just a few more pennies," Pelton groaned, "and we could take Hayes's own state away from him."

"More pennies *and* a better organization." They mentioned names of important politicians who might be sent out. Was Bigler too ill? would Kernan go? and what about the infinitely corrupt, hence infinitely persuasive, Senator Barnum of Connecticut? is he not the ideal person to charm the sly Indianians?

The subject turned then—as always—to the South. "We'll carry every state south of the Mason-Dixon line." Bigelow was emphatic.

Pelton was equally emphatic, and deeply uneasy. Eight states of the former Confederacy have self-government. Of the eight, five have secure white majorities. But three of the self-governing states (I begin to think that one should use quotes about the phrase "self-governing")—Alabama, Georgia, and Mississippi—have black majorities.

"Grant can always put the pressure on. They can force those Negroes to vote against us."

But Bigelow is certain that "The Negroes are as apt to support us as them. Besides, the whites will—to a man—vote for us and against Grantism. Oh, we'll carry those states all right. By the way, Colonel, they want the Governor at the Alabama state fair. If you can arrange it . . ."

Smoke from Pelton's cigar had by now so filled the closet that I was beginning to feel ill. But I stayed where I was, eager to find out what I could. After all, *my* future (the United States can go hang!) depends on a Tilden victory.

"I've had another alarming letter from Louisiana."

"The famous Returning Board?"

Pelton nodded. I tried to look intelligent but had no idea what they were talking about. "The Republicans have complete control over the board, and no matter what the Democratic majority they will report that the state voted Republican, and the Supreme Court has already ruled that there can be no appeal from their decision."

"But they would never dare. This isn't Mexico."

"My correspondent also says that in the parish of Baton Rouge, the Republicans can and will vote the same Negro twenty-two times, and no one will ever have any way of catching them at it."

"But there is still such a thing as public opinion . . ."

"There are also, still, Federal troops in Louisiana . . . as there are in South Carolina and Florida. And these troops report directly to the commander in chief. To President Grant."

"Grant is always ill-advised, but I cannot see him subverting the Constitution."

By now the room was dim with blue smoke and I was beginning to see double; had difficulty breathing. The voices of my companions came to me as if from far away; it was like the moment just before one slips into unconsciousness from nitrous oxide.

"I think we should send some of our people to Louisiana, and to Florida. Make sure that they don't steal us blind."

"But who will go? And the money . . ."

Always money. To date, Jamie estimates that Tilden has spent close to half a million dollars on this campaign. The Republicans have spent perhaps twice that amount, but then the party's chairman, Zach. Chandler, and secretary William Chandler (no relation to Zach.) have resorted to the ever-useful spoilsman's tactic of requiring all Republican officeholders to contribute to the party. Obviously there is a good deal to be said for being the party in power, particularly after sixteen years.

When Pelton left, I insisted that the door be kept open. New air revived me. Bigelow told me that he does not take seriously the possibility of fraud at the South or, rather, "They will of course *try* to steal the election. Then they will be caught *in flagrante* and even *The New York Times* will have to admit that this is not the way to conduct the affairs of a democracy."

Bigelow changed the subject. "I do wish the Governor would take a holiday, go to the White Mountains—"

"He prefers Gramercy Park?"

"And running every detail of the campaign. He wears himself out. He has spent more time on that damnable report on his taxes than on anything else. It's been a nightmare. I've never seen him so irritable. But," Bigelow quickly added, "he is extraordinarily strong, physically as well as mentally."

I rose, unsteadily, to go. "Is there anything I should know about Governor Hayes?"

Bigelow nodded. "Something odd. When we were preparing our paper on Governor Tilden's tax returns, we asked the government for Governor Hayes's returns, too. The government refused to make them public. That's interesting."

"I'm not excited by taxes, John. What I really want to know is whether or not Hayes shot his mother."

"I should think not." Bigelow was droll. "But you might wonder—aloud, as it were—in print, if such a terrible thing could ever have happened."

4

ELECTION DAY: November 7, 1876.

In October Ohio went Republican by a mere six thousand votes. Bigelow and Pelton were right: with more money and more industry, the state would have been Democratic. On the other hand, the October canvass in Indiana was heartening. The Democrats won the state by five thousand votes.

I have been too busy to make any notes in this book. I make them now only because I am nervous; have nothing else to do; can no longer assist the Governor, whose fate is presently in the hands of the electorate.

At this very minute, millions of people who will never so much as get a glimpse of Tilden or of Hayes or understand what either represents are now choosing between them, and, I fear, there will be votes cast for Hayes because he is thought to be against the

Roman Catholics and votes for Tilden because he is the opposite. Hayes himself has been responsible for thrusting religion into the campaign because, as he told an intimate, "Hard times is our deadliest foe." So bait the Catholics. But the phrase "Tilden and Reform" *seems* to have caught on. Proof? President Grant has appointed 11,501 deputy marshals and 4,813 supervisors to police the polls, particularly in the Democratic wards of the Northern cities and in the Democratic South. Word has just come that Grant's supervisors in Philadelphia are wearing Republican badges and making things difficult for those who want to vote Democratic.

Emma is staying with Denise in the Sanfords' half-completed Fifth Avenue mansion. Sanford has been in the West working for Hayes. If Sanford is sufficiently industrious, the West is bound to vote for Tilden.

With suspicious docility, John Apgar has agreed to a postponement of the October wedding at Grace Church. Somewhat guiltily, we have made occasional forays into Apgar-land; and detect there a slight chill in the air—premonition of harsh winter?

But Emma is plausible. She has told John that she worries about Denise's health (which is actually excellent), as well as that of her beloved old father (which is probably failing rapidly but I do not allow it to preoccupy me). In any case, John knows how important the election is to us and he has made no serious demur. I have not really had him to myself since our evening with Mr. Clemens.

As soon as this day is over—if it ever ends!—I must have that deep, serious talk with John and Emma about marriage, about the future, about France, where—God willing—I shall be the American minister once Tilden is inaugurated president in March.

It is now noon. I sit in my single room at the Fifth Avenue Hotel, writing these notes in bed. A dark sky over Madison Square. A cold rain falling. Traditionally, bad weather is a good sign for the Democrats, since it means that the Republican farmers upstate will stay home while the loyal party members in the city will get out the vote. Presently I shall go to the Everett House, where Tilden is expected to make an appearance. Betting in the city is that Tilden will be elected. Odds: 100 to 80.

I caught a glimpse of Zach. Chandler this morning, entering the Amen Corner with some Stalwarts.

"How does it look?" I could not help but ask.

"Simply terrible," was the honest answer. But then he can be
as candid as he pleases now, for no word to the press from me or
from anyone else can make a difference. The voters are at the
polls.

A note of minor interest: Boss Tweed has been arrested in
Spain, and will be returned to a New York prison. People take
this to be a good omen, recalling to the nation Tilden's first
victory over the powers of darkness.

My hands are shaking so much that I can barely decipher my
own handwriting. For once I do not ascribe this tremor to ill-
health but to a quite normal *crise de nerfs.*

Midnight. November 7 to . . . No, now it is November 8.

Shortly after noon Governor Tilden arrived at the Everett
House, having himself just voted. I was amongst the crowd that
greeted him with an ovation as he entered the ballroom.

Tilden looked calm, and presidential; he wore a black frock
coat with a red carnation in the buttonhole. I tried to get to him
in order to shake, idiotically, his hand. But the crowd was too
dense for me to penetrate. Luckily I found Colonel Pelton, who
said, "Come back to Gramercy Park with us. We've got a direct
wire there. The returns will be coming in pretty soon."

So at about four in the afternoon, I drove in Pelton's carriage
to Gramercy Park, where a small crowd had braved the cold and
the rain for a glimpse of Tilden.

The parlours and study were crowded with members of the
inner court. Green crushed my hand. Bigelow was almost giddy
with anticipated victory. An euphoric Mrs. Pelton was still sufficiently polite to ask for Emma.

"She's with Mrs. Sanford, playing nurse."

Actually Emma seems to have got over her African phase, at
least, temporarily. I think that she lost heart after the defeat of
her favourite chieftain Blaine. "Besides," she said, "I don't know
General Hayes. And as for your Governor Tilden . . . Well, I
want so much for him to win."

"But he does not excite you?"

"He lacks true savagery, Papa. I'm sorry. The fault is mine. In
Washington I dined too long on raw flesh."

Tilden was applauded as he entered his own drawing room: a
ludicrous thing to do, but we were all—we *are* all—still afire with
excitement.

As I pressed Tilden's hand, the drooping left lid rose slightly and a faint smile began. "We have had an unconscionably long summer and autumn, haven't we, Mr. Schuyler?"

"To be followed by a winter of absolute contentment."

"I hope you are right. But tell me"—the low voice became a whisper—"of *your* symptoms. The seeing of images doubled . . ."

"Quite gone," I lied, since no president wants a moribund minister to France. "I am rejuvenated."

"Curiously enough, so am I. My headaches have quite gone." He lied, too, for the same reason: no republic wants a valetudinarian president.

Although no returns had as yet been reported, messages kept coming in over the wire, congratulating the new president.

Amongst the first to be heard from was General McClellan, Lincoln's opponent in the election of '64. Since McClellan had been a disaster politically as well as militarily, I took this to be a bad omen. But Bigelow cheered me. "We're now certain to carry the city. And who wins New York wins the country."

After we had dined, the Governor led us in procession back to the Everett House, where crowds were beginning to fill all the lobbies.

In a room just off the main ballroom, Tilden seated himself comfortably near the ticker-tape machine. Hewitt sat on one side of him; Green on the other. The rest of us served as Greek chorus to the grand single Aeschylean protagonist.

First returns: Tilden carries New Jersey. From the ballroom, a roaring sound like that of a wave bursting on the shore. Cheers from us in the small room.

Tilden's eyes begin, ever so slightly, to glitter while in each cheek a touch of pink suddenly appears like a plague spot. No, like the stigmata. No! No similes! I am plain recorder tonight.

The next returns: Tilden carries Connecticut. Waves again break on the shore in the next room. Green shouts, "It is going to be total, Governor!"

But Tilden shakes his head and murmurs something that I cannot hear.

"New York will be the key," says Bigelow for the hundredth time. And so we waited for New York until about eleven-thirty, when the word came.

Tilden has carried New York City. Tilden is sweeping the state.

Hewitt turns to an aide: "Telegraph *The New York Times*, and ask the editor what majority they will kindly concede us." Much laughter.

The door to the ballroom is thrown open by enthusiasts. "Tilden, Tilden, Tilden!" the chant has begun.

"Go on," says Hewitt, helping the not-entirely-reluctant Tilden to his feet. "They want to see you—Mr. President!"

That got us cheering too: and in a daze as close to that of sexual ecstasy as anything that I have ever known, we accompanied Tilden into the crowded, smoky ballroom, where a thousand people cheered themselves hoarse as the small figure in black made his way amongst them, creating in some magical way a certain space about himself, for no one actually tried to touch him as the crowd usually wants to do when the hero has, thanks to Demos, become for at least a quadrennium their god.

I went back to the hotel and found the lobby nearly empty. One of the night managers told me, with a wink, that the entire staff of the Republican headquarters had vanished when word came that Tilden had carried New York. "Nobody's up there except Mr. Clancy the clerk, tidying up!"

"And the two Mr. Chandlers?"

"Mr. Zach. Chandler went to bed." The manager lowered his voice. "Had a bottle of whisky in one hand . . ."

We were interrupted by a powerful and, to me, ominously familiar voice. "Which way to Republican headquarters?"

I turned and saw the one-legged General Daniel E. Sickles. This colourful creature, whilst in Congress, killed his wife's lover in cold blood; then took her back. Later, in the army, he lost a leg at Gettysburg; he also came close to losing the war for the North. In recent years he has, simultaneously, been American minister to Spain as well as chief minister to the voracious sexual appetites of the exiled Spanish queen, whose house in the Avenue Kléber we all avoid, as we do *le roi américain de l'Espagne*.

I bowed to General Sickles, who bowed to me. He owns a wooden leg but prefers to use crutches. "Your man Tilden's made a very decent showing." Sickles was patronizing. Once a Tammany Democrat, he is now a dedicated Republican, hoping no doubt to obtain *my* post at Paris.

"Yes, General. President Tilden's majority is a most decent one."

Sickles snorted through walrus moustaches; then followed the night manager in the direction of the perpendicular railway. I looked into the Amen Corner and saw Collector Arthur. He conceded defeat gracefully and together we had a nightcap. Arthur was on his way home to nurse a sick wife.

November 8. Midmorning.
I slept heavily, thanks to drugs, and feel somewhat unreal this morning.

Did last night really happen? or was Tilden's victory simply one of the many strange and often unpleasantly lurid dreams that I have been lately having?

The morning papers reassured me: Tilden is the president. The *Tribune* is certain that he has been elected while the *Evening Post* estimates that Tilden may have as many as 209 votes in the Electoral College as compared to 160 for Hayes. Characteristically, *The New York Times* refuses to acknowledge defeat.

The *Times*'s headline: "A Doubtful Election." The editor made much of the fact that Oregon had gone Democratic by only 500 votes; also, of the fact that the crucial states of Louisiana, Florida, and South Carolina were being claimed by Hayes's electors—as we had always anticipated.

I was startled, however, to read the *Herald*'s headline: "The Result—What Is It? Something that No Fellow Can Understand." (Pure Jamie, that style). "Impossible to Name Our Next President. The Returns Too Meagre." But then the writer declared that the key states of Louisiana, Florida, and Oregon had indeed gone Democratic, and so it did *look* as if Tilden was elected.

During a quick breakfast in my room, I received a telegram asking me to dine tonight at the Sanfords', no doubt to meet my daughter. I have just sent a telegram of acceptance; am off to the *Herald* offices.

November 8. 4:00 P.M.
The *Herald* offices are in an uproar. Even the printers are quarrelling about the returns.

I found Jamie in his baronial office, wearing a polo helmet and holding in one hand a polo mallet. On the splendid mahogany desk was a crystal decanter, containing the morning's ration of absinthe.

"Ain't it a mess?" Thus he greeted me. As we talked, editors

came and went whilst messenger boys delivered telegrams that
Jamie would glance at and then drop to the floor.

"But what's wrong? Surely he's won? He's carried New York."

"New York's New York. Lot else going on."

"But your own story said he's carried Louisiana, Florida, Oregon . . ."

"*New York Times.*" Jamie said the three words with distinct
emphasis.

"What have they got to do with the *Herald* or with the election?"

"They've got an inside, Charlie. My God, I'm tired. I've been
here for close to two days. In this office." He took a quick swig
of his terrible liquid.

During a lull in the traffic of editors and messengers, Jamie
explained what had happened.

Around four o'clock this morning, the ever-alert editors of the
Times discovered that one of Tilden's aides had sent out a telegram to all state chairmen, asking each state what the electoral
vote was going to be.

The *Times* decided that this telegram displayed anxiety on the
part of the Democrats; therefore, the election might still be in
doubt. Although the editors knew that the popular vote at the
South had gone for Tilden and the paper had already grudgingly
conceded him New York State, they preferred to act as if the
Democratic majorities in Louisiana, Florida, and South Carolina
had already been reversed by the Republican Returning Boards.
This explained the headline in the first morning edition of the
Times.

At 6:00 A.M., the second *Times* edition arbitrarily gave Hayes
two of the "doubtful" Southern states and threw in Oregon for
good measure while admitting that Florida was in doubt. Tentatively the *Times* gave Tilden 184 electoral votes and Hayes 181,
making the point that if "doubtful" Florida should go Republican, Hayes would be elected by one vote in the Electoral College.

"But all of this is invention."

"I know. I know. And Tilden *has* won. But you asked me why
I had the *Herald* say the election was in doubt. Well, the *Times* and
now Zach. and William Chandler are deliberately putting it in
doubt. With the help of General Dan Sickles."

I sat down, feeling ill, confused. An offer of brandy was accepted. Promptly my brain clouded over and I felt—though I am
sure that I was not—the better for it.

At dawn this morning William Chandler returned from New Hampshire, where he had voted. He assumed the election was lost. At Republican headquarters he found the clerk Clancy who told him that General Sickles had gone through all the latest returns on Zach. Chandler's desk and decided that the election was close enough "to fix up." Sickles then wrote telegrams to the state leaders of South Carolina, Louisiana, Florida, and Oregon. The text: "With your state sure for Hayes, he is elected. Hold your state." Sickles wanted to send out these telegrams over Zach. Chandler's signature. Clancy demurred. At that moment Chet Arthur (having just left me) entered and said that he would take responsibility. Arthur then went home to his wife whilst the infernal Sickles remained at his post. At 3:00 A.M. South Carolina responded favourably. Close to 6:00 A.M. Oregon did the same. Sickles sent off another round of telegrams, and then stumped off to bed.

Needless to say, William Chandler was delighted. He was even more delighted when that rabid Republican the editor of *The New York Times*, John C. Reid, materialized, with ambiguous news reports declaring that Oregon and Florida had chosen Hayes. Both Reid and William Chandler were convinced that with time and the Republican Returning Boards, the election might still be reversed.

After some difficulty they found Zach. Chandler's bedroom. After even more difficulty, they roused him from a despondent, drunken slumber. He gave them carte blanche, and went back to sleep. The conspirators went back to headquarters, where it was decided to telegraph once more each of the Republican leaders in Louisiana, South Carolina, Florida, and Oregon as well as those of California and Nevada.

The burden of this urgent message from national headquarters was: "Hayes is elected if we carry South Carolina, Florida, and Louisiana. Can you hold your state?"

"How on earth do you know all this, Jamie? When this was only—what? three hours ago?"

Jamie hit a wastebasket with his polo mallet; the basket crashed into the wall and more papers joined the litter on the Turkey carpet. "Well, it's the damn fool unimportant things that give people away. Chandler and Reid went down to the telegraph office in your hotel but it wasn't open yet. So they had to go to the main office of Western Union. When they handed over their messages, Chandler said 'Charge these to the Republican National Committee.' But the clerk was a good Democrat who knew as how Tilden had been elected, so he said, 'No, sir, I can't do that.' So Reid said, 'Well, charge them to *The New York Times.*'"

"And the telegrams were sent?"

"They were sent. And the clerk passed the word on to us. Now we're waiting to see what skulduggery's going to result." Jamie poked with his mallet at some papers on the floor beside my chair. "Take a look at that one there. Just got it a few minutes ago."

I picked up a telegram signed by the Republican National Committee: "Despatches received at these headquarters report that Louisiana, Florida, South Carolina, Wisconsin, Oregon, Nevada, and California have given Republican majorities. There is no reason to doubt the correctness of those reports. And if confirmed the election of Hayes is assured by a majority of one in the Electoral College."

"But none of this is true."

Jamie shrugged. "Not yet. In fact, early this morning, old Zach. got word from his chairmen in Louisiana and Florida that their states had gone Democratic. So far he's been suppressing the bad news, waiting for them to get his message . . ."

"A message which clearly means: Falsify the vote."

"That's the size of it, Charlie."

I felt suddenly weak, and ready for the grave; particularly when Jamie told me in a most matter-of-fact way, "The Democrats say they carried Louisiana by some twenty thousand votes. The Republicans say *they* carried it by four thousand. This makes for what they call a doubtful state, which is to say that the Democrats actually won the most votes but the Republicans who control the election machinery are now going to reverse the vote."

"But that is—fraud."

Jamie laughed cheerfully; his interest is not good government but good drama of the kind that sells newspapers. Well, he has now come into a gold mine.

One of the editors entered—no one stands on formality today. "The President has sent in the troops."

"Where?" Jamie removed his helmet as though to hear—think? —better.

"Where, sir? Why, General Grant is in Philadelphia, staying at the house of a Mr. Childs . . ."

"I don't mean where *he* is." Jamie was irritable, excited. "The troops—where are they being sent? To what states?"

"Grant has ordered General Sherman to send Federal troops to Louisiana, to—"

"To Florida and to South Carolina," Jamie finished. "Am I right?"

"Yes, sir."

" 'To keep order'."

"Yes, Mr. Bennett."

"How did we find this out?"

"The President used Jay Gould's private telegraph wire to get the word to General Sherman."

"Good work."

"Thank you, Mr. Bennett. We've also heard a report that the President personally believes that Louisiana has definitely voted for Tilden, and that Tilden has been elected." The editor departed.

"But if Grant thinks Tilden is elected, why the troops?"

"That, Charlie, *is* why."

5

M IDNIGHT: November 8–9.

Before I went to the Sanfords' for dinner, I stopped at Gramercy Park, where an enthusiastic crowd still holds vigil. With some difficulty I convinced the police on guard that I was one of the Governor's advisers.

Tilden was in the main drawing room; he looked uncommonly grey and strained; the left eyelid droops more than ever. But his manner was easy.

"So glad you could come to dinner."

This was embarrassing, since I had not been invited to the "Victory" dinner for the inner court. Even as I spoke to him the courtiers were beginning to arrive.

"I'm afraid I've not come to dinner but . . ."

"But surely you were invited. If not, you are now." Just behind

Tilden, I saw several would-be Cabinet ministers moving purposefully towards us; my audience would be short.

"No. Thank you. I am with my daughter tonight. But there is something you should know." Rapidly, I told him everything that I had learned in Jamie's office. Tilden listened most intently. In fact, when Mrs. Pelton tried to draw him away to greet the other guests, he motioned for her to leave us alone.

"I knew about Mr. Reid of the *Times*," he said, when I had finished. "He is a man of absolute zeal, and of a perfect dishonesty." This is the harshest reference I have heard Tilden make to any opponent. "But I don't think there is any chance of the majorities we have gained at the South being reversed. "But"— the deep lines between his brows were now like trenches—"I did *not* know that Grant had despatched the troops."

"Surely it is too late to change the vote. Everyone knows you have carried Louisiana by twenty thousand votes."

"Less, I fear. But our majority is a large one. Unfortunately, there is still the Board of Registration and there is still the Returning Board that has the power to decide just what the vote is. And both boards are controlled by Republicans. Add Federal troops to this equation . . ." Tilden did not finish the sentence.

As I said good night, Tilden shook my hand warmly. "You have been a good friend, Mr. Schuyler." That cheered me, I must say. In fact, I am generally in a good mood, and convinced that there is now no way to keep Tilden from the presidency, short of a military coup d'état on the part of Grant.

Although the Sanford house is not yet finished, they are "camping out" in some splendour, if not total comfort.

Twenty guests were assembled in a drawing room where that which is not tapestried is gilded.

Although Denise must be in her sixth month, her condition was disguised by a beautiful rose-velvet creation that flared almost as much in the front as fashion requires the bustle to flare at the back. "Tell us everything! Emma says you've been with Mr. Tilden all day."

"I've just come from Gramercy Park." I fear that I allowed everyone to think that I had indeed been at the hero's side not only all day today but every day since the campaign began.

"What does he say? Has he gone and bought his ticket on the cars for Washington?" Sanford loomed before me. The other guests were, as usual, possessed of familiar faces and of familiar

names, but I am now reconciled to the fact that I shall never sort
out the New York gentry, and so go to my grave believing that
what looked to be the true Beekman was instead mere Fish.

"He's noncommittal. Of course he's won."

"Noncommittal?" Emma joined the group that had attached
itself to me as I stood in front of a Gobelin depicting Charle-
magne. "I have just read the *World*. Mr. Tilden says that he has
won because he was able to attract so many Republican votes."

"In the name of reform," added Sanford. "Well, I could've
sworn we had him beat all hollow. Fact, I told General Hayes on
my way back from California, 'The West is yours, General, particularly Oregon, where I've made a special effort.' Lord knows,
we did spend a lot of money up there. Anyway, I'm still hoping
that Tilden's measly five-hundred-vote majority will just go
away."

"Happily, it won't." I was firm, knowledgeable.

"Well, sir, soon you'll be in France." I turned on this, and there
was John Apgar. With my permission, Emma had confided to
him my dream.

"Don't tempt fate!"

"Oh, Mr. Tilden has won. The Family all agree. They're very
sad of course."

"And you?"

"Well, that depends on Emma, doesn't it?" John was suddenly,
unexpectedly wistful.

"I think that now that all this is over . . ." I stopped, not
wanting to commit Emma, who was watching us from across the
room; there was a warning look in her eyes. "Life will resume a
more normal course."

"I'm very happy for you, sir, anyway."

I have no idea what Emma intends to do, nor can I get her to
give me a straight answer. She will neither set a date for the
wedding nor break off the engagement. "I'm paralyzed," is the
very last word she has had to say on the subject.

I suspect that if Emma is truly out of the idea of becoming Mrs.
Apgar, she will keep putting off John until we know whether or
not I am made minister to France. Should I get the post, she will
then go back with me to Paris as my official hostess. I cannot say
that I find this arrangement anything but paradisal. Yet I do feel
sorry for John, for the limbo that she has put him in.

Denise looks forward with much excitement to motherhood.

"In February. What is it they say of February babies?"

"Nothing good. But then I feel toward babies much the way good King Herod did."

"Not this one. You will be his godfather. And Emma his god-mother."

"It *is* a he?"

"Oh, yes. One can tell."

"What does Madame Restell have to say?"

"I've not seen her. But Emma's talked to her. And Madame's sent one of her best women over to look at me and the verdict is that all's well. Touch wood." We touched wood together.

"Certainly you've never looked more beautiful." This was true.

"Then you must like the Rubens style. I am *very* fat, and never look at myself in the bath. I can hear him, you know. Right now, inside me. Rapping to be let out. He's very impatient."

"Poor boy! What a world to come into!"

"What a marvellous world! And the things that he will see that we won't. I do envy him."

"Unless it's a daughter."

"Impossible. But if it is, I shall call her Emma."

In my hotel room, I found a note from Jamie: "You must start writing again. The Republicans are sending their leaders—and their money—South. They're going to steal the election if they can. Popular vote: Tilden's beaten Hayes by more than 250,000 votes. This *used* to be enough to make anybody president."

I feel very secure tonight. There is no way of denying the presidency to a man who has won by such a popular majority no matter what tricks are played, bribes given, troops mustered.

Admittedly, the Electoral College—that ridiculous invention of the founders—can be manipulated to some degree but not sufficiently at this late hour to cheat the people of what they have so overwhelmingly voted for: the Tilden Administration.

On the floor beside the table I saw a newspaper slip which must have fallen out of Jamie's letter. With difficulty, I picked it up. A statement from Governor Hayes in Ohio to the New York *Sun*. "I am of the opinion that the Democrats have carried the country and elected Tilden . . ." My eyes blur. We have indeed won.

Eleven

1

THE UNITED STATES is now on the verge of civil war.

During the week since the Governor was elected president, the Republican press and the Republican party and Federal troops commanded by the Republican President have been openly at work trying to reverse the popular vote. It is a truly marvellous scandal, and deeply alarming.

As of this morning, Tilden is certain of 184 electoral votes, while Hayes is certain of only 166. Nineteen electoral votes are "in doubt," despite Tilden's plain and overwhelming victory at the polls.

Every day, new reports from all over the country excite the people dangerously. There is talk of a march on Washington. The South is reported to be arming. The better sort of Republicans are appalled at what's happening, and the Democratic majority in the country has suddenly acquired some very odd allies, amongst them Senator Conkling, who has declared Tilden the duly elected president but warns that desperate Republicans may yet steal what is not theirs. Conkling says that if Tilden will put himself forward promptly to claim what is his by right, then Conkling and a number of other influential Republicans will support him.

But will Tilden put himself forward—promptly?

This afternoon I made my way through the watchful crowd in Gramercy Park. After showing my special badge to the police who stand guard permanently at the house of the president-elect, I was allowed to enter. I found the downstairs rooms crowded with political leaders from every part of the country. I was pushed this way and that by strangers until, luckily, I saw Bigelow on the stairs. He motioned for me to follow him up to Tilden's study. To my question "What is happening?" he replied, "Nothing. Everything."

With Tilden were Hewitt, Dorsheimer (the lieutenant governor of New York State), and a Southern politician from Louisiana. Tilden rose from his desk, and greeted me formally. I noted that the left eyelid is drooping more than usual, which gives one the disquieting sense that Tilden is winking at those who would defraud him. Then the Governor sat down and said, "Mr. Hewitt has some figures for us."

I should note here that thus far Hewitt has proved to be a disaster as party chairman. Tilden selected Hewitt because he himself intended to administer the campaign, which he did with perfect success. But no one foresaw that in the aftermath Tilden would be forced to rely upon a party chairman who was elected to the House of Representatives less than two years ago, after a career in metallurgy. I suspect that the only true bond between him and Tilden is dyspepsia: he, too, belches, breaks wind, suffers.

But Hewitt reads figures impressively. "Gentlemen, the national popular vote is as follows: Tilden has received 4,300,590 votes. General Hayes has received 4,036,298 votes. That gives Mr. Tilden a popular majority of 264,292 votes. We have overwhelming—and uncontested—majorities in New York, New Jersey, and Connecticut. We also unexpectedly—but happily—carried Indiana. As a result, the true vote in the Electoral College is Tilden, 196 and Hayes, 173. It is not, as the Republicans claim, Tilden, 184; Hayes, 166, with 19 in doubt . . ."

"But while we're sittin' here, they are out there in the hen house stealin' our chickens from us—" began the Southerner.

"So it would appear." Tilden cut him short. "Go on, Mr. Hewitt."

"The Republicans hope to reverse our victories in Florida and Louisiana. In Florida we won by the narrow margin of 92 votes out of 48,774 cast. But in Louisiana we swept the state, enjoying a majority of 6,549 votes. Now the Returning Boards that will decide the elections in these two states are Republican. They are made up of uneducated, docile Negroes and of transplanted Northerners as well as—"

"You describe 'em in what I call a real polite way." The Southerner was grim. "What you mean are damned carpetbaggers with their burr-headed nigger friends."

"Sir, we allow the *other* side the passion." Tilden was delicately droll. "We can afford to, since we have the votes."

"For the present." The Southerner was drinking whisky from a beer mug.

"For the present." Hewitt echoed, and again referred to his memorandum (from which I have copied these statistics). "The combined electoral vote of Louisiana and Florida is twelve. Should those two states go to Hayes, he would be elected president by one vote in the Electoral College. Or 185 votes for Hayes and 184 votes for Governor Tilden."

"It does not seem to me possible that the Louisiana vote can be reversed—even by 'uneducated docile Negroes and transplanted Northerners,' " observed Tilden. "But we are getting disquieting news from those states. Bribery, intimidation . . ." He paused, and took yet another pill, drank mineral water. Unmedicated, Hewitt held back a rising belch with a strangling sound.

Tilden continued: "Gentlemen, a trap was prepared for us a year ago by the Republicans in the Senate. I was aware of what was happening at the time but since I was at Albany I was not in a position to—affect events. And our party in the Senate allowed themselves to be outmanoeuvred." For an instant Tilden's cold eye rested on Congressman Hewitt, who looked uncomfortable.

"Our success last year in the various state elections was a clear warning to the Republicans that this year we would carry New York and the other major states, which we have done. They also knew that the South was ours, which it is. How, then, could they prevent us from winning? Of course they had—they *have*—their troops in three of the Southern states with"—Tilden turned to the Southerner, and smiled—"carpetbag regimes. So they figured that if worse came to worse those illegal state governments could simply throw out our votes and add as many fraudulent votes as would be needed to make for a Republican victory."

"But this *can't* be done after the popular vote is already known!" Bigelow is innocent in ways that surprise me. Even I could see the events that are now in train.

"But it can. Our majorities will be—are being—challenged. There will be 're-counts.' There will be bribes given, and taken, and we shall certainly lose our majority of ninety-two in Florida."

"But you won't lose Louisiana, Governor, if you fight, and fight now!" This from the Southern politician.

"Fight, yes. And also pay?" Tilden was delicate, ironic.

"I'm afraid you'll have to pay, Governor. Everybody back home is for sale, no matter what party they belong to."

"You see my problem?" Tilden was suddenly hard; also, sad. "I have done what I set out to do. I have been elected president by a clear majority of the people who are as revolted as I am by the state of affairs in this country. Now, if I want the office to which I have been elected, I must outspend General Grant and his friends."

We were all of us silent. Bigelow looked uncommonly wretched, but then he is an idealist. Tilden did not speak for some minutes; instead, he stared at the clock over the mantel. With each movement of the second hand, we are propelled nearer and nearer to December 6, when the Electoral College will be convened in order to decide the fate not only of us in that room but of the United States as well.

From outside we could heard several male voices shouting, "Hurray for Uncle Sam," as the people have taken to calling Tilden. The Governor bit his underlip. Some sudden emotion stirred beneath that cool exterior.

"Yes, the trap," Tilden remembered. "Let me explain it. In 1865 a Republican-dominated Congress passed something called the Twenty-second Joint Rule. It was intended to clarify the Constitution, which says that the final vote of the Electoral College shall be delivered to the president of the Senate. Then with both houses of the Congress as witnesses, he will declare the vote of each state and have the total counted. The Constitution is silent on the question of what happens if a state's vote is disputed."

Suddenly, plunged into a matter of law, Tilden became almost cheerful. The voice strengthened. "The Twenty-second Joint Rule declared that should there be disagreement as to any state's returns, the matter would then be resolved in a joint session of

the Congress. A most statesmanlike solution to an ancient am-
biguity." The clock over the mantel struck five o'clock, and
Tilden stopped speaking. I suspect that each of us counted to
himself, foolishly, the five strokes.

"Now a joint rule of Congress is an absolute law, which cannot
be rescinded save by both houses. But last January our sly Republican friends in the Senate, anticipating defeat in this election,
and wanting to carry those Southern states, unilaterally abolished the ten-year old Joint Rule and—"

"Unilaterally and illegally?" Bigelow was looking more cheerful.

Tilden nodded. "It was all done swiftly, without debate. Our
party never knew what was happening until too late."

"But there must be some means of arbitration, even without
the Joint Rule." Hewitt was doing his best to appear knowledgeable in the one field that is the most remote from metallurgy.

"That is my hope. There is bound to be new machinery. We
must find some way to see that it is honestly established."

"Well, I say go and tell those who elected you to take to the
streets of New Orleans and Baton Rouge! And then you go there
yourself, as the president-elect, which you are, and with some
fifty thousand Louisiana Democrats in the streets, armed to the
teeth, the carpetbaggers won't dare steal your vote from you."

"There will also be fifty thousand Federal troops, ready to
re-commence the late war." Tilden was outwardly serene.

"But what am I to tell our people, who are even now waitin'
to hear from me at the telegraph office in New Orleans?"

To this challenge Tilden merely responded with his famed
mumble, "I'll see you later." If there is to be civil war, Tilden
does not want the credit for firing the first gun. I find his attitude
entirely admirable, and perfectly maddening.

"Well, sir, I'll tell you what will happen if you *don't* take a firm
stand this very minute." The Louisianian (must get his name) was
harsh. "There are a number—maybe as high as forty—Southern
Democratic members of the Congress who will desert you and
support Hayes if he promises to take the troops out of those states
where they now are and give us back our liberties."

"But, sir, you have overwhelmingly elected me to do this very
thing, and I will do it." Tilden was equally hard. "I cannot believe
that any Southerner will ever put his trust in the party of General
Grant."

At this point, Tilden was called downstairs to meet with a

number of constitutional lawyers. Disconsolately, we stayed on
in the study. The Louisianian proceeded to get drunk. Hewitt
examined charts.

In a low voice Bigelow told me some of the latest developments,
which I am *not* to write just yet for the *Herald*. "We can have
South Carolina's electoral vote for eighty thousand dollars."

"That's not unreasonable."

"Pelton's dealing with the members of the Returning Board
right now. They want the money in Baltimore by Sunday night.
In cash. In one-thousand- and five-thousand-dollar bills."

"Will the Governor pay?"

"No. At the moment the Governor is sending every honest and
distinguished man he can think of to the South to counteract the
Republicans, who've already sent half their leadership down
there, including your friend Garfield, who is in Louisiana right
now, wooing a Mr. J.M. Wells, the head of the Returning Board
for Louisiana."

"Is Mr. Wells expensive?"

Bigelow shuddered: not just a figurative shudder but an entire
true convulsion of the body. "I am told Mr. Wells will give us
Louisiana for one million dollars. Cash."

"The Governor . . .?"

". . . does not wish to pay for what he has already won."

"And Florida?"

"W.E. Chandler arrived there on the ninth. To date he has
been sent seven thousand dollars in cash from New York.
Meanwhile, just in case, the Republican governor of Florida
has asked General Grant for troops. We've sent some good
men there, too . . ."

"Armed with cash?"

Bigelow looked ill. "I pray not. But Hewitt *has* told me that the
price for Florida is two hundred thousand dollars. To be paid
directly to the Board of State Canvassers."

"That seems to me to be modest."

"That seems to me to be of a horror beyond belief!"

"John, you have spent most of your life in this city. Why are
you surprised that the politicians elsewhere come as high?"

"I have always thought of our native city as unique, due to the
Catholic influx." Bigelow's hobby-horse briefly pranced. "Still I
cannot see how the Republicans can steal Louisiana or Florida."

"If they pay the money that Tilden refuses to pay, they will have both states, regardless of the popular vote." This struck me as bleakly reasonable.

"Well, Pelton has gone underground." Bigelow was cryptic and sad.

I was heartened; and hope that while Tilden continues to speak of legitimacy and honesty in government, his brother-in-law will be busy buying the votes already won.

At the moment, Bigelow is assisting Tilden in the writing of a definitive study of *The Presidential Counts* since the time of George Washington. They believe that this scholarly work will absolutely prove to the Congress that Tilden has won the election.

If Governor Tilden has a fatal flaw, it is his curious notion that men can be compelled by good argument to be honest, to show disinterest where there is only interest and greed.

2

DECEMBER 13: Congress is now in session. The Senate has a Republican majority of 17. The House of Representatives has a Democratic majority of 74.

After a month of confusion, of money given and of money taken, of Federal troops on the alert, and of fierce Southern whites arming themselves to those famous proverbial teeth, there is still no resolution.

On December 6, the electors in the various states of the Union met. There were no surprises. As we have known all along, the Republican masters of Louisiana, Florida, and South Carolina have obliged their states to send two sets of returns to Congress; as has Oregon. One set favours Tilden, and reflects the actual vote; the other favours Hayes, and reflects fraud. Tilden still has 184 undisputed votes; Hayes, 165 (he has lost one vote); in dispute, 20.

This morning Hewitt declared Tilden to be the president.

Although many Democrats want the Governor to take the oath of office immediately, there has been no response at all from Gramercy Park. Tilden is busy preparing his legal case. Pelton is underground, spending money, I pray. Out in Ohio, Hayes is now silent while at Washington City President Grant is more than ever mysterious. On instructions from Tilden, Hewitt went to see the President last week. Like all of us, Tilden is alarmed at the way people speak so casually and so openly of coups d'état.

Hewitt found General Grant surprisingly straightforward. In Grant's view, Hayes has carried South Carolina (which may be true) and Florida (which is not true), but he agrees that Hayes has plainly lost Louisiana to Tilden.

The President then went on to observe that since Louisiana is such a peculiarly corrupt state and that since both sides have made complaints of irregularities, all sets of returns from Louisiana should be thrown out and the election decided in the House of Representatives, as prescribed by the Constitution. Since the House is Democratic, Grant tacitly accepts the fact that Tilden is his successor. We are much encouraged.

Yet in every corner of the land storm warnings sound. "Tilden or Blood!" is a cry more and more heard not only at the South but here in the city.

Although my last piece for the *Herald* examined our electoral process in order to make the case that "due process of law" is all that keeps us from becoming another Mexico, I am by no means certain that this terrible business is going to have a peaceful resolution.

Item: this morning Company D, 35th Battalion, of the New York National Guard declared themselves ready to march on Washington. And the South is arming.

"Tilden or Blood!"

I think of Paris—of the Communards—of the slaughter.

3

THIS EVENING at Chickering Hall I addressed a large audience of Europeans come to observe the election. Apparently I was the choice of both Democrats and Republicans to address those foreign personalities (to a man, lovers of liberty) who have converged on New York to observe the way our republic manages elections in its hundredth year.

Since the opening of the Centennial Exhibition, the foreign press have been writing paeans to the United States. Now—for more than a month—they have been astonished witnesses to the complete breakdown of our electoral system. There were elements of high comedy, I fear, in my glum performance.

I was introduced by August Belmont, whose Eighteenth Street mansion is just across Fifth Avenue from the Hall. Although, like me, Belmont is a Tilden supporter, it was agreed that tonight neither of us would be partisan as we did our best to explain the constitutional crisis to our country's well-wishers.

Belmont was brief, gracious; he spoke in both French and German. I spoke only in French.

As I crossed the stage, the calcium or limelights full upon me, my heart's pounding was far louder in my ears than the polite applause that greeted me.

I had a written French text. Unfortunately, the lights had been so cunningly arranged that I was quite dazzled and could not read. So I improvised, not too badly, using my very special, very resonant sententious manner, reminiscent of Flaubert's *idiot* and thus entirely suitable for this peculiar occasion.

When I came to the matter of corruption, I was delicate. The audience, however, knew perfectly well what I was talking about.

"It *is* mysterious," I said, "how many flaws can be found in the actual process of voting. It should be a simple matter for a voter to mark his ballot Democratic or Republican. But ever since the

election last November, the good people of Florida—or at least
their Republican guardians—have discovered that Tilden did not
win that languorous, tropical state by ninety-two votes, but lost
it to Hayes by nine hundred and ninety-two. Since these margins
are small, it is possible that the first count *was* incorrect. But now
we are told that Louisiana—also languorous, tropical—after giving Tilden a majority of six thousand five hundred and forty-nine
votes in November, has now, on second thought, elected Hayes
with a majority of four thousand eight hundred and seven
votes . . ."

By this time there was some laughter and a good deal of mur-
muring in the audience. Squinting hard, I was just able to see
Emma, sitting with Mrs. Belmont in the central box.

"These curious last-minute changes in the voting of the two
states caused the Electoral College on December sixth to elect
Hayes—by one vote—president. But since Hayes has clearly lost
the election by more than a quarter-million votes to Tilden, the
Congress must now decide which of the two sets of disputed
returns from the contested four states are valid: the first set that
elected Tilden in November or the second set that elected Hayes
in December."

Just below me, in the first row, an angry Frenchman was now
on his feet. He is one of a group of workmen sent to observe the
ways of Democracy, their passage paid for by a popular subscrip-
tion. As the party of workmen left France they were blessed by
none other than Victor Hugo himself, whose prose style is even
more emptily splendid than the one I resort to in French.

Hugo had roared, "The future is already dawning, and it
clearly belongs to Democracy, which is purely pacific." Apparently the great man has not yet been told of America's attack on
Mexico in the forties or on Canada in 1812. Hugo spoke confi-
dently of the coming United States of *Europe* and bade the good
workmen to go forth, bearing a torch (how rhetoricians love that
torch!), "the torch of civilization from the land where Christ was
born to the land which beheld the birth of John Brown." It would
seem that the master's genius stops short of elementary geogra-
phy.

"Explain to me, sir," said the workman, "in what way this
election differs from that infamous election where Louis Napoleon destroyed the French republic, and made himself emperor."

Much cheering and applause. Out of the corner of my eye, I

saw Belmont nodding his head in a most demagogic way at the audience.

"The difference," I said, when the audience had again grown quiet, "is that General Grant will leave office in March—"

"But Grant's party . . ."

"But Grant's heir . . ."

"But Hayes . . ."

From various parts of the Hall the discouraged—no, the enraged—lovers of democracy started to shout their slogans and their maledictions.

In a last desperate effort to maintain control, I shouted back: "In February the Congress will declare that Samuel Tilden—already elected president by a majority of a quarter million votes—is indeed our president. And the American republic will continue, and will flourish!" I managed to create a sufficient ovation at that point to get myself offstage. I was soaked with sweat, and shaking as if from fever.

Emma and I went back with the Belmonts to their house—no, palace—where supper had been prepared for half a hundred people, of whom a number had been at Chickering Hall. I was complimented on my performance. But I was not allowed to bask for very long in much-needed praise. Before I could do more than drink a glass of champagne, Belmont had led me into his library, where beneath acres of fine morocco bindings, he delivered himself of an impassioned speech, his guttural accent every bit as reminiscent of Bismarck's as was his startling theme. "That workman was correct. What's happening now *is* like what Louis Napoleon did when he made himself Napoleon III. But I want Tilden to play the part of Louis Napoleon. I want him to take the crown. Because it's his, by every right. So let him seize it. And let him use force if necessary!"

"But he has no force. *They* have the troops." I settled back in a leather-covered chair of the new deep sort. My clothes were clinging to me most disagreeably as the sweat began to dry. All I need now is to contract pneumonia.

"They are worse than Jacobins!" Belmont inveighed against the Republican leadership, shifting the historic analogy to yet an earlier epoch.

"Everything," I said soothingly, "will be resolved by some sort of electoral commission."

"But we don't know *what* the commission will be. Or who will be on it. But we do know that every day that passes, our position weakens. For a month the country has thought of Tilden as the next president. But now they begin to doubt. They read the *Times* . . ."

"*And* the *Herald*," I added softly; ours is the larger circulation.

"I want Tilden in Washington. Now!"

"Taking the oath of office?"

"No. He'll do that in March, as the Constitution prescribes. But I want him directing our party in the Congress. He can't leave anything so important to Hewitt, who's a good man but . . . well, Tilden is a master of politics. He also has legitimacy. And the combination . . ." And so on.

Finally, I was released; and had my supper. Just as I was leaving the Belmont house, I was stopped by a plainly dressed middle-aged woman who had been waiting for me in the street. "I am a cousin of your late wife, Mr. Schuyler." And so she was (her grandmother was a Traxler; she, too, is called Emma). She lives in Wisconsin where she has supported herself and five children by writing for the foreign press ever since her Austrian husband left home one day. I promised to give her an interview.

"My oldest daughter is very like yours," she said wistfully. Emma was kind to her unfortunate cousin and namesake.

Emma dropped me off at the Fifth Avenue Hotel on her way to the Sanford house, where she dwells in lonely state. Denise is in South Carolina. Sanford is in Washington, meddling in the electoral process. Most genially he invited me to stay in the house during his absence but I said that I prefer living at my hotel with its private telegraph office and its milling throngs of Republican politicians. I am able to learn more during a half-hour in the Amen Corner than I can from a reading of all the newspapers.

"You were superb, Papa!" Emma was comforting.

"I was adequate, which is superb given that audience and all that I could *not* say."

"You must spend Christmas with us, in the South. Denise insists. So do I."

"I know she does." Denise writes me nearly every day to report that her spirits and health are both good.

"I must stay here with the Governor."

"But all this could take a very long time."

"Not too long. By March fourth, there must be a new president. That is the law."

"So that means there will be two months of—disturbance, doesn't it?"

"I'm afraid so."

"Will there be revolution?" The question on Emma's lips was very real. We have lived through so many desperate bloody times at Paris.

"No one knows," was my wise response. "It depends on the Governor. At the moment there are supposed to be more than a hundred thousand men at the South, ready to fight."

"Now I know why one visits but does not actually *live* in Africa."

Emma goes South tomorrow. I assume she will be safe enough on the Sanford plantation, where Denise plans to stay until her child is born in February.

In a letter waiting for me when I got back to my room just now, Denise writes, "Emma thinks it safer here. Certainly it's comfortable. And she has sent me Madame Restell's most comforting and certainly most expensive 'assistant' . . . is that the word? to see me through the *accouchement*. But you'll be here long before then. By New Year's Day at the latest, or I shall be furious and deprive you of your godfatherdom!"

Twelve

1

I write this on the cars from Albany to New York. The parlour car is nearly empty. In the seat next to me is Governor Tilden, as of this morning governor no longer. At the moment Tilden is sleeping in an upright position, the expression on his face politely expectant. Bigelow is across the aisle from us. Nearby, the detective is reading a novel with a yellow cover. Our several fellow travellers stare with some interest at the president-elect. It is New Year's Day, 1877.

I must say that I have never been so tired in my life. In fact, all three of us are beginning to succumb to the never-ceasing strain.

Our day began when the outgoing governor of New York, Samuel Tilden, escorted his successor, one Lucius Robinson, into the Assembly chamber of the state capitol to take the oath of office.

Bigelow and I sat in the back of the chamber, and I fear that Bigelow slept through most of Tilden's graceful speech. But then Bigelow had helped write it.

I was on hand in my capacity as official Tilden-watcher for the

Herald. The national press was represented hardly at all.

Bigelow remarked that the number of journalists in attendance was about average for the inaugural of a New York governor. This is ominous, considering that today Tilden gave his first major address since being elected president.

With altogether too much delicacy Tilden referred to the current "subject of controversy," making the point that in the twenty-two previous presidential elections, the Congress had simply recorded the votes sent them by the Electoral College. But now the Congress must choose between two absolutely conflicting sets of votes sent them by four states.

Tilden reminded the audience that three years ago the Congress had declared illegal the present government of Louisiana, whose Returning Board has just seen fit to reverse the state's popular vote. Tilden also spelled out the illegality of the South Carolina and Florida boards. But where he ought to have thundered his contempt for the most corrupt and now tyrannous Administration in our history and unfurled his banner as our rightful lord, he was throughout his address very much the dry constitutional lawyer and in no way the outraged tribune of a cheated people.

Tilden made no reference to the two congressional committees (one from the Senate, the other from the House) whose task it is to create a solution. The House Committee on Privileges has already declared that the election must be resolved *within* the Congress. Tilden concurs on the ground that the Constitution requires disputed presidential elections to be decided in the House of Representatives, as was done in 1800, when Colonel Burr and Thomas Jefferson each received the same number of votes for the presidency. The House chose between them, and in my prejudiced view chose unwisely.

Another solution is to form some sort of special agency *outside* the Congress, and let it decide. Tilden thinks such an agency would be contrary to both Constitution and custom. Well, we shall know soon enough, for there will be a joint session of the two committees on January 12. Jamie insists I go to Washington.

After the inaugural of the new governor, Bigelow and I accompanied Tilden to the house in Eagle Street where some trunks were assembled, as well as half a dozen well-wishers (*not* including the new governor), and a representative of the New York Central Railroad.

"We shall go back to the city in the five P.M. cars," said Tilden.

"Then we'll check these trunks straight on through for you, Governor."

"Straight through to Washington City. To the White House," I heard myself say. There was general if strained laughter, and even Tilden smiled, though he said nothing.

Just before 5:00 P.M. of this grey, freezing day, we arrived at the depot. To my astonishment no one had come to say good-bye. Awkwardly we stood by the potbellied stove in the nearly empty station, trying to make conversation.

I found it suddenly hard to believe that this lonely small figure was the president of a great nation and the center of a national crisis. "Tilden or Blood!" Well, beside me in the parlour car at this very moment dozes the first part of that rallying cry. When comes the second?

There are, I suppose, explanations for the lack of a crowd. Today is New Year's Day and everyone is home or paying calls. Certainly the cars are nearly empty but . . .

We are rattling through the town of Hudson. Between red-brick houses I can see the river, frozen solid. A single iceboat with a blue sail skims swiftly over the ice, close to where boys have built a bonfire. Smoke from the chimneys of Catskill downriver gives an infernal aspect to a frozen landscape that lacks only the slow unfurling of the great cold leathern wings of Dante's Satan to match my mood.

I have just moved across the aisle. I sit next to Bigelow, who is now wide-awake. "What do you make of it?"

Bigelow knew exactly what I meant. He spoke in a low voice in order not to disturb Tilden. "The Governor was never popular at Albany. They just didn't care for him."

"But he is the president."

"I know. Strange, isn't it? To win such a victory and watch it all leak away."

"Except it hasn't."

"We're in the hands of Congress now." Bigelow looked forlorn. "And of Hewitt. I have no idea what he'll do when the House meets tomorrow."

"Can't you persuade the Governor to take charge, directly?"

"He won't. 'Separation of powers,' he says."

"Are the Southern Democrats in Congress apt to defect?"

"Not yet. Not until Hayes and Grant make them an irresistible offer."

Across the aisle Tilden's eyes are now open. Neutrally, he watches us. The three of us look at one another as the cars hurtle south through the icy evening. For some time now not one of us has had anything to say.

2

JANUARY 14, 1877. A Sunday. I am still in New York. Jamie was much put out that I did not go to Washington City but I think that now he sees the wisdom of my having stayed close to Tilden.

I ought to note that in the midst of all this high political drama there has been some comedy. On New Year's Day, while I was at Albany, Jamie made the rounds of those houses that still receive him.

By the time he got to the house of his fiancée, Miss May, he was so drunk that he pissed in the front parlour fireplace. Last week a male relative of the now former fiancée accosted Jamie in front of the Union Club and horsewhipped him.

I found Jamie still bruised, and very grim. He has said nothing to me about the matter, but then he does not have to, since New York talks of nothing else.

Until two days ago, when the committees met in joint session, there was no news at all out of Washington City. The members of the two committees had conducted their affairs in absolute secrecy. This uncharacteristic continence has alarmed us all.

Last night Hewitt came up from Washington, bringing with him a draft of the joint resolution which the two committees will submit to the whole Congress. Apparently Tilden and Hewitt sat up most of last night, going over the various articles of the bill.

Just before noon Tilden and Hewitt appeared in the downstairs parlour, where a half dozen advisers (and myself) were gathered. Tilden looks uncommonly serene. I have now come to recognize that the more serene he looks the more furious he is.

"Gentlemen, the joint committee of the Congress have decided that there is to be an electoral commission. Although members of Congress will sit on the commission, this . . . novelty will exist outside the Congress, as well as outside the Constitution."

"But this is only a proposal." Bigelow was quick. "The Congress can still reject it."

"Mr. Hewitt tells me that the Democratic members of the Senate committee have already accepted the principle of such a commission . . ."

"But, Governor, after consulting you, the House—which is controlled by us—can still reject what the joint committee propose." This from one of the legal advisers.

Tilden turned to Hewitt, "Isn't it rather late in the day to consult me?"

Hewitt looked wretched; he has been constantly but softly belching all day. Like Napoleon, he keeps his hand plunged inside his coat, rubbing his dyspeptic stomach.

"Well, Governor, the House committee isn't actually *consulting* you even now. I mean they have their constitutional and separate duty to perform. *I* consult you of course."

We then sat at a baize-covered table and the plan for an electoral commission was gone over carefully. As always, in matters of detail, the Governor is impressive. During the night he had mastered the contents. "*Personally*, I find this totally unconstitutional."

"Then oppose it!" Although a lawyer, Bigelow has not the legal temperament. "The House will support you."

"John, I cannot openly thrust myself into the deliberations of the legislative branch of the government."

"Then, secretly!" Thus Bigelow, devotee of all that is right.

A suggestion of a smile on the arched blue-grey lips. "I don't think that you've quite understood Mr. Hewitt. Since our party in the Senate favours this commission, he thinks that the House will follow suit. It is now too late to stop this . . . thing."

"But what *do* you advise?" Hewitt looked like a man who has failed; which he has.

"I certainly will not advise you to agree to this bill. But I am willing to advise you about details."

The proposed electoral commission was then carefully examined. There is to be a tribunal of thirteen worthies. Nine members will come from the two houses of Congress. Four will be Justices of the Supreme Court. Each house of the Congress will choose five members, of whom one is to be eliminated by lot.

Tilden regarded this last example of congressional ingenuity as typically frivolous. "I may lose the presidency," he said in a hard voice, "but I will not raffle for it."

"Then how *should* the commission be chosen?" asked Hewitt.

"Certainly not by chance, and not through intrigue. I would advise you to move slowly, deliberately. After all, we have a month in which to negotiate."

But Hewitt has a fearful nature. "There is a danger, Governor, that—well, of a collision with General Grant."

Tilden showed some amusement. "I can think of nothing more helpful to our cause than the President ordering Federal troops into the Capitol. But he won't. My point is why surrender *before* the battle? There will be plenty of time for surrender *if* we lose. No, we must hold out for the best terms."

"But they're meeting tonight at Washington, our Democratic committee members. They will want to know if you will personally adhere to this plan."

"Since you put it on a personal basis, no, I will not adhere." Tilden suddenly bared his teeth. A good deal of rage has been accumulating behind that most reasonable and decorous façade.

"This commission is purest mischief. But should it be adopted by the Congress, I will help in any way I can to minimize the dangers of their inept and hasty work. Meanwhile, you may say that, personally, I do not accept any part of this and that I deeply deplore"—and here he glanced meaningfully at me—"the secrecy in which the Congress has concocted what, in effect, will be an extralegal presidential election, contrary to all custom."

"I'll telegraph our leaders that you oppose the plan." Hewitt looked most unhappy.

"But do tell them how much I appreciate their courtesy in consulting me, even after the fact." The cold gaze of a tiger glared across the baize-covered table. "I can see why they would like my blessing on their unsatisfactory labours, but *that* I am obliged to withhold. Personally, I would suggest placing the whole matter before a court of arbitrament. But then I am just a lawyer and not a revolutionary."

"Governor, if you *absolutely* disapprove of the bill, it will not be passed." Hewitt was abrupt, and startling.

Bigelow and I exchanged a look. Now was Tilden's chance. But suddenly lawyer replaced tiger at that table. "I cannot be put in the position of appearing to oppose an arbitrament by the Congress when our present dilemma *does* call for something of the sort." On that legal ground, Tilden gravely undermined his own position.

Later in the day Bigelow remonstrated with him, but Tilden was firm in his principle. He would accept, in theory, the electoral commission, but would change, if he could, the means by which its membership was chosen.

Shortly before midnight a messenger arrived from the glorious Charles Francis Adams himself. The great man proposed that Tilden and Hayes jointly call for a new election.

Tilden was amused. "The Republicans having stolen three states from us without rehearsal, can now, thanks to their recent criminal practices, efficiently steal six. My compliments to Mr. Adams," he said to the messenger. "I will see him later."

"What," I asked, "may I say about all this for the *Herald*?"

"I would appreciate it if you would give the impression that I am neutral, at present."

"But may I say that you do plan to fight for the office you have won?" I grow more alarmed by the minute. Tilden the lawyer is actively working against Tilden the leader, who has fired with a rage for reform a majority of our countrymen.

"The word is not 'fight,' Mr. Schuyler. At least not yet. The word is 'arbitrate.' "

3

JANUARY 25. At Willard's Hotel, Washington City.

On January 17, details of the electoral commission bill were published. That night I asked Governor Tilden the obvious question: What was his view of the bill, which must now be voted on by the Congress?

"Unchanged." The voice was weary; he has lost entirely his famous "snap." "I stand by the Constitution, by custom, by the twenty-two previous elections for president. If neither Hayes nor I has a majority in the Electoral College, then the Constitution prescribes that the president be chosen by the House and that the vice president be chosen by the Senate. If the House should name me president, as it is inclined to do, then I would go immediately to Washington and take the oath of office, even though I were to be shot five minutes later."

"What of Governor Hayes?"

A smile flickered on papery lips. "The only thing we have in common is that we each detest this commission."

"Then why don't you jointly denounce it?"

"For one thing, we cannot—either of us—control our parties in the Congress. Particularly now. Also Governor Hayes is— obligated to the Senate, whose Republican president counts the electoral votes. Anyway, the thing is done."

"But Congress could still reject the joint committee's bill."

"Congress will accept the bill. And the loudest objections to it will come not from our party but from the Republican Stalwarts." This was most surprising. I tried to pursue the matter, but Tilden only shook his head and smiled a cryptic smile. Despite what he says officially, I have the impression that he is not displeased with what is happening.

As we parted, Tilden said, reflexively (will "automatedly" soon become a post-centennial neologism?), "I'll see you later."

The night before I left New York I had a long talk with Jamie, and found him uncharacteristically sombre—and sober.

Apparently the famous event of New Year's Day has made the greatest impression on him. I am still not quite certain as to what happened on that ill-omened day; but then no one else seems to know either. In fact, New York is now divided into quarrelling factions. The largest group maintains that Jamie urinated in the cannel-coal fireplace of Colonel May's front parlour. The second largest group bitterly protests this version, declaring that in actual fact it was a china umbrella stand that received the transmuted razzle-dazzles. A small but dedicated sect does not merely believe but, magically, *knows* that Jamie pissed into a *blue Delft Chinese* bowl. The identifying adjectives are always repeated in exactly the same significant order, like the Hail Mary. A number of sturdy nonconformists think that a grand piano also played an important part in the sacred story.

In any event, on January 3, a member of the former fiancée's family named Fred May accosted Jamie outside the Union Club. Mr. May was armed with a cowhide strip. Through the windows of the Union Club a dozen horrified members like a Greek chorus observed with pity and awe the terrible *agon*, which ended with the two men falling into a snowdrift.

Wanting to salvage honour, Jamie then proceeded to challenge Mr. May to a duel. On January 7 the two heroes met at something called Slaughterer's Gap, a fashionable place for duellists, since it is possible for one would-be assassin to stand in Delaware whilst the other stands in Maryland, causing no end of juridical problems should murder be committed.

But there was no murder that day. Mr. May saw fit to express his contempt for bold urinaters by firing into the air. Jamie was too nervous to fire at all. Honour was satisfied.

Jamie made only one reference to the duel. I, of course, made none. I noticed that he kept wriggling uncomfortably, and tugging at his shirt.

"What's wrong?" I finally asked.

"May!" Jamie retorted, assuming correctly that I knew who and what he was talking about. Then Jamie unbuttoned his shirt. "Look!" And he bared for me a metal-mesh inner waistcoat. "This can stop any bullet. Pure high-quality steel. But it pinches something fierce."

"But is a bullet apt ever to be fired?" I asked. "At you?"

"Oh, yes. He's waiting for me. Skulking about in alleyways. Climbing up on fire escapes. But I'm ready for him." Jamie withdrew a small pistol from his coat pocket. "I sleep with one eye open, you can bet."

"Do put that thing away." Since I am at best nervous in the presence of all firearms, a pistol in the hand of Jamie Bennett was altogether a most alarming experience.

Jamie put away the pistol and without a change in tone said, "*He* ought to be keeping that one good eye of his open, too. Your friend Tilden."

"I was just with him. He seems—surprisingly—pleased with the commission."

"Watch Davis. That's the man."

"The Supreme Court Justice?"

Jamie nodded. Then contrary to his new rule, he shut both eyes and began to recite: "The commission will be composed of fifteen members. Five will come from the Senate. Of the five from the

Senate, three are for Hayes and two are for Tilden. Of the five members from the House, three are for Tilden and two are for Hayes. So House and Senate cancel each other out. Four Supreme Court Justices have been appointed to the commission. Two are for Hayes. Two are for Tilden. These four Justices are now obliged by the electoral commission law to pick a fifth Justice as an independent judge, and that will be Davis."

"You are assuming that Congress is going to accept this novelty."

"Oh, yes. No doubt of it. And the fifth Justice is going to be Davis. And he's going to decide the election. He's an Illinois man. A founder of the Republican party who was put on the Court by Honest Ape. But Davis sounds like a Democrat a lot of the time because he wants to be the Democratic candidate for president some day."

"Then he'll vote for Tilden."

"Maybe. Anyway, watch him. He's sly."

Nordhoff confirmed Jamie's estimate of Davis. "But it's too early to tell. We haven't got the electoral commission yet." That was yesterday. Today, January 25, we are halfway to getting the commission.

By a vote of 47 to 17, the Senate early this morning approved the bill. I was greatly heartened by the fact that sixteen of the seventeen senators who voted against the bill were Republicans, amongst them Blaine, who warned his party that this electoral commission will disarm them of their principal weapon: the fact that the Constitution requires the president of the Senate (currently the Republican Thomas W. Ferry) to *count* the electoral votes. But Conkling spoke magnificently in favour of the bill, a good sign, since he not so secretly supports Tilden. Speaking for Hayes himself, Senator Sherman bitterly opposed the commission. I take this to mean that the all-important fifth Justice is bound to support Tilden.

In any case, the reason for the Republican dismay is apparent: twenty electoral votes are in dispute. Tilden needs to win only one of the twenty to be elected president. Certainly, there seems no way that he could lose all twenty, since most of them were his to begin with.

At about noon this afternoon, I was in the cloakroom of the House, talking to Hewitt. He was enormously pleased with this morning's vote in the Senate. While we were talking, the bill for

the electoral commission was being introduced into the House.
"And tomorrow we'll pass it two to one!"

We were interrupted by a page with a telegram for Hewitt. As
he read it, his mouth fell open like a landed fish. "My God."

One of the congressmen at his side took the telegram. He, too,
was appalled. "But they can't. It's not possible."

"Well, they have. And it is possible." Thus was I privileged to
be amongst the first in Washington to know that the Illinois
legislature had that morning elected Justice Davis to the United
States Senate, with heavy Democratic support.

"But Davis can still serve on the commission." Hewitt was
emphatic. "He won't be obliged to take his seat in the Senate until
March."

"But will he serve?" That urgent question spread through the
cloakrooms, the lobbies, the city, the nation.

I dined this evening with the Garfields, and a dozen Republican leaders. The only lady present was the noble Lucretia who
seemed not at all distressed by her singularity.

Needless to say, the talk was of the commission and of Davis's
sudden election.

"Mr. Schuyler is a Tilden spy." Garfield genially warned his
friends. "We must not plot too openly." Garfield waved a damp
handkerchief in my direction. He has been suffering from a bad
cold.

"We don't plot at all. We're too stupid," was the sour observa-
tion of an elderly Stalwart. "That Tilden of yours has just gone
and put Judge Davis in his pocket, by making him a senator like
that."

After dinner Garfield puffed on his cigar and Lucretia did
needlepoint. From time to time she thrust the needle of her own
analysis into the glum stuff of the evening's mood. Defeat was
palpable in that company.

Garfield and I, momentarily excluded from the general conversation, sat in a corner of the family parlour. In a low voice Garfield told me, "We're going to lose tomorrow in the House.
That'll be the end of Hayes."

"But doesn't Tilden deserve to be elected? I mean, isn't it usual
to grant the office to the man who gets the most votes?" Possibilities of a play on the verb "grant" in this particular context occurred to me, but I let them swiftly go. We are all of us so trapped

by the desperate struggle for power that any sort of wit is a kind of blasphemy.

"I don't think he *is* the winner. Not truly." The beautiful blue eyes glittered with their usual sincerity; as always, I was captivated.

"But what about Louisiana? Tilden won the state by a large majority?"

Garfield shook his head. "I don't think he did. Not really. After all, I was there. The President sent me. And I am truly convinced that in a *fair* election Hayes would have won Louisiana."

"The first returns were twenty thousand for Tilden."

"I admit there were errors on both sides."

"Errors or crimes?"

Garfield looked unhappy; he never likes to hear or say the hard accurate word if he can find a soft euphemistic replacement. "Crimes, too. Yes. After all, the state in question *is* Louisiana, and I've never seen anything like those people. Did you know that the head of the Returning Board . . ." But he stopped himself. "I mustn't go into that since I'm apt to be a member of the electoral commission."

"You don't have to go into it. I already know the man's price. He wanted a quarter-million dollars, which I assume your party paid him, since he gave you the vote."

"What I find unfair," said Garfield, moving with his usual quick grace from the dangerous to the anodyne, "is the way that the press ignores real issues. For instance, in almost every parish of Louisiana the Democrats kept the Negroes from the polls. They threatened them. Beat them. Terrified them. So even if the first vote in Louisiana had been accurate, it would not have been honest or representative, since the Negroes were almost entirely excluded from the canvass."

I must say that Garfield was as plausible and as charming as ever. There is no crime that his party can commit that he will not find some way of . . .

4

I AM IN THE TELEGRAPH OFFICE at the Capitol, where Nordhoff is transmitting the news to the New York *Herald*.

The Associate Justice of the Supreme Court, Mr. David Davis (on whom, Jamie said, to keep an eye), has just announced that he will *not* serve on the electoral commission, even though he intends to stay on the Court until March 4. According to his statement, "I can say without the least reserve" that the mysterious translation to the Senate was "entirely unsought and unexpected."

Nordhoff is much amused by that last word. "Davis has known for at least two weeks that he would be elected to the Senate. And he certainly wanted it."

"But did Tilden know it two weeks ago? Did Tilden arrange it?"

"You tell me. He's your friend. I do know that Hewitt was kept in the dark until yesterday."

Davis went on to say that he has been "anxious for two years to retire." I am writing this in a corner of the crowded telegraph office, waiting for Nordhoff to finish with the telegrapher. I shall begin my own story tonight.

As Garfield predicted, the electoral commission bill passed the house on January 26. One hundred and ninety-one voted in favour of the bill and eighty-six voted against it, amongst them Garfield.

On January 29 President Grant signed the bill, and the electoral commission now exists. Until yesterday's bombshell, the Democrats were euphoric. They had counted on Davis to be the deciding vote in their favour. Now he is (mysteriously?) gone. Piously, Davis tells everyone that he could not bear the responsibility of deciding a presidential election. For one thing he is sensitive about having been born at the South; for another, he has taken positions on the Court displeasing to many Republicans; finally, he is somewhat embarrassed at having been so "unexpectedly" made a senator not so much by his friends the Greenbackers but by the Democratic party of Illinois.

The defection of Davis has created perfect confusion. After all, the only reason the Democrats in Congress supported the electoral commission was because they believed that Davis would have the decisive vote.

Nordhoff thinks that the Republicans have known all along that Davis would not serve; and that Hewitt and the Democrats in Congress fell crashing into a trap which Tilden helped contrive by arranging a Senate seat for the Machiavellian Davis.

If this is true, was Garfield—of the luminous, honest, loving blue eyes—once again lying to me?

January 29. At Willard's.

This morning I had a few minutes with Hewitt in the cloakroom of the House. He has every reason to look as harassed as he does.

We stood trapped between two desks by a crush of lobbyists and representatives who made it suddenly possible for me to have him to myself: there were so many who wanted to take my place that none did or could in that mass of black-coated tobacco (and worse)-smelling political flesh.

"Did you ever ask Davis—before all this—if he would serve?"

"Certainly not." Hewitt was emphatic. "That would have been unethical. Besides, it never occurred to us that he would *not* go on the commission." I believe Hewitt.

Yet Nordhoff tells me that Tilden knew as early as January 13 that Davis would go to the Senate. Why then did Tilden not tell Hewitt? Is it possible that Tilden secretly prefers not Davis but one of the four remaining Justices available for appointment?

From the beginning the leading Democratic senators have favoured, officially, the commission because they believe in the essential impartiality of any and all Supreme Court Justices on the ground that when faced with fraud, these noble men will say it is fraud. I think this naïve and see no reason to exempt these high jurists from the universal corruption, since theirs, too, is an African provenance. Nordhoff thinks that the Democratic senators, secretly, dislike Tilden and would like to see him defeated.

The remaining four Justices are all Republican, at least nominally. Currently, the Democrats would like the crucial fifth Justice to be one Joseph P. Bradley, of New Jersey. Bradley was appointed to the Court by Grant after a long and somewhat shady career as a railroad attorney and Western judge. Originally a radical Republican, Bradley has lately presided over the Southern Circuit for the Court and has given satisfactory "justice" to the Southern whites.

Apparently Tilden and Hewitt have confidence in Bradley. At least, that is the word going around.

January 29. At Willard's.

Justice Bradley is the fifteenth member of the commission, and his vote will decide the election, since the votes of the other fourteen members (amongst them Garfield) are already known to be split seven to seven no matter what evidence is presented them in their lofty capacity as keepers of the national conscience, as duly sworn detectors of fraudulent election returns, as sole electors of the nineteenth president.

I am so nervous that I sleep soundly, dream not at all, and enjoy perfect health, or its appearance.

Thirteen

1

FEBRUARY 8. 2:00 A.M. At Willard's Hotel.

    I have just got back from Hewitt's house. We have won!

I feel like a boy again—though why it is always assumed that any boy, by definition, feels good I do not know. I certainly never did.

On January 31 the electoral commission met in more or less solemn state in the Supreme Court's chamber at the Capitol, a small, elegant, rather ominous-looking room.

On a high dais sit the empty thrones of the Justices. Overlooking this dais is a small gallery where the press and interested parties normally sit. The small well of the chamber contains a large table at which sit the fifteen members of the electoral commission, chaired by the most ancient of the Justices, Mr. Clifford. Solemnly he receives the various lawyers representing Tilden and Hayes, and accepts their lengthy learned briefs.

The principal objective of Tilden's lawyers has been to determine whether or not the commission has the power "to go behind the returns." In other words, to produce witnesses and evidence proving Republican fraud. Tilden's lawyers maintain that he was plainly elected in the disputed states but that later "jugglery" denied him the election.

The Republicans deny any "jugglery" and declare piously that to "go behind the returns" would be an invasion of states' rights! So much for the party that fought one of the bloodiest wars in all history to prove the absolute primacy of the Federal government over any of its component states.

Nordhoff and I sat in the crowded gallery looking down on the commission, neither able to follow any of the first day's proceedings. But Nordhoff did tell me that "From the beginning the entire joint committee was in favour of going behind the returns. That was the whole point to having an electoral commission. Unfortunately, Friend Hewitt never got the Republicans to agree publicly to what they had agreed to in secret session."

"Hewitt is not the greatest party manager, is he?"

"I think," said Nordhoff, as if translating at sight from an old German text, "that this man is a wanting fool."

From the well of the chamber Garfield waved at us. He looked more cheerful than he did the other night. I take this to be a very bad sign indeed.

Nordhoff pointed out Bradley to me. The arbiter of a nation's (and my) destiny is a nondescript creature, with a perpetual half-smile. I take this to be another bad sign, too. But then I was collecting ill-omens all that day.

The next day, as well.

On February 1, the two houses of Congress met in the chamber of the House of Representatives. Since the press gallery was overfull, Garfield got me a place in the Distinguished Visitors gallery, where I was surrounded by what looked to be the entire diplomatic corps, including Baron Jacobi, who was squeezed between me and the British minister Sir Edwin Thornton.

"What nation do you represent, dear Schuyler?" The Baron whispered in his *boulevardier* French.

"The kingdom of good government," I whispered back.

"Then I fear that, presently, your small state will be annexed by this gorgeous, this unique democracy."

I feared as much, too. Yet I found myself admiring the unexpectedly dignified way in which the republic's rulers were now confronting the constitutional crisis.

Before the anxious gaze of the entire world . . . at last I am beginning to sound like a true journalist! Let me be precise. Before the anxious gaze of those of us who will benefit directly from the election of Tilden or Hayes, the solemn drama began to unfold at one o'clock when the doorkeeper of the House of Representatives announced in a loud, trembling voice the approach of the United States Senate.

Through the chamber's central entrance the senators walked and marched, strolled and strutted. Most eyes were upon the two continuing antagonists, Blaine and Conkling; yet each is now peripheral to the last act of that high drama whose early acts they dominated. Conkling looked, as ever, superb. It is said that Kate Sprague is in the city, but I have not seen her. Conkling wants a Tilden victory, so that he can then take over the Republican party and either be the candidate himself in four years' time or, it is murmured, create yet another administration for General Grant.

Blaine is very much the loyal party man today, plainly on excellent terms with everyone save Conkling. Should Hayes be elected, it is said that Blaine will be given a high place in the Cabinet.

A number of *very* distinguished visitors have been allowed the courtesy of the floor. Amongst them, I saw General Sherman—fortunately, in civilian clothes (people still speak seriously of a military coup d'état by General Grant should Tilden be elected). I also recognized the celebrated New York jurist Charles O'Conor, a handsome old man, who is Tilden's chief spokesman before the commission. Baron Jacobi pointed out to me the historian George Bancroft; the sage was listening gravely to a long disquisition from Garfield—no doubt on the ease with which *true* history can at last be written in this marvellous candid age of telegraph and newspaper.

Once the senators and the guests were seated on the extra chairs that had been set up in the aisles, the President of the Senate, Thomas W. Ferry, climbed to the high throne where usually sits the Speaker of the House of Representatives. But today the Speaker is secondary, and occupies a chair at the President's left. Incidentally, the Speaker is no longer the alleged West Point–cadet salesman of last summer but one S. J. Randall, a Democrat from Pennsylvania and a friend of Tilden. Mr. Randall's face is decorated with nothing more than a discreet moustache—unlike the President of the Senate, who wears attached to his lower lip an inordinately long beard that halfway down his chest divides in two; it seems to be made of grey tweed.

The ceremony's early stages differed in no way from the usual quadrennial joint session of Congress that receives the Electoral College's confirmation of the popular vote for President.

In alphabetic order the roll of the states was called, beginning with Alabama. The returns from each state are given to the president of the Senate, who then gives them to the tellers, who announce the vote and prepare the ultimate tally. During the votes of Alabama, Arkansas, California, Colorado, Connecticut, and Delaware, members of Congress, distinguished visitors, and journalists all talked amongst themselves, drowning out the tellers' announcements of each state's vote. But with the naming of Florida the voices stopped, and there was absolute silence in the chamber.

Senator Ferry tugged at his beard; cleared his throat. "The chair"—the voice was loud—"hands the tellers a certificate from the State of Florida, received by messenger, and the corresponding one by mail."

The teller came forward and took the documents from the President of the Senate. In an equally loud voice the teller announced that Florida's four electoral votes for president and vice president had been cast for Hayes and Wheeler.

The Republican Senator Ferry looked for a moment satisfied. The room was silent, expectant. Then, looking *dis*satisfied, Senator Ferry gave one of the tellers a second set of returns, and we were told that Florida's four votes had been cast in favour of Tilden and Hendricks.

For what seemed to be a long time, there was silence. Then Ferry asked, almost casually, "Are there any objections to these certificates from the State of Florida?"

A sudden roar from every side of the chamber, and the battle was joined. Members of both houses were on their feet. Finally a New York congressman was recognized. He objected to the returns favouring Hayes. A Californian and an Iowan each objected to the returns favouring Tilden.

The President of the Senate then asked, "Are there any further objections?" Hearing none, Senator Ferry referred the matter to the electoral commission, vacated his throne, and led his fellow senators from the chamber. So the curtain fell on Act One.

During the week since the electoral commission was given the two (actually, because of a technicality, three) sets of Florida returns, things did not appear to go well for us despite the brilliance of Charles O'Conor.

For one thing, the commission has never seriously tried to examine any of the initial voting frauds in Florida. The Republican case is based on the fact that the Hayes returns are the only valid ones because they have been signed by the carpetbag Republican governor of the state, while those favouring Tilden were only signed by the state's attorney general. For a whole week the number of angels able to dance on that pin's head have been counted and re-counted. All in all, it has been a discouraging time until tonight—Wednesday, February 7—or, rather, this morning, February 8.

I have just come from a late supper at the house of Hewitt. Tomorrow—today—the commission votes for the first time on whether or not to go behind the returns. Everything hinges on Bradley. If he votes with the Democrats to go behind the returns, Tilden is elected.

Two hours ago, after supper, Hewitt sent a common friend named Stevens to talk to Bradley.

Stevens returned with good news. "Bradley read me his opinion. He thinks the commission is obliged to go behind the returns.

"And Florida's electoral votes?" asked Hewitt, kneading his stomach in a positive ecstasy of dyspeptic contraction.

"Belong to Tilden!"

"Then we've won." Hewitt let go his stomach, and offered us champagne.

I shall sleep well tonight.

2

FEBRUARY 8.
    According to Nordhoff, right after Stevens left Bradley, the Republican Senator Frelinghuysen (a member of the electoral commission) and Secretary of the Navy Robeson arrived at Brad-

ley's house. Both are fellow New Jerseyans and friends. The railroad interests were also heard from, the flag was appealed to, and Mrs. Bradley is reported to have wept when she begged her husband to support Hayes (how Nordhoff finds out these things I do not know).

In any case, whether or not Nordhoff's information is correct, it is a fact that Bradley today voted *against* going behind the returns.

The seven partisan Republicans are now eight partisan Republicans versus seven partisan Democrats.

Hewitt is stunned. "Something—or someone—changed Bradley's mind," he said to me, "between midnight and sunrise."

3

FEBRUARY 10. The electoral commission met *in camera* for most of the day. They have just now announced that they have accepted the Hayes electors from Florida. The vote was eight to seven. Bradley has sold out.

Nordhoff is curious what form the thirty pieces of silver took. "I hear he was paid two hundred thousand dollars to change his vote. But that," Nordhoff admitted, "is unsubstantiated gossip."

Each newspaper responds to the scandal in its own characteristic way. The *Times* lauds the noble Bradley. The *Sun* hints ominously at money changing hands and reminds the nation of Bradley's corruption: when he was a West Texas circuit judge, he was bought by the railroad interests. The fifth judge is not Bradley, according to the *Sun*, but the Texas Pacific railroad who will award the presidency to Hayes. The *Sun* says that seventeen carriages containing Republican leaders and Texas Pacific railway men converged on Bradley's house after Stevens's departure.

February 16. The electoral commission has accepted the Hayes electors for Louisiana. The vote: eight to seven.

A few days ago Bradley admitted to Hewitt that he had indeed written an opinion favouring Florida's Tilden electors, but that this was no more than his usual practise as a judge. Apparently Bradley often writes two opinions, one for and one against. How he arrives at his ultimate opinion he regards as no one's business.

One of Bradley's fellow Supreme Court Justices on the commission told Nordhoff, privately: "What Bradley says is nonsense. You don't need to write two opinions as to whether or not to go behind the returns. The arguments were all set before us. So either you behave morally, or you don't."

"Tilden or Blood!" Someone is shouting below my window. But there is only silence from Gramercy Park.

Meanwhile Grant has called out the troops (to defend the Capitol?), and soldiers are constantly, pointedly on display. Recently an overwrought local journalist wrote that if Hayes were to go in safety from White House to Capitol for his inauguration, then the people of this country are indeed fit for slavery. This morning the journalist was arrested. The government has indicted him for sedition.

"Tilden or Blood!" I now favour the second if we are to be, by conspiracy, denied the first.

February 19. The commission's recommendation that the Hayes electors for Louisiana be accepted was passed in a stormy session of the Congress.

Two Republican members of the House voted against their own party, maintaining fraud.

The roll of the states continued after Louisiana until Oregon . . .

Fourteen

1

I HAVE NOT HAD THE HEART to write in this book since I received, on the evening of February 19, the following telegram: "*Denise died this morning we are all devastated her son survives the funeral is tomorrow here on the plantation my love and shared anguish Emma.*"

I suppose it is in the nature of things that, as one ages, one is obliged to witness the gradual loss of all that one has ever cared for until the laggard self slips into what is, at the end, an altogether commonplace and so common darkness.

I have telegraphed condolences to Sanford, to Emma.

I feel as if it were Emma who had died.

I persevere for the *Herald*, for Tilden, for my own . . . but it is absurd to write the word "future" now. Nothing *will* be ever again; and what has been is all that's left.

To date, March 2, I have still received no letter from Emma—only a second telegram to say that she will be at the Fifth Avenue Hotel March 5.

I do my best not to think of Denise. Fortunately, there is a good deal to distract one here as, one by one, the pretensions of this ludicrous republic collapse into ruins.

Tilden was originally thought to have won Oregon. But, perhaps legitimately, his 500-vote majority vanished and the state's three electoral votes went to Hayes. But the law says that no state elector can be an officeholder. Since one of Oregon's three electors for Hayes is a postmaster, he has been forced to withdraw. The Democratic governor of the state then appointed a new elector who is pledged to Tilden, proving that the Democrats are as devoted to fraud as the Republicans.

During this squalid contest the Southern Democrats in Congress are daily wooed by the Republican leadership in tandem with the railroad interests, and a number of those wooed have been won.

Two conditions exacted by the Southern Democrats. One, Hayes has agreed to appoint two Southerners to his Cabinet. (Nordhoff thinks this an excellent idea; he has also confessed to me that he has been in correspondence with Hayes since last summer. "A weak but honest man. I voted against him of course, but even so . . .") Two, the Republicans agree to remove all Federal troops from those Southern states that are still "unreconstructed."

Even more compelling than the Republican politicians are the railroad lobbyists; they swarm through the Capitol like maggots through a cheese, openly buying Southern votes for Hayes (they fear reform; they fear Tilden). They are even trying to push their own special legislation through a Congress supposedly dedicated to the sublime task of electing a president.

From about February 19 on, the tide has been turning in favour of Hayes. Tilden may have won the election, but the party that has been in power for sixteen years has no intention of surrendering the presidency. Aside from the buying of Bradley (and God —or the Texas Pacific railroad—alone knows how many members of Congress), the Republicans constantly wave the bloody shirt of rebellion. Daily the nation is reminded that the Democratic party having once gone into rebellion might do so again.

Simultaneously, the rulers praise those "good" Southern statesmen who do not want to see the precious Union, for whom so many died, torn once again asunder by civil war. Even Jamie has been taken in by the atrocious rhetoric. A few days ago he praised the Southern members of Congress for their "patriotic submission."

On February 24 the Speaker of the House, Mr. Randall, joined the Southern Democrats for Hayes. Hewitt then rose and denounced the electoral commission as a fraud; nevertheless, he was forced to admit that this prolonged political crisis is having a bad effect on every aspect of American life, particularly on the nation's business. In other words, four years of Hayes is better than four years of civil war.

On February 27 a number of Southern Democrats met with the Republican leadership in a suite at Wormley's Hotel. The next day the Associated Press gave the official version of the meeting which, amongst other things, emphasized that Hayes would support the claims of the *Democratic* candidate for governor of Louisiana!

Nordhoff tells me that Garfield was present at the meeting, and that he had the grace to be appalled. In fact, he left early. Yet he is to be well rewarded. He is to be made Speaker of the House, with the support of the Southern Democrats.

"Even so," said Nordhoff, "there he is, one of the electoral commissioners who is on record as saying that the Republicans won Louisiana. Now, to get Hayes elected, he's forced to say that the Democrats really did carry the state after all. Oh, it was a precious bargain!"

On February 28, as the votes of Vermont were being recorded for Hayes, someone asked (out of curiosity?) if there had been any other returns from that state.

Hewitt sprang to his feet, waving a thick envelope in the best Blaine tradition. "I hold in my hand a package which purports to contain electoral votes from the State of Vermont. This package was delivered to me by express about the middle of December last." Apparently a similar package had been sent the President of the Senate, who denied to Hewitt he had received it. "I then tendered him this package, the seals of which are unbroken. He declined to receive it!" Much shouting and confusion at this point.

Nordhoff explained. "One of the three Hayes electors is—what else?—a postmaster. So he has to be disqualified. Those returns that came to Hewitt were sent by the Democratic elector who lost the election but now claims he won it because his rival was ineligible."

"Nonsense, then?"

"Not if there was more time. Tilden needs only one out of the twenty disputed votes. This could be it."

The joint session divided to consider the matter of the Vermont returns.

2

ARCH 1. The joint session has now sat continuously for
eighteen hours. Without a doubt, it has been the stormiest and most confusing session in the country's history. The galleries are packed with noisy partisans. The floor is so crowded with lobbyists that at times the members of the Congress are outnumbered by their masters. Around midnight whisky bottles appeared openly. Around one in the morning, a revolver or two was noted.

The mood of the joint session was not improved when it was discovered that Hewitt's Vermont returns had been mislaid. For some weeks now, a continuing filibuster has stopped dead the work of the election.

Finally a Louisiana congressman named Levy took the floor and asked his fellow Southerners to continue with the count of the states because, "I have solemn, earnest and, I believe, truthful assurances . . . of a policy of conciliation toward the Southern states . . . in the event of Hayes's election to the presidency." A removal of all Federal troops from the South has been guaranteed not only by Hayes but, yesterday, by Grant himself. The deal has been made.

I sat with Nordhoff until the joint session of Congress ended at 4:10 A.M., this morning, Friday, March 2, 1877.

A number of times during the eighteen hours of the joint session, the two houses separated in order to vote amongst themselves.

At the last session of the House, Speaker Randall read a telegram from Tilden, saying that he would like the roll of the states to be continued—that is, to its foregone conclusion. Thus Tilden surrendered to *force majeure*. The House then declared Wisconsin for Hayes, and that was that.

At four o'clock, the Senate straggled into the House chamber to renew the joint session. For the last time Senator Ferry sat in the Speaker's chair.

Nordhoff and I rested side by side, arms on the railing of the press gallery. We were all of us half asleep as the tragedy came to its end.

Senator Ferry got to his feet. He looked up at the sleepy and somewhat drunken people in the public galleries. He spoke firmly. "In announcing the final result of the electoral vote, the chair trusts that all present, whether on the floor or in the galleries, will refrain from all demonstration whatever . . ." When he spoke of the necessity for dignity, there was a soft bark from Nordhoff at my side.

In silence the votes of each state were read and tallied. Hayes was elected president by a single vote. Nor was the silence broken as Ferry intoned, "Wherefore, I do declare: that Rutherford B. Hayes, of Ohio, having received a majority of the whole number of electoral votes, is duly elected president of the United States for four years, commencing on the fourth day of March, 1877 . . ."

There was no applause. Only a long weary sigh from the embattled Congress. Then a sudden thick sound.

Just beneath us, Abram S. Hewitt had collapsed. Like Hamlet in the last act of Shakespeare's play he was carried out of the chamber. All in all, Hewitt has about as much understanding of politics as Shakespeare's prince, and far fewer good speeches.

3

MARCH 3. By a vote of 137 to 88, a still-rebellious House of Representatives today adopted a resolution declaring Samuel J. Tilden, the duly elected president of the United States, and giving him 196 electoral votes. But no one pays the slightest attention to the House, which, in any case, belongs to the railroads, who never intended for Tilden to be elected. I daresay this meaningless resolution relieved the consciences of these grubby Fausts.

Today, for the first time since Lincoln's murder, the front page of the New York *Sun* appeared with a band of mourning. There are rumours that General McClellan is raising an army in order to ensure that Tilden will be inaugurated day after tomorrow. If McClellan moves with the same despatch that he did during the Civil War, we can expect to see him arrive in time for the inaugural of 1881.

4

MARCH 5. This is my last night in Washington City. Travelling cases are packed. Tomorrow morning I take the cars to New York.

Earlier today, Rutherford (now popularly known as "Rutherfraud") B. Hayes was duly inaugurated at the Capitol before a crowd of what looked to be some thirty thousand potential Republican officeholders. But then who am I to complain of those who seek office? I tried, and my candidate failed. Two members of the Supreme Court refused to attend the ceremony.

Fierce-looking troops lined every approach to the Capitol. There is rebellion in the air, but nowhere else. Here on the ground all is peaceful.

The new President looks like a back-country preacher, and sounds rather like one. He was plainly nervous, and when a shot or firecracker went off nearby, he winced noticeably—no doubt aware of all those heavily armed whisky-filled Southern congressmen on the warpath.

Hayes's speech was conciliatory and designed to appeal to both Southerners and reformers. It would appear that he intends to continue the Administration of Grant with the rhetoric of Tilden.

The outgoing President looked more than ever puzzled, and

hurt. Mrs. Grant looked as if she had just peered into a coffin and seen her own remains. *Sic transit gloria Grantium.*

Nordhoff and I dined at Welcher's. Sentimentally, we sat at the same table where we had first made each other's acquaintance one year ago. One year! It seems a century.

The dining room was crowded as a result of that quadrennial Washington phenomenon, the convergence on the city of would-be officeholders which resembles nothing so much as a blight of locusts. The wealthy locusts come to the tables at Welcher's.

Despite the company, we dined well, drank far too much, and were in the best of spirits. I cannot think why. I suppose the more harrowing the experience the more delighted one is that it is over. I remember how Emma and I could not stop laughing when we finally realized that we had survived the bloodletting of the Communards.

With the first course (a complicated dish of Maryland crab garnished with creamed mussels), Nordhoff and I toasted one another in hock, which I had ordered in honour of Tilden.

"To the President across the Mason-Dixon line." I said.

"To good government!" Nordhoff's bark became a roar. For some reason the phrase "good government" struck us both as so hilarious that we laughed until we wept.

After that we drank "To His Fraudulency," as Nordhoff calls Mr. Hayes. Nordhoff told me that the new President has been in Washington since March 2, hidden away in Senator Sherman's house, wondering whether or not he was going to be inaugurated.

"Not that there was ever any real doubt. Over a week ago Grant invited Hayes for dinner on the night of March third. So when Hayes came skulking into the White House, he found that the Chief Justice had also been asked to dinner. Then Grant and his son and the Chief Justice led Hayes into an empty parlour where the Chief Justice administered the oath of office, just in case."

"So today was simply . . ."

"The religious ceremony. The real, the civil wedding was last Saturday night when, with ravishing stride, the republic was bedded. Let's drink to the future children of that wedding bed. To the dwarf Reform—"

"To the hunchback States' Rights . . ."

"To the idiot Hard Money . . ."

"To the twins Texas and Union Pacific . . ."

"What a lovely family!"

Whilst we were enjoying ourselves with gallows humour, a familiar figure suddenly appeared at the door to the dining room. For a moment Garfield looked uncertain. But then, when he saw me looking at him, he decided to brazen it out. Smiling, he came to our table and sat down. "I was on my way upstairs . . ."

"To a private dining room. To celebrate with the Republican leadership the great victory. And divide the spoils." Nordhoff was beginning to show the wine he had drunk.

"Nothing so exciting." Garfield was warm, even affectionate— at least with me. But then I cannot keep myself from beaming fatuously at him, like a senile father with a lovely, lovely son. "Actually, I'm entertaining constituents. Just about everyone I know from Ohio is in town."

"Looking for jobs?" Nordhoff remembered to smile.

"Only *pro bono publico.*" Garfield's mock-gravity was almost worthy of Blaine himself. "One or two *have* confided to me that they are at liberty to take on, at great personal sacrifice, government labour."

Nordhoff relaxed somewhat. I preened myself in the light of so splendid a son.

"A terrible time," Garfield observed. "I know you're not happy with the result."

"Are you?" Nordhoff was quick.

"Yes. I also think that the disputed states would have been ours if the Negroes had been allowed to vote . . ."

This familiar speech was cut short by Nordhoff. "But surely you're not happy about a *Democrat* being elected governor of Louisiana."

Garfield was all blue-eyed innocence. "But we were assured that he was indeed the winner."

"At Wormley's Hotel?"

"At Wormley's Hotel. So we agreed not to dispute his election."

"But how could a Democrat have won the governorship of Louisiana when, according to the electoral commission, according to *you* as a commissioner, the state voted overwhelmingly for the Republicans?"

Garfield's face did not for an instant lose its beautiful candid expression. "Mr. Nordhoff, when you are dealt the cards, you play them." So Caesar must have sounded when he set aside the old republic.

Nordhoff was absolutely silenced. The waiter poured the three of us claret. Garfield raised his glass to drink, blue eyes aglow in the candlelight.

Nordhoff proclaimed the toast. "To good government."

Garfield nodded. "To good government, yes. And to President Hayes." Garfield drank; as did I.

But Nordhoff did not drink; he continued the toast. "To President Hayes, yes. And to James G. Blaine. To Roscoe Conkling. To General Grant. To the Returning Boards of Louisiana, South Carolina, and Florida. To Jay Gould. To the Texas Pacific Railroad. To the Federal army. To General Sherman . . ."

Garfield laughed, most genially, considering the vastness of the insult. "You will make me quite drunk, Mr. Nordhoff, with so much good government." He put down his glass and got to his feet. I did the same. He and I shook hands.

"I go tomorrow," I told him. "You will say good-bye to Mrs. Garfield for me?"

"Only if you will give our very best regards to your daughter." The crooked arm had slowly turned me toward him, and the fine face looked down into mine.

"I shall, with pleasure." I have no idea what cupboard of memory was suddenly at that moment sprung, but I not only remembered but said that haunting line: *"Brevis hic est fructus homullis."*

Garfield frowned; let go my arm. "Horace?"

"No. Lucretius."

"I must answer that, mustn't I? Well, then . . ." Garfield paused; shook his head. "I'm afraid all my Latin is in my library. I can think of nothing except *Gaudeamus igitur.* Will that do?"

"Why not? It has always done."

After Garfield left us, Nordhoff and I continued to drink.

Shortly before midnight, I came back to the hotel and in the *vase de nuit* relieved myself of both dinner and wine.

I am now sober, tired, apprehensive. How am I to live? and why?

Fifteen

1

AGAINST THAT JUDGMENT sometimes dramatized as "better," I have allowed Emma to stay at the Sanford house in Fifth Avenue, with myself as chaperone.

I suppose it is the right thing to do. Certainly it is the kind thing to do. Sanford was close to weeping when he begged us to move in. He appears to be quite out of control. Suddenly, faced with genuine grief, with true tragedy, he has no convincing performance to give. He vacillates from glum silences to unnatural gaiety; worse, he likes to take me aside at regular intervals to tell me how devoted Denise was to me, how she asked for me when she was dying. This naturally puts me in a terrible state; the heart pounds as the pressure of the blood increases; the tears stream down my face, though I am not actually weeping, a phenomenon of age and illness. Curiously enough, Denise is never mentioned when the three of us are together. But when I am alone with Emma, or with Sanford (not, thank Heaven, often), we talk of nothing else.

The first night at the Sanford house, Emma came into my

bedroom, which is separated from hers by a charming small drawing room with grey walls à la Pompadour.

Emma looks pale, is listless. Although I want to know nothing, she means for me to know everything.

"I've never seen anyone die, Papa."

"Your father-in-law . . ."

Emma gestured impatiently. "He was old. Besides we weren't there—in the room—the way . . ." Emma stopped. She had caught a glimpse of herself in the glass opposite my bed. Abruptly she pushed the hair out of her eyes, and for the first time I saw white hairs in that splendid auburn mass. I felt guilty, disloyal for having noticed.

"Well, at least we were both there. With her. And I don't think there was much pain. But when there was, near the end, the nurse gave her chloroform. Sanford's a good man. I do think he loves Denise. I mean, loved. In his way, of course." Emma spoke disjointedly but resolutely. As if she was in court and obliged to give complete evidence, no matter how terrible.

Deliberately I slipped into French, thinking that this would make it easier for her, but she continued in English—like a penance.

I asked, "How was Denise? I mean before the—before the last part?"

"Marvellous. She had never looked better. Felt better. The day before the pains began we drove into Savannah. She wanted to buy flowers. There's a conservatory there. Have you ever seen an azalea?"

"I don't recall an introduction, no." No. No lightness is possible, ever again.

"She liked azaleas. The pains began in the early morning. She screamed. That woke us all up. The nurse was with her. Denise was overdue. By a week. Maybe two weeks. That was when I started to get uneasy. Sanford too. But Denise ignored it. Except for once, when she said of the baby, 'I think he's growing irritable. He's so old now.' But that was all. Nothing like Newport. No terror. Thank God. She was unconscious when the doctor came. He cut out the child. And that . . . was . . . that."

Emma sat very straight in the chair beside my bed, deliberately *not* looking at herself in the mirror.

"What now?" I broke the stillness.

"Oh . . . now." She shook her head, as if there was to be no more

life. "I don't know. You saw Sanford. You heard him. I must stay
to help him. Because of Denise. He has collapsed."

"Men are not as strong as women."

Emma gave me a long thoughtful look. Then she nodded. "It
is true, Papa. So, for now, we stay here until he is himself again."

"And John?"

Emma came close to a smile. "There is no John. The funeral
service for the Princess d'Agrigente has been indefinitely post-
poned."

"So," I said, without tact, I fear, "what do we do now?"

"It is very bad, isn't it?"

"It is very bad." I agreed. "Mr. Tilden is not the president. And
I am not American minister to France."

"The *Herald* . . ."

"Jamie is deserting America. Forever."

"Because of the horsewhipping? That was droll." And Emma,
finally, smiled; normal life insists that we pursue it.

Certainly I have been in hot and desperate pursuit of normal
life for some weeks now.

"It's all over, Charlie. There's nothing left." Jamie kept repeating this refrain to me, as we sat at his special table in the bar of
the Hoffman House. Not even the elegant appearance of the
Collector of the Port could do more than, momentarily, disrupt
Jamie's gloom.

Arthur complimented me on my election reports. "You made
me feel I was right there in the Capitol."

"You could've been, Chet. Only you were hiding out at Wormley's." Jamie was suddenly his old mocking self.

But Arthur took no offence. "I'm afraid I'm not that important.
I was right here the whole time, tending to the port."

"Watch out for Hayes, Chet. He's going to have your scalp."

Jamie's cryptic *non sequitur* was ignored by Arthur, who said,
"There is a rumour that we are in for an austere administration.
Mrs. Hayes refuses to serve wine or spirits at the White House."

"One more reason for going," said Jamie darkly, drying with
the back of his hand those absinthe drops that forever cling like
seed pearls to his moustache.

"A friend of mine just came from a dinner at the White House
and he said that the water flowed like wine."

I was grateful to the genial Arthur for praising my articles in
front of Jamie. But to no good end. I can write for the *Herald* from

Paris as I do for the *Evening Post;* but I cannot begin to support myself on what either paper is willing to pay.

I continue to make the rounds.

My second day in the city I called on Bryant at the *Post.* The old man is beginning to look transparent with age but appears to possess all his faculties. I listened to more praise for my election articles. Then: "I suppose that you will be going back to Europe soon?"

"Yes. If I find nothing to do here."

The Jovian head turned toward me with some curiosity. "You *want* to live amongst us?"

"I want to live, my dear Bryant. And I must do that by my pen."

"But you are, permanently, our valued European contributor."

"For which I am grateful. But I have a daughter and two grandsons to provide for." I rather laid it on.

"Oh, dear. I see what you mean. If only Mr. Tilden had been elected."

"But he was elected. He was simply not inaugurated. Did you vote for him?"

At the center of that Sinaean bush, a smile began. "I never say. The paper . . ."

"Supported Hayes."

"A decent man. With the makings of a good Cabinet. Particularly now that he has taken on Carl Schurz . . ."

"Not to mention Mr. Key." Part of the deal at Wormley's Hotel was that the postmaster-generalship (the most copious source of patronage in the land) go to a Democrat. Hayes's choice was the Democrat Senator Key of Tennessee.

"Well . . ." Bryant looked straight ahead.

We agreed that I would, from time to time, write on matters of general interest while I am still in New York. Once back in Paris, I shall continue my valued contributions, assuming I do not, meanwhile, starve to death. Despite the general impropriety of staying with Sanford, I must confess that it has saved our lives, for, despite a year's hard work, I now have exactly the same amount of capital that I had when I arrived here on the *Pereire,* less all the prospects that I had then.

I dined last week at Gramercy Park with Tilden. Bigelow and Green and the Peltons were on hand; the other courtiers seem all to have vanished. No longer is the front door importantly guarded by police.

I was warmly received not by the nineteenth president but by a nice old bachelor-lawyer, happy in the bosom of his family, his books—his numerous dollars.

"You must have had a most exciting time in Washington." This was Tilden's understatement as he ushered Emma and me into the family sitting room, where the last loyalists were gathered. It put me in mind of our poor Emperor and Empress at Chislehurst.

Bigelow shook my hand. He has taken this defeat hardest of all. Well, not as hard as I have, since, of the lot, I am the only one without a penny or a future. But I did my best to appear as unruffled as the others.

"What news of your friend the Princess Mathilde?" Like the others, Bigelow avoided any reference to the election.

"She has just sent me her first book. A biography of Didi, her late dog."

"An instructive life?"

"For a dog, yes. I'll lend it to you."

"I'll read it to our dogs."

We did our best. Emma was subdued but sufficiently herself to excite Mrs. Pelton. Everyone envies us "for going back to Paris." Green sighed. "Wish I were going. The Governor is."

Tilden nodded. "Bigelow has consented to be my cicerone. We sail in July when the Atlantic is, reputedly, calm." Bigelow told me that the bookings were made the day they learned that the commission had accepted the Hayes electors for Florida.

We made all sorts of plans to meet in Paris, assuming that I am not in debtors' prison. Bigelow suggests I write a book about the election. "After all, you've already got most of it written, your pieces for the *Herald*."

At first I thought this not a good idea, but since that dinner in Gramercy Park, I have changed my mind. When I proposed the subject to Mr. Dutton, he was enthusiastic. Yesterday at the Lotos Club I mentioned the matter to Gilder, who says that he will present the idea to Scribner's. I mean to get them all bidding against one another, just as if I were Mark Twain!

As I was leaving, Tilden said, "I overheard Bigelow. Such a book might be very interesting."

"Would you be helpful?"

"Oh, yes. I have"—the bleakest of smiles arched the upper lip —"a great deal of information. I might even say evidence. For instance, one of the fifteen commissioners was paid one hundred thousand dollars for his vote. This seemed to me odd, since the

going price throughout the election has been two hundred thousand dollars. But perhaps he did not know?"

"I wish *you* had paid him!" I spoke from the heart.

"It's as well I did not. Besides, four years is a short time. And
Mr. Hayes insists that he will serve one term and no more."

I could not say that for me four years is the equivalent of all
eternity. Tilden can look forward to a future election. But I have
not that luxury.

Meanwhile I have decided to write the book. Bigelow promises
to tell me *all*.

One incident: after the House of Representatives passed its
resolution confirming Tilden as president, Hewitt tried to get the
Governor to issue a proclamation declaring that he would present himself at the Capitol on March 4 to be inaugurated as the
duly elected president. According to Hewitt, armed troops in
fifteen states were ready to march. Tilden responded by asking
Hewitt to resign as Democratic national chairman, which he has
done.

2

ODAY HAS BEEN both disturbing and splendid.

At noon Blaise Delacroix Sanford was baptized in the
drawing room of the Sanford mansion by a Roman Catholic
bishop with, as they say, the map of all Ireland writ large upon
his red face.

Emma and I stood as godparents for the baby, who roared
agreeably. Sanford was in an exuberant mood, made only slightly
more distasteful than usual by a newfound religiosity. He has
taken to exclaiming in a loud voice and at odd moments, "Praise
God." He has not yet asked us to drop to our knees and pray with
him, but I feel it is only a matter of time.

Some fifty people had been invited for dinner after the ceremony, amongst them Ward McAllister. "*She* could not come," he

breathed into my ear. "But *she* has sent a most beautiful cup. So tragic, the loss of the beautiful Mrs. Sanford. He has taken it very hard, hasn't he?"

"Very hard. As we all have."

"So good of you and the Princess to stay with him. He has no family. She had Family, of course. But they are at the South, don't you know?"

Due to my gentle insistence, the Gilders (wife and sister as well as book-man) had been invited to the christening. I fear that I have taken to literary society in the biggest way. One day finds me at the Lotos Club, the next at the Century Club. I fawn relentlessly on publishers.

I now have, according to Gilder, "a truly princely offer from Scribner's. They will pay you five thousand dollars for the rights to your election book." Gilder was as pleased for me as I am for me. "Naturally, you'll let me publish as much as I can in *Scribner's Monthly.*"

"We *are* thrilled," said Jeanette Gilder, but whether by my sudden good fortune or by the Gilders' finding themselves in the same drawing room as the August Belmonts, I could not tell.

I now work every day on the book. Bigelow provides me with all sorts of information, and Tilden himself promises to give the final manuscript a careful reading.

I was well on my way to survival, until this afternoon, when my life was most unexpectedly changed.

After the guests had departed, I sat with Sanford and Emma in the pseudo-Renaissance library with its view of Fifth Avenue, bright and new-looking in the early April light. Sanford and I continued to drink champagne while Emma poured herself cup after cup of coffee from a massive Georgian silver pot.

"A good party!" Sanford lit a long cigar. "Praise God!" This last was addressed to the ceiling that, presumably, separates Sanford from his much-lauded Deity.

"I hope my literary *confrères* did not lower too much the 'tong.' "

"They give variety. Say, it sure was nice of Lina to send us that cup." Sanford has lately taken to referring to the Mystic Rose by her family nickname—no doubt, on the ground that the less he sees of her the greater the intimacy.

Then Emma put down her coffee cup and said, "Papa, William and I were married this morning."

"Praise God in Heaven!" Sanford addressed this prayer not to the ceiling but to me.

"My God!" I said, contaminated by so many celestial references.

"The Bishop married us, before anyone came." Emma was nervous . . . from too much coffee, I decided dumbly.

"Why didn't you tell me?" I heard my own voice, as if from far away; and noted that it was the querulous voice of an old man.

"Because—" Emma stopped.

"Because," said Sanford, "you might have objected. I mean it is . . . so soon . . . after—"

"Yes. It is *too* soon after." I was sharp. On the one hand (why deny it?), I am delighted that Emma has not only saved herself but released me from a burden that has been threatening to crush me entirely; yet, on the other hand, I cannot stop thinking of Denise, only three months dead. "Why couldn't you have waited a few more months?"

"The child," said Sanford. "He needs a mother. And I"—Sanford's small pretty mouth suddenly delivered a spontaneous if somewhat girlish, even coquettish smile—"*I* need Emma."

"The orchids," I said, not meaning to. But neither one of them was listening to me. They were looking at each other.

"We thought it the right thing to do, Papa." Emma shifted to rapid French, and I don't think Sanford was able to understand us. "William wants to get away. To go to Paris. As soon as possible. With the child. With me. Obviously, I can't travel with him unmarried. So last week we asked the Bishop, and he was most agreeable. He arranged it all."

"But it seems to me to be—and I'm not exactly punctilious in these matters—much too swift. Too . . . insulting to Denise."

"You will make me weep." Emma's eyes were indeed filled with tears.

"I'm sorry."

"*I* think Denise would have approved. She loved us both. William *and* me. And you, too, Papa. If you had been there, with us, you'd understand better what I've just done."

"No matter." I spoke again in English. "Well, congratulations, Sanford."

My son-in-law was on his feet. "Praise"—I fear he shouted—"God!" as he lunged forward to shake my hand.

I kissed Emma. She burst into tears. And so, on this lovely

April day we at last buried the celebrated Princess d'Agrigente and attended the *accouchement* of the second Mrs. William Sanford, who will depart next week for France with her husband aboard his yacht.

I stay behind in the mansion, writing my book and living a life of perfect luxury. For the first time in years I am free. I feel the way a life-prisoner must when his heavy chains are suddenly, inexplicably, struck from him.

3

WE PARTED THIS MORNING. My son-in-law shook my hand firmly; he looked surprised when Emma and I did not embrace. Emma gave me a long look; started to speak, and then thought better of it. She got into the waiting carriage. Two wagons were needed for the Sanfords' trunks.

"You'll join us soon. That's all agreed, isn't it?" At least Sanford does not call me Father.

"Yes. I'll join you soon. When the book is done."

"The Lord be praised."

Then they were gone, leaving the butler and me standing in the grey light of what promises to be a rainy day.

I have not a curious nature; do not read other people's letters; do not eavesdrop. Since I can usually imagine with the greatest ease the worst, I need not know it. In fact, I avoid confidences and hate all secrets. I assume that there are things even in the lives of those one loves that are dark, and I for one would rather not have them brought to light.

The greater the ascent, the longer the fall. Yes. All platitude is truth; all truth platitude. Unfortunately, it takes a long life to learn this, at the end.

I spent last night with Jamie, at his insistence. "I need company, Charlie. Because I hate everybody."

"That's normal."

"I can't wait to leave this city. It's bad luck for me."

We dined together at an obscure French restaurant back of Steinway Hall. Jamie will not go to any place where he might be recognized by the gentry. I had rather hoped that he would want to go on to the Chinese Pagoda, but like most people who hate everyone, he desperately needs company.

Although Jamie won't go to the new Delmonico's, he will go to shady places where the people are lively, and if he should meet any of the gentry there—well, they are fallen, too. He thinks of himself as Lucifer, and all because of a schoolboy tussle in the snow with young Mr. May.

My pen delays . . . Stops. Why write any of this? Why make a record? Answer: habit. To turn life to words is to make life yours to do with as you please, instead of the other way round. Words translate and transmute raw life, make bearable the unbearable. So at the end, as in the beginning, there is only The Word. I seem to be making a book of maxims.

Jamie took me to Madame Restell's house, where the usual charming women and eager men were gathered in her comfortable rich salons.

Jamie promptly went to the card room to gamble, leaving me with Madame Restell; she affected to be glad to see me once again. At her insistence I took brandy from a waiter, despite the bad effect it always has on my heart.

"We're neighbours." Madame grinned at me; her bright knowing eyes are like some quick flesh-eating bird's, forever on the lookout for provender.

"You do know everything."

"Well, I do see you coming and going from the Sanford house. But"—she frowned—"I don't really know *every*thing. For instance, the charming Mrs. Sanford. I liked her so much."

"What about her?"

"Well . . . She is dead."

"Absolutely. And horribly so, for us."

"But why?"

"You tell me." I was hard. "*You* know. I don't. I do know that Denise wanted a child and that you told her that she could have one, safely, if she followed your regime. Well, she followed it, and she died."

Madame Restell was silent for some minutes. Past her shoulder I could see the gaming room. Handsome women stood back of the intent card players, no doubt giving signals to their partners.

Then Madame Restell said, "I saw Mrs. Sanford for the last time a year ago when she came here to ask me if she could ever have a child and I said, no, never. I was as blunt as I have ever been to anyone in my life because I liked her."

The room began to enlarge and contract. I thought I might faint or, better yet, die. "But last summer when my daughter came to see you, didn't you say . . ."

"I have never met your daughter, Mr. Schuyler."

I should have stopped right there, for I saw dawning in those old bright bird's eyes a truth that no one must ever know. But I could not stop myself. "The special nurse. She came from you, didn't she?"

"I sent no special nurse. And I have played no part at all in what has happened."

I have no memory of walking home. Although not drunk, I was not sane.

I went straight to Emma's room. She was reading in bed. She smiled; looked lovely.

"I've just come from Madame Restell."

Emma put down her book. She looked at me, and her face did not change expression.

I sat down in a chair because my legs had given way. I looked at Emma; saw her as she had been that evening in Philadelphia at the desk in Sanford's railway car. I saw two figures entwined in a summer gazebo and I knew exactly what had happened. I knew what Emma had done. Or thought I did.

Emma was to the point. "Madame Restell does not like failure, Papa. It is bad for business."

"Was she lying to me?"

Emma sighed; made a bookmark of her comb. "If it was only you, I wouldn't mind. You know the truth. You know I was devoted to Denise and that if I had had to choose between her and Sanford . . ." Emma stopped; took the comb out of the book and kept her place with one finger. "Anyway, to save her professional reputation Madame Restell is going to tell everyone in New York her terrible story. That's why we're running away to France."

"What did happen?"

"Nothing except what you already know. Madame Restell thought that Denise, with care, had a good chance of surviving—"

"Only a good chance?"

"Yes. Denise insisted that we pretend that there was no risk at all. But there was. That's why I begged her not to—go ahead. But she did."

"Madame Restell says that she never sent anyone to look after Denise."

"For a woman who does not exist, Madame Restell's assistant demanded a very large salary. She can be produced—though *I* never want to see her again."

"Madame Restell says that she has never met you."

Emma smiled. "Never having met people is Madame Restell's usual form of tact. Shall I describe the horrors of her drawing room?"

"No. I am relieved." I got to my feet. Emma kissed her hand to me, and as she did I saw between us, for a brief hallucinatory moment, a single white locust blossom spinning slowly, softly, like a summer snowflake.

"*Bonne nuit, cher Papa.*"

"Sleep well," I said, and meant it.

Emma opened her book and began to read.

I came back to this room.

I have just taken a double draught of laudanum.

4

I HAVE MOVED into a pleasant room at the Buckingham Hotel (seventeen dollars a day, with excellent meals) across the avenue from St. Patrick's Cathedral. My room at the back looks out upon the large vegetable garden of a very pleasant farm just west of Fifth Avenue.

I work with Bigelow on the book. I write occasional articles for the *Post*. I dine out every night but, miraculously, I am losing rather than gaining weight and so I feel, at times, almost young again. Certainly the loss of excess flesh makes all the more intense, even rapturous, my cigarine interludes.

Bryant, I fear, is not long for this world, but then he is—what? eighty-two, no, eighty-three years old. I do worry what will happen to me when he is dead, since I have lost the *Herald* now that Jamie has turned Coriolanus and gone into exile whilst the young editors at the *Post* know me not.

Bryant has asked me to do an article on our old friend Fitz-Greene Halleck. "Because I simply haven't the time. Besides, I've already paid him lengthy homage at the New York Historical Society."

This morning—a fine May day—I was both journalist and memorialist, for I was called upon to say a few words at the unveiling of a statue to Halleck in the Central Park.

Bryant also spoke, as did that luminary, His Fraudulency himself, the President of the United States Rutherford B. Hayes, a true lover, to hear him tell it, of our home-grown American sweet-singers or warblers.

We sat on a wooden platform beside the bronze statue that looks not at all like the Halleck I knew, but then the best statues, unlike the best words, always lie.

I read my short, short speech, recalling the Shakespeare Tavern group of which Halleck was the presiding genius. On my feet, I was so much at ease that I am half convinced that I should attempt, at last, the lecture circuit once the book is finished.

I did not get a chance to talk to the President. Bryant had seen to it that no one could get at Mr. Hayes without first stepping over Bryant's long legs.

Hayes is an impressive-looking, rather stout man with a naturally fierce expression. I stared at him with some fascination, for he is, after all, my creation, a major character in the book that I am writing. It is not often that writers are actually able to see their fictional creatures made flesh.

∽

A Special Despatch to The New York Evening Post
by William Cullen Bryant

It is with the greatest sorrow that I am obliged to record here the sudden death of Charles Schermerhorn Schuyler, a friend, a colleague, one of the last sharers with me of the old times in Knickerbocker's town.

I saw my old friend the morning of the day he died, May 16,

1877, in the Central Park, where we were both present at the unveiling of a statue commemorating our common long-dead friend the poet Fitz-Greene Halleck. In fact, Mr. Schuyler was writing a description for this newspaper of that memorial service when he died.

I find it peculiarly poignant, always, when a colleague of so many years dies. I had known Mr. Schuyler since he first wrote for the *Evening Post*, nearly half a century ago. But his true fame rests securely upon those valuable historical works that he composed during a lifetime spent for the most part in Europe. Perhaps the most exemplary of his works is that compelling and incisive study, *Paris under the Communists*.

At the time of Mr. Schuyler's death, he was at work . . .

ꝏ

Afterword

A s in *burr* and *washington, d.c.,* I have mixed real people with invented ones. Charles Schermerhorn Schuyler and his daughter, Emma, are invented (though by now Charlie seems very real to me). Also made up are Mr. and Mrs. Sanford, as well as the atrocious William de La Touche Clancey. Readers of Henry Adams will duly note the resurrection of Baron Jacobi.

The other characters all existed, saying and doing pretty much what I have them saying and doing. The year 1876 was probably the low point in our republic's history, and knowing something about what happened then is, I think, useful to us now as times are again becoming rather too interesting for comfort.

Although I have a deep mistrust of writers who produce trilogies (tetralogists are beyond the pale), I have done exactly that. *Burr, 1876* and *Washington, D.C.* record, in sequence, the history of the United States from the Revolution to—well, the beginning of Camelot. Certain characters from *Burr* reappear in *1876* while *Washington, D.C.* records the doings of, among others, the son and grandson of Mr. and Mrs. William Sanford.

Professor Eric L. McKitrick and E. McKitrick have together gone over the text of *1876*, firmly pointing out inadvertent errors and anachronisms. My thanks to them.

August 15, 1975

BOOKS BY GORE VIDAL

BURR

Alternating the narrative of journalist Charles Schermerhorn Schuyler with the Revolutionary War diaries of Aaron Burr, this novel begins Vidal's history of the United States on a note of intrigue and scandal.

"A dazzling entertainment . . . a devastating analysis of America's first principles." —*The New York Times Book Review*

Fiction/0-375-70873-1

LINCOLN

This novelistic portrait of Lincoln and his era—which nearly created its own civil war among historians when it was first published—is perhaps the pivotal work of the series, illuminating Vidal's theory of the transformation of America from a republic to an imperial state.

"An astonishing achievement." —*Harold Bloom*

Fiction/0-375-70876-6

1876

The centennial of the nation's founding is the occasion for Vidal to bring back the narrator of *Burr*, Charlie Schuyler, and reintroduce his family line as a force in the history of the nation.

"Superb. . . . Simply splendid. . . . A thoroughly grand book, must, must reading for anyone." —*Business Week*

Fiction/0-375-70872-3

BOOKS BY GORE VIDAL

EMPIRE

The end of the Spanish-American War, the beginning of the "American Century," and the burgeoning power of the American press—represented by William Randolph Hearst and the fictional Caroline Sanford (Charlie Schuyler's granddaughter)—continue the transformation of the empire.

Fiction/0-375-70874-X

HOLLYWOOD

The future movie capital of the world and the nation's capital begin their long and checkered relationship (and Vidal's own grandfather, Senator Thomas P. Gore, makes an appearance) as Vidal continues his saga into the first decade of the new century.

Fiction/0-375-70875-8

WASHINGTON, D.C.

Although the most recent historically, this is the first novel Vidal published in what he later conceived as the Narratives of Empire series. Set in the period surrounding World War II and FDR's presidency, *Washington, D.C.* also concerns the ambitions of a young John Kennedy–like politician.

Fiction/0-375-70877-4